"Welcome to the seat of my kingdom," Norgard said behind her.

Kayla had the feeling few humans had ever seen this much of his lair and lived to tell about it. "Desi would have loved this." Her sister's involvement with the Drekar suddenly made sense. But she would have known Kayla wouldn't believe her; no rational person would. Kayla felt some of her anger ease. Desi had kept her secrets to herself simply because the truth was too fantastic, too terrifying to grasp.

"She was beautiful," Norgard said. "Full of light and laughter." There was a slight wistfulness in his voice that caught Kayla off guard.

"Were you the father of her child?"

Norgard's eyes changed. An ancient being peered out, one too old to understand the petty cares of mortals.

Kayla shivered. "Did you ever love her?"

"Enough. What is love but a tool we use to bend another to our will? You'll take her place. One is the same as another. Return to me what is mine."

"I'm not an object you can take!" She stood, but there was no one to help her. "Hart will come back for me."

"Darling, Hart delivered you in exchange for his freedom. You are now mine to do with as I please."

"Liar." She didn't want to believe it. She had trusted Hart, and he had betrayed her. If, no, *when* she got out of here, she would skin that wolf and wear him as a muffler.

Books by Kira Brady

Hearts of Fire: A Deadglass Novella
(available only as an e-book)

Hearts of Darkness

Hearts of Shadow
(coming soon!)

Published by Kensington Publishing Corporation

WITHDRAWN

Hearts of Darkness

A Deadglass Novel

KIRA
BRADY

ZEBRA BOOKS
KENSINGTON PUBLISHING CORP.
http://www.kensingtonbooks.com

ZEBRA BOOKS are published by

Kensington Publishing Corp.
119 West 40th Street
New York, NY 10018

Copyright © 2012 by Kira Brady

All rights reserved. No part of this book may be reproduced in any form or by any means without the prior written consent of the Publisher, excepting brief quotes used in reviews.

If you purchased this book without a cover you should be aware that this book is stolen property. It was reported as "unsold and destroyed" to the Publisher and neither the Author nor the Publisher has received any payment for this "stripped book."

All Kensington titles, imprints and distributed lines are available at special quantity discounts for bulk purchases for sales promotion, premiums, fund-raising, educational or institutional use.

Special book excerpts or customized printings can also be created to fit specific needs. For details, write or phone the office of the Kensington Special Sales Manager: Attn. Special Sales Department. Kensington Publishing Corp., 119 West 40th Street, New York, NY 10018. Phone: 1-800-221-2647.

Zebra and the Z logo Reg. U.S. Pat. & TM Off.

ISBN-13: 978-1-4201-2456-9
ISBN-10: 1-4201-2456-0

First Printing: August 2012

10 9 8 7 6 5 4 3 2 1

Printed in the United States of America

For Ryan,
for making me believe in Happily Ever After

and

for Juniper—
the dreams that you wish will come true
(with tenacity, resilience, and elbow grease)

and

for my parents,
for their unwavering support,
no matter what madcap
milk-carton-and-duck-tape scheme I propose

ACKNOWLEDGMENTS

Heartfelt thanks to my family for encouraging me down this bumpy road less traveled, to my friends who read early drafts and cheered me along the way, to Joy for her optimism and steadfast help, and to the Lusty Wenches Book Club for indulging my love of tea and romance novels. Special thanks to Cherry Adair for encouraging me to finish the damn book, to Shelli Stevens for her advice, and to Cherry's Plotters and the Greater Seattle RWA chapter for their camaraderie. Thanks to Peter Senftleben and Kensington for believing in the Deadglass Trilogy. Thanks to my agent, Miriam. Last, but certainly not least, thanks to Sherida and Rachael for introducing me to the romance genre and sending me off on this mad quest.

This book was inspired by ghost stories of my beloved city, but the Seattle depicted herein is fictional. I've taken liberties with the geography and peopled it with figments of my own imagination. I hope you enjoy this alternate world!

Chapter 1

"*These shores will swarm with the invisible Dead of my Tribe. The White Man will never be alone. Let him be kind and just to my People, for the Dead are not power-less. Dead, did I say? There is no death, only a Change of Worlds.*"

—CHIEF SEATTLE,
Washington Territories, 1854

Seattle, Present Day

The drowning world was gray through the riflescope. From the exposed rooftop across the street, Hart watched the Seattle morgue. Charms to guard against the dead were woven into the cyclone fence. They whistled in the harsh March wind—a low haunted noise, like the keening of spirits.

Hart hunched in his worn bomber jacket. Rain sliced his skin and pummeled the broken asphalt far below. Soggy leaves and cigarette butts raged through overflowing gutters toward distant Puget Sound. Wiping the water out of his eyes, he watched a woman come into view. She fit the profile of his target: midtwenties, short, curvy, with smooth latte skin, generous eyebrows, and a high forehead. She shivered in a thin jean jacket that did nothing to shield her from the rain. Did she have the necklace with her? Her body tensed when she caught sight of the morgue. She wrapped her arms around herself, hesitating momentarily as she took a shaky breath.

She pushed the thick brown hair out of her face, and he saw her eyes. Framed with wet-clumped lashes, they were golden brown and red from crying. Nothing special, and yet for a moment he forgot himself. Forgot his stiff aches and his cold fingers. Forgot the job and the madness and the constant stench of blood on his hands. Forgot his one driving goal: freedom.

Then she turned her head and the moment was lost. He felt the rain again beating on his face and the familiar burning in his chest. He tamped it down before it consumed him, before the thing inside him clawed out of his skin.

She continued down the sidewalk. Her generous ass swayed in the soaked jeans plastered to her body. Hart swallowed.

Around her, the Aether roiled—a sure sign she was not alone. The shining water that surrounded all matter didn't take kindly to ghosts on the wrong side of the Gate to the Land of the Dead. Spirits were supposed to pass peacefully through those Gates, leaving this world to the living, but the Gate in Seattle was busted. Dark spirits slipped free through the crack formed by Chief Seattle's curse to wreak havoc among the living.

Hart pulled a small spyglass out of his pocket. Holding the Deadglass to his eye, he adjusted the cluster of gears to focus the glittering cut-glass lens. The murky sight that emerged sent a jolt of fear to his gut. His lips peeled back, baring his teeth, and the beast inside him sat up and growled.

He knew the spirit world was alongside him, but it was another thing entirely to see it with his own eyes. The damned souls who refused to pass through the Gate swarmed around the woman on the street below. Her grief attracted them like moths to the flame. He could almost taste their hunger. The ethereal forms floated around her. Craving her touch. Coveting her senses.

She unconsciously waved a hand in front of her face as if

brushing away fog, but was unaware of the danger. Why did humans choose to ignore their instincts?

For some reason the sight of the woman trapped by the wraiths affected him more than it should have. His beast strained forward, trying to catch her scent across the water-logged street. Energy tingled through his core. Fur rippled beneath his skin. He hung on to his human form, snuffing out the glow that preceded the Change. Sweat broke on his brow. His pulse raced. With three days until the full moon, he should have more control.

The crows chose that moment to show up and distract him, which for once was a good thing. Gossiping in their guttural tongue, they landed on the telephone wires and rooftops. Watching. Waiting. Spying on him for their Kivati masters.

Lady be damned.

Kivati sentinels couldn't be far behind. An ancient race of shape-changers, the Kivati were legends in their own right: Raven, Cougar, Coyote, Thunderbird. Wolf. They once protected the land and humankind. Still did, officially. But they did little to prove it, too caught up in a bloody war with the Drekar to waste time on humans.

At least the Drekar's intentions were honest. Cursed with no souls of their own, the dragon-shifters fed on human souls. They weren't always careful to leave their food alive. Who cared how many humans died, as long as there were enough to feed on? Better the weak were culled from the flock, leaving the strongest souls to provide sustenance. The Kivati felt honor-bound to defend humans, and the Drekar gave as good as they got.

It was a secret war, carried out in the shadowed alleys and boardrooms, behind the backs of the humans. The battles might be hidden, but the damage was everywhere. Outright neglect as resources were diverted into the war. A failing power grid as ghosts fried electrical circuits. Midnight explosions made to look like accidents. The shining skyscrapers deteriorating as soon as the last nail was hammered in. People disappeared and murder splashed across the nightly news, but humans chalked it up to gang violence. Other major metropolises had similar problems of urban decay and crime. It was the high price of city living. Those who didn't like it were welcome to leave, and they did.

The damage accelerated every time some damn fool tried to open the Gate, cracking it farther, letting more ghosts and demons slip into the living world. The last time, it caused Mount St. Helens to erupt. Next time, who knew? From his vantage point on the roof, Hart could count three more volcanoes just waiting to blow their tops.

He could take care of himself. Always had. He aimed his rifle at the north end of the street where Kivati sentinels were sure to appear. Their crow scouts gave them away. Odds were good they were here for the same necklace he was. He had to get it first. Norgard wouldn't take no for an answer.

Once Hart completed this job there was a single task left to pay off the blood debt that bound him. He could taste his freedom on the bitter north wind. After fifteen years in Norgard's service, Hart's soul was a dark, twisted thing, but it was his.

Down on the street, the woman glanced briefly up at the cackling crows, before stepping through the fence gate. The whistling charms that hung from the wrought-iron bars kept the dead from following her. Too bad the Kivati weren't so easily put off. She climbed the steps, heaved open the morgue's heavy iron door, and slipped inside.

Hart didn't have time to follow and interrogate her about the necklace. All he could do was train his rifle on the two black jeeps that screeched to a halt on the street below. Black titanium scales plated the sides and tops of the vehicles. Two long tailpipes trailed from the undercarriage, one puffing black smoke from the firebox, the other a cloud of white water droplets. The Kivati had kept their old technology and adapted it to the new era. Though the large armored vehicles resembled modern cars, they ran on steam.

The Kivati sentinels moved with the grace and speed of their animal counterparts. Six tall, muscled men untucked themselves from the cramped vehicles and spilled onto the sidewalk, long black dusters swinging in the wind. Even though the sun hadn't been seen in a good week or more, they wore dark sunglasses—the better to hide eerie violet-ringed pupils. The Kivati believed in secrecy at any cost. Humans could never learn of the monsters that battled for control of their city.

Hart recognized the Fox and his usual crew of hotheaded young Thunderbirds and Crows. Rudrick was shorter than the others, with the lean build of a runner, red-streaked hair and a tuft of fur at his chin. Cocky too, as he wore no glasses. The look in his beady black eyes was crafty and calculated, his inner Fox brought to the fore by the pleasure of the hunt.

Hart had a clear shot of the sidewalk and anyone trying to walk past the fence to the morgue front door. He raised his rifle, aimed at the ground in front of Rudrick, and fired. The bullet nicked the concrete. The sentinels scattered, dodging his bullets as they ran behind their jeeps for safety.

The bastards might not have time to pull their own guns, but they weren't without weapons. From the sky, a crow swooped, talons extended, straight at Hart's face. He shot it. On the ground, a sentinel cried out as his mental connection to the bird was severed.

The other birds attacked, slashing and clawing. Razor-sharp beaks aimed at Hart's eyes.

He was too quick. He rolled onto his back and came up blasting. The guns he kept strapped beneath his jacket settled into his grip as if he'd been born with them instead of hands. Black feathers rained down. Screams like rusty violins filled the air. A few crows slipped past his bullets, and he felt his scalp tear and blood splatter his cheek.

He relished it, though it wasn't a real battle, just a game. A bit of professional courtesy between one killer and another: *This target's mine.*

Message received, thank you.

Crow blood sprayed his tongue, bitter and warm and disgustingly familiar. More and more came until the sky was black and beating wings obscured his vision. His ears rang with the blast from his guns.

The attack stopped all at once, after a single mental command from their Kivati masters. The birds—the survivors—limped off to sit on the telephone wires and clean their wounds. Hart's jacket had held up well against the assault, shielding him like a tough leather skin, but his face and hands stung with talon marks. He rolled onto his stomach and pulled himself to the edge of the building so that he could look down on the street and assess the damage.

Behind the cover of the jeeps, the sentinels waited with firepower ticking in their hungry fingers. One man clutched his right shoulder; blood welled slowly from a hole shot through the black wool coat. Another lay moaning on the cold, wet ground, hands pressed to his temple, his consciousness ripped apart by the loss of too many crows. Mental wounds were hard to stitch up.

Sucked to be him, but what did the man expect, connecting himself to another being like that? Kivati felt the death of their familiars like the loss of a limb, keen as a knife to the heart. Dumb bastards. Attachments were weakness. Hart would give his left nut—hell, both nuts—to be rid of the crazed beast inside him.

The rain washed the blood from his skin and swept broken feathers into the clogged gutters in the street below. In the distance, beyond the stormy Sound, sunlight broke over the Olympic Mountains.

To Hart's surprise, the Kivati gave up. With an order from Rudrick, they loaded into the jeeps and drove off in a cloud of smoke, the chug of the steam engines echoing in the empty, waterlogged street.

Strange. Either they weren't here for the necklace after all, or they didn't want it as badly as he'd thought. Maybe it was only sentimental junk, but he doubted it. His instincts said Norgard was holding out on him, as usual. Norgard wouldn't lift a claw to save his own mother.

Dead crows lay where they had fallen along the rooftop and the asphalt below. Hart pulled the Deadglass out of his pocket and held it to his eye. Through the glass he watched shadows pull away from the small broken bodies. They condensed and solidified, feather by translucent feather. A pathway through the Aether began to shine, guiding the way home. One by one, the spirit birds flew into the sky and disappeared beyond the shimmering veil.

Rising, Hart shouldered his rifle. He slipped the Deadglass into his pocket, slid down the fire escape, and headed to the morgue. Nothing could keep him from finding that necklace. No Kivati. No wraith. He'd earn his freedom if he had to fight hell itself.

Kayla entered the dimly lit morgue and bit her lip to keep from crying. She had to hold it together. If she allowed the swelling sorrow to shatter her into a million bits, there would be no one left to pick up the pieces. Seattle, this godforsaken, desolate city, had stolen everyone from her. Her mother in a violent "accident" that Kayla only vaguely remembered. Her father from the heartbreak of it years later. Now her sister, who was shockingly, mysteriously dead. A yawning chasm opened in her chest, threatening to suck her down into the black abyss. She couldn't let it.

Instead of harsh fluorescents, the Seattle morgue was lit with soft gaslights. A fire hazard, but the warm glow was strangely comforting. It made everything seem less real, like she'd stepped back in time.

A skinny, middle-aged woman with sallow skin manned the welcome desk. Her shirt had a vaguely Edwardian air with a short collar and lightly puffed sleeves. She was filling out forms by hand, holding the pencil awkwardly with her long pink nails. She didn't look up when she asked for Kayla's name. Too tired to care, perhaps.

"Friday," Kayla said, proud that her voice didn't shake, "Kayla Friday. I'm here to identify my . . . sister."

The woman set the pencil down and raised her head. She was younger than she had first appeared. Her salt-and-pepper hair and the weary sag of her shoulders were deceptive. "I.D.?"

Kayla fumbled with her purse to pull out her driver's license and handed it over.

The woman eyed the Philadelphia address. "Long way from home."

No kidding. Seattle might be a six-hour plane ride from Philly, but Kayla felt like she'd traveled halfway around the world to some war-torn, third world country where electricity was rationed. She'd never seen so many old diesel cars or broken traffic lights. Half-empty skyscrapers lorded over roads strewn with uncollected trash and abandoned vehicles. The few brave souls out on the streets of the once-great city scuttled about with creased foreheads and downcast eyes.

Desi should have taken one look at this dump and come back home, but she hadn't. The contrary kid had *liked* it. She had started taking mythology classes at the university. Useless degree, Kayla thought. But for the first time Desi was excited about school, so Kayla let it slide.

Until recently. In the past few weeks, Desi had grown distant. Preoccupied. She hadn't returned Kayla's last two phone calls.

The receptionist tapped her pencil against the desk and thinned her lips. "You took longer than you should have to show up."

"I got the call yesterday," Kayla protested. "Took the first flight I could." She was going on thirty hours without sleep. The policeman's voice haunted her, repeating those terrible words in her head: *Your sister is dead.*

"Dangerous to let a body sit empty and whole overnight." The woman stood and unlocked the cabinet behind her.

Why? In her two years of nursing, Kayla had never heard of such a thing. Perhaps if Desi had died of something contagious—bubonic plague or smallpox came to mind—but then she would be quarantined.

The receptionist pulled a paper bag out of the cabinet and handed it to Kayla. "The deceased's effects."

Kayla licked her lips, trying and failing to say thank you like her mama had taught her. Her mouth was dry as bone. She clutched the bag to her chest, the last articles found on her sister, the only clues to solving the mystery of her death.

The woman stabbed one long nail down the dim hallway. "Body is waiting. First door on your left." Washing her hands of the matter, she returned to her paperwork.

The deceased. The body. The words were so impersonal, detached from the loving, bubbly girl who was her sister. *Had been* her sister.

Strength of will held Kayla together and carried her down the long empty hallway to the exam room. A wave of formaldehyde and a blast of freezing air greeted her when she opened the door. Unforgiving metal covered every surface, and—despite the soft glow of the gas lamps—the air felt stagnant and dead. Dead as the body beneath the sheet.

How could her heart hurt so much yet still beat so quickly? She could do this. She was a nurse, for goodness sake. Dead bodies were nothing new. Approaching the exam table in the center of the room, she reached out to touch the cold cotton sheet. Her hand trembled. With a deep breath, she yanked the cloth back.

It took a few minutes for her brain to recognize the

blue-tinged figure on the slab in front of her. At first she
thought there'd been some mistake. This wasn't her sister. This
was some alien body: lips purple and cracked, belly swollen
and distended, dark veins clearly outlined as if they'd been
drawn on the skin in magic marker.

Pregnant? Her sister wasn't *pregnant*.

But that small hope that this wasn't her sister shattered as she
took in the familiar cheekbones; wide-set eyes; the rich, wavy,
mahogany hair; proud nose; and delicately pointed chin. Desi.

A sob burst from deep in her chest. How could Desi be so
still? Desi was always full of life, overflowing with passion.
A little touch of the devil in her twinkling brown eyes. How
could a life so vibrant be snuffed out?

It couldn't. No, it was impossible. There must be some
mistake.

Her brain quit and all her rational, logical thoughts flew out
the window. She watched herself as if from a distance, detached
yet frantic. She ran her hands over the frozen blue skin, searching automatically for a pulse. She needed a defibrillator. A shot
of adrenaline to inject in the heart. Something, anything to
make her sister move again.

The chest muscles were hard beneath her fingers when she
placed them over Desi's heart.

"Please," she whispered. Hot tears streamed down her
cheek, but she ignored them. All she wanted was to have her
sister back. She didn't want to be left behind. Not again. Not
when there was no one left.

Grief opened a door deep inside her, and a pulsing, shimmering light poured out. She'd never seen or felt anything like
it. In her panic, one thought became clear: if she could warm
Desi with that light, everything would be okay. Instinctively,
she grabbed hold of it and pushed. The viscous light slid up her
nerve endings and tingled along her arms. A liquid flow of
her own essence, pouring out through her fingertips and into
her dying patient.

Except this patient was already dead.

She pulled and pushed at the unreal, impossible light. Yanked until the room spun and her eyes could no longer focus. Poured everything into the empty shell beneath her palms.

Only to watch the light die when it left her skin. Desi's life force was long gone. There was nothing left. Not a flicker. Not an ember. Not a whisper of the laughter and love and heart that had once been a giving, brightly burning soul.

Instead there was an emptiness in Desi, and it sucked at Kayla until she thought she might leave her body and jump headfirst into the cold corpse beneath her hands.

Out of nowhere, strong hands yanked her away from the table. A deep, gruff voice penetrated the haze in her brain. "Stop it."

Kayla found her sobs muffled against a broad warm chest. She didn't want it. Her hands flailed against the stranger, but it was like hitting a boulder.

"Stop," he growled. "Lady be damned. You got a death wish?" His fingers gripped her biceps like iron bands. She wasn't strong enough to push him away. She hadn't been strong enough to help Desi or her parents. What was the point of being a nurse if she couldn't save the ones closest to her?

"Let go of me!" she demanded.

He complied, and she stumbled back. It was foreign, this helplessness. She was supposed to be the strong one—the rock. At the moment, she was weak as a kitten. Desi wouldn't recognize her. Embarrassment burned across her cheeks. How long had this guy been watching her? She hadn't heard him enter. "Who are you? What are you doing here?"

"Name's Hart." The stranger leaned back against the metal door, aloof and detached. He was big—almost a head taller than she and shoulders twice as wide—and seemed to take up half the oxygen in the room. Even with fresh scrapes on his skin, he was a rugged sort of handsome. His face was compelling, as if his features had been hewn by wind and rain from some lonely mountain crag. The rain had plastered his coal-black hair over his forehead. His dark eyes studied her, wolflike, from under shaggy brows. The gaslight warmed his copper skin, giving him a sun-kissed glow at odds with the gloomy winter skies outside. He seemed dressed for combat in a dark brown leather bomber jacket, worn and patched with age and hard use; charcoal-gray pants with bulging pockets; and heavy black boots. The butt of a rifle stuck out over his shoulder and a holster hung at each hip. How did he get in here armed?

In spite of the weapons, he made her think of a wild animal, graceful yet predatory. It was in the wise wildness of his gaze; the inquisitive tilt of his head; the way he held himself, perfectly still, muscles clenched, poised to run at a moment's notice. He had a definite air of danger, and the weather-worn creases at the corners of his eyes only made his face more intriguing.

A shock of blinding white marked his dark hair on the right side. A memento of some injury? She reached out to explore that thick mane, but caught herself before she touched him.

How embarrassing. First she cried on the man's chest, then she almost molested him—what was next? What was wrong with her? She rubbed the ache between her eyes. "I'm Kayla, Desiree's sis—"

"I know who you are. Just what do you think you were doing?"

Of course he had to notice her mental breakdown. Grief had made her completely irrational. There was no door inside her. No magical light. "I . . ." She couldn't answer. Couldn't explain something that didn't make sense to herself. Logic, for the first time in her life, failed her. "I don't know." She turned away, trying to hold together the last shreds of her dignity.

She felt Hart step nearer. The heat and energy that radiated from his body was like a living thing. It skimmed along her skin and down her spine.

"Don't do it again." He grasped her chin and turned her head to examine her. His gaze bore into her with an intensity that stripped her to blood and bone.

"Don't touch me."

He leaned closer and *sniffed* her. What the hell? "You're human." He sounded . . . confused.

Well, duh. Her raised brow said it all.

"Never mind. Doesn't matter." He dropped his hand abruptly. "Where is the necklace?"

"What necklace?"

"Be straight with me, and this will go down easier."

"Are you one of Desi's friends?"

"Never met the chick." He shook his head and glanced down at the paper bag she had dropped beneath the table. "I need to search the belongings found on her."

"Why?" She didn't want him touching her sister's things. "You think she has a necklace that somehow belongs to you?"

He hesitated, as if debating to tell her the truth. "She stole it from my boss."

"Bull." Desi was a little wild, but she would never steal.

"How well did you know your sister?"

She pointed her finger at him, but her lips wouldn't form words. Desi had been her best friend, the sun to her moon. They'd known all each other's secrets. Didn't they? "I want to speak to your boss. The police have stopped asking questions, but I know there's more. I want the truth."

"The truth?" His expression went flat. He glanced at the body and back at Kayla. "Looks like a drug overdose."

"I don't believe that." *And neither do you.*

"The coroner's report not good enough for you, is that it?"

"Not for me. Not for anyone with half a brain."

He stepped around her and picked up the fallen bag that held Desi's effects. She fought down the urge to snatch it back.

"She ever mention Norgard? The Drekar? The Kivati?"

Kayla shook her head at each. Sorrow washed over her, and

a strange sense of betrayal. She had thought she and her sister were close, but none of those names sounded familiar. Desi's stories had involved wacky new friends, grumpy professors, and off-the-hook parties. At least in the beginning. Since Thanksgiving, she'd talked solely about her coursework: the mythology, legends and folklore of the Pacific Northwest. Finally growing up, Kayla had thought. Getting serious. Pulling all-nighters in the library, not the clubs. And then Desi had become distracted. Distant.

A hint of worry had germinated at the back of her mind, but Kayla hadn't pushed. She'd figured her sister would talk about it when she was good and ready.

But maybe Kayla should have pushed in this instance. She might have done something to avoid this outcome if she had known. Peer pressure, a bad relationship, depression, addiction. These things were solvable, with help. If only Desi had asked.

Hart lifted the paper bag to his face and sniffed it. What was it with the sniffing?

"The necklace is a piece of jade carved with Babylonian cuneiform. Doesn't matter how it got into your sister's possession, but it belongs to my boss and he wants it back."

"What's your boss's name?"

He ignored her and rifled through the paper bag.

"Yo, buddy, I'm talking to you." She tried to snatch the bag back, but he restrained her easily with one hand while he dumped the bag's contents on the metal table. She struggled against him. It was like trying to move a mountain. "Stop it! I'm calling security."

"Good try, babe. Things work a little differently here. Now when I drop my hand, you're going to stay right there like a good little girl while I go through this."

"Screw you." She kicked him in the shin.

"Tempting." His eyes scoured her body. "Against the cold metal wall? Or should we dump the dead girl off the table and bend you over it?"

Kayla swallowed the bile that rose in her throat. She couldn't stop the hot tears that welled in her eyes. "Bastard."

Hart looked away uncomfortably. "Yeah, that's the truth. Just . . . just stay there."

When he let go, she stayed where she was.

He separated the pile of belongings on the table, pulling out a change of clothes, two hollowed silver needles with rust-colored tips, a club ID bracelet, which read "Butterworth's" in elegant gold foil, and an envelope addressed to her in Desi's loose scrawl. Inside was a single business card. He took it out and read the name. The muscles in his jaw clenched. She almost expected him to bare his teeth and snarl.

"What is it?" she asked.

"Nothing."

She snatched the card out of his hand and read, "Emory Corbette, Kivati Hall." On the back Desi had written *Give him the key.*

She glanced at Hart. "What key? Who is this guy?"

"Your sister never mentioned him?"

"No." And it hurt. "Who is he?"

"The Raven Lord. A ruthless son of a bitch."

"The *what* now?"

One edge of his mouth kicked up.

"What exactly is the Raven Lord? What would my sister be doing with some crackpot who makes up titles for himself?"

"You might not want to call him that."

"What, Raven Lord?"

"Crackpot."

"Whatever. Is this a friend of yours?" Hart shook his head, but he looked amused. Kayla couldn't tell if he was joking or not. She tried to veer back to the topic. "You think this guy had something to do with my sister's death?"

Hart began to stuff the clothes back in the bag and didn't look at her. "Lady, I think you should accept your sister died of a drug overdose and leave it at that."

"As a nurse, I can tell you she didn't. Do I look like a chump?"

He thrust the bag at her, and they both held on for a moment. The pupils of his strange eyes were encircled by a thin band of violet. His gaze raked her body, head to toe and back again, taking extra time to visually fondle her chest. She resisted the urge to cover herself, proud she didn't back down. But when he took a step forward, she couldn't help a hasty step back. Her shoulders knocked against the cold metal wall.

"Naw." He leered, towering over her. "You look smart. Are you smart, babe? 'Cause nothing you do can bring her back." The half smile dropped like a mask. His pupils dilated until his eyes shone, two pools of violet-black, otherworldly and somehow inhuman. He bent down to whisper in her ear, breath hot on her sensitive neck. "Take some advice." His lips brushed her ear. "The smartest thing you can do?"

She smelled musk and pine, thought of dark forests and the wild hunt. A shiver that had nothing to do with fear raced down her spine.

"Run."

Chapter 2

Kayla licked dry lips. "Are you threatening me?"

Hart opened his mouth to answer, but the door crashed open. Men burst through. There were six of them, all hulking brutes with chiseled features and dark hair. The long black dusters swept out like wings as they moved. The black sunglasses were laughable against the dim indoor gaslight; the guns were not.

This was not her day.

"Too late, babe," Hart said softly. "The cavalry has arrived. Another damsel saved from the big bad wolf." He straightened and adopted a half smirk. "Ladies."

Three men rushed to restrain him. They pulled him away from Kayla and yanked his arms roughly behind his back, one man on each side. The third man pressed a rifle barrel to his temple. Hart grinned, daring them to shoot him.

The leader of the band was a wiry, red-haired man with a goatee. He strolled forward, all lanky, oiled grace. "Hart. Getting sloppy, aren't you? Johnny, please."

One of the younger men—early twenties with crow-black hair pulled back in a ponytail—stepped up to Hart and smashed the butt of his rifle into Hart's head.

Kayla screamed.

Hart crumpled to the ground, blood running from his forehead, unconscious.

She rushed forward to help him, but steely arms caught her and swept her off the ground. She couldn't move.

The red-haired man made soothing noises in her ear. "Don't trouble yourself, Miss . . . Friday, is it?"

"He's hurt! I'm calling the police." The arms around her squeezed, almost cutting off her air.

The man only laughed. "Let me introduce myself: Rudrick Todd. I'm part of the city's security force. I'm the guy the police call in situations like this."

"I don't believe you."

He shrugged.

"Please," she begged. "Let me help him. I'm a nurse. Head wounds are serious. You don't want him to die."

"Forget him," Rudrick said. "Benard, be quick about it."

The largest henchman—a hulking brute with long brown hair and a monstrous unibrow—approached the metal table. He yanked the sheet off Desi's body, exposing her naked limbs to the frosty air.

"Don't touch her!" Kayla's stomach rolled as she watched the man run his large hands from the top of Desi's head, over her breasts and distended belly, and down each leg. His movements were impersonal and cold, but he was still groping her sister.

"Stop. What are you doing?" she asked.

"Desiree was in possession of an artifact of immense value when she died," Rudrick said.

"So I've heard."

Rudrick scowled. "She was bringing it to me. The Drekar can't be trusted with it—"

Benard whistled, cutting Rudrick off. "This could be trouble." He held up Desi's hand to show the inside of her wrist, where a rough symbol had been carved into the flesh. "It's Norse."

Kayla had missed that. It brought to mind cults and satanic rituals, but that was even crazier than Desi using drugs.

"Copy it down and move on," Rudrick ordered. "The girl was too smart by half."

Benard checked Desi's body cavities next. He opened her jaw and felt the inside of her mouth. He stuck his thick, ugly hands between her thighs.

Kayla looked away. "Let me go. I don't know anything about the necklace."

"Let me put this in simple terms your little human brain can comprehend: Hart works for a man who would suck out your soul and leave you to die in a heartbeat. I'm one of the good guys. So I'm going to ask you one more time: Where is the necklace?"

"I don't know."

"She's clean," Benard said. He bent and picked up Emory Corbette's business card from the floor. "Take a look, Red." He handed it to Rudrick, who read the message on the back.

"I see." Rudrick's fingers tightened on her arms. "You're holding out on me, Miss Friday."

"I don't know what you're talking about."

"Perhaps." He searched her face. "Perhaps not."

On the floor Hart groaned. He was coming around. Two men picked him up by the arms. Hart was a big man, but they dragged him between them like a rag doll.

"Let's take this outside." Rudrick hooked Kayla's elbow and escorted her toward the door. "Take care of the body," he ordered over his shoulder.

"What—" Kayla tried to turn back to her sister, but Rudrick wouldn't let her.

Benard whipped out a flask and poured it over Desi's body.

She knew what was about to happen, even before he lit the match. Fire erupted, greedily consuming the accelerant, spreading across her sister's poor corpse.

Kayla froze, a scream caught in her throat. She would have

run to beat out those terrible flames, but Rudrick grabbed her shaking shoulders and dragged her out of the room. She fought, uselessly. Shock set in. Her vision blurred.

Her last sight was the pyre. The smell of burning flesh followed them down the hallway and into the wet dusk outside. The rain had slowed to a light mist. Clouds still obscured the sky, but the air seemed bright after the dark of the morgue. The cold wind slapped her wet cheeks. The pavement was littered with dead crows.

"Why?" she screamed. "How could you? You . . . monster!"

"Shut up, human." Rudrick shook her.

"Human? What are you talking about? You're crazy. All of you." Pain thickened her voice. "You can't do that to her. She's my sister! My baby sister."

"It's what she would have wanted," Hart said from behind her. His tone was soothing, but his words made no sense. "You don't want her to come back that way."

Come back? There was no return from death.

Rudrick's goons didn't relax. They formed a loose circle in the street, guns ready. More crows than she'd ever seen were perched on the telephone lines above. Their grating calls seemed tinged with laughter.

"Right, then." Rudrick released her arm abruptly, and she staggered.

She wrapped her arms around herself, looking to Hart for guidance, but he had his own problems. Rudrick ordered the two men to release him, and they shoved him into the center of the circle. He quickly caught his balance and brushed off his arms, smirking at the men surrounding him, insolent and cocky despite his bruises.

She had to admire his bravado.

He turned toward her and their eyes locked. His strange violet-ringed pupils held danger and desire. The connection burned hot and fast. Her breath caught. She wanted to run to him. A stranger. A dangerous, unpredictable man.

Surprise flickered across his face, and she knew he felt it too. He looked away, unable to hold that vulnerable connection.

"Our lord and master," Rudrick told Hart, "still harbors this delusion that you will rejoin the fold."

Hart spat on the ground.

"Funny, I had the same response," Rudrick said. "The rest of us don't want your filth. The moon madness is a blight on our sacred bloodline. It doesn't excuse your behavior." His lip curled. "A traitor to your own kind."

Moon madness? Sacred bloodline? What the hell was he talking about?

"I work for whatever fucker pays me," Hart said. "You want something done? I'll work for you too. I don't discriminate."

"How you could be so stupid as to voluntarily enslave yourself, I can't imagine. I should put you out of your misery."

"I'll be there to welcome you on the other side. Cross my heart." Hart drew an X over his left breast.

Were these people for real? Kayla searched the street and crumbling buildings on either side, half expecting a movie camera to pop out of the shadows. Nothing. She decided shock must be messing with her hearing. When everyone around you seemed delusional, it might just be you.

"Fortunate for us that you heal quickly. The necklace, dog." Rudrick motioned for his men to tighten ranks around Hart. "Tell us what you know. Johnny?"

Behind Rudrick, the younger man who'd hit Hart with the rifle stepped into the circle. He took a pair of leather gloves from his coat pocket and made a big show of pulling them on.

Hart didn't seem worried, though blood still trickled down his forehead. His powerful shoulders cocked back. Amusement played along the crooked line of his lips. "How does Corbette feel about the girl dying under your watch? One human life for a sentimental trinket."

Rudrick showed a mouthful of pointy white teeth. "Sentimental? Hardly. Don't tell me you don't know what it does?"

Laughing, he stepped back into the circle. "Single combat. No weapons."

Kayla felt sick. What was this—*Mortal Kombat*? What kind of people had her sister been involved with? "You can't do this," she protested. "It can't be legal."

No one paid her any attention.

Hart began unloading weapons. The rifle strapped to his back went first. The broadsword at his hip, next. Beneath the jacket he wore a holster with two pistols. Out of his pants pockets he pulled a strange brass spyglass, throwing stars, and small knives. She'd never seen such an arsenal except in the movies. He stacked them, lovingly, on his jacket at the edge of the circle.

Hart and Johnny stripped to the waist. And—oh!—if she hadn't been so anxious she might have admired all that fine muscle and shimmering copper flesh. Both men were ripped. Johnny was younger by about ten years, his sleek body unmarred by battle and time. Black geometric tattoos covered his back and shoulders. Inked feathers twisted up his spine.

Hart was larger, but battered. Purple blotches decorated his ribs. He looked about thirty, but his body had seen a lifetime of fights. Where Johnny was tattooed, Hart bore old white scars that crisscrossed like lace over his tanned skin. Gold bands with runic marks circled his impressive biceps. A silver disk on a leather thong hung from his neck. Both men were exotic and mysterious, but Kayla couldn't keep her eyes off Hart.

The two contenders circled each other, dancing lightly on their toes. Quick as a whip, Hart lashed out, not with his fist but with his fingers, as if swiping with claws. Johnny managed to dodge back by a hairbreadth.

"No shifting," Rudrick growled. "Or I'll let the Thunderbird at you. It's in your favor, dog."

Shifting how? They couldn't fight if they didn't move from foot to foot. That couldn't be what he meant. Was Thunderbird some sort of gang caste?

Hart shrugged as if to say, "Who the hell cares?"

After that, the action went so fast it was all Kayla could do to keep track of the combatants. They lunged and dove in sync, partners in some impressively coordinated dance. The movements were a strange mix of martial arts and barroom brawl—anything goes, yet smooth and efficient. Each punch was a close shave away from serious damage.

Their shadows blurred, until Kayla could swear she saw not two men fighting, but two animals—a giant bird and a wolf, snatching at each other with tooth, claw, and razor-sharp beak. It was the oddest sight. First her hearing, now her vision. She was losing it inch by inch.

The gunmen watched the fight hungrily. Out of the corner of her eye, their cheekbones seemed to widen and their eyes glowed.

She tried to laugh it off, but couldn't shake the feeling. She couldn't watch. Couldn't drag her eyes away. Two gladiators locked in combat, sweat and rain-slicked muscles glistening. Sleek and graceful. Vicious and wild.

Hart was tiring, and no wonder, given his recent head injury. His reaction time slowed, so that she could actually see the movements of his hands and legs.

Johnny swiped out with his fist and Hart brought his arm up seconds too late. The fist connected with his nose and Hart crashed to the ground. Johnny followed him down. Punching. Kicking.

Wetness splattered the concrete, and Kayla realized it was blood.

Blood.

Johnny was going to kill Hart while these lunatics watched and did nothing.

Shock might be wearing on her system, but she couldn't let that one go. She refused to stand idly by while murder was committed in front of her. How would she live with herself? "Leave him alone!" she shouted. "Stop hurting him!"

Johnny didn't stop. Running forward, she threw herself on top of Hart and shielded him with her body. He was so much bigger than her; it was laughable that she would try to protect him with her small frame. But she had to do something.

Johnny's foot came an inch from connecting with her head. She cringed. Stupid move, running into danger like that. She'd never been an act-first, think-later sort of person—that had been Desi's suit—but adrenaline made her reckless. "Stop hurting him," she repeated. The jagged asphalt cut into her knees. "Please stop."

The circle of men was icily still. Disapproving. Dangerous. She tried not to shake. Beneath her, Hart lay still, his body hot and hard, smelling of sweat, blood, and the forest. She was uncomfortably aware of her breasts pressed against his solid muscle.

"You'd risk your life for this bastard?" Rudrick asked. "He killed his own mother."

Kayla paused. Was that true? If she let Rudrick distract her, she was going to chicken out. Raising her head, she looked him in the eye and played her only card. "I'm Desiree Friday's sister. Her confidante. I know her better than anyone. If Desiree hid this necklace you want so badly, I'm the only one who'll be able to find it."

Rudrick stared at her. She stared back. He had the same weird violet-rimmed eyes as Hart. Must be some freaky contacts.

The moment stretched out. A billion thoughts raced through her head. If he called her bluff, would he kill her too? Would she die trying to rescue a stranger? Who would the police call to identify her body? There was no one left. Was this how Desi died, recklessly throwing herself into someone else's problems?

She swallowed her fear. She'd already stuck her foot in. There was no backing out now. "The necklace for his freedom."

Rudrick glanced from her to Hart. His eyes were calculating. "Is he a friend of yours?"

"I . . . yes." Hart's chest vibrated beneath her. Was he laughing?

"I wonder," Rudrick said, studying Hart, "if you'll be allowed to pass through the Gate if you die before the blood debt is repaid."

More nonsense, Kayla thought. But apparently it meant something to Hart, because he tensed.

Rudrick smiled. "I admit the thought of endlessly fighting your enslaved ghost is the only thing that keeps me from killing you. So be it, Miss Friday. You can have your Wolf."

Wolf? Another strange reference that shot over her head. Ghosts and bogeymen aside, she didn't trust these men. "Promise you won't hurt him anymore." As much as a promise from a lunatic would get her.

Rudrick held up three fingers, scout's honor. "You find me what I want, Miss Friday, and I promise not to harm a hair on his furry hide—"

Kayla let out a breath.

"—but only if you bring me the necklace by the full moon."

"What?"

"Three days, Miss Friday. After that all bets are off, and I'll be forced to make an example of you. Remember that as you hunt." Rudrick pulled out a business card and bent down to hand it to her. On it was a number, nothing else. "My private line. I'm handling this matter personally. Don't talk to anyone else."

He motioned to his men.

And they began to change. Their pupils expanded, growing outward over their irises and covering the whites of their eyes. Their noses lengthened, either to sharp points or hooked beaks. The black of their dusters stretched and split, changing before her eyes into feathers and wings. Their bodies morphed grotesquely. Men, no longer, but giant birds. Three, including Johnny, became man-sized crows. Two others were monstrous *things*. Feathered and avian, but the size of a pterodactyl. Twenty-foot wingspans. Long, hooked beaks the length of her arm. Claws large enough to pick up a small whale.

Rudrick and the brute Benard—who had remained human—swung themselves onto the necks of the two monster birds. Rudrick gave a mock salute.

Beautiful and terrible, they launched into the air. Gale-force wind rocketed through the street behind them. The giant crows followed closely behind.

Kayla blinked, hard, but it didn't clear the sight from her eyes. She watched in horror as they soared across the sky and disappeared behind Capitol Hill.

"Oh, my God," she murmured. "Oh, my God."

Her brain—her logical, ordered, rational brain—had shorted out.

Chapter 3

"You can get up now," Hart said, his breath hot on her sensitive neck.

Her cheeks flushed, and she scrambled off him. "What the hell? That did not just happen. I'm seeing things. It must be shock. It must be . . . no. I must have hit my head." That had to be it.

Stiffly, he pushed himself to his feet. He reached down and grabbed her hand. She focused on the sight of his long, strong fingers and the feel of calluses and heat. It made sense.

Men turning into birds did not.

Fear sunk its claws deep into her gut. What if she really had hit her head and was in some sort of coma? She raised her hands to cover her temples as if she could hold together the tatters of her sanity. The world was too crisp to be a dream. Other than her eyes, her senses were functioning. The wind scraped her skin. The salt air chafed her nose. She bit the inside of her cheek and tasted blood. She must be hallucinating. There was an explanation for those birds. There had to be. Grief. Stress. Sleep deprivation. Concussion. Fever. She was too pragmatic to believe in fairy tales. Her mind—the thing she prized most—had cracked.

Hart tugged her up, and she practically flew into the solid

wall of his chest. She found herself staring at his collarbone.
Another thing that made sense. She understood collarbones,
though she'd never before seen one quite so nicely shaped. A
sleek pelt of light brown hair covered his chest, running up to
the hollow at the base of his throat. Those pecs, even battered,
made her mouth go dry. He was too close. She could stick out
her tongue and lick him.

What was wrong with her?

"You're not crazy," Hart said. His eyes held understanding
and pity. Or was it only a shared madness? "You're not."

"How . . ." She licked her lips and watched him watch the
movement of her tongue. "How can you be sure?"

His hand shot toward her. She reared back. Too slow. He
clamped his fingers around the back of her skull, anchoring
her. Suddenly his mouth was on hers. Hot and wet. Domineer-
ing. Their teeth collided. Her jaw dropped, and he took advantage. His tongue, tasting of coffee and mint, thrust savagely,
once, twice. It thawed the cold shock that had shrouded her
body. Her core heated. *Yes,* she thought. *More.* Forget the monsters. Hart was human and male. Temptation beckoned, more
alluring, more powerful than she'd ever felt it.

Before she could react, it was over. He dropped his hand and
stepped back, leaving her dazed and strangely empty.

"Don't know if that proves I'm dreaming or what," she murmured.

One corner of his mouth turned up. "Dreaming, definitely."

He was a contradiction: violent one moment, flirting the
next. She didn't know whether to fear for her life or her vir-
ginity.

She looked away. *Focus,* she told herself. Now was not the
time to be distracted by a chiseled jaw. There had to be a logical explanation. Mental disorder. Brain cancer. *Anything.*

But there on the ground, only an inch from her sensible
black clogs, lay a feather, long as her leg and shimmering black
like an oil slick. The silver tip narrowed to a razor-sharp point.

She nudged it with her shoe. There was no bird big enough to grow a feather that long. "What is this?"

"Thunderbird feather."

"Thunderbird," she repeated. "Are you in some sort of gang?"

He snorted.

"No? This is a bird feather."

"Yup."

"What kind of bird is a Thunderbird?"

He raised his eyebrows and pointed one finger at the sky in the direction those monster birds had flown in her imagination.

She swallowed. "You saw that too?"

He rolled his eyes.

"Don't roll your eyes at me! What is going on here? Is it . . . is it drugs?"

"Well, now, that's what the medical examiner wrote, ain't it?" He stretched, half turning away from her. Under his breath, he added, "Chump."

She didn't need that thrown back in her face.

When he turned back, his eyes were crinkled in humor. He met her glare with an easy, conspiratorial look, like they were sharing some inside joke. He knew it wasn't drugs. He didn't act like he thought she was crazy.

She glanced at the sky. The clouds lay strewn across it like dirty snow. The birds had disappeared. If she ignored the feather at her foot, she could pretend it had never happened.

Listen to her! For someone who prided herself on scientific reasoning, she was being awfully closed-minded. How could she ignore the evidence in front of her? "I know what I think I saw. I just don't believe it."

He huffed out a breath. "Shocking."

"I mean—" She scrambled to recover. "I saw those birds, and I can't think of an alternate explanation. It just doesn't make sense. You're telling me that those men really changed into Thunderbirds, which are"—she searched her memory of

Desi's mythology lectures—"some kind of Native American myth. I might accept the reemergence of some sort of lost species, but men turning into birds? It defies all logic."

He made a noncommittal noise and bent to pick up his shirt from the wet ground.

"What are they? How can they exist? I saw them change. If I'm not delusional, that is—the jury is still out on that one. But seeing is believing, right? So I have to believe it, but . . . what the *hell*?" She watched him shrug painfully into his shirt, and her eyes caught on the exotic gold bands around his biceps. "What are those?"

"None of your damned business."

Okay then. She pulled her jean jacket tighter. The cold was worse than in Philly. Not by degree, but by intent. It took on a life of its own, damp and insidious. It seeped into a person's bones, and she could imagine it lingering there until a body rotted from the inside out. "Let's humor each other. Let's say you're telling the truth. So tell me what I'm up against. Who are those men? How are mythic monsters flying around Seattle, and it hasn't made the news?"

He studied her for a long moment. "Who's gonna believe it?"

"But with camera phones and the Internet—"

"You can't capture the supernatural on camera, any more than you can measure the Aether." At her blank look he sighed and glanced out to sea. He ran a hand unconsciously over his bruised ribs. Finally, he turned back to her. "Okay, I'll bite. Rudrick and his clowns are Kivati shape-shifters. Those stories about Crow, Raven, Thunderbird, and Wolf are all based on the Kivati. Ancient humans worshipped them as semi-deities, because the Kivati protected them from the *Unktehila*."

"Unka-what?"

"Dragons. It's what the local people called them. You'll hear Drekar now. Old Norse."

"Dragons," she repeated. Desi would have been thrilled. For

a girl dubbed "the Chatterbox" in school, she sure had kept a closed lid on this secret. They weren't supposed to have secrets, not from each other. It had always been the two of them against the world. "Giant birds are easier to believe. I've seen unexplainable things in medicine, but this is huge."

He shrugged. "Humans. If you can't see it, it doesn't exist."

Guilty as charged. She explained away things that seemed impossible. She wanted to do the same to this, but those birds—she couldn't forget them. They were burned into her retinas.

"So let's make sure I have this right: Rudrick and company are shape-shifters who are saving humanity from modern-day dragons? But I'm human—why would they threaten me? I'm really struggling here."

"You're right. Sounds stupid. Forget it." With brisk efficiency, Hart loaded the pile of weapons back into his pockets.

"I didn't mean that." He was clamming up again. She had so many questions. "Desi had a symbol carved into her wrist—"

"A Norse rune."

"I thought you were unconscious."

"Faking it."

"Who would do that to her?"

He picked up the holster and slipped the leather straps over his broad shoulders, wincing briefly as the straps dug into his wounds. It must hurt a lot more than he let on. "That's the question, isn't it?"

"Do you think Desi's key and the necklace are the same thing?"

"Do you?"

She fought to rein in her temper. "Look. I'm sorry I'm having trouble understanding this whole story, but I'm trying. Can't you share any information with me? Rudrick—whatever he is—gave us three days to find the key. We're on the same side. We need to work together."

He fingered the gun strapped to his waist. He didn't need

the weapon to be intimidating. Didn't need the bruises or the cut at his temple to proclaim to the world he was a fighter. Violence flickered in his eyes. Every self-preserving instinct she had screamed, *Run. Run fast and run hard.* But she couldn't. She had to find out what had happened to Desi.

She remembered her little sister at eight, hair pulled back in a dozen mismatched braids, an endless parade of scrapes on her knees and hands, inquisitive eyes straining to take in the world all at once. While playing hide-and-seek in sprawling Fairmount Park, Desi strayed too far and got lost. A late-summer storm hit, and Kayla searched the forest through a wicked downpour, at times fording knee-high water. Hours later, she found Desi shivering under a wilting cardboard box in the deep underbrush, teeth chattering, raindrops dripping from all those braids, big eyes full of relief.

"You came," Desi said as Kayla pulled her from the soggy cardboard.

"Always," Kayla promised. She stuck to it, no matter how much trouble Desi found herself in. Kayla was always there to dig her out.

Until now. She'd failed her baby sister. There was no way in hell she could leave Seattle without knowing why.

"You owe me one," Kayla told Hart. "Tell me what you know."

He ran a hand through the white patch in his unruly dark hair, letting the silence lengthen. She forced herself to look him in the eye. Finally he spoke, "The necklace could be a key. I don't know, but it's a good guess. I'll ask my boss—"

"Who is?"

"A businessman." His eyes slid to the side. "He owns a tea house."

"And?" She motioned for him to elaborate.

"And . . . he's a politician. And patron of the arts. Respected civic leader." The mocking curve to Hart's lip said he didn't think much of his boss's fine reputation. He shrugged into his thick jacket. The light rain beaded on his long eyelashes. "Look, your sister made some bad friends. Forget the Kivati, the Drekar are worse. They eat souls. Stay away from them. Stay away from my boss. Just get out of town."

"Thanks for the heads-up, but—"

"There's nothing I can say to convince you to leave, is there?"

"Nope."

"Hell." He took off down the hill, holding his left arm tightly against his side. "I tried."

"I consider myself warned, so you can clear your con-science," she called, hurrying to catch up. He might not need her, but she, unfortunately, needed him. He was her only guide in this crazy place. "Maybe Desi left more clues in her apart-ment. We should check there, then track down her friends and professors at the university. Then, well, your boss probably knows something." She paused to note his injured stance. "But if you've got a broken rib, first stop should be the hospital."

He shook his head. "No hospitals. I'm fine."

"You're hurt. I can help."

The look he shot her was incredulous, and a little angry. "Forget what I said before—you *are* crazy. You know that?"

She got the feeling offers of help, in his experience, were either nonexistent or plagued with conditions. "She's my sister. I'd do anything for her. Can't you understand that?"

"No. And you can't trust me." He seemed deadly serious.

Of course not. The day she trusted a stranger who carried a gun was the day she'd ice-skate in hell. But she didn't have a choice. She didn't know Seattle. She didn't know about Thun-derbirds and dragons and things that went bump in the night. She didn't know what the mysterious necklace looked like. Where was she going to find another person who did? Rudrick was out of the question. She had to find Desi's key. Hart was her only hope.

"But you can trust me," she said. It would have to be enough.

Emory Corbette narrowed his eyes at the Thunderbird general who sat across from him in the silver steam car. "But would Norgard let him go?"

"None of the Regent's operatives have lived long enough to get this close." Like Corbette, Jace Raiden wore a sharp three-piece suit and heavy wool duster. Though younger than Corbette by a century, Jace and his brother, Kai, had proved themselves in the war with the Drekar. Strong physically, emotionally, and magically, they had risen quickly through the ranks, becoming the Raven Lord's trusted advisers and each a leader of one of the four Kivati Houses. Every man, woman, and child had a job and a place within the hierarchy of their House. Each House contained a balance of warriors, craftsmen, and strong Aether workers. If anything should happen to him, Corbette trusted his Thunderbirds to take control of their Houses and carry on the fight. The Kivati would not fall apart. Not like last time.

"Unbound, the werewolf will be even less stable," Jace said. "Do you want to reinstate the kill order?"

Corbette's gaze shifted to the young blond woman to his right, but his fiancée stared out the rain-streaked window, oblivious to their conversation. She watched the short-lived humans scurrying through the haunted downtown streets. What could they possibly have that she wanted? He turned back to Jace. "No, there are too few of us left. We can't afford the mistakes of the past."

His joke of a father had traded Kivati lands and their sacred duty to protect the Gate for a nickel of gin and a pair of twos. Under his watch, the blood had been diluted. Their ancient enemies—the Drekar—had moved in. The Kivati had been scattered like grain beneath a scythe. A territory that once stretched from northern California to Alaska was now split into small, disparate enclaves in and around the Cascade Mountains. Worse, under his father's rule the Gate that separated the worlds had been cursed and cracked. How much longer could it hold?

Corbette would wrest his people back from the brink. No half-mad Wolf would get in his way. "Every man has a weakness." He didn't look at Lucia, but he was keenly aware of her delicate fragrance floating through the trapped confines of the car. Orchids, he thought. A fragile bloom, suitable to her elegant beauty but not to the steel-spined leader she must become if she were to be his mate. "We must find his."

Jace's nostrils flared. He favored direct attack over the subtle manipulation of pawns on the game board.

"The Wolf is Kivati. He is blood. Some thread of honor must lie at his core, however decrepit it has become." Corbette's anger was a living thing, heating the air of the car. With effort, he restrained it, before Lucia saw in his eyes the iridescent purple light of a killing edge.

She wasn't paying attention. Her narrow upturned nose hovered next to the glass. Her gloved hands were clasped tightly in the folds of her skirt. He glanced out her window to see what had put the wrinkle in her elegant brow. "Penny for your thoughts, Lady Lucia?"

Lucia started, as if she had forgotten he was sitting next to her, though the crisp sleeve of his coal-black suit brushed the edge of her navy sailing gown. It ticked him off. He certainly hadn't forgotten her. The corset pushed up her small perfect breasts. Lace covered them just enough to be proper, but allowed a tantalizing hint of curve and cleavage beneath.

"Forgive me, my lord." She tucked an errant blond curl behind her ear. "My thoughts wandered."

Buttons ran from her slender waist up to a high lace neck. In his mind he slipped them free, one by one, to expose her alabaster skin. *Damn propriety*, the animal in him growled.

But the man knew his tenuous hold on his people and his world was a wing tip away from chaos. He couldn't afford to let down his guard. In a month he could slip those buttons free and flip up her skirts as he liked. Thirty long days. Patience might kill him.

"You seem fascinated by the humans," Jace commented.

She blushed. "Just wondering why they can't feel the Land of the Dead hovering all around us. The Aether is so . . . *alive*, but they insist it doesn't exist. I don't get it."

The Aether was a weightless liquid that filled space, allowing for the propagation of light, electricity, and magic. It separated the worlds and wove the fabric of time. Human scientists from Newton to Einstein had accepted it in one form or another, but more recent theorists had decided the concept was "unnecessary" to explain their measured phenomena. Their brains were too narrow-minded to envision Aether in its entirety. It required an acceptance of the divine, and to humans, faith and science were oil and water.

"Self-deluding idiots," Jace muttered.

"You're more sensitive than most," Corbette told Lucia. Sensitive, but lacking the ability to manipulate the Aether like she should. He could feel the power inside her, trapped like a hive of angry bees. So much potential. What would it take to unleash it? He would enjoy finding out. *After* they were wed.

"But solar flares—I just don't think they're a strong enough explanation for the electricity winking out here and there. Some of them see ghosts. Surely some of them must know the truth?" she asked.

"You expect too much from humans."

"Besides, solar storms do take out satellites, radio communications, and power grids," Jace said. "It happens in other cities around the world. It's not too unbelievable."

"More believable than ghosts?" she asked.

Jace snorted.

"What rational human believes in ghosts?" Corbette gave a

half smile. "I can't explain the stupidity of——" He broke off as he felt the subtle tap of wings against the iron bulwark of his mind. Reaching out across the Aether, he located the crow flying above them and connected to the bird's consciousness. The vision slid into his mind as if he were seeing it himself, the focus clear and bright, but the edges murky. A city street appeared below him, and he knew the crow had watched the scene from a wire overhead. He recognized the sculpture park with its monument to lifeless art, the twisted metal trees and bloated technological instruments standing testament to the barren wasteland of modern imagination.

Below him, Mayor White stood grinning in front of a giant boring machine. The metal blades glistened in the flashes from the press. White waved to the crowd and cut a crimson ribbon in front of the machine. A bead of sweat slipped over his temple. His gaze flicked to the crows overhead, and something ugly flashed over his face.

So. The poor fool had finally done it. After months of courting both sides, the profit-hungry mayor had thrown in his lot with Norgard and his hell-bred kin. Going behind the back of the Kivati-controlled city council, White had approved that idiotic and dangerous drilling project. He assumed that Norgard would return his loyalty. Maybe for a time. As long as he played the fool, Norgard would keep his wallet heavy.

The project would build a light rail tunnel deep beneath the city streets from Ballard to Redmond, passing through downtown. White claimed light rail was the green solution to the city's traffic woes, but it conveniently connected Norgard's main bases of operation. He claimed burying the line prevented a costly land grab; the economic and environmental benefits outweighed the potential disruption of historical and religious artifacts hidden in the earth. Corbette seriously doubted Norgard had any interest in saving the environment. There was another reason the Drekar Regent wanted to dig

through the churned bones of Kivati ancestors and into the
secret lair of the Spider.

What is your plan, Norgard? Corbette wondered. He let the
vision go as the drill came roaring to life. Lucia's anxious face
clicked back into place in his sight.

"Another attack?" she asked.

"No. White has started digging his tunnel."

"Into *her* caves?" Lucia whispered, both afraid and awed
by the ancient being that inhabited that sacred earth. Corbette
had been a child when the Spider had last prophesied the fate
of the race. Now, after a lifetime of waiting, the subject of that
prophecy sat in front of him, her blue eyes solemn, elegance
and innocence wrapped around every last square inch of her
lovely body. Even her name seemed perfect for her role: Lucia,
light bearer. Lucia, harbinger of destiny.

"Don't let it worry you," he said. There would be blood
tonight, he would see to it. "But I'm sorry." He spoke the words
even though Lucia knew them by heart. "I must take a rain
check on our sailing trip."

Something flashed over her porcelain features—relief
or disappointment, he didn't know. He didn't have time to
find out.

"Jace, call a meeting."

"Kai—?"

"Fill your brother in on the situation. Norgard thinks he's
pulled one over on us. We need to move fast while he's busy
gloating."

"There's his assembly plant in Kent—"

"Not now," he said. Lucia didn't seem like she was listening, but he didn't want death weighing on her conscience.
Whatever Drekar target they chose, there would be human
casualties.

He ordered the driver to take them home. The familiar
weight of responsibility adjusted itself on his broad shoulders.
He reminded himself that he was doing this for Lucia so that

their future children could grow up in a world free from Drekar violence and human stupidity.

A world they could rule in peace.

Hanging half out of the driver's side door, Hart push-started his old diesel Mercedes down the steep hill toward the churning sea below. He pulled himself into the moving car and released the clutch. The engine turned, sputtering like an ancient crone, and coughed to life.

Kayla sat in the passenger seat. Her fingers were white-knuckled on the armrests. "What's wrong with your car?"

"Nothing's wrong with it." It was half-truth. His car drove fine, as long as there were no ghosts around. This close to the morgue, electricity rarely worked. Humans had a lot of explanations for the blackouts. The city blamed lack of funds for their neglected power grid. Scientists blamed an abnormal patch in the earth's magnetic field that triggered solar storms, which in turn caused electromagnetic pulses that fried electrical circuits. Conspiracy theorists blamed the government's nuclear bomb testing over Puget Sound, which also caused EMP. They were partially right—EMP was to blame, but most humans would never accept that ghosts were the cause. The few "crazies" who tried to investigate the paranormal in Seattle quickly learned to keep their yaps shut.

Whatever the imagined cause, Seattleites—human and non-human alike—had learned to cope with the electricity problem. They rode bikes and drove old diesels. Environmental, yes, but practical too. With a diesel, he could start his engine by running his car downhill; no electric spark required. If he parked on the flat, he was screwed. Fortunately, downtown was one steep hill after another. The entire city stank of French fries because of all the homemade biodiesel. Importing companies made fast money shipping mechanical tools from other cities' antique shops. Hand-push lawn mowers, vintage rotary egg beaters, and typewriters were a real hit.

The Kivati had their fancy steam cars. Biodiesel fueled the fire that heated water for steam. They could start on the flat no problem in a battlefield full of ghosts. Steam, wind, and the sun powered most of the fancy machines that did their dirty work, all designed and built by Kivati hands. But the stingy bastards didn't share their technology. Not with the humans, and not with the likes of him.

The drive north to Desiree's apartment took half an hour. Seattle crowded a narrow strip of land, squeezed between the salty Puget Sound to the west and the freshwater Lake Washington to the east. The Ship Canal cut through the earth like a gouge from the Sky God's staff, connecting the two bodies of water. Salt meets fresh. West meets east. A dividing line splitting gritty downtown from the peaceful residential neighborhoods of the north. Four drawbridges and two soaring freeways spanned the canal like gear and steel rainbows.

Just north of the Ship Canal, Desiree's apartment crouched beneath two massive fir trees. It had a beaten-down look, with old fieldstone siding, missing shingles, and a slick patina of moss. It clashed with the surrounding artsy neighborhood, where steel sculpture clung to buildings like metal spiders. Corner coffee shops abounded, each proclaiming, WE HAVE LOKI CHOCOLATES! in the window.

Hart pulled into the parking lot and shut off the engine.

"I'm not even going to ask how you knew where my sister lives," Kayla said.

"Babe, I'm a thief and a murderer. You do the math."

She swallowed, but shook off her fear. "Right."

Part of him admired her persistence. Part of him wondered what god he had pissed off to get stuck with her trailing his ass. She shouldn't trust him. The beast prowled around the barrier of his skin. Growling. Growing violent by the minute. It had Kayla in its sights. Her scent filled its nostrils. Her lush curves beckoned. Hart didn't know what the beast would do if let free, but he couldn't take any chances. The curse hung about his heart, heavy as the gold manacles that bound his upper arms. Blood coated his memories—the drapes of the small apartment hanging tattered and dripping red-brown, the sodden carpet squishing beneath his feet, the red stain creeping up the sides of his white sneakers. His fault.

He unleashed his claws into his thigh. The jagged pain brought him back to the present. The Lady help him. He had to find the necklace, and he needed Kayla alive to do it. Desiree Friday had left her sister clues to the hiding spot, he was sure of it. He would make Kayla find the thing and he would steal it from her. Wouldn't be the worst black spot on his record. Not by far.

Opening the car door, he pushed himself out and almost fell.

"Let's get you cleaned and taped up," Kayla said, sounding genuinely concerned. "You won't make it farther in that condition. You must be exhausted."

"I'm fine," he snapped. He was in rough shape, but a little R and R would do it. He didn't want to waste the Drekar blood he had left; Norgard extracted too high a price for refills. Inside him the beast crouched, ready to lash out if she made any threatening moves toward him.

She didn't. Instead, she gave him her back and led the way into the building. She thought him honorable. He wasn't, but her regard warmed something deep inside him. He found himself wanting to prove her right.

He took a moment to admire the way her damp jeans molded to her curvy backside. She had a real figure, the kind a guy could grab hold of. That kiss flashed into his mind. He had meant only to snap her out of her shock, but it had backfired. He could still taste her, and wanted to again.

Three crows perched on the telephone line outside the apartment building. One flew off when he and Kayla approached the building entrance. He didn't give it another thought. The Kivati always had crows tailing him. Sometimes he amused himself giving them the slip. Sometimes he just shot 'em.

He caught the scent of Fox, Crow, and Thunderbird, and followed it inside and up the stairs, straight to Desiree's front door. At first he thought they'd left the place in shambles, but the lay of the mess wasn't quite right for that. He realized Rudrick had put everything back the way he'd found it— Desiree had been a pig.

He quickly swept the two-room apartment for surprises Rudrick might have left behind. Desiree hadn't been in Seattle long, but she had jumped in with both feet. Posters covered every inch of wall, advertising the Drekar's Babylonian New Year festival, anachronistic punk bands, Rainier Beer, and the Port Townsend Victorian Fair. A stack of essays sat on her bedside table, *Raven and the Spirit World*, *Thunderbird and the Whale*, and *Prophesies of the Spider*, next to two hurricane lanterns and a mob of candles for the frequent blackouts. She had matches from Butterworth's and a Thunderbird feather tacked above her bed. Unlike her sister, Desiree Friday hadn't been scared of the supernatural.

He returned to the kitchen. Kayla had rolled up her sleeves and attacked a dirty pot in the sink, brows knit in furious concentration as if banishing grime could make sense of the madness her life had become.

"Place reeks of Kivati," he said. "Rudrick's been here, but didn't want you to know. He slipped up. Didn't count on me tagging along."

She wiped her hands on a dish towel. "He didn't find anything, or he wouldn't have gone to the morgue."

Hart shrugged. "Or he found another clue your sister left you. He agreed to your bargain pretty quick."

She turned away, but not before he caught the sudden sheen in her eyes. He should comfort her or something. *Lure her in*, Norgard would say. *Gain her trust*. Act sympathetic even as he plotted her downfall. There was no room for pity in his empty shell of a heart.

Apparently Hart still had room to feel like a jackass. Naively, Kayla had gone to bat for him and promised to give Norgard's necklace to Rudrick. Hart couldn't let that happen. His freedom, and his life, depended on returning Norgard's treasure. But maybe he could soften the blow. Keep her safe until they found the necklace. Convince her to get out of Seattle before Norgard discovered she was here.

He could smell her grief. The wraiths, too, would smell it, like blood in the water, and come circling. "You need to get your shit together," he told her.

"Excuse me?" She wiped her eyes with the back of her hand and turned. A few strands of hair had worked their way free of her ponytail to wave chaotically about her face. His fingers itched to free more.

Banishing that wayward thought, he pulled a medallion from under his shirt and over his head. "We've got a real wraith problem in Seattle. They're the reason electricity doesn't always work here. Why you'll see gaslights and steam engines and coal bins." He ran his fingers over the comforting silver disk, worn smooth as a polished stone over years of handling. His mother had given it to him. The protection rune carved into the surface tingled as Aether poured through.

"What is a wraith?"

"An evil spirit. Some people just don't want to go when it's their time. They cling to the Land of the Living. But the dead can't taste. Can't touch. Can't experience any of life's little pleasures." His eyes ran along the curve of her lip. "Can't let go, either, like they should. They need a body to feel alive again, so they hunt for weak beings to take over." He tossed her the medallion before he could change his mind. She needed it more than he did.

She fumbled, but caught it. "Like a zombie?"

"You got it. The Norse call them aptrgangr—those who

walk after death. Nasty things. Hard to kill. Your emotional mess paints a big red bull's-eye on your forehead." Stepping forward, he pulled the medallion from her limp fingers. Her soft skin smelled lightly of lilac. He wanted to run his tongue between her fingers and taste her delicate flesh. Wanted to bite the soft pad of her thumb.

Was it the beast's desire, or the man's?

He shook himself. Wrong time. Wrong place. Wrong woman. She wasn't his type. He liked Ishtar maidens who asked no questions and expected nothing in return but hard coin. Mercenaries. They spoke the same language.

The last thing Kayla needed was a tumble with a guy like him. He'd lie, steal, and cheat, but he didn't mess with good girls. Maybe he had a smidgen of honor left after all.

He quickly slipped the leather thong over her head before he did something stupid. The disk landed smack between her lush breasts. They cradled it, the silver contrasting nicely with her smooth latte skin.

He tore his eyes away. "It'll protect you from possession. Don't take it off."

She seemed about to thank him, but he interrupted her. "Let's search this dump."

Kayla rubbed the smooth metal disk. Energy sparked off it, but that was impossible. She didn't want to ask Hart. He blew hot and cold. One moment he was telling her not to trust him, the next he was offering her protection. She was still unsure about his crazy story. As the minutes ticked by, it was easier to explain away what she had seen. Stress could make a person hallucinate like that. She was almost sure of it.

Desi's living room was a mess, but it didn't take long to search. Her fingers itched to clean it. A galley kitchen took up one wall, opposite a battered couch and coffee table. Hart seemed determined to keep her at arm's length, avoiding eye contact, but they kept bumping into each other in the small room. Every time she turned around his broad back blocked her path.

Her mind wouldn't stay on the task at hand. It kept jumping back to that kiss on the street. He hadn't meant anything by it. Couldn't. The scene replayed in her mind: his warm mouth pressing against her own, the shock of heat ricocheting down her spine, the arousal pooling low in her belly.

She would chalk it up to another symptom of emotional strain. It couldn't mean anything else. He was alpha—arrogant, overbearing, aggressive—the type of guy who would use her up and spit her out. Wham, bam, thank you, ma'am. She had enough on her plate without adding sex to the mix.

Kayla pulled herself from the low kitchen cabinet and hit her head on his as he leaned over her. He was too close, invading her space. His wide shoulders blocked out the light, until all she could see was his intense gaze piercing her own. Something wild flickered within. The hair on the back of her neck rose.

Run, her instincts screamed.

The wild thing in his eyes heard, and urged her on. He would chase her, and he would catch her. She had to be strong. She would not back down.

"I don't need you checking up on me," she said.

Slightly chagrined, he straightened abruptly. "I can smell better than you humans."

Kayla pressed her back against the cabinet. "You're not human?"

His lips pulled back from his teeth. "Hell no."

"So what Rudrick said about you 'rejoining the fold'—"

"I'm Wolf. But not Kivati. Not anymore. They leave 'damned' kids like me on Rainier for the elements."

His story was getting weirder and weirder, but all she could think was how terrible that must have been for him. Betrayed by his own people. "Who could do such a thing?" She put a hand out, but he brushed it aside.

"They had good reason. I'm moon-marked. See?" He tugged at the stripe of white hair over his brow. "I can't control the beast. Think of the bloodiest Hollywood werewolf movie and multiply it by ten."

His anger boiled in the air between them, warding off any pity she might feel for the child he'd been. She didn't know how to read him. He was either serious or trying to scare her off from asking more questions. What kind of man had she allied herself with?

"Forget it," Hart said. "The only thing that keeps the Kivati alive is their secrecy and self-control. Imagine rabid animals with human cunning running around killing people. Hard to cover that up for long. If an adolescent goes through the Change and comes out moon-marked, he's sacrificed to the gods."

"But you escaped."

"My mom disagreed with the ruling." He pulled a dagger from a pocket and threw it. It flipped end over end, the silver blade glinting in the lamplight, and embedded itself to the hilt in the wall. "I don't need them or their straitjacket rules. Don't fancy asking every time I want to sneeze." He strolled across the room and yanked out the blade.

She shivered. Werewolf. She didn't want to believe it. *Show me*, she wanted to say. *Prove it*. But she could imagine a werewolf, and she had no wish to see one in the flesh, if it was true. It was hard to discount his obvious belief in his story. She thought she'd seen the beast lurking behind his eyes. Hart might not hurt her—at least he hadn't yet—but she didn't think a werewolf would be so accommodating.

His cell phone rang, breaking the tension in the room. He dug for it in his pocket and snapped it open. "Hart," he said, no emotion in his voice, his face once again impassive. The dagger disappeared into his jacket.

She stood, walked to the window, and pulled back the cherry-print curtains. The top of the Space Needle and the downtown skyline peeked over the building across the street. Streaks of color lit the clouds above. It was hard to imagine giant animals running wild through the city. Hard to believe wraiths and zombies stalked the alleys, or dragons, with or without souls. Hard to understand a culture that would sacrifice its children.

A beautiful land, hiding such deadly secrets.

"The mountain is out," she whispered. Desi used to say that when the clouds parted enough to reveal the view of Mount Rainier from her window. How many times had her sister stood like this while chatting to Kayla on the phone? Desi had wasted precious time describing the scenery. She should have told Kayla about the monsters that hunted in the mountain's long shadow. Kayla felt her grief give way to anger. Anger at her sister for coming here on some harebrained whim. For keeping secrets. For getting herself killed.

Anger at herself for not helping Desi before it was too late.

"Yeah. Understood." Hart snapped shut the phone.

Her pulse sped as she felt him approach. Fear . . . or excitement? He claimed he was a werewolf. A crazed killer. She forced herself not to scoot away as he glanced over her shoulder at the view.

"The Lady watches even through the mist," he said.

"The Lady?"

"Our Goddess. Her milky-white breasts, from which She nurtures Her people." He pointed to the two snow-covered humps of the mountain. Offering information freely was an apology of sorts. She was more than willing to make peace.

"Your cell phone works?" she asked.

The edge of his mouth kicked up. "Seattle gives 'dead zone' a whole new meaning, but, yeah, it works when there are no ghosts around. We need to find that necklace."

The sooner they found the necklace, the sooner she could go back home. "Time to tackle the bedroom."

"After you, darlin'." Hart waved her forward, making sure she caught him staring at her backside. The flirtation released the tension of his earlier anger, but the lust in his eyes was unfeigned. The werewolf probably wanted to eat her. The man *definitely* wanted to.

The knowledge made her uncomfortably aware of his every move. She swallowed, hard, and threw herself into searching the bedroom, trying to ignore the way his eyes followed her.

Next to her bed, Desi kept a framed photograph of their parents' wedding. Kayla couldn't help picking it up. They looked so happy. So young. Her father wore a stylish three-piece suit. His shoulders were straight and proud, not bowed with the weight of grief that he carried in her memories. He turned from the camera to look at his new bride, as if he couldn't get enough. The love shining from his face punched Kayla in the gut. Would a guy ever look at her like that? Her mother was gorgeous in a high-necked white gown, lace-covered buttons up the side. She smiled infectiously at the camera. Desi had inherited that wicked gleam in her eye and exuberant spirit. Kayla was more like their father: patient, meticulous, serious.

How different would her life have been, if not for her mother's accident?

"Who's that?" Hart asked.

She quickly put the picture down, slightly embarrassed to be caught mooning over the past. "My parents."

"They'd worry if something happens to you. You should go—"

"They're dead." She turned away before he could start the argument again.

It seemed almost sacrilegious, tearing apart Desi's things like they were so much garbage. Overturning her drawers and unearthing her secrets. Kayla knew she couldn't keep the apartment untouched—a museum to her sister's last days—but she desperately wished for an hour or two to sit peacefully among Desi's things and reflect on her life. A life that boiled down to a closet full of dirty laundry, a pile of old receipts, and a missing piece of jewelry that someone would kill to possess.

"Desi was always the dreamer," Kayla said as she dug under the bed after an hour of searching every drawer, loose floorboard, and shoe box with no luck. Nervous energy made her overly loquacious. "Head in the clouds, following rainbows and butterflies—*that* was my sister. She had a dream one night about Mama, and bought a plane ticket to Seattle the next day."

Desi should have listened to her and stayed in Philly. Nothing good came of Seattle. Nothing good came of following silly dreams instead of rational plans. "That was a year ago." Kayla pulled out a last box and wiggled out from beneath the bed. She could feel Hart's gaze boring into her back.

"Why Seattle?" His voice was gravelly, even deeper than before. She imagined the Wolf trying to get out.

"Mama was born here, and she died here. I barely remember it. I was five, Desi three. My dad packed us up the same day and moved to Philly. Haven't been back since. I used to have these nightmares of my mother bursting into flames. The fire didn't kill her. Only burned her flesh as she screamed." She hadn't told anyone that story, or about the dreams. And here she was telling her deepest secrets to a stranger. There was something compelling about him, as if she knew he would understand and wouldn't call her crazy. He had known stranger things.

"Did that really happen?"

"I don't know, but the dreams never made *me* want to come back here and find out."

"And your old man?"

"He never recovered from her death. He lived just long enough to see me through nursing school."

"That's rough."

"Yeah." Kayla swallowed back a tear and focused on searching through the box of loose notes and newspaper clippings. She found an article about an archaic Babylonian festival. At the top in large red letters Desi had written *Gate stabilization—Ask Sven*. On an essay about Chief Seattle, Desi had written *Curse—Ask Sven*.

Who was Sven?

At the bottom of the box was their mother's obituary. Desi had written the plot number, K-9881, next to the cemetery address. Maybe she had visited, leaving flowers on the grave. She must have been searching for closure.

"Well, that's it. No dust bunny left unturned." Kayla sat back against the bed and wiped the dirt out of her eyes with the back of one hand. Fatigue wove cobwebs three feet thick in her brain. "If I don't find it by the end of the week, will those guys really come after us?"

"Me? Please, those idiots are the least of my worries." He paused and rubbed his bruised ribs. "You, however, should watch your back."

"Gee, thanks."

He grinned. It softened the sharp edges of his face and lit up his eyes, making him striking, if not beautiful. Kayla had the strangest desire to kiss him again, which was crazy. *He thinks he's a werewolf, remember?* Fur and fangs at the full moon, not to mention the arsenal of weapons strapped to his muscled body. Too much stress had her brain malfunctioning. She needed a good night's sleep. She had a job to do, and then she was out of here.

"You mentioned," she said, "back at the morgue, that your boss dated Desi. I need to talk to him. He should know who her friends were. They might have some insight to where she would hide something valuable, or someone she might have given it to."

Hart shook his head. "Don't even think about it. You're not going anywhere near Norgard."

She narrowed her eyes. "Norgard, huh? Even if I didn't want to find this mysterious necklace, I'd still want to ask him about my sister's death. I didn't even know she was pregnant. If they dated, Norgard was probably the father. I want answers."

He opened his mouth to argue, but seemed to change his mind. A curtain descended over his face, hiding all emotion except indifference. He shrugged. "Do whatever you want, babe. It's no concern of mine."

"I will."

She followed him into the main room. "We aren't finished. How will we contact each other if we find anything?"

He snatched a pen off the counter and turned to her. He pulled the cap off with his sharp white teeth and picked up her hand. "I'm giving you my number." The pen tip tickled her palm. "There you go." He dropped her hand and recapped the pen.

Kayla watched him stroll to the door, feral grace in his stride, cocky arrogance in the set of his shoulders.

"Don't get in any more fights," she called after him. "Stay out of trouble."

He snorted and left without a word. Opening her hand, she read what he had written.

For a good time call . . .

Oh, brother.

Chapter 4

Butterworth and Son's Mortuary first opened in 1903 as a one-stop shop for the dead: morgue, funeral parlor, and crematorium. Before that, the land had been an Indian burial ground. The result was one seriously haunted chunk of earth. The number of dead passing through the Gate in this spot had forever warped the Aether, so that even humans could sense the otherworld. Various bars and restaurants had come and gone, quickly driven out of business by strange happenings and ghostly vandalism.

Butterworth's, as it was now called, was the longest-running business to occupy the building, thanks to the owner, Sven Norgard, who understood how to manage otherworldly inhabitants. No one, living or dead, crossed Norgard. He'd turned the place into an opium parlor and tea house. Those of Seattle's famous musicians who were unlucky enough to die in Norgard's debt performed nightly, putting a new twist on "live" music.

All were welcome, but for a price. Guns were checked at the door, no exorcisms allowed, yet the air reeked of violence. Shadows slithered in the flickering glow of the candelabras. Clouds of opium puffed from the deep, red velvet booths like sweetly scented, miniature volcanoes.

Hart pulled himself up to the massive mahogany bar that took up one wall. Hand-carved dragons decorated the imposing piece, a nod to the owner and his kin. Every muscle protested from Hart's earlier fight. He was getting too old for this crap. In the fifteen years he'd worked for Norgard he'd watched countless other men die. Two more jobs, he could do it. The Lady had never done him any favors, but maybe She'd take pity on him this once.

Doc, the bartender, saw him and ambled over. Charms tinkled from the man's portly belly, warding off spirits intent on breaking his bottles of alcohol.

"Happy Nisannu," Doc said in greeting. "May Tiamat aid you in the coming year."

Nisannu—the celebration of the Babylonian New Year— was in full swing. Norgard had gone all out with fountains of fermented honey wine and free chocolate. Red streamers hung from the ceiling and stalks of barley decorated the walls. Stone Babylonian gods, illuminated by red lanterns, leered over the dance floor.

"What'll it be?" Doc asked.

"The usual," Hart said. "Tell Norgard I'm here."

Doc nodded and poured him a cup of Darjeeling with a shot of gin. Hart gingerly raised the porcelain cup to his lips. The delicate handle felt ridiculous in his thick fingers. As he waited, he watched the grinding bodies on the dance floor, keeping his back to the bar and an eye on the door so no one could catch him off guard. The thick air, clogged with sweat and opium, threw off his nose. Without his sense of smell he felt blind and vulnerable. If it were up to the beast, he would avoid all crowds and closed spaces. Too bad he had no choice in the matter.

Like most Drekar and Kivati haunts, Butterworth's was wired for gas. Red plates of glass covered the chandelier and wall sconces. The bloody glow of the lights illuminated an empty chair on stage. In front of it sat an old-fashioned microphone flanked by two large amplifying horns that pumped out music from the ghostly entertainer. Hart dug out his Deadglass and raised it to his eye to see what the dancers, high on opium and alcohol, could see: a thin young man with stringy blond hair, torn jeans, and a flannel shirt sitting in the chair and strumming a beat-up guitar. He looked not much different from the way he had in life—same paper-pale skin, same hollow eyes. He played with a demonic flare that roused the crowd to a frenzy.

Hart pocketed the Deadglass and surveyed the room. Politicians made deals in the booths that lined the walls. Ishtar's Maidens, in lace garters and little else, slipped through the crowd selling their wares. He caught sight of Oscar's blond head at the back of the room and raised his teacup in a mock salute. His fellow operative saw him and touched his forehead in return. Norgard discouraged camaraderie. It was practical, given the short life expectancy of his blood slaves.

Speak of the devil. The tall blond Viking glided through the crowd toward him. His beautiful face made people trust him. In his left eye, he wore a Deadglass monocle. His right eye was clear blue, icy as his heart. Unless feeding, fighting, or fucking, the oval iris looked mostly human. Usually by the time anyone noticed its irregularity, it was much too late.

Norgard owned half the city and controlled most of the territory across the western United States. His business interests covered everything from technology and aeronautics to chocolate. All of his ventures flourished; Norgard had the Midas touch.

Behind Norgard stalked the head of his personal guard, Erik Thorsson. Civilization might have advanced, but Thorsson hadn't. He was a bloody, violent individual, better suited to pillaging by longboat than running a business. Norgard indulged him, especially if that violence was directed toward the Kivati.

Norgard slid gracefully onto a stool next to Hart, engulfing him in a wave of iron-scented air. The beast inside Hart strained forward at the sight of his alpha. Norgard had taken something natural and twisted it, leashing the beast. But Hart's mad totem couldn't be fooled for long; this alpha and make-shift pack were tainted. Once the blood debt was repaid, the beast would make its move. Hart found himself eyeing Norgard's throat, saliva pooling along his sharp canines. He wrenched his gaze away. Soon.

"What could be so important that it could not wait for later?" Norgard asked. A hint of Norse tinged his voice.

Hart waited for Norgard to order a drink—*glögg,* aflame as usual—before telling him the job had changed. Norgard's nostrils flared, but Hart didn't give a damn. The Dreki had left out a dangerous amount of information.

"Losing your touch, mad dog?" Norgard smiled, showing a mouthful of sharp teeth. "What could be so difficult in robbing a silly chit?"

"Seems you're not the only one interested in this so-called sentimental trinket."

Norgard had the grace to look away. It was as much an admission of guilt as Hart was going to get. "Corbette. I had hoped he was unaware of its existence. What does he know?"

Hart shrugged.

"The man is a stuffed shirt," Norgard said. "His reactionary tactics will never restore the glory of the Kivati. Their gilded age is over. He needs to accept that and move forward. Open up, rather than isolating his people like some damned Victorian commune. I will not let him interfere in my plans."

Hart took a sip of his tea and waited. It was a rant he'd heard before, and privately agreed with. Corbette thought a few generations of exacting protocol and rigid societal laws could keep his people from fading completely into the Shimmering Lands. But nothing could wash the taint from the blood. Nothing could restore the integrity of the cracked Gate. That didn't mean Hart agreed with all of Norgard's views.

Humans wouldn't accept the supernatural races unless the hellfire of the apocalypse was raining down around their shoulders.

Norgard sighed heavily. "I suppose this means the original price will no longer suffice."

"You suppose right." Hart had never figured why a man so filthy rich could be such a penny-pincher.

"Fine. So close to freedom," Norgard said. "What will you do, little Wolf, when you no longer bear the leash?"

Hart wanted to tell him to go to hell. He'd follow the packs north to Canada, last of the great wild spaces, and then he didn't know what he'd do. Anything. Everything. No one to answer to. Nothing to keep him here. He'd find somewhere he could run free.

"Can you taste it? The tang of blood coating your palate? Free to let its magic feed your own soul once again?" Norgard leaned in, a seductive purr in his voice. "Or is it fear that haunts you? Knowing that once the leash is gone, the madness will take you, faster and stronger than ever. What will stop it from destroying you? What will stop you from destroying everyone around you?"

Hart growled low. The beast waited beneath the surface, hungry and aching to be let free. His skin itched with the need to Change. His mouth watered. He wanted to rip the Dreki's throat between his teeth.

Norgard smiled and leaned back. "I rest my case."

Hart reined in the beast. "Tell me about the necklace," he bit out. "What's it a key to?"

"Ah." Norgard paused to adjust his French cuff sleeves under his crisp black jacket. The gold cuff links glittered under the flickering gaslights. "I didn't lie when I said it was sentimental."

Hart knew that. While the Drekar were experts at manipulating the truth, they couldn't outright lie.

"Two centuries ago," Norgard said, "I took a grand tour

through Asia, along the Silk Road and into the uncharted interior, seeking the great Babylon Gate. I never found it. The ancients hid it too well. But I discovered a small shrine where nomads still left offerings to the gods. It was heavily warded. Surprisingly enough, it wasn't a benevolent spirit they worshipped, but Tiamat's lover Kingu."

Shit. While Norgard paid homage to the Norse gods of the land of his birth, they were only the incarnation of an older, more violent pantheon. His true sovereign was Tiamat, the Babylonian goddess of chaos, mother of all dragons and the demon horde. No Norse word existed for her. She was the beginning of the world, and she would be its end.

"The price of this job is rising with every word," Hart said.

"Don't I know it." Norgard ran a hand through his long blond hair. "Can't depend on your overwhelming concern for mankind to do the right thing, can I?"

Hart raised an eyebrow. Norgard should be glad, since that meant Hart wouldn't have a problem returning the damn thing to him. The world was doomed if its fate rested in the soulless, profit-hungry hands of either of them. "So this necklace does what exactly?"

"Don't ask."

Lady be damned. Nothing connected to the Gate to the Land of the Dead could be good. The Gate in Seattle wasn't the only one, of course, but it was vulnerable. A Gate could open wherever a mass exodus of souls tore a hole in the Aether. It usually took centuries of bloodshed to open a new one. The Kivati's job was to keep this one closed, but it seemed like Norgard had an ace up his sleeve.

A commotion at the entrance to Butterworth's prevented Norgard from providing more details—probably to his relief. Hart followed his gaze over the undulating mass to a clique of skinny young teenagers. Their leader was a willowy girl with a long, thin nose and pouty red lips. The Kivati's future queen. Her hips were cocked at a haughty angle as if she had every right to be here. Her companions looked nervously at the crowd, as well they should. The Kivati youths had left behind their regimented bustled gowns and corsets for the skanky threads of the modern age. If only the Raven Lord could see them now: midriffs exposed by halter tops, platform shoes, and fishnets pulling eyes up to thighs tantalizingly bare under short black skirts.

"Well, well. What have we here?" Norgard's brilliant white teeth flashed in the dark parlor. "Has the princess evaded her bodyguards? Such rebellion. Such spark." His forked tongue slipped out to lick his lips. "I would be a poor host if I didn't indulge her little indiscretion. Perhaps return her to Corbette in a less than pristine condition, hmm?"

He laughed and stood up. His Drekar pheromones pulsed outward, a beacon calling his prey. Part metallic, park enthralling musk. Humans throughout the parlor turned with dazed, hungry eyes. The room swayed toward the towering blond man, like iron to a lodestone. He used the attention to glide unhindered through the crowd.

The noise was dimmed enough that Hart—with his heightened hearing—could eavesdrop.

"Princess," Norgard said, "welcome to my humble establishment."

The girl raised her haughty nose as the large predator stalked her way. She hid her fear well, but not well enough.

Hart shook his head. He felt a brief moment of pity for the girl. She was what, seventeen? Sheltered, spoiled, and rebellious made for a dangerous combination. Dangerous for her, that is. Stupid kid was going to get killed, and it would set off a new, bloodier round of Kivati-Drekar wars. More work for him, but shit.

He still needed more info about the necklace. Was it a key to the Gate? Seemed likely. Chief Seattle's curse had cracked the Gate in Seattle. This was the perfect place for someone to attempt to free the demons that waited hungrily on the other side.

Hart didn't want to still be here when that happened.

* * *

"Missed you."

Kayla opened her eyes from a deep sleep. She lay in Desi's bed, in Desi's tiny apartment. The faded patchwork quilt was the same one Desi had as a child.

Her sister lay beside her.

Kayla smiled. "Where did you go? I thought you had left me."

Moonlight spilled onto the pillow from the open window, bathing Desi's face in a pale, milky glow. "Come with me," she whispered.

"Oh, yes." Kayla tried to raise her hand to smooth Desi's braids, but her arm wouldn't move. Something wasn't right. Her sister was with her; surely that was a good thing.

"Forever," Desi said.

"Yes, forever." Kayla smiled at the thought.

Desi's eyes were darker than Kayla remembered. Flat black instead of twinkling mahogany.

Kayla wanted to pull up the blanket to warm her suddenly cold arms. "It's been so lonely without you, sweet girl," she said.

"You must find it," Desi said. "Come."

A knocking started from somewhere outside. Desi's lips thinned. Her eyes narrowed.

"What is that?" Kayla asked.

"No time," Desi said in a voice lower than Kayla remembered. "No time, my Kayla. You must find it. Blood will out."

"Blood will what?"

The knocking got louder, like hammers upon tin. Kayla imagined she heard the ruffle of feathers.

"No time," Desi hissed. "Let me in—"

Kayla tried to turn her head to see where the noise was coming from, but her neck wouldn't move. The hammering became a thundering inside her skull, like Athena's birthing pangs. She winced under the assault. The edges of the room began to blur.

"Desi?" she asked.

Her sister looked sorrowful. She opened her mouth, but no sound came out.

"Desi?" Kayla started to panic. The thundering sounded like cannons, bursting through her eardrums.

She woke with a start.

Her window was a mass of black feathers. Huge wings brushed the pane, again and again, blocking out light as the crows dove, trying to break in. Their beaks pounded against the glass, *rat-a-tat-tat, rat-a-tat-tat*. Her heart jumped in time. It was like a Hitchcock movie. With each swoop, they pinned her with their beady black eyes.

Fear seized her. She held her breath, praying the window wouldn't break. The crows screamed. Macbeth's witches, weaving spells of terror.

She swallowed and forced herself to move. Quickly, before she could change her mind, she jumped out of bed and ran to the window. She pulled the shutter closed and secured it. Moving to the other side of the white dresser, she shoved it with her back and shoulder until it shifted across the floor and barricaded the window. It was only particleboard, but it would have to do.

"Peck through that, suckers," Kayla said to the unseen assailants still cawing outside. She wiped her forehead with the sleeve of the T-shirt she had slept in. It was an old one of Desi's, the Soundgarden logo faded from washing.

Desi—

She spun to the bed, but it was empty. "Desi?"

No one answered in the empty room.

She let out a breath. "Only a dream." But it had been so vivid. She could have sworn she could reach out and touch her sister. Goose bumps broke over her skin. The dark bedroom seemed suddenly menacing. She flipped the light switch. The bulbs flickered once, buzzed angrily, and died. From the dresser Kayla grabbed a candle and matchbox. The matchbox read *Butterworth's*, and Desi had ten more like it scattered around the apartment. She must have spent a lot of time in the club. Kayla lit the candle, and it sputtered in a phantom breeze. The tiny wavering light was too weak to fight back the darkness.

Here among Desi's things—her clothes that smelled like gardenias, her childhood teddy bear, her framed photos showing Desi hamming it up for the camera—the truth came home.

Desi wasn't coming back.

Kayla choked back a sob. "Buck up, girlfriend," she muttered to herself. "If you can't survive staying in Desi's apartment without going crazy, how are you going to find the truth about her death?" The last word caught in her throat, but she ruthlessly pushed on.

After Hart left, she had knocked on every door in the apartment complex asking for information about Desi. No clues. It seemed her sister had spent little time at home. Disheartened, she returned to Desi's apartment and crashed. Too little sleep and too many emotional hits. The clock on the bedside table was dead, but her windup watch gave the time at 11:30 PM. She'd slept for six hours. Jet lag hung from her brittle bones like lichen.

The crows had reminded her of all she would prefer to forget. Dragons. Thunderbirds. Werewolves. Weapon-toting thugs who were madder than a hatter. Why couldn't that part of it have been a dream?

She gingerly picked her way over to the bed, hardly wanting to look at it—the memory of Desi's face cut deep. After setting down the candle, she pulled the blankets on the bed, gripping the quilt with white knuckles. She whacked her pillow against the wall to smooth the lumps. She reached forward to grab the second pillow, and froze.

There was an indent where a head might have rested.

Kayla hadn't used that pillow. No one had recently.

"I don't believe in ghosts," she said out loud. It was reflex. Hart said they did exist. Wraiths, he called them. Ghosts and electricity don't mix, he'd said, and now the lights were out and the clock broken. Evidence, maybe. Hard to call him a liar with her heart jumping in her chest and her hair standing on end. Her rational half wanted to dismiss his entire story, but her instincts warned her to stay alert. She couldn't afford to ignore him just because she didn't want it to be true.

Her hands shook. She carried the candle into the bathroom and splashed water on her face. The reflection in the mirror above the sink was pale and thin. Her eyes were red. Her skin sallow.

She glanced at her palm where Hart's message was now blurred. *For a good time.* Right.

It was late, but perhaps there was still an hour or two left to hunt down leads. She pulled her phone out of her pocket to search the Internet, but it was dead. Great. She went into the living room and was surprised to find a phone book and a pile of bus schedules beneath the coffee table. It seemed like Desi had had to resort to old-fashioned methods to get around in a city with unreliable electricity. Butterworth's seemed like her best lead. It was located in Pike Place Market; a bus could get her there in half an hour. She would snoop around and see if anyone had talked to her sister before she died.

This day was so bad, something had to go right for her eventually.

Right?

Right.

A shower did wonders for her confidence. She raided Desi's closet—just like the old days—and found a pair of matchstick jeans and a jade-green silk shirt. It was sleeveless with toggle buttons down the left side of her chest. Dragons, embroidered in red and gold, danced along the high Chinese collar. Bright colors and expensive fabrics, just like Desi liked them. A little makeup cheered her skin to its usual luster.

Only two crows greeted her outside the apartment. Creepy, but at least they didn't attack. She checked the ground below the bedroom window out of habit. It was clear of injured birds, even though the crows had thrown themselves repeatedly against the glass. Her mother had had an unnatural talent for patching up injured creatures. Kayla had once caught her kneeling in the flowerbed over a robin, its neck bent at an odd angle, its soft wings wriggling helplessly in the dirt. But a moment later it flew off as if nothing had happened. Her mother had seemed embarrassed.

Kayla often thought this cloudy memory had influenced her decision to go to nursing school. Her father had always said Desi was just like their mother. Kayla had wanted some connection of her own, however tenuous. Her mother was a healer in her memories. Now Kayla continued the tradition.

The crows followed her as she hopped a bus downtown, arriving at Butterworth's a little before midnight. The older red stone building had three arches marking three separate doors. Tiles on the porch spelled out MORTUARY, CREMATORIUM, and CHAPEL. The morbid décor didn't detract from its popularity, if the line out the door was any indication. She waited for twenty minutes in the cold before a bouncer let her in.

Cloyingly sweet air met her inside, mixed with the smoke of many candles and gas lamps. Shadows hovered in the depths of the recessed booths. The flicker of a match briefly lit a long silver pipe below a gaunt face and glazed eyes. Though the stage was empty, the crowd on the dance floor seemed to press closer as if straining to touch the vacant chair.

It would be tough to find anyone who knew Desi in this crowd, but she had to try. She pulled out a photo of her sister and began asking around. No one had information—at least that he or she was willing to share. People glanced at her sideways and then away, dismissing her easily. Recognition flickered in a pair of eyes, but was quickly shuttered. She got the feeling that death and disappearance were common occurrences here. People accepted it like they accepted rain for nine months of the year. It happened. They moved on.

Eventually she found two college-aged kids, tucked in an alcove, who admitted to knowing Desi.

"Beautiful girl. Smart too." Adam put the end of an ivory pipe between his lips and bent to hold the bowl over a small lamp. He wore an old olive-green army uniform. A multitude of straps buckled up his knee-high boots. He looked barely old enough to shave, though his downy whiskers tried gallantly to form muttonchops. His cheeks expanded as he inhaled the sickeningly sweet smoke.

His companion, Caroline, wore a black dress with a bright red bustier. Her goth-black hair cascaded down her back in ratty ringlets. "She won that mythology fellowship. That's how she met Norgard, when he came to present it."

Kayla had to lean closer to hear her over the noise. She pretended she didn't see the pipe. She was not here as a nurse, but to get information about her sister. Her tongue hurt from biting it. "Norgard endowed the fellowship?"

"Yup," Caroline said. "He's real generous with our department. Thinks mythology is an underappreciated field."

"Well, it is, Caro," Adam said.

"Do you know anything about Thunderbirds?" Kayla asked.

Adam and Caroline exchanged a look. "Maybe. What do you want to know?"

"This is going to sound silly, but have you ever seen one? You know, flying. Like a real one."

"There are lots of strange birds around here," Caroline said.

A curl of smoke escaped Adam's lips. "A poet once wrote, 'Old myths, Old gods, Old heroes never died. They are only sleeping at the bottom of our mind, waiting for our call.' Do you believe that, Desiree's sister?"

She watched him pass the pipe to Caroline. "I'm not sure. Goethe said, 'We see only what we know.'"

Adam's face lit. "Ah! A philosopher, Caro. We have us a philosopher."

Caroline blew a smoke ring.

"And tell me, Desi's sister," Adam said, "have you seen only what you know? A narrow viewpoint, I think."

"You would never see more than your own arse," Caro added helpfully.

"And Thunderbirds?" Kayla asked. She felt a little silly pressing the topic, but she needed to know.

"Ah, Thunderbirds." Adam took the pipe back. He lounged back in the booth and studied the velvet drapes hanging from the ceiling. "There are a couple good bird-watching spots in the city at dusk and dawn. The water tower at Volunteer Park gives you a fine view of Queen Anne and the Space Needle, and, best of all, some cover. The beach at Shilshole is another place, for another kind of rare bird sighting. Look up. Stay in the trees."

"So you're saying you have seen one," Kayla said. "It's not some hallucination on my part."

Adam chuckled. "Hallucination? Damn straight it's a hallucination, a trick of the light, a plane or whatever." In the flickering lamplight, his eyes were bloodshot. She was asking about hallucinations from an opium smoker. What did she expect him to say?

"That's right," he said more softly. "I'm just a dragon chaser, so what do I know?"

Her face must have given her away. "I just want . . . I don't know—"

"Proof?" Caroline suggested.

"You won't find that here," Adam said. "Let me tell you something. Seattleites are an odd lot. We will be perfectly polite to your face, but if you're not from around here, you don't get to be part of the club. The club is a tight-lipped bunch, but that's what you get from a city built by Scandinavians. Now, I'm not a native either, so I can let you in on our little secret."

"Adam—" Caroline said.

"You and me and Caro, we're on the low end of the totem pole. No one cares about you as long as you keep your head down and stay out of the way. But once you throw in your lot with either team—the prudish, but powerful animal gods, or the dangerously seductive soul stealers—then your clock is wound and the timer set."

"That would be the Kivati and the Drekar?" Kayla asked.

Caroline drew in a sharp breath. "The squeaky wheel gets the ax, *Adam*."

"Exactly." He offered Kayla the pipe. "So join us. Open your mind. Watch dead musicians through the smoke. Search the horizon at dusk for unnaturally large flying birds. But it's good to be seen as delusional. You know how these things go, don't you?"

Kayla refused the pipe. "Not really."

"My old man calls me a pothead, and I'm okay with that," Adam said. "I don't have a leg to stand on. Because I am a nobody, I'm not a threat. I like my little pleasures on this side of the Gate."

Someone might kill her if she asked too many questions, was that it? Is that what had happened to Desi? "Can you tell me about my sister?"

"Desiree," Adam said. "We're all a bit jealous of her. With Norgard as a tutor, she's getting a damn fine education. She'll be big someday, you can count on it. Kiss ass and live forever."

Present tense. Kayla took a deep breath. "I'm sorry, you must not have heard. She's dead. She died almost two days ago."

Adam gave her a long look and drew another breath from the pipe. He must have known already. He let it out slowly. "Did she now?"

Caroline slapped him on the arm. She turned to Kayla. "Sorry for your loss. May her spirit rest peacefully on the other side."

"Thanks." Kayla wondered if Desi had been afraid to die. Death frightened Kayla. Perhaps that's why she had studied medicine, to seek some control over life and death. Useless, really. Modern science had found ways to postpone death, but couldn't put it off forever. Perhaps Desi had found comfort in the supernatural, because it meant death wasn't an ending. It was only a change of status. Kayla wasn't sure she believed that yet, but these kids obviously did. Hart, too. "Is there anything else you can tell me? Who her best friends were? Who she might have gone to if she had a problem? A professor, maybe, or—"

"Norgard," Caroline said. "She was always talking about him. He knows everything. He's got the power to fix any problem she might have had."

Kayla needed to talk to Norgard. The man had answers. But if Desi had been running from him, he wasn't going to be forthcoming. "Anyone else?"

Adam settled back against the booth, his limbs relaxed, his eyes half closed. "There was a girl she mentioned once or twice. Was teaching her Norse mythology, I think. What was her name?"

Caroline took the pipe from Adam's limp fingers. She tapped it against her lips. "I saw her once, but her face was shadowed. Short. Had a cat following her."

Kayla filed that information away. A short girl with a cat. Why couldn't anything be easy?

Adam seemed to have fallen asleep. Caro's heavy eyelids indicated she would soon follow. Kayla turned to go.

"Adam's wrong, you know," Caroline called after her.

Kayla stopped and glanced back. "About?"

"He's a cynic, because it's cool. It doesn't take great magic or wisdom to cheat death." She blew another smoke ring. The opium lamp lit her face from the bottom. Her eyes suddenly looked older, and a bit sad. "'For love is immortality.'"

Kayla gave her a brief smile. Desi had been a romantic

too. All clues seemed to point to Norgard, and his reputation was growing bigger by the minute. She wondered if Desi had loved him.

She didn't find anyone else who knew her sister. She needed a break, and found her way to the ladies' room. The lavish powder room was surprisingly empty—a welcome respite from the noise and heat. A brass, nine-headed dragon statue stood at one end of the room. It was serpentlike, but with glittering wings that stretched out to the ceiling. She recognized the hydra from Greek mythology. Each head arched over a shell-shaped basin. The mouths were closed, but when she drew in front of one, the jaws snapped open with a small whir and steaming water poured out.

The toilets were, thankfully, more traditional. While she was in the stall, someone else entered the room, shoes *clickity-clacking* on the tile floor. Whoever it was slammed the stall next to her and commenced vomiting.

Kayla exited her stall and washed her hands in the sink. She wondered if she should assist. Alcohol poisoning was a serious danger. She'd seen her share of deaths in the ER. After a minute the sounds tapered off to dry heaves.

She tapped on the door gently and asked, "Can I help you?"

"Go away," came back the slightly breathy voice. "Ugnh."

A teenage girl with pin-straight apricot hair and a black leather miniskirt that barely covered her butt stumbled out a moment later. She was classically lovely, with an oval face, wide cheekbones, and large blue eyes. Her nose was perhaps a trifle too long. Fishnet stockings covered her impossibly long legs. Her cute high-heeled half boots jingled with small bells at the ankles.

"Ohhh, I feel gross," she moaned. "I'm quite drunk."

That much was obvious. The girl's eye makeup had smudged circles below her eyes. She clutched the shell washbasin to hold herself up. With her free hand she cupped water from the spewing dragon and rinsed out her mouth.

"You want me to call someone for you?" Kayla asked.

"No!" The girl straightened and wobbled. "No. No-no-no-no-no. They'll find me soon enough. I don't wanna go back yet. I'm not done being terribly improper."

"Improper?" If she were back home, Kayla would probably find the bartender and discuss the medical and social ramifications of underage drinking. But this wasn't Philly. This was a strange place with strange rules.

The girl nodded with the earnestness of the very drunk. She lunged toward Kayla and threw an arm around her shoulders. "You'll be my friend, right? Friends don't turn friends in. I haven't been this amused in *aaaaages*."

"Sure. Why don't you drink some more water? How many alcoholic drinks have you consumed?"

"It was just tea. Very proper. But I think he spiked it. He keeps pouring me another. Don't have to pay for a thing."

"Let me call someone for you—"

"No!" The girl let go of Kayla and fell against the sinks. "You promised."

Kayla hadn't, but it seemed rather irrelevant.

"Want some chocolate?" the girl asked. "I just *llllove* chocolate." She opened her purse and pulled out a small box covered in gold foil.

Kayla's stomach rumbled painfully. When had she last eaten? A day ago? She hadn't felt like eating, not when grief clawed its way through her gut. Suddenly, she felt a bit faint.

"He doesn't look evil," the girl mused, popping a chocolate in her mouth and chewing thoughtfully. "He's too pretty. Pretty. Pretty. Pretty. Don't you think?" She held out the box. The chocolates lay temptingly in gold foil. Each one heart-shaped with six red dots decorating the top.

Kayla politely refused, though she was starving. She didn't accept candy from strangers.

"You sure? Persephone's Delight. They're shpecial. Special." The girl laughed. She picked up a fine linen towel embroidered with a B, wet it in the sink, and rubbed at the smudges around her eyes, but only succeeded in spreading them farther over her wide cheekbones. "I didn't ask to be the Crane Wife, you know. Didn't want to. I thought Crow, yeah, or Eagle. My parents are birds, you see? But not a *Crane*."

A Kivati, Kayla realized. She tried to imagine this slight girl turning into a giant bird, and failed. No one had ever accused her of an overactive imagination. On the bright side, at least this delusional person wasn't over six-feet and packing heat. This was her chance to get data without getting her head blown off.

Pumping a drunken teenager for information. She stooped to new lows. "What's wrong with a Crane?"

The girl made a face. "What thirteen-year-old wants to be engaged?"

"You're thirteen?" Kayla asked, horrified.

The girl—who was too filled out to be thirteen—laughed. "Nooo, no. I Changed then. Changed into a Crane. Lady be damned."

"You Change first at puberty?"

"Duh." The girl grew solemn, her moods shifting like the wind. "Only a few more weeks till the wedding. Eighteen. Happy birthday to me."

Thank goodness. A young woman, not a child. Still, too young to be married. Too young to be drinking, for that matter. She seemed resigned to her fate. "They can't make you marry someone you don't want to marry." At least it was true for humans.

"What planet are you from?"

"You can declare independence at eighteen," Kayla suggested. "The courts won't allow your parents to marry you off."

"Shhh. He's got spies everywhere." The girl lowered her voice and glanced furtively around the bathroom. They were alone. "There are no courts. The Raven Lord makes the laws. He is the law." She dropped the towel in the sink. Her lower lip trembled. "I don't wanna marry him. He frightens me. Have you seen him? Frightening. He only wants my ovaries anyways."

This girl knew the Raven Lord, the mysterious figure listed on the business card Desi had left behind. Finally, after hours of searching, a clue landed in Kayla's lap in the bathroom of all places. Did the girl know about the key? Kayla tried not to let her sudden, desperate excitement make her smile too sharp. *Slowly*, she warned herself. She couldn't scare the girl off. She offered her hand to shake and tried to keep her tone light. "Sorry, let me introduce myself. Kayla. What's your name?"

The girl looked startled, then delighted. "You don't know who I am? That's splendid. Splendid. Call me Lucy, my friends do."

"Pleasure."

"Have a chocolate?"

"I don't know—"

"Come on. We're celebrating." The chocolate box shook in Lucy's hand.

Kayla hesitated. There was a knock on the powder room door.

"Who's it?" Lucy called out.

"Lucia, my darling," a man's voice said. "Come out and play."

Lucy—or Lucia—giggled. "He thinks he's so dashing, but I know his shecret. Secret." She wrapped her arm around Kayla and led her to the door. "He just wants to screw me to spite the Raven Lord," she whispered conspiratorially. "And for that stupid prophesy. No one wants me for me."

Lucia swept Kayla out of the ladies' room and into the dark club. Beneath the red lights the walls glittered like rubies. A towering blond man waited for them. His elegant midnight-black suit and shiny high boots would have looked ridiculously over the top on anyone else, but he pulled them off with an elegant old-world charm that was somehow Regency rake and Viking marauder all rolled into one. A strange lens surrounded by brass gears covered his right eye.

"Would you do me the honor of an introduction?" he asked, the perfect gentleman.

"Regent Norgard, may I present Kayla," Lucia said with a sudden show of manners. "Kayla, may I introduce Sven Norgard."

So this was the infamous Sven Norgard. Hart's boss. Desi's lover. The probable father of her unborn niece or nephew. He seemed larger, somehow, than she had imagined him. Strikingly beautiful with sleek blond hair and high, sculpted cheekbones, he had a compelling smile and an intense, appreciative gaze. She could see how Desi had fallen for him. If Norgard turned on the charm, it would take a stone-cold heart to be immune.

He ordered both Lucia and Kayla drinks at the dragon-carved bar. There was a definite theme to his décor; Norgard was either in love with dragons, or he was one. *Thanks for the heads-up, Hart*. She shivered and watched the bartender pour tea into two green porcelain cups. She was usually a coffee drinker—four cups at day, minimum—but it didn't seem to be on the menu. Unexpected, given what she knew of Seattle.

"Sugar?" Norgard offered.

Stalling, she took one lump, stirred, and took two more. The tea had a floral aroma, with hints of chocolate and vanilla. She didn't want to drink any. She didn't trust what was in it.

"Try it," Norgard said. "I promise you'll like it."

He smelled really good. No sooner had the thought passed through her mind than she found herself swallowing a mouthful of the tea. How had that happened? But he was right; it tasted delicious.

Kayla watched Norgard flirt with Lucia. He was heartbroken over her sister's death. Obviously. Perhaps Norgard had swept Desi off her feet, but he hadn't loved her. Kayla concentrated on maintaining her social smile, while inside her anger rose. Maybe things had ended badly between them before Desi

ran off with his necklace. Maybe he hadn't wanted the baby.
Maybe he had killed Desi himself.

"So what brings you to Seattle?" Norgard asked, after pouring her more tea.

"Family." She ran her finger beneath her high collar. The
temperature of the room had risen dramatically. Sweat trickled between her breasts.

She was glad she hadn't told Lucia her last name. At the
moment Norgard didn't know who she was. She wondered if
he would care. At best, he would pretend sympathy. At worst,
he would—what? Kill her in a room full of witnesses? She
shook her head. Seattle was making her paranoid.

There was a commotion at the door. Familiar large men in
black dusters stormed inside, guns at the ready. She recognized Rudrick—face almost purple with rage—and his goons.

Not again.

Kayla didn't duck this time, or cower. Maybe she'd found
her backbone. Mabye she'd inhaled a whopping dose of Idiot.
Who didn't duck when guns were pointed in their direction?

Norgard didn't blink at the intruders, or the guns. "It has
been a delightful evening." He swept up Lucia's hand and
kissed it. "I am so disappointed that you could not stay longer."

"Get away from her!" Rudrick yelled over the crowd. He
scattered patrons left and right in his effort to reach the girl.

Norgard ignored him. There was a pleased gleam in his eye
as he bent over Lucia's hand. "Please join us again anytime."

"Oh, I will—"

"Shoot him!"

That got Norgard's attention. He twisted a large malachite
ring and a blast of arctic air bowled through the room. Candles
flickered and went out, leaving only gas sconces for illumi-
nation. Screams echoed off the arched ceilings, a haunting
noise that scraped over Kayla's eardrums and left trails of icy
fingerprints down her spine.

Chapter 5

The hair on Kayla's arms stood on end. It wasn't just the cold; it was something else, something that felt like a low volt of electricity and fear all in one.

"Don't tempt me," Norgard told Rudrick over the noise. "My servants can't be killed."

"Hold your weapons." Rudrick shoved against some invisible force until he reached Lucia's side.

He didn't acknowledge Kayla at all. She didn't want to talk to him again either, not even to ask him about the birds. She had three days. Time enough to find the necklace and screw up her courage to face him again.

Rudrick and Norgard stared at each other, an invisible battle warring between them. Tension rolled and Kayla almost imagined she could see the air molecules boiling with it. A truce flickered, unspoken but understood. She wondered if they were more concerned with violence or showing themselves before the human patrons of the tea house.

"Give us the princess and we'll leave," Rudrick said.

Norgard lowered his hand. Instantly the temperature in the room resumed to normal.

Lucia crossed her arms, but didn't protest when Rudrick grabbed her.

"You don't have to go with him," Kayla said.

"Stay out of this, human," Rudrick snarled.

As he led her away, Lucia called over her shoulder, "Lovely to meet you, darling. I had a smashing good time."

Kayla watched the Kivati leave. She should have felt more anxious about it, but her limbs were warm and tingly. Buzzed, she would say if she had been drinking. There was something about Norgard that made her forget what she was doing. She couldn't stop thinking about his cologne, and she found herself drinking more and more tea. She needed to confront Norgard about Desi.

Norgard clapped his elegant hands. "Free drinks all around," he announced. It appeased the tea house's patrons, who were quick to forget the incident and crowded the bar. Hart was right. Humans ignored what was right in front of them. They were eager to return to their comfortable, oblivious existence. Or maybe this was normal behavior at the club. Maybe, like Adam suggested, they were in on the secret and chose to turn a blind eye.

Norgard turned back to Kayla with a brilliant smile. "Shall we see if this evening can be salvaged? Let me treat you to something special. Quite the theatrics for an evening, wasn't it?"

Beneath the fatigue that muddled her brain, she knew she shouldn't follow him. But she needed answers. If only she could remember the questions.

He led her to the bar. Two stools suddenly opened up in front of them. He swept out his hand to offer her a seat. She took it. He swiped a gold box from behind the counter and offered it to her. "Chocolate?"

"No thank you."

"One can never have too much chocolate."

She bit into a piece. She hadn't remembered accepting any.

"Are you familiar with the story of Persephone?" Norgard was beautiful, but cold. His skin seemed to shimmer beneath the lights, almost as if it were made of a million tiny scales.

"Greek girl kidnapped by Hades." Her eyes were drawn to him. She watched the muscles of his neck swallow, the skin shimmering as it shifted. A little voice urged her not to take another piece of chocolate, but her brain was slow. She was swimming through molasses. The lights were brighter, yet the room was darker too. Besides, she was starving. She took a heart-shaped piece. "Delicious."

"I am so glad you think so." Norgard's smile was indulgent, like a teacher praising a small child. "Yes, the Greek god fell in love with her and made her queen of the underworld."

She'd pleased him, and suddenly she wanted nothing more than to please him again. Something was wrong with that thought. Struggling to remember, she refused another piece of chocolate. "I don't think Persephone had a choice in the matter."

"Oh, but she did. She chose to eat some pomegranate seeds, which sealed her fate. Six months in the underworld as queen, and six months with, God help her, her mother. Personally"—Norgard leaned in conspiratorially—"I believe she was happier with Hades."

Every bit of Norgard's ten-kilowatt smile was aimed in her direction. His left eye, blindingly sky blue—like Paul Newman's—with a strangely oblong iris, was set on her and only her. She could almost feel his gaze rake over her arms and breasts and legs, until she felt naked and very desirable. Under his attention, her plain jeans and borrowed shirt turned into silk and lace. The silk and lace seemed to slide away, until she could have sworn she was naked.

She giggled.

She never giggled. Somehow she felt free, giddy even. All the pain she had been carrying around with her for the past two days suddenly lifted. Her soul flitted in her chest, light and buoyant. She wanted to laugh out loud.

Why shouldn't she? She was young and alive. Desi couldn't laugh anymore. So Kayla laughed for her. Kayla would have to live for her too; from now on she would really live. She would not be scared to flirt and laugh out loud. She would be wild and carefree.

She caught a flash of something speculative in Norgard's eye. Calculating. Despite her happy haze, she shivered. There was something she should remember. Someone she should remember.

Norgard put his arm around her, and she snuggled into his side. "You smell so good."

The crowd parted in front of them like they were royalty. His arm clasped her. Tight. Possessive. She didn't have to put much weight on her own legs; he practically carried her through the parlor. She couldn't bring herself to care.

She felt too good. Full of chocolate. At ease for the first time in forever. On the arm of a handsome, charming man who looked at her like she was the only woman in the world.

He must love her.

Where had that thought come from? Her brain struggled beneath the thick spiderwebs that caged it. "Where are we going?" she asked as he brought her through the back door. She didn't want to go. Her legs wouldn't stop walking.

"More chocolate?"

"Gee, Norgard, you really know the way to a woman's heart."

"Sven. Call me Sven." His voice poured into her ear and she realized he was close, so close those elegant lips were almost brushing her ear. He was tall, but not as broad as . . . someone.

She couldn't remember. Someone big, with big shoulders and big arms and . . . gold. That's right. The memory was coming back to her. Gold bands around his muscular biceps.

But she still couldn't remember whom.

Sven placed something in her mouth—another piece of chocolate, she thought. So good she might have moaned.

Sven chuckled, his chest vibrating against her breasts.

"You are so beautiful." *Stop talking*, she ordered her mouth. Her prized control slipped, slid, and shattered against Norgard's shimmering scales.

"I have a feeling about you." His low voice purred in her ear. "How would you like to be the mother of my children?"

Kayla laughed. He was joking, right? But it was hard to filter through the haze of her brain. *Smack him upside the head*, she ordered her arms. They flatly ignored her.

"Perhaps you've had a bit too much. I told him to reduce the dose." He didn't seem to be talking to her.

Outside the cold air pulsed against her overheated skin. She was on fire. Hot. Wet. Her clothes were too tight. Her skin was too tight. Suddenly the wall pressed against her back, and she was trapped between brick and a very large, very hot male. His lips were firm on hers.

She didn't want to kiss him.

"I . . . drunk." Her voice sounded very far away.

"Be still," he said. "You taste of affection, at least."

Something was not right. She needed air, needed space, but her arms were lead weights.

Her eyelids drooped. Waves of light seemed to flow through her. Fire where his hands touched her skin. Her core self was sucked upward, leaving her body, and she screamed.

When the Kivati sentinels showed up, Hart was obliged to get his ass off the bar stool and run interference. So much for a leisurely night. Oscar met him at the door, and together they politely escorted the Kivati and their wayward charge out of Butterworth's. The princess batted her long eyelashes at him just to piss Rudrick off. Always helpful, Hart leered at her. She turned white and scooted closer to her babysitters.

"See you next time, sweetheart," Oscar called after her.

The girl gave him a thankful smile. Nonthreatening, Oscar was. He could be a regular gentleman, if one ignored his penchant for scamming old ladies out of their retirement funds.

Rudrick tugged the girl into a black jeep and gave Hart the finger. Hart saluted him good-bye, and the Kivati sped off.

"What are the odds she gives Corbette a heart attack before the honeymoon?" Oscar asked. He scratched the underside of his jaw with the tip of his knife.

"Three to one."

"Bet you three ounces he won't say 'I do.'"

Hart considered it. He could stretch that much Drekar blood a long way, especially if he was free. But if he lost, replacing three ounces would cost him a shit ton. He wouldn't put it past Oscar to cheat. "Why not? Deal."

"You working the drill this week?"

"No, I'm on a special." Thank the Lady. Providing security for the new deep bore tunnel would kill a guy from boredom.

"Luck to you." Oscar ambled off, presumably to work on his latest con.

Hart returned inside and met the suffocating iron smell of Norgard's rage. Patrons started to trickle out. No one wanted to be in the way when the storm broke.

Hart thought he caught a glimpse of Kayla Friday's curvy form, but couldn't be sure. The memory of her smooth skin still burned his fingertips. The image of her large caramel eyes brimming with unshed tears haunted his thoughts.

If she couldn't help him find the necklace, she was no longer his concern.

He was still baffled that she'd intervened in the fight with the Kivati and made Rudrick promise not to hurt him. No one had ever stood up for him. Well, his mother had, and look what that got her.

Rudrick was right—the world would be a better place without Hart in it. Hart wasn't interested in pleasing other people, however. Rudrick could kiss his ass.

Hart stood and pressed his way through the sweaty dancers,

who were too drunk to know to get out of his way. He showed his teeth at the back door and was quickly released into trash-strewn Post Alley. It had once been a trendy lane occupied by restaurants and knickknack stores, a block from the tourist Mecca of the Pike Place Market. These days, with the number of wraiths slipping through the cracked Gate, dark narrow alleys like this one were safe only for the likes of him.

His breath formed clouds in the cold salt air. The odor of urine and rotting food overwhelmed his nose. It was disorienting. He almost ran into the couple pressed against the brick wall, but stumbled away just in time.

It was Norgard pressing up against some chick. He must be really hard up to take her in the alley. Her limbs were limp, her knees bent in such a way that Hart could see they no longer held her up. Norgard steadied her with one hand and tried to pry off her pants with the other, but it looked like her marionette arms kept getting in the way.

Hart would have walked past, left the lovebirds alone, but over Norgard's sharp metallic scent he caught something sickly sweet, like rotting fruit. Unnatural.

The woman moaned, the sound edged with panic. The familiar voice hit him in the middle of his chest.

Kayla.

Inside him, the beast rose bristling and spitting. It didn't like another man touching her.

Norgard paused feeding. "Run along, little doggy," the Dreki said between nips of Kayla's smooth skin.

Hart didn't move. Stupid, he knew. This was the Drekar Regent. His employer. The man who owned everything and everyone. The man who owned him.

Kayla struggled faintly, like a butterfly flapping its wings.

He really should leave, but his feet wouldn't move.

"Let her go," Hart said. The beast looked out through his eyes, scenting its prey.

Norgard turned his head. His irises were completely slit,

snakelike. It was like looking at death himself. The Dreki was as far from human as he could get without Turning. Hart was no coward, but he wasn't suicidal.

Hart turned away. Norgard was right; it wasn't any of his business. He'd watched Drekar feed before, plenty of times. The girl would recover as long as Norgard didn't take too much. He strolled to the end of the alley, but her weak scream caught him between the shoulder blades and he stopped. Most Dreki victims were moaning in pleasure at this point, their senses overwhelmed by the iron musk that soothed their waking minds. It seemed Kayla was strong enough to resist.

Hart took another step, listening to the rustle of clothing and the distant crash of waves against the seawall. He needed to leave and get on with his work. There were shipments to guard, people to kill. Pissing off a Dreki? Bad idea. His boss? Terrible idea. Especially when he was so close to paying off his blood debt. He needed to find the necklace and complete one more job; then he'd be free. Last thing he needed was to fuck it up playing some Lady-be-damned hero. Ha. He was the furthest thing from a hero.

Fog seeped into the alley, coming toward him. Behind the garbage cans and in the crawl spaces between brick fronts, shadows collected. Around him, the Aether rippled and twisted. The hair on the back of his neck rose.

Wraiths waited for their turn. Once Norgard drained the girl and left her here in a crumpled heap, the ghosts would push aside her weakened soul and possess her body. She'd be worse than dead before the first rays of sun split the horizon.

The sound of ripping fabric cut through the dark alley.

Hart didn't know what hit him. The decision wasn't conscious—it was instinctive. The creature inside him took over, vibrating with the need to hurt and kill. *Enemy*, it growled, and Hart felt the sharp pain of claws slicing through his fingertips. Aether flowed through him, waves of magic transforming him from nose to tail, a blinding light rolling over his body to Change skin and man to fur and Wolf.

Norgard never saw it coming. The blow to his head sent him sprawling to the pavement. Hart was on him, tooth and nail, struggling to push back the madness that burned through every cell. His need to kill warred with the part of him that was still human. His body was Wolf, but he couldn't give the beast free rein of his mind. No one would be spared if he did, not even the girl.

Even through the bloodlust he could feel the girl behind him, could hear her whimpering, could smell the salty tang of her femininity and the sweet decay of the drug.

A strange possessiveness crept through his anger, but before his brain could make sense of the feeling, Norgard attacked, claws extended. Norgard had a height advantage, but Hart weighed more and was built like a brick, boulders for shoulders and a rock for a head. His totem was twice as large as a wild wolf, but he was no match for a full-grown dragon. He couldn't give Norgard time to Turn.

Norgard landed a punch to Hart's rib, and the Dreki's poison-tipped knuckle-spikes felt like a red-hot poker.

Hart compartmentalized the pain, shoving it ruthlessly aside as he fought against the onslaught. There was no room for anything but pulverizing his opponent and protecting his prize.

Where had that thought come from?

Shock made him slow, and his head snapped back from an uppercut to the jaw.

Norgard danced on his toes. His inhuman irises glowed. His skin sparkled with thousands of tiny green-tinged scales. He was a hairbreadth away from sprouting wings and breathing fire.

They circled each other, each breathing heavily.

"Think, mutt. Why would you jeopardize your freedom,

your very life, over some dumb bitch?" Norgard asked. He spit on the ground, his saliva tinged red with blood.

Hart's lips pulled back over sharp white teeth.

Norgard blinked. "This is really over the chick?" He laughed in disbelief. "She'd never look at you twice, you deranged illiterate mongrel."

Hart didn't care about the girl. He didn't care about anyone. All he wanted was to pay his debt and get the hell out of here. But he couldn't deny the low growl that emanated from his throat at Norgard's mention of her.

"No? That explains why you're pacing now in front of her like a fucking guard dog. You would give her—a stranger—your back."

Lady be damned, Hart couldn't deny it. He attacked, teeth ripping the sleeve off the Dreki's coal-black suit.

"Think carefully," Norgard said. "I was robbed of the Kivati princess, and this female's soul is almost as pure. I won't be denied a second time tonight."

Hart silently agreed. He knew Norgard was playing with him. If the man shifted there was no way Hart could beat a twenty-foot-tall dragon. He surged forward and snapped at Norgard's jugular, but missed as the Dreki spun out of the way.

Norgard's back slammed into the brick wall behind him. He used the wall as leverage to push himself forward in attack. "By Tiamat, you really are crazy, aren't you?"

Hart didn't have a response to that bit of truth. He let blows glance off his muzzle like rain, unlike Norgard, who guarded his pretty mug and left his groin unprotected.

It was the opening he'd been waiting for. Hart used his powerful back legs to strike the poor schmuck in the balls. Couldn't do permanent damage to a Dreki unless you cut off his head, but Norgard was still man enough that the move dropped him like a stone.

"Dishonorable," Norgard wheezed.

Hart would have laughed if he could. The Drekar had such a warped sense of honor.

Norgard had had enough; he began to Turn. His skin glittered as his body grew. His shoulder blades widened, extended. His face lengthened to a snout. A ridge of razor-sharp spikes broke out of his skin from the tip of his flat head, down his scaly back to the end of his long, muscle-bound tail. The spike on the end thrummed against the ground and, with a *whoosh*, it crashed into the brick wall behind him. Steam puffed out of wide, slit nostrils.

It was terrible to watch, ugly and twisted. A creature of nightmare. Dragon.

Hart had one chance as death transformed before him—he had to reason with Norgard. He Changed, embracing the pain that tore his bruised ribs and battered limbs. The shock to the beast caused his vision to black in and out. Panting with exhaustion, he crouched on the cold cobblestones, naked but for the slave bands. "She's Desiree's sister," he rasped. "Kayla Friday. You need her. Desiree left her clues. You can't kill her until I get the necklace back."

A lie, but it was the only thing he could have said that would get through to the dragon. Nothing stood between a Dreki and his treasure. Anger, lust, hunger, revenge—all fell before the creature's overwhelming avarice.

Norgard towered above Hart, considering his options. Norgard could eat his prized operative, but Hart was as much Norgard's possession as the necklace. Or, Norgard could force Hart to stand down with the power of the blood debt. The gold bands would burn Hart's biceps, pulling his blood out through his skin, filling the magic runes along the surface of the bands until Hart fell unconscious from blood loss.

The gamble came down to the necklace's value. If it truly belonged to Kingu, it was worth hundreds of pure souls.

The dragon breathed out a hot rush of air that smelled of burnt meat and cinnamon. His tail thrashed once, twice. He was angry, but he turned away from Hart and launched into the sky. The ground shook as the huge beast pushed off.

Hart dove to the side to escape being crushed.

Norgard spread his membranous black wings and soared silently into the air. He disappeared against the cloud-dark sky over Elliott Bay.

Hart lay on the hard, cracked asphalt and let his heart slow to a normal rhythm. He was still alive. Little surprised him anymore, but this did. The old Dreki must have a soft spot for him buried deep in his cold, unfeeling heart.

He turned and found Kayla half propped against the brick alley wall with her shirt unbuttoned to her waist and no pants. Shit. He exhaled quickly at the sight of her naked legs. They went on for miles, all smooth latte skin that went up and up and . . .

He tore his eyes away and clenched his fists at his side. The beast was too close to the surface. One look at that naked skin made the beast strain to burst free in a lust-crazed frenzy. Hart was drained of energy, too spent to Change. It was the only thing that saved her. A fine sweat broke out on his forehead and every nerve ending buzzed with energy. He had to get away from her. Lady be damned, he'd never come so close to losing it outside the full moon.

He rose stiffly and collected his weapons from where they had fallen. His clothes had shredded when he Changed, but he had an extra set stashed inside the club, which he retrieved and quickly donned. He considered leaving her there in Post Alley—he certainly couldn't trust himself to get near her—but he made the mistake of glancing one last time at those plump curves that screamed at him to touch and taste.

On the other side of the alley, partiers came out for a smoke. The noise made his hackles rise. A growl rose in his throat.

What was wrong with him? He wasn't a damn taxi service, but he couldn't very well ditch her here, half naked with those drug-clouded caramel eyes. Her pink cotton panties were all that stood between her and a good hard fuck.

He picked her up, and she moaned. She was light, despite her generous body. He threw her over his shoulder in a fireman's hold with his hands on her smooth thighs to hold her steady. But then her round ass was right in his face. Her scent—arousal and wildflower—went straight to his head.

This was a mistake.

Too late to change his mind, he bounded off down the alley, his unnatural speed hidden in the dark night. Gloom cloaked the city like a blanket. Comforting, even as it hummed with midnight creatures.

Ghostly skyscrapers loomed over him like drunken bones, the mausoleum of a once-great city. He ran past crack addicts and meth heads huddled in doorways. The mist ensured he would only be a passing blur. A dream. A nightmare in the endless depredation of the streets.

He couldn't leave her unprotected at her sister's place. Instead, he ran south, under the broken streetlights, past the glass and steel structures, to Pioneer Square. It was the oldest part of the city and the most haunted. Metal fire escapes clung to the brick buildings like black skeletons. Beneath his feet twisted the Underground, the labyrinth of tunnels created when the streets were raised two stories after the great fire over a century ago. Milky glass cubes had been set into the sidewalk to let light down below.

The shadows were thicker here, writhing and condensing in the pitted landscape. The Aether rippled. Death stalked.

Just off King Street, near the old train station, he stopped and propped Kayla against the wall of an abandoned building. The empty windows leered down on them, but he couldn't smell anyone—human or otherwise—nearby.

Her head rolled to the side, but she managed to cling to the wall in a standing position. She whispered something through those bedroom lips. It sounded like a sigh, but not one of sadness or pain. A heated sigh. Breathy and wanting.

The tempting bit of pink cotton between her legs had a small ribbon of lace circling each creamy thigh.

He pulled his eyes away. "Wait here."

"Here," she repeated, but it was obvious she had no idea what she was saying.

"Don't go anywhere," he said slowly.

She rubbed herself against the wall behind her. Up and down. Side to side. Like a cat needing a pet. Her eyes were unfocused. The sick sweet smell came off her in waves.

He had little choice left. Leave her to die or bring her to his place. She couldn't exactly tell anyone how to get there if she wasn't conscious enough to respond to her own name. The thought of her among his things—exposing his secrets, invading his personal space—made him want to growl.

But another part of him wanted to claim her. He'd found her, spared her, fought for her. She belonged with his other possessions, stashed away from the world.

Hart banished that thought as soon as it came.

An alley opened off to his left. A small cat-sized shape with a waving tail peeled out of the shadowy interior. A larger shape—small and androgynous, but clearly human—soon followed.

Hart froze with a hand beneath his jacket.

"A good night for hunting, I see." The voice was low and female. She tossed something in the air and caught it again. The streetlight glinted off a spinning blade.

"Stand aside, Grace," Hart said.

Grace laughed and tossed the blade. "Or what?" Another operative bound by blood in Norgard's service, Grace had a special affinity for hunting aptrgangr. She sensed the Gate—unusual for a human—and could send the damned back through it. She stepped forward into a pool of light, illuminating almond eyes and sleek blue-black hair. A black hoodie and black jeans enabled her to blend with the shadows. Her too-seeing eyes were out of place in her youthful face. She took another step toward him and held out her knife, point forward. "Or what? How do I know you aren't one of them?"

"Stop pulling my tail," he said. "The cat would tell you." He looked pointedly down at the long-haired black-and-white cat.

It brushed against his leg and purred.

Grace sighed. "You're no fun."

"You're testy. Something up?"

"Yes." Grace cocked her head as if listening to a voice he couldn't hear. She licked her lips nervously. "Gotta be careful. Something's coming. I can taste it."

Hart sniffed the air experimentally, but caught nothing unexpected. He didn't understand Grace's gift. He picked Kayla up again.

"What've you got there?" she asked.

He shifted Kayla on his shoulder, uncomfortably aware how he must look with a half-naked, barely conscious woman over his shoulder. "A job. I'm pressing her for some, ah, information. For the job."

"Information," Grace repeated. He wasn't sure, but he thought he saw a flicker of disappointment cross her face. He suddenly felt guilty.

Kayla moaned and squirmed. He had to clamp his large hand more firmly on her rounded ass to keep her in place. He swallowed hard. His cheeks warmed uncomfortably.

"Sure. Whatever." Grace dropped into a crouch, dismissing him and his warm-blooded prize.

A booty prize. Literally.

"Got a question for you," he said. "What's a rune like an upside down R?"

Grace brushed her knife against her thigh. "Raidho, reversed. Where did you see it?"

He tapped the inside of his left wrist. "Carved here on a corpse. Silver needles found with the body."

She breathed sharply through her teeth. "Prevents the last journey. Anchors the soul to this side of the Gate."

Now why would a good girl like Desiree Friday want to haunt Seattle?

"Bad juju, that. Especially at Nisannu." Grace held out her hand to the cat. When he trotted over, she scooped him up in her arms and buried her face in his long fur. The cat stared at Hart. His little brown mustache twitched.

"How do you set the ghost free?" It didn't matter to his mission, but he couldn't help asking. Kayla would want to know.

"Hard to brand a ghost. If it goes aptrgangr you can brand the new body before you kill it. Draw Ehwaz to release it." She drew a rune like a letter M in the air with her knife. "Then Raidho, right-side up, to send it on its journey. Draw it in blood."

"I owe you one."

"Hurry." Grace raised her head again and her eyes flashed silver. "The Gate is restless."

A shiver ran down Hart's spine. Kingu waited on the other side, Norgard had said as much. Lady be damned.

"Watch your back, Reaper."

"Stay to the light," she murmured, stepping into the darkness.

He swallowed his unease and strode into the dark alleyway. If anything had lurked there recently, it was now dead on the end of Grace's spell-tipped blade.

A Dumpster blocked the end of the lane. After setting Kayla down, Hart pushed it back to reveal a rusty green door, which creaked when he eased it open. He grabbed the girl again, entered the musty stairwell, and barred the door securely behind him. He hit a hidden switch, and outside, the Dumpster slid back into position. There were no lights to illuminate the rickety stairs or the peeling walls. The beast looked out of his eyes; he was born to stalk the night.

Spiraling into the bowels of the earth, he carried the girl down and into the maze beneath the city streets. The gaslights shone through the thick glass plates in the sidewalk above, casting patches of murky light into the tunnel. Water leaked through, forming sewage puddles the rats played in. The trickle grew to a pour in the wet season—spring, fall, and winter—but he had found a dry enough set of rooms in a long-forgotten basement.

Norgard ran a cartel of killers and thieves based in the Underground, far from the respectable Drekar business front in north Seattle. Cameras and runners monitored every entrance to the illicit lair, though no sane person came down here anymore.

Hart avoided the traps that guarded his tunnel, dismantling and resetting them as he passed. He hesitated at his door, sniffed the air for signs of intruders. The only unusual smell in the musty air was Kayla. She squirmed like an eel on his shoulder. It was all he could do to hold on to her as she rubbed her thighs and stomach and chest against him.

Lust grabbed him by the balls and held on tight.

He stumbled through the door and slammed it closed with his heel. The locks set on their own. The familiar click of gears and thunk as the bolt slid home made him relax, but only an inch.

He had to regain control over his body and mind. Control was more necessary to him than oxygen. His whole adult life, since puberty when the Change had first hit him, he'd sought control over the beast inside. Fight the instincts. Fight the moon's call. Fight the bloodlust and rage.

He tried breathing deeply, which usually helped center him, but this time Kayla's scent filled his nostrils, hijacked his brain, and set his skin on fire.

He swore.

"Need," Kayla moaned. "Need more."

Her voice was breathy with want. It sent shivers over his skin, hot and cold.

"I know," he bit out. He knew what she needed. A dead man would know. Sweat dripped down his back from fighting his body's instincts, but he couldn't give in. He didn't have that much control.

His small four-room apartment wasn't much, but it was warm, dry, and safe. Someday, when he was free, he'd go north. Somewhere far away from everyone and everything.

Where it'd take a few days' hike through the snow to catch sight of a neighbor. Build himself a log cabin. Fill it with . . . stuff. Didn't really matter what, as long as it was new and *his*.

The main room of his apartment had a small kitchen and a sitting area with a lumpy, faded armchair. Torn paperbacks, falling apart from use, spilled out of a wooden bookcase against the far wall. The only nice features were two oriental rugs spread over the dark oak floors. They looked the same to him, but he knew one was red and one was green.

Hart decided to put the girl on the chair, but when he tried to set her down she clung to him. The drug Norgard had given her seemed to have amped up.

"No," she groaned. She was no longer catatonic, but she wasn't lucid either. Her arousal scented the room, heavy and thick, overpowering the smell of the drug. "I need—"

"Shh." Hart tried to disentangle her arms from around his neck, but she clung on like a drowning man. "Let go. Kayla, let go." He was afraid to hurt her. Her name sounded foreign on his tongue, and he tried to recall the last time he had called a woman by name. "Kayla." He liked that. "Kay-lllah." It rolled through his mouth and flicked off his tongue.

She rubbed herself against him. Breasts smashed against his chest. She purred, a deep throaty sound that made all the blood rush to his groin. He'd seen chicks like this before. It wasn't ecstasy. It was something new and much more powerful. An aphrodisiac on steroids.

"Need more," she begged. Rubbed. Writhed.

Lady be, he wasn't a saint. It was so tempting. Her heady scent overwhelmed his nostrils until Hart became drunk with it. It wasn't like he was Norgard—planning to screw her and suck out her soul.

He just wanted to screw her.

She tilted her head up and tried to reach his lips. Her pupils were dilated.

"Hell." Hart swept her into his arms and carried her into the bedroom.

Chapter 6

Sven Norgard spread his thin membranous wings and caught an updraft over Elliott Bay. He left behind the carnival of the city, where a million lights blazed gaudily from every surface. A cheer painted on the city like a cheap trick. Even at this hour, humans buzzed to and fro with their gaggle of technology and gas-guzzling machines. While the power worked, wireless signals created a constant annoying buzz, throwing off his navigation. A mosquito in his ear that he couldn't shake.

Humans, *bah*. Sometimes he wanted to kill them all.

He flicked his powerful tail and burst through the cloud cover into the ruddy glow of a pregnant moon. He stretched his wings above the clouds and plunged back down into the wet sky below. Ballard perched on the cliff edge like a tottering old man. The small town he'd founded over a hundred years ago with his flock had long since been annexed in Seattle's hunger, but his people had maintained their old ways. The cafés along Ballard Avenue served pickled herring and lingonberries. The boats of Fisherman's Terminal unloaded fresh salmon from Alaska daily. Celebrations of Yule and Tivoli turned the town into a colorful mass of Scandinavian flags.

His lair was built directly into the cliff face overlooking Puget Sound. Giant glass windows were eyes into the earth. He flew through one of the windows into the Great Hall. Landing, his claws gouged furrows in the gold-plated floor. It took but a thought to Turn. Shivers of Aether raced over his skin, peeling back scales like a butterfly emerging from its cocoon.

He snapped his fingers and a servant brought him a change of clothes. He dressed in his preferred fashion, blending vintage styles with the technologically advanced fabrics of the modern era. The gold buttons on his tall leather boots glittered in the light from the gas wall sconces. He patted the pocket of his iridescent black waistcoat, where a gold chain secured a sparkling, diamond-encrusted compass. Shiny things. Sparkly things. Precious gems and golden talismans. One could not fight one's nature.

And why should he? The top of the food chain was a glorious place to be.

He twisted the large malachite ring on the third finger of his left hand three times and commanded his servant to appear. An arctic breeze fluttered the tapestries on the walls. He adjusted the iron gears in his monocle. Through his naked eye, he saw a faint orb rippling in the air. Through the monocle, Mr. Nils looked like a portly man in a striped suit and bowler hat. The indistinct lines of his body dissolved and solidified, as if he hadn't quite decided on the form. Haunting black eyes stared, unblinking, out of a corpse-white face. His slash of a mouth showed no inkling of emotion.

"Accompany me, Mr. Nils," Norgard ordered. He strolled down the sloping tunnels to the laboratory on the lowest level. Below it, more tunnels ran into bowels of the earth, some, it was rumored, to the very heart of the Spider's lair. At the laboratory door, he placed the skeleton key that hung about his neck into the complicated lock. Gears grated on the other side. The lock slid open with a long whine.

"Come, Mr. Nils," he said and held open the door. Not that he needed to. Mr. Nils had no need of corporal fripperies.

On either side of a long aisle, whirring steel monsters belched steam, obscuring the cavernous room. His skin greedily drank the heat of the machines. It was a pity humans weren't designed to withstand the more agreeable temperatures. A deficit, he mused, he might fix when his current project was complete. Making humans strong enough to carry his offspring was the first order of business. Damned fragile things. Unfortunately, a necessary evil. If only Drekar could mate with their own kind, but one needed a soul to carry life. A human woman could nourish the dragonling in her womb with her own life force; a dragon female couldn't. Unless, legend had it, that dragon female had found and bound herself to her eternal mate, thereby sharing his soul.

Romantic drivel, if you asked him.

Norgard rapped on a nearby boiler.

"Hullo, little brother!" he called, projecting his voice to be heard over the clanging and whizzing machines. "Come out, come out, wherever you are."

A clatter of instruments answered his summons, and a moment later a disembodied face appeared out of the steam. Disorderly dirty-blond hair stuck out over large goggles. A square, stubbled jaw smudged with grease. A prominent nose, like the prow of a longboat.

"Sven?" the face asked, as if it could be anyone else.

"The latest batch of serum did not work as desired," Norgard said. "I am forced to descend into the dungeons to report on your failure."

"My apologies." Leif stepped forward and pushed the goggles to the top of his head. His brilliant green eyes were distant, as if his brain still attended his experiment, rather than focusing on the here and now.

"It was too strong," Norgard said.

"What size dose did you administer?"

"How should I know? I gave the chit a box of chocolates. I assume she ate them all."

Leif rubbed his eyes. "Measuring is important. Precision. I need details. Please describe the response."

As always, the detached scientist. Why couldn't his brother see the bigger picture for once? He often exploited Leif's narrow focus to his own ends, but occasionally it became inconvenient. The man was too young, only two hundred compared to Norgard's fifteen hundred. Leif had an irritable honest streak, unusual in their kind, and needed to be carefully managed.

"The serum was too strong," Norgard repeated. "She lost function in her arms and legs. Became incoherent. Almost passed out. I wanted an imitation of love, but the flavor was completely off."

The soul of a human in love satisfied like nothing else. It could reach crevices in his cold heart that had never known light. A soul in love was almost too pure to ingest. Almost, but not quite.

"It's strange that it's still too strong. Our metabolisms are so high, I would have thought . . ." Leif muttered to himself.

Originally the drug had been intended for Drekar. After centuries of soulless wandering, most slowly went insane. Norgard had discovered quickly that the drug was better administered through humans.

Leif took a deep breath and focused, for once. He looked serious. Norgard felt a trickle of foreboding.

"I heard about Desiree," his brother said. "I'm sorry."

Desiree. The memory rose, like a puff of steam from one of the nearby machines, only to float, ethereal and untouchable, in the echoing turbines of his mind.

Mechanically, he examined it. His chest tensed for only a heartbeat, then once again relaxed. He felt nothing, only the familiar sucking darkness in his breast, swirling emptiness that contracted and expanded with the currents of the Gate.

"It's nothing," he said. And it wasn't.

Leif frowned. "But—"

"She has a sister." Norgard cut him off before he could embarrass them both with some insipid emotional drivel. "If the first Miss Friday was strong enough to conceive my child, the second should be as well."

"Ah." Leif studied the toes of his boots. "Well, I'm glad to hear it."

"There is only one problem. Desiree died in possession of Kingu's Stone."

"How? When?"

Norgard shrugged, loath to admit such failure under his watch. "I wore it on a leather thong around my neck. She must have lifted it when I was screwing her that last time."

He remembered the girl's smooth skin, glowing with a sheen of sweat, those little noises she made in the back of her throat when he thrust into her. He remembered her belly growing round with his child. His gut tightened.

Must be indigestion.

"I set the werewolf upon its trail once I realized it was missing," Norgard said.

"When—"

"Two days ago." Norgard refused to think of her. She was nothing, but she dared to steal his child. Dared to steal his treasure. Dared to run from him—he who razed empires. He who raised kings.

"You set the werewolf on her, and now she's dead."

"His target was the necklace," Norgard said. He didn't have to explain himself. He would do the same if the situation repeated itself. "He wouldn't terminate the suspect before locating his target."

"How can you be sure? You know he's unstable," Leif said. "What if the Stone falls into the wrong hands? If someone breaks open the Gate with it—"

"You think I haven't thought of that? I told him it was only a sentimental trinket. No one knew I had it, but the necklace's connection to Tiamat will call to any Drekar who finds it."

"You think one of our own would open the Gate to gain power." It was not a question.

The Drekar were naturally solitary creatures. They disliked Norgard's rule on principle. The current political bonds, with Norgard as the Regent and all Drekar organized into a clan hierarchy, was necessary to succeed on a crowded earth, but unstable. Any one of their number would jump at the chance to seize power.

"Free Kingu, and we could return to the glory days when we rode at the head of the Demon Horde. When humans knew their place and dragon-kind ruled the world. When the skies were our domain, and we could fly free with the sun upon our wings. Who of our kind would not want that power?"

"Not me, thank you." Leif scrubbed a hand through his messy hair so that it stuck straight up. "I like civilization. You're talking about Ragnorök. The battle to end the world—"

"Don't be dramatic. It wouldn't be that bad."

"Unleashing Kingu and his horde? Of course it would be!"

"I'll take care of you, little brother. If you don't want to see the stone in the wrong hands, then we better find it first."

"Lovely." Leif's voice showed he thought it was anything but. "And the Raven Lord knows about this?"

"The Kivati also seek it."

"Corbette wouldn't use it. He's sworn to protect the humans."

"He cares more about secluding his precious Kivati from the evils of the outside world. Since we arrived on this cursed earth, Corbette has sought to destroy us."

They stood in silence, contemplating the immensity of the Gate breaking.

"I suppose," Leif said, his scientist brain returning to the nitty-gritty of solving the fallout of such a situation, "the Aether problem is more important with the Gate under peril."

"Yes." But Norgard was prepared for the worst. He had food and supplies stockpiled for the coming reign. Clean drinking water and medical supplies would be the currency of the new Dark Age. He had learned centuries ago that the true wealth lay in holding a monopoly on limited nondiscretionary resources. "I need to know that I can control my spirit servants if the Gate falls. I need to know how much power an Aether flare of that magnitude will give wraiths and demons that cross over."

"If the Gate falls altogether, that isn't just a flare. The very makeup of the Aether would change. At the very least, there would be no more electric charge in the land of the living. I don't have the technology to test something of that scope—"

"Do your best with what you've got. Start with the effect of a flare on Mr. Nils here. He is most eager to be of service."

Mr. Nils shimmered in the air in acknowledgment.

"Fine." Leif led the way to the back of the laboratory, where a giant engine lurked in the corner. It was the size of a barn and made of burnished brass. Wires fanned out from steel knobs, sparking up to the distant ceiling. On the front side spanned a series of levers and dials, some marked with tape on which was written, in his brother's distinctive scrawl, *Pull me first!* and *Touch me gently!* and PUSH ONLY IN EMERGENCY.

Leif pulled the goggles back down over his eyes and handed Norgard a matching pair. "Put these on."

"But—"

"It's not worth the risk," Leif said. "I've never tried it at the highest setting."

Norgard took the goggles. They fit over his monocle, but only just.

"Besides," said Leif, in a smug younger-brother tone, "I've no interest in ruling should anything happen to you."

"You'd do a rotten job of it anyway," Norgard muttered.

"Too true." Leif strode to a raised pool of water to the right of the engine. "Mr. Nils, if you please."

Without removing his clothing, Mr. Nils climbed into the pool. The water didn't ripple. He didn't get wet.

Leif hummed under his breath as he set about connecting wires from the engine to the pool. One for every direction of the compass, each bristling with energy. He moved to the panel to push buttons and twist knobs. The machine coughed, belched, lurched to life like a mechanical Frankenstein.

"Brace yourself," Leif shouted over the noise. With his left hand, he pulled a gold pocket watch out of his lab coat and studied the steadily ticking second hand. When it reached twelve, he yanked a chain dangling over his head. The engine screeched like a stuck pig. Green fire burst from the steel dials, descending down the wires in every direction. It snaked toward the pool where stoic Mr. Nils waited with a gallows-bait expression.

Norgard plugged his ears against the shrieking pipes. Time seemed to slow while the fire burned down the wires, closer, closer, until finally they hit the pool with a sizzle.

Water exploded into mist and the world went dark. An Aether wind tore through the airtight room, a storm swirling in the darkness. It pulled at their clothing and tore at their skin. Over the noise of the storm rose a howl, growing louder, until it filled every cranny with the sound of its pain.

The green fire flashed. Once. Twice. Three times. Each one bigger than the last. Each one a momentary reprieve from the terrible darkness.

In the midst of the gale, Norgard felt a ghostly presence. It brushed the outside of his consciousness, the lightest knock to the hollow house of his missing soul. Beneath his woolen coat and linen shirt, cold fingers touched his spine. Slowly, they rose, growing longer and icier, caressing his naked skin, freezing his marrow, stealing his will.

He tensed against the invasion. "Mr. Nils," he bit out. The wind whipped the words from his lips, but he knew his words had been heard. The fingers paused.

"Mr. Nils," he said again, louder, an edge to his voice. "I bind you, Mr. Nils, not the other way around."

The cold fingers turned to claws. They scratched, angry, down his skin, tearing the flesh beneath their electrically sharpened nails.

"Leif! Turn it off!"

With a bang, the machine blew. It wheezed and sagged and moaned, a crone stuttering at the top of a steep hill. Acrid smoke filled the lab, making both men cough. Mercifully, the wind stopped and the icy fingers disappeared. The gaslights flickered back on.

Norgard leaned against a nearby boiler to catch his breath, weakness be damned. He pulled a handkerchief out of his breast pocket and mopped the water out of his now-sopping hair.

"Needs more work," Leif mumbled. His face was black with soot and grease. He yanked the goggles off his eyes, exposing wide, white circles like a raccoon. He pulled off a leather glove and ran a hand through his filth-streaked hair.

"Indeed." With measured precision, Norgard folded his wet handkerchief and tucked it back into his pocket. Removing the goggles, he handed them to his brother. He straightened his damp jacket and squeezed the excess water from his dripping cuffs.

"Apologies." Leif glanced at him sideways. "I told you I'd never tried it at full speed. That's not a fraction of what would happen if the Gate fell—"

"You just need to find me a solution." Norgard ran his tongue over his sharp teeth. Next time he would await the report instead of observing the experiment in situ. He would send an underling to play the damned guinea pig. "Mr. Nils," he bit out.

Mr. Nils's face displayed no remorse at having tried to kill his master. He calmly climbed out of the now empty pool and stood silently next to Norgard. The only show of disturbance was the undulating edge of his ghostly form.

"I'm a scientist, not a magician." Leif turned to the machine, already lost in his calculations.

Norgard resisted the urge to gut his brother with a carefully aimed claw.

"Come, Mr. Nils," he said, spinning on his heel and marching back down the cluttered aisle. "We've something to discuss. A few relatives of yours, who are—unfortunately for you—very much alive."

They wouldn't be for long.

Kayla woke with cotton balls in her mouth, sand in her eyes, and a hammer terrorizing the inside of her skull. She lay on something soft, but could see nothing in the absolute darkness. Entombed alive.

Breathe. She had to keep breathing. Had to figure out where she was. Images flashed in her mind: grinding bodies beneath the red glow of gaslights; a striking blond man with a strange mechanical eyeglass offering dark sweets; leathery wings unfolding across the sky; claws; teeth; terror.

Her fingers searched over her body, checking to make sure every piece was still there. Beneath a sheet she was naked.

Oh God, oh God, oh God.

She couldn't panic. She had to think clearly. Her body was sore. Shifting her legs, she felt gingerly between her thighs. Would she know if she'd been assaulted? She had to remember what had happened last night. The city had passed by in a blur while she clutched a hard warm chest. Hart's face, frozen in an expression of surprise. Heat in his eyes. Heat in her core.

God, the heat.

She had to get out of here. Slowly she sat up and braced

herself against the sudden rush of blood to her head. The sheet tangled about her legs. She wrapped it around her torso and waist like a sarong. Her legs didn't want to hold her, but she pushed herself to a standing position by propping her shoulder against the wall. Her limbs were jelly. Her stomach wanted to reintroduce her to last night's dinner.

Kayla stepped off what she assumed was a mattress and felt a rug beneath her feet. Running her hand along the wall, she inched her foot forward, slowly feeling for obstacles. When her fingers found the end of the wall she turned, and two steps later encountered a rough door frame. Fumbling for the knob, she found a cold iron handle instead. Something old-fashioned, with a lock for a skeleton key beneath it.

The door wouldn't budge.

Behind her the blackness thickened. She felt eyes on her back. Imagined a cold breeze teasing the skin on her neck. The darkness felt alive.

Nonsense. She wasn't afraid of the dark. Except she'd gotten the proof she asked for last night, and suddenly ghosts were real. Shape-shifters. Dragons. Aptrgangr. Who knew what waited in the dark?

"Let me out!" She banged on the wood. She clawed at it with her short fingernails. "Please!" There wasn't enough air. The walls were closing in on her.

On the other side of the door, heavy footsteps approached. Someone was coming for her. She banged louder. The door opened, and she fell into a hard body. A bare chest. Muscular shoulders. Strong arms wrapped around her. She buried her face against his hot skin and breathed deeply, smelling the astringent mint of shaving cream and pine.

She recognized that forest scent, and, damn it, he smelled so *good*. After the fear and the darkness, all she wanted was to lean into that strong, familiar embrace, to cling to Hart's muscled chest and let her racing heart calm. But she couldn't kid herself for long—he wasn't her friend and he wasn't safe.

And the blood galloping through her veins didn't slow at the soothing scent of him; it just moved south to call forth other arousing and unwanted desires.

Her cheeks burned. Yet again, he saw her at her weakest. Her coworkers back in Philly had nicknamed her "The Rock" for her solid, steady nerves. Not in Seattle. She'd never felt so out of control. Never struggled beneath the weight of so much fear, uncertainty, and doubt. She liked things black-and-white, but nothing here was clean cut. Everything was lost in shadow.

Steeling herself, she pulled away from his solid chest and pressed back against the door. "Please tell me there is a logical explanation for this." She indicated the sheet.

"Calm down. Nothing happened." Large bruises—new since she had seen him last—purpled his ribs and chin. His face was freshly shaven, and a dab of shaving cream clung stubbornly to his ear.

"Nothing?"

"Norgard didn't have time." He turned abruptly, giving her space, and strode across the cramped living room to an open door where a small pedestal sink was partly visible. He examined his face in the small mirror above the sink and wiped the shaving cream off his ear.

"And after?"

He glanced at her in the mirror. Hurt flickered deep in his eyes, but was shuttered so fast she might have imagined it. He covered with a sardonic grin. "That good, was I? Memorable. Just what a guy likes to hear." He pulled a green and brown plaid flannel shirt off the bathroom door and stiffly slipped it on. He met her eyes as he did up the buttons.

Somehow she believed him. "Thank you."

His gaze shifted, and he shrugged one shoulder. "You should get out of here. Norgard will be looking for you after I finish this job."

Norgard. She remembered a spiked tail slashing through the alley. Norgard was a dragon. It still seemed so unreal.

"About that—thanks for the warning. Upstanding businessman? Pillar of society?"

"Hey, I never said that."

She glared at him. "Forget the fact that he's not human. He sells opium, pushes prostitutes, and drugs women—*minors* even. How does he get away with it?"

"He's the Drekar Regent. He owns half this state."

"Fuck." She ran her hands through her tangled hair. "Listen to me asking the wrong questions. I've clearly lost my mind. What's a little crime, if the big secret around here is that he's a dragon?"

"Most people don't know that."

"Don't know what?"

"That he's a dragon. Only a small group of humans are clued in."

That made her feel marginally better. "Why do you work for him?"

"None of your business," Hart growled.

Maybe not, but she wanted to know. Wanted him to have a good excuse, or some proof that he wasn't a bad guy, despite his employer. She shouldn't care, as long as he helped her find Desi's necklace. But, she realized, she *wanted* to trust him. Around him, her body developed heated desires of its own; it didn't care what he did or who he worked for as long as he took his shirt off a couple more times in front of her. Gawd, what a mess she was. As if his motives could somehow justify her lust.

She needed to get her head on straight. She hadn't held out this long to throw herself at the first guy with nice cologne and a really big *gun*.

She glanced around Hart's small living quarters, which were sparse but clean. With a single chair in evidence, it didn't appear he did much entertaining. In the corner, a small puddle of water collected beneath a mini-fridge. A bookcase overflowed with tattered paperbacks. Science fiction, thrillers, classic literature, nonfiction treatises. The man might act like a thug, but he was well read.

"Joseph Conrad?" she asked, changing the subject. "And here I had you pegged as the Jane Austen type."

"Oh, I've got Austen." He walked to the bookcase and pulled a novel from the top shelf. The cover showed Jane Austen with half her face ripped off. "The zombies add a little realism. You want illogical? Illogical is happily ever after."

"You're a cynic."

"A realist. Nothing lasts. But back to the subject. You should leave." On the floor, his weapons lay spread out on a thick woolen blanket. He picked up a curved six-inch knife and began sharpening it.

Trying to intimidate her? Yes, weapons made her nervous, but he knew diddly-squat about her if he thought she would run now. "I'm not going anywhere. We need to find that necklace for the Kivati—"

The knife scraped along the sharpener. "We're even."

"Who's keeping track?"

Disbelief flashed across his angular features. "I don't need your help. Go home."

That hurt. She steeled herself. "You think you're a one-man army. I get it. But I need your help to find out what happened to my sister, and I made a promise. I don't break my promises. Ever. The Kivati will—"

"You don't get it."

"Then explain it to me."

He inspected the sharp edge of the knife. "Forget the Kivati. This is bigger than both of us. The Drekar worship an ancient Babylonian goddess named Tiamat. You heard of her?"

Kayla shook her head. Mythology had been Desi's specialty, not hers. She'd never bothered with the stuff until now.

"Goddess of primordial chaos. She takes the form of a monstrous dragon. She and Apsu gave birth to the gods and goddesses of ancient Babylon, but when one of them offed Apsu she swore revenge. She birthed the monsters of the world—dragons, giant sea serpents, maelstrom demons, shark men—you name it. Then she gave her lover Kingu the Tablets of Destiny and, with this army of monsters, he waged war on the younger gods, decimating the world."

"But someone stopped him," she guessed.

"Another god slew Tiamat and trapped Kingu and his horde behind the Gate to the otherworld." Apparently satisfied with the knife, he set it back on the blanket and moved on to the rifle. He unloaded large silver-tipped bullets, the surfaces etched with strange markings. "Imagine that happening again. Imagine Kingu gets released from his prison. He's had a few millennia to plan his revenge. He's become stronger. He's got cooler toys this time around, thanks to the humans."

"Like—"

"Atomic bombs. A world population of six billion. That's a big army for his demons and wraiths to inhabit." He removed the bolt and scope from the rifle, inspected the interior, and wiped it down with a handkerchief. His movements were gentle, caring even.

"A zombie army," Kayla said.

"Yeah, you imagining that? Genghis Khan had nothing on this guy. Kingu leads his army of monsters across the globe, leaving nothing alive behind him. The slaughtered get back up and join his forces." His large hands caressed the pieces as he reassembled the rifle. A man and his gun. Go figure. "Nothing could stop him."

"Then what?"

"He declares war on the gods, retakes the Tablet of Destiny, and uses it to wake Tiamat."

"The goddess of chaos."

"You got it." Hart smiled and popped a bullet into the rifle barrel. Even though his words were terrifying, his smile drew her closer.

"And that, I assume, is the end of the world as we know it." Her voice came out flat. She didn't want to believe him.

"Knew you were a smart girl."

She took a deep breath. His story sounded like tales of the bogeyman, but she couldn't afford not to believe him. "Let me guess, this necklace of my sister's plays a part?"

"It belongs to Kingu. I'm pretty sure it's the key to open the Gate."

"Then you need my help more than ever."

He blinked. She liked that she could surprise him for once. He had shocked her quite enough.

"Desi left me more clues. I know it. It'll be something only meaningful to me. Something you would overlook. We're wasting time." First things first. "Where are my clothes?"

He ran a hand through his thick hair. "Shirt and panties should be in the bedroom. Last night you couldn't get naked fast enough. Your pants are ruined." He grabbed a pile of black fabric off the armchair, and tossed it to her. "Catch."

She caught the bundle before it hit her in the face, but dropped the sheet. "Don't look!" Her knees crumbled under her, and she frantically grabbed at the sheet on the floor. Mortification flooded her from her roots to the tips of her toes. "I said don't—"

"You don't have anything I haven't seen before." Hart took a toothpick from his pocket and stuck it into his mouth. He chewed it thoughtfully, not looking away.

Kayla felt her cheeks flame. She clutched the sheet to her chest. "Some gentleman."

He pulled his lips back in a grin, displaying even, white teeth with sharp, pointed canines. "Didn't say I was."

She licked her lips, and his intense gaze rose to her mouth. She suddenly felt like Little Red Riding Hood facing the Big Bad Wolf, and—wow—for the first time in her life she understood why Red had succumbed. Beneath the sheet her nipples tightened.

What was wrong with her? *Werewolf*, remember? Violent, weapon-toting maniac. Not to mention Armageddon looming on the horizon. Sex was not on the agenda.

A rebellious little voice asked if she wanted to die a virgin. She ignored it. She was good at that.

The fabric bundle he had thrown her was a pair of huge sweatpants. She quickly pulled them over her legs beneath the sheet. They hung from her hips like pantaloons, but stayed up. She raised her head to find him watching her sideways. His eyes were half-lidded and secretive, but he couldn't hide the hunger in his gaze. His grip on the rifle barrel was white-knuckled. His nostrils flared.

That look made her feel naked again. Her pulse hummed beneath her skin. "Stop."

"Stop what?"

"Just stop it."

He smirked.

She turned her back on him to retrieve her shirt from the bedroom. When she emerged, he was tucking the last of his weapons into the holster on his back.

"We need all the facts so that we can make a logical plan of attack," she told him. "Why did Desi have the necklace? How did she get it? Who knew she had it? Would someone have killed her to get it? Why did—"

"Hold on there, Sherlock. One at a time."

"I'm serious. You need to share all your information with me. Otherwise I won't be able to help."

He stuck the toothpick out the side of his mouth and thought for a moment. "Okay."

"Okay?"

"Okay." He settled into the armchair and stuck his long legs out in front of him. "Your sister was scrogging Norgard—"

"Please—"

"Hey, you wanted the facts."

She didn't want to talk about scrogging, not with Hart

lounging in front of her, muscles bulging beneath a soft flannel shirt. His tongue flipped the toothpick end over end between his lips.

Hart continued. "Don't know how she found out about the key. Norgard kept it on the D.L., but who knows what he said in his sleep? He was hung up on her."

"Did you ever meet her?"

"Maybe." His eyes shifted away. "Hard to keep track of all Norgard's bitch—er, lady friends."

She let that slide. "She wanted me to give the key to Corbette. But Rudrick said she was bringing it to him. Do you think that's the truth?"

"Could be. Kivati can lie, but they've got a strict code of honor. Unlike the Drekar, who can't lie, but bring the art of deception to a whole new level."

"Is there anyone else who wants the key, besides the Kivati and Drekar? Any other factions I should know about?"

"The power to open the Land of the Dead? Plenty of people would want it, if they knew about it."

She hesitated. "With this key, a person could bring the dead back to life?" Adam and Caroline had hinted that Desi was searching for immortality. Perhaps Desi had a different goal in mind: with the power to raise the dead, she could resurrect their parents.

Hart frowned. "Not life like you mean it. You can bring them back through the Gate—necromancers do—but it's unnatural. They aren't 'alive,' not like you and me. Which reminds me." He stood and approached the bookcase. He rummaged around until he found a pencil hidden between the pages of a book. "The rune on your sister's wrist is ancient Norse: Raidho, reversed. It anchors her spirit here." He drew the strange marks on the back of the book cover.

"Desi's still here?" Kayla didn't know whether to be happy or horrified. "Can I talk to her?"

"Maybe. Spirits trapped on this side of the Gate become

warped. If we can find the ghost, it won't be your sister like you remember her. She'll be a shade. A shadow of herself. Depends on how strong she was."

"Who would want to anchor her spirit here?" She imagined Desi stealing the necklace and running, with Norgard hot on her trail. If he caught her and killed her, wouldn't he want to silence her permanently so no one would know? "You think she did it to herself."

"Could have, to pass a message on."

"She could tell me where the key is hidden."

"That's our best-case scenario, but sometimes it's done as punishment. A wraith finds no peace in the grave." His jaw tightened. It wasn't a pleasant thought. "Another possibility: in ancient times, warriors were sacrificed and their souls anchored at tombs and treasure holds as undead sentinels. Her ghost could be guarding the key."

"But she wanted me to find the key and give it to Corbette. Wouldn't she hand it over, if that's the case?"

"Maybe, but wraiths become twisted. They forget their humanity, their living connections. She could just as easily attack you. Hard to fight a ghost. Hard to kill something that's already dead, or wound something with no body."

Kayla shivered. Desi wouldn't hurt her, would she? It had only been two days. How quickly could her sister forget their bond? She hated the idea of Desi's corroded ghost haunting the streets of Seattle. Her sister deserved peace.

He drew another symbol on the book that looked like the letter M. "This is called Ehwaz. It should free her, if you get the chance."

"How will I know?"

He shrugged. "If the Lady is willing, you'll know."

"Trust my instincts, you mean?" They were still screaming, *Run fast, run hard.*

"These things aren't an exact science. Magic depends on the quality of soul. The power to manipulate the Aether. Even the weather. Dangerous stuff, magic." He tossed the book on a shelf. "The ghost will be strongest at the death site. You know where that is?"

"Not exactly, but I've been wanting to ask the officer who discovered the scene more questions," Kayla said. "We can call him on our way to the hospital and ask him to show us the exact location where she died."

"The hospital?"

"For a rape kit. I might trust you—"

"You shouldn't," Hart growled.

"—but I don't trust Norgard. Come on, wolf man, let's get this over with."

The hospital gave Kayla a clean bill of health—thank God. Hart had told her the truth. He might tell her not to trust him, but he hadn't lied to her yet. They met Detective Cortez at Gas Works Park that afternoon. The old coal gasification plant was located on a spit of land that jutted into Lake Union. Gloom shrouded the park. Brown cylindrical towers rose from a sea of mist. A solitary seagull squawked overhead and flew off, abandoning them to the deserted factory. Yellow crime tape fluttered in the wind, the only cheery color amid the gray and brown.

"This place gives me the creeps," she said as Hart parked next to Cortez's unmarked police cruiser.

Hart got out of the car and sniffed the air. "Watch your back."

Cortez joined them. A younger officer with sandy brown hair, he had tired rings under his eyes and a persistent smoker's cough.

"I'm going to sniff around, see if I find anything." Hart motioned to the water's edge. "Yell if you need me."

"But—"

"Scared, babe? He'll take care of you, won't ya, pal?"

Hart's black gaze seemed to pierce straight through Cortez. His smile showed all his teeth.

Cortez swallowed. "She's safe with me."

Hart took out a small brass spyglass and held it to his eye. He surveyed the park in a quick circle and came back to rest a beat on Cortez. "All clear." He handed the glass to Kayla.

She accepted the glass. "What is it?"

"A nightlight of sorts. I search better alone."

He must need to change his shape, she realized. He didn't want to do it in front of Cortez. She made herself smile. She didn't need Hart to hold her hand. Really. She watched him fade into the mist and turned back to the policeman. "Ready when you are. This weather is weird. How did it get so dark so quickly?" She rubbed her arms.

"Your guy's a little intense, huh?"

"He's not mine."

Cortez made a noncommittal noise and motioned for Kayla to follow him into the park. They approached the main site of the factory: six rusty steel-plated towers connected by teetering walkways high in the air and numerous pipes. The stench of fish and salt blew in from Puget Sound. The wind passing between the towers howled.

Kayla pulled her jacket tighter.

"It's always like this in the winter and early spring," Cortez said. "Least we got sun breaks this morning. That's pretty good for April. Anyway, two nights ago my partner and I got an anonymous tip that something big was going down at the Pump and Boiler Houses." He pointed to two large wooden sheds to the left. Inside the shadowy doorways, pumps, steel-plated compressors and pipes huddled together against the dark. "Around dusk. Weather about like this. Low visibility. Damp. As soon as we parked, I got this twitch I get sometimes. You know, sixth-sense type of thing." His tight expression dared her to disagree.

She nodded. "I know what you mean." She wouldn't have,

before. She would have discounted her instincts and convinced herself there was some other logical explanation.

Cortez relaxed slightly. "Yeah, well, Sanders, he doesn't hold with my twitches. Can't file them in a report, see? He's a good cop, but there isn't enough manpower to follow up every time someone gets a feeling. My twitches, they've saved my ass more than once on the street. After the preliminary reports are in, though, most cases are locked tight."

"So, it's not just my sister's case. Your force doesn't follow up any cases?"

Cortez scowled. "Hey, there aren't enough of us. Limited resources. Limited funds. We do our best. Dead people—they aren't getting up anymore, no matter what we do. We focus on the murders we can prevent."

Kayla grudgingly admitted he had a point. She had seen the news reports. Worse than fictional Gotham. What could a bunch of half-crooked cops do against so much bloodshed?

"I do my best with what I got, Ms. Friday," Cortez said stiffly. "You people don't hear about the ones we do save. The young girls in shipping containers we intercept before they disappear into the underground brothels. The perps so hyped up on drugs they got superhuman strength. For every one that slips through the cracks, we take down five more. But you only pay attention to the one that got away."

"I know. You do a great job. Thank you," she said. A hostile Cortez could quickly turn into an unhelpful one.

He led the way to the Pump and Boiler Houses. More rusty towers flanked the buildings to the right. "We found your sister in here." The field light overhead sputtered and died, casting the industrial towers in gloom. He pulled a heavy flashlight out of his waist holder and switched it on. "I'll tell you the truth: it looked like she was fleeing something. There were signs of a struggle. Scratches on her arms and neck, though my partner thought they were self-inflicted—"

A shadow passed in the doorway of the Pump House, the silhouette of a woman. There and gone in the blink of an eye.

Cortez froze with one hand on his holster. "Who's there?"

No one answered. There was no sound but the soft splash of water against the bulkhead and the whine of the wind through the towers.

"I saw it too," Kayla whispered.

"Probably just a park-goer, but you never know. You stay here. I wouldn't want your boyfriend on my case—"

"He's not mine," she insisted. She wasn't eager to follow Cortez. She didn't want to be left alone in the mist, but Hart hadn't returned. She didn't have much choice. "I'll be fine," she said, more to herself than Cortez.

"Sure, sure," Cortez said.

She heard a muffled clang. There was definitely someone— or something—out there.

"Hello in there? This is a crime scene. You need to leave." Cortez drew his weapon and, flashlight in one hand, gun in the other, ducked under the yellow police tape, entered the building and disappeared behind a fire engine red boiler.

Minutes ticked by, but it felt like hours. A few drops of water fell from the sky onto Kayla's face, startling her. "There's nothing to be afraid of." Maybe if she ignored the fear creeping up her spine it would go away. She turned Hart's spyglass over in her hand. A nightlight, he'd said. She held it to her eye and adjusted the small gears until her vision came into focus. Still, it was a little blurry. Lights and shadows played over the machinery of the park. She wasn't sure what she was supposed to see.

A groan slid through the air. A scream should have been more alarming, but somehow that groan packed more terror.

"Cortez?" It was too quiet. "Hart?" She looked around for Hart, but there was no sign of him. She called out again, but no one answered. If Cortez was injured, she could help. If Cortez was in danger, she couldn't. If this were a horror movie, this is where the heroine would stupidly leave the house to investigate the strange noise outside. So many ifs.

Her instincts said to wait, but her inner nurse said, "Get off your butt and go help the man." If he was injured, every second counted. She tried calling again.

Nothing.

Crap.

This was the moment that defined a person. It wasn't enough to have the skills to save a life; you had to have the guts to act. She held up Hart's spyglass one more time and peered into the Pump House. More flickering light was visible through the glass, but what did it mean? Pocketing it, she entered the doorway and concentrated on putting one foot in front of the other. Cortez probably hadn't heard her. Any minute now he would step back into view with a smile on his face and an all-clear. Nothing to be frightened of.

"Cortez?" she called. Her voice echoed tinnily against the silent steel structures.

Still nothing.

The shed was a mausoleum of a bygone industrial age. The machines were silent sentries, fashioning aisles and rows the length of the building. The air felt heavy with dust and disuse, yet somehow alive. She could almost imagine energy crackling around her. She wiped her sweaty palms on her pants.

Up ahead, a light bounced off a series of brass pipes. She circled around a massive boiler and found Cortez standing in the center of the aisle, flashlight hanging limply at his side, his back to her. He didn't move, didn't seem to hear Kayla coming up behind him.

"Detective Cortez." She reached out and touched the man on the shoulder.

Cortez turned, slowly, awkwardly, as if his limbs weren't quite coordinated with his brain. He stared at Kayla blankly.

And she knew that something was hideously wrong.

Chapter 7

Cortez's eyes were dead. Lifeless, and yet hungry. As if that made any sense. Christ, the man looked like he was in a waking coma. The edges of his mouth unfurled. There was a whole lot of scary in that smile. She swallowed.

"Kayla," he said.

Detective Jake Cortez had never called her by her first name.

"Are you all right?" she asked.

Cortez didn't blink. "Come with me." His voice was different. Hissing. Breathy.

Then he spasmed. Groaned. His hands came up to his neck, scratching, clawing, trying to peel off his skin. "Get it out!" he cried, his voice normal once again. Angry red grooves appeared on his neck and face. Blood beneath his fingernails.

Kayla rushed to help him. "Stop hurting yourself. Stop it!"

He flicked her off like an ant, and she tumbled to the floor. The concrete scraped her palms and knees.

"I can tassste your fear, sssissster," he hissed. He closed his eyes and breathed in deeply.

This wasn't Detective Cortez. Something else peered out at her. Kayla licked her lips. "Who are you? What have you done to Detective Cortez?"

His eyes popped open so wide the whites showed all around. His legs moved, awkwardly, as if pulled by strings of an invisible puppeteer.

He had called her *sister*.

"Desi?" Kayla crawled backward. Desi wouldn't hurt her.

He lurched forward.

She flipped to her feet and bolted toward the entrance. The semi-aisles had turned into a maze. She tripped over a lever and slid on a steel plate in the floor. Dead ends all around her. She glanced back and saw the creature reaching for her. Grabbing the spoke of a giant wheel, she let momentum swing her around the corner. Not fast enough. Hands gripped her legs. She clung to the wheel as she was yanked back. The cold metal cut into her skin. Her shoulder joints stretched painfully. No letting go. She kicked and felt her foot connect with a sickening snap.

The creature hissed and raked its claws down her leg. Her sweatpants ripped.

"Help!" she screamed. "Help, Hart!" The deserted shed soaked it up, played it back. No one could hear her. The creature squeezed, and pain radiated up her leg. Oh, Lord. Her eyes watered. Its grip was an iron vise, cutting off circulation to her foot, crushing the delicate bones until the verge of breaking.

Her sweaty hands slipped free of the wheel. The world flipped. Gravity pulled at her head, her body suspended in air. The monster clutched her ankle and shook her upside down. Her hands raked the ground, but there was nothing to grab on to. She could only hang like meat in a butcher's rack. Helpless.

"Desi," she pleaded, "if you're in there, if you can hear me, please, let me go."

The thing didn't answer. It dragged her as it marched back down the aisle. Its limbs were becoming more coordinated, as if with practice it was learning to use Cortez's ligaments and muscles. Kayla's head thumped against a brass pipe. Her vision blurred as pain shot through her skull. Something wet ran down her hairline.

This was it. Twenty-five years of planning, saving, reasoning. All for nothing. Meticulous. Rational. Practical. She'd always been proud when those words were applied to her, but suddenly they lacked heat. She'd missed out, always playing it safe.

She should have kissed Hart when she had the chance.

The creature stopped at a giant engine. She closed her eyes and immediately sensed a blackness reaching toward her. It seemed to be attracted by her helplessness. Shadows rippled within Cortez's body, down his arm to where he gripped her ankle. They pulsed against her skin, slimy and tainted.

Hart's medallion still hung from her neck. It banged against her forehead as she was jostled upside down. Now it heated. Light sparkled through it, like a thousand tiny stars. Reacting instinctively, she pulled at that light and reached deep inside herself to find more. A light that *was* her. Soul or essence or life force, she wasn't sure. She only knew that she couldn't let the blackness overtake her.

She grabbed hold of that light and pushed against the shadows with all her might. The creature startled. It stumbled, and they fell together, hitting the metal pipes that fed the engine on the way down. She grabbed a pipe and felt skin scrape away. Her blood splattered the floor.

Suddenly, a large timber wolf sailed over her and slammed into the creature. His black fur stood on end. A white stripe ran between his ears and down his neck. Hart had come for her. She'd never seen him shift before, but she knew it was him.

The Wolf growled and snapped its jaws over Cortez's arm. The thing in Cortez's body roared. It swept its other arm around the Wolf's throat and squeezed. The two rolled across the aisle, locked in combat.

Kayla crawled out of the way. Her leg burned. She was pretty sure it was broken.

The Wolf ripped out a chunk of skin, spraying his muzzle and the front of Cortez's uniform with dark red blood. By all logic, the human should have fallen easily under the Wolf's attack, but Cortez was no longer fully human. The thing possessing his body seemed to grow stronger on the pain. She imagined it would keep fighting until the Wolf severed every ligament, effectively cutting the strings of its puppet.

A shot rang out and the Wolf stumbled. Somehow Cortez had managed to shoot his gun while partially holstered. Hart whimpered in pain, but dove again at Cortez, this time knocking the gun away. The weapon ricocheted off the engine and spun toward Kayla, stopping inches from her outstretched fingertips.

She pushed forward and grabbed it. A gun. She didn't know how to shoot a gun. It shouldn't be hard—just aim and pull the trigger, right? Sweat dripped into her eyes, blurring her vision. The Wolf was in the way. Locked together, they moved too quickly. Blood flowed from the Wolf's foreleg, leaving a trail crisscrossing the aisle.

She abhorred violence. She aimed. The gun shook in her hand. Her finger squeezed the trigger.

Nothing happened.

She was almost dizzy with relief. She hadn't shot Hart or Cortez. Hadn't taken anyone's life, aptrgangr, werewolf, or whatever.

The Wolf tore out Cortez's throat. The fight was over in an instant. Blood coated the cement floor. Blood dripped from the brass boiler. Blood ran in rivulets down the pipes that fed the engine.

She wanted to vomit.

The Wolf collapsed in a pool of blood. She crawled forward until she could see his chest rise and fall in shallow breaths. Pain made her eyesight fuzzy. She thought she saw a firefly alight on his nose, then another and another until he glowed. The glow flowed up his muzzle and fell down his back, a golden wave that dissolved fur and fang and left sun-kissed skin in its wake.

When the glow faded, sprawled on the floor lay a thoroughly masculine, completely naked, gorgeously familiar man. His skin was rosy from cold and exertion. The gold armbands did nothing for modesty. If anything, they accentuated the godlike perfection of his muscled physique.

"See anything you like?" Hart growled. His eyes were closed, but a smirk lurked in the corner of his mouth.

Kayla had to swallow twice before her voice would work. "What took you so long?"

He scowled, but instead of a snappy comeback he launched himself. One moment he was on the ground, and the next he was on top of her. His large, hot body pressed her into the floor. His hungry lips descended on hers, tasting of mint and pine.

She couldn't help herself. She needed reassurance that he was alive and whole. Her fingers searched for injuries, but all they found were the chiseled muscle and taut skin of his back. Adrenaline rushed through her veins, relief and madness all coiled together. The world narrowed to touch and taste. His tongue in her mouth. Mint and pine. His calloused hands on her breasts. Kneading and wanting. His leg pressing open her thighs. Wet heat and tingling need. The hard masculine part of him settled firmly there, where the heat centered, where the wanting built, like a puzzle piece falling into place.

Touch me, she thought. She stroked his arms. Her fingers slid over those strange gold armbands that never seemed to leave him, even when he Changed. His left arm was wet and sticky. He jerked his arm away.

"You've been shot," she said, guilt swamping the heat in her belly. How could she forget he was injured? He made her lose all sense. Her own aches and pains rushed back to her. "I'm so sorry. You shouldn't let me maul you like this. You must be in terrible pain."

Hart gave a wry smile. "Must have slipped my mind." He

rested his forehead against hers for a moment. His breath came as fast as her own. The sky peeked through a hole in the roof of the shed. He slowly pushed himself up and achingly stood, naked and proud in the gray light.

She looked away, face hot. She didn't have to see his face to know he was laughing at her. It was too late for modesty after she'd had her hands all over his naked skin. Her hand rose nervously to the medallion around her neck. It had broken in two. "Hart, I'm so sorry!" She held the pieces up to him. "It saved me."

"Don't worry about it." He waved off her concern, but his fingers tightened around the twin pieces when she handed them back. "Just some old thing of my mom's."

"I'm sorry," she said again, knowing it was inadequate.

He shrugged. "But I want my Deadglass back."

She pulled the spyglass out of her pocket and handed it over. "What's it for?"

"Lets you see the dead. Didn't I tell you to use it?"

"I did. I didn't see anything."

"No river of light? No looming shadows?"

"But what does that tell me?"

"It's the Aether. Takes some practice to read the currents, I guess." He glanced at the Deadglass and then down to his naked body. He had nowhere to put it. "On second thought, hold it for me a bit longer, will ya?" He offered her his good hand. His left forearm showed an angry red tear where the bullet had shot clean through the muscle. Otherwise, he seemed *extremely* healthy.

Her body was another story. Her foot hung at a crooked angle. Deep scratches ran up her exposed leg.

"I don't know if I can stand," she admitted. "My ankle."

He growled low in his throat and swept her up in his arms.

"Don't! You'll hurt yourself."

"Save it, babe." He started down the aisle, but something about the engine caught her eye.

"Stop. Look at the blood." She pointed to the engine, where splattered blood ran over the burnished metal. It didn't drip toward the ground, as it should. The droplets separated and spread, against gravity, coating the sides and lingering in grooves carved into the thick metal. Scripting across the engine like a ghostly fountain pen, a message emerged: *K-9881*. The last number was half formed, as if the writer had been interrupted.

"Blood will out," she murmured.

"Does that mean anything to you?"

"It looks familiar, but I can't place it."

"Think harder." Hart set her on the ground. "Memorize it." He strode to Cortez's body and tore the uniform off. Using it as a rag, he scrubbed the blood off the engine. The writing disappeared as if it had never been.

He swung her back into his arms, and she settled against his naked chest. *Again.* Her brain worried that this position was becoming all too familiar. Her body purred, happy to rub against him like a cat in the sun. She glanced back at the corpse. "What about Cortez?"

"He knew the risks."

"The police will find our fingerprints."

"No, they won't. Norgard owns enough of them. They'll find a rabid dog attack, nothing more. We've a real problem with rabid animals in this city."

Party to manslaughter, obstruction of justice, police bribery. Kayla was on a roll. She hardly recognized herself. The straitlaced nurse had been left far behind. Maybe she'd fallen out of the plane on the ride here.

Hart carried her to his car, set her down, and opened the trunk where he'd stashed his clothes. Now that she wasn't pressed against his naked chest, she had a great view of the rest of him. She caught his grin and forced herself to stop staring. "Who knew you were such an exhibitionist?"

"What's to be embarrassed about? This is the way the Lady made me. A hundred percent natural."

"Lovely," she said, tongue in cheek.

"Thank you." He winked at her.

Her face burned scarlet. "How do your clothes stay together when you Change?"

"I took them off before I Changed, to search for clues. The beast has a better nose. Didn't want to miss anything." He dressed more slowly than strictly necessary, covering all that beautiful skin inch by inch. She felt a strange sense of disappointment.

After dressing and loading his weapons, Hart handed her a vial of viscous black liquid. Faint specks of gold floated in it, like Goldschläger. "Drink this."

"What is it?" It smelled like cinnamon and . . . iron? She took a sip and choked. Fire raced up her tongue and down the back of her throat. Immediate. All-consuming. She cried out.

Hart caught the vial before she dropped it. "Careful. It's all I have."

The fire burned brightest in her injured ankle. She could almost feel the tendons and bones melting and being reforged in the flame.

"Breathe," he ordered. "It helps."

After a few agonizing minutes, the fire died. She stretched experimentally. Her ankle moved as if it had never been broken. She gently searched for cuts and bruises, but they had disappeared.

Hart took a swig of the black vial. He scrunched his nose, but stoically let the fire heal him. The bullet wound knit together before her eyes. The muscle stretched and closed; skin regrew in seconds. She blinked, and there was nothing left to show that he had ever been injured. It was a miracle drug. Scientifically impossible, but what she wouldn't give for a bottle of that in the emergency room. Magic. "What is it?"

"Dragon's blood." He corked the vial and stowed it. "Highly

valued for its healing qualities. In the Middle Ages dragons were almost hunted to extinction for it. One reason they went into hiding from the humans."

"Why didn't you use it yesterday when the Kivati injured you?"

"Wouldn't waste it on a little scratch like that. This shit's hard to come by."

"How did you get—"

He silenced her with his lips. His kiss was hard and hot, stealing the thoughts right out of her head. Her legs melted, and he swept them out from under her. She clung to him. His mouth tasted of cinnamon and passion, blatant sin and carnal delights. His arousal pressed insistently against her belly, and she wanted to climb higher to settle it where it belonged.

He pulled back an inch and smiled, a real, broad grin full of masculine satisfaction. It lit up his face.

Her breath caught. "So why did—"

He kissed her again.

Hart forced himself to set Kayla down and take a step back. Lady be, he wanted her. He'd never wanted anything so badly. Wanted to nuzzle into that soft skin where her neck met her shoulder. Wanted to bend her over the hood of the car, push down her pants, and bury himself inside her. Over and over, until the world melted away.

Even the beast wanted her, but its hunger was sharper and feral. It wanted to dominate, to dig its teeth into her shoulder and mark her as his. It wanted to hold her down and knock her up. It wanted to taste her blood on his tongue.

If that wasn't enough to scare him shitless, nothing was. Sure, she might give in to his advances, but it was only momentary insanity. After all she'd been through, the poor girl was twisted around so bad she didn't know which way was up.

Kayla deserved far better than a dangerous, broken thing like him.

He'd kissed her to shut her up, plain and simple. He didn't need her asking questions about Norgard. She still thought Hart would hand the necklace to Rudrick in exchange for sparing his life. Yeah, right.

She looked at him with those huge golden-chocolate eyes as if he could slay dragons for her.

So naïve. He was more likely to feed her to them.

"So." He cleared his scratchy throat. "K-9881. Sounds like a location."

Her lips parted. Comprehension lit her face. "Of course. The obituary. My mother's plot. Desi wrote that number on the newspaper clipping."

"Get in the car." She grimaced at the order, probably hurt by his abrupt change from kissing, but she climbed dutifully in the passenger seat. Maybe she understood the danger she was in. He could only hope.

"Where is Mount Pleasant Cemetery?" she asked.

"Queen Anne. The Kivati own everything on the hill, from the Space Needle on up. I wonder why she was buried there. Humans usually aren't."

They crossed the Ship Canal and drove up the hill. Gables and elegant front porches replaced the split-levels and ramblers of lower Queen Anne. The century-old Victorian houses gave the hill its name. Gingerbread and ornamental spindles made the houses seem delicate, but Hart knew inside each one was enough firepower to level a city block. The chimneys spouted steam to power the complex inner workings of the electricity-free, yet incredibly advanced, mechanized house systems. Crows perched in every tree, watching.

"I hate crows," Kayla murmured. "Why are there so many here?"

"The Kivati own them. They're smart birds. Good spies. Not as sharp as ravens, but easier to control."

She shivered. He liked seeing Kayla in his car. Liked it far too much. Her scent filled the enclosed space. He rolled down the window and focused on the road.

A funeral was in progress at the Mount Pleasant Cemetery, giving them light cover to slip in among the guests. It was packed with out-of-towners, obvious from their more liberal dress, so he and Kayla didn't stick out. They listened to the Spirit Seeker's eulogy, some poetic shit about the deceased's good deeds and safe passage through the Gate. Hart picked out the man's widow from her straitlaced black gown and her high-pitched wails. She wept next to the pyre, at times drowning the Seeker's words, surrounded by her grown children, also in black.

No one would mourn at Hart's grave. Oscar would show up, but only to empty his pockets. Maybe the Reaper would say a few words over his body. "Hart was a damn fine shot," or something equally complimentary and uplifting.

He wondered if Kayla would shed a tear for him. She seemed the sentimental type, but they'd only known each other a day or two. Funny, he felt like it'd been longer. They got on well, and then there was that inconvenient attraction.

"The plot is this way," Kayla whispered in his ear. She had located a map and was pointing to a section on the far side of the cemetery. "Let's go."

Then again, maybe not. She had a no-nonsense streak a mile wide. She probably thought funerals were a waste of precious time.

The cemetery was divided into four sections, one for each sacred Kivati House. Four large totem poles marked the center of each section. Kayla's mother was buried at the western edge behind a patch of huckleberry bushes. It was a ragged, forgotten corner of an otherwise pristine park.

Kayla searched the small gravestones. "I don't see it."

"There." Hart pointed to a short totem pole topped with the Watchmen—three men in tall hats who warned the village of danger. At its foot, hidden in the grass, was the door to a small crypt. He pulled out his sword and cut away the sod from the marble.

Kayla rubbed her nose with the back of her hand, but she was doing her damnedest to keep it together. He should give her a moment or something. This was her mother's grave, after all. His mother didn't even have a grave. He'd burned the body, like she'd taught him, and then he'd run like hell. Her ashes were probably still fluttering around that sad little apartment.

He kicked a huckleberry bush.

"Now what?" Kayla asked.

"How should I know?" He sniffed around, but all he found was salt air, wet grass, and mud. "You still got that Deadglass?" She pulled it from her pocket, and he showed her how to turn the gears to focus the lens. "What do you see?" He held his breath. Wraiths didn't scare him, but he avoided them if possible. He didn't like the thought of being stuck in limbo, neither alive here nor free in the Land beyond. Cursed worse than he was now.

"Nothing," Kayla said.

"What do you mean, nothing? It's a fucking graveyard." He grabbed the Deadglass back and took a look. She was right. No ghosts. He watched the shimmering Aether, stronger than he'd seen it in years, swirl around the totem pole like a small tornado.

"So, big guy, see anything interesting?" Kayla leaned against the totem pole and crossed her arms over her chest. It stretched the fabric of her T-shirt taut across her breasts, giving him a fine view.

"Yup."

She scowled. "Give me your sword."

Like hell. He raised an eyebrow at her.

She cocked her hips at an angle, planted her right fist, and held out her left hand. "Stretch it out."

Bossy. He kind of liked it.

He held out the sword, point first. She grabbed the blade with her bare hand. The smell of blood was sharp and sweet. Blood. *Her* blood. His head was dizzy with it. He breathed short and fast through his mouth. The beast clawed at the inside of his skin. "Little girls should stay away from weapons for exactly that reason," he bit out.

"I'll keep that in mind next time I see a little girl." She cradled her bloody hand and knelt by the crypt door. He saw where she was going with this idea. Smart woman. He liked that about her. She might have started the game behind the eight ball, but she was catching up fast.

Blood dripped from her fist and splattered on the cool white marble. Around them, the Aether heated. He could feel it singeing the air, filling his nose with ozone like an approaching storm. Sweat broke on his brow with the effort of controlling the Change.

She opened her fist and smacked her bloody hand to the stone, palm down. She waited a beat. Nothing happened. "I thought it would open, or something." A worry line creased her forehead. "Open sesame?" she tried. Still nothing. "It's got to be in the crypt, right?"

Hart raised the Deadglass to his eyes and watched the flow of Aether again. It circled the totem pole. He had a weird, itchy feeling that he was missing something. They probably taught this shit in Kivati high school. He'd know how to read the Aether, how to manipulate it, how to weave weather patterns and put the dead to rest if he'd stayed. If he hadn't been kicked out. His mother had taught him just enough to know what he was looking at, but she didn't like to talk about the Kivati. Not after what they'd done. He shook his head, trying to keep his mind clear. The blood made his canines descend.

"Weren't totem poles sometimes used for burial purposes?" Kayla asked. She had risen from the crypt door and was examining the carvings on the short cedar pole. Her hand still dripped.

The beast yanked at the flow of Aether and almost forced the Change. She had to cover that thing. Hart pulled a handkerchief from his pocket and grabbed her hand. Her skin was soft and smooth beneath his calloused palm. He forced himself to be quick, holding his breath as he bound the cut. "Now stay there." He dropped her hand before he could give in to the urge to lick it.

Following the flow of Aether was easy. It wound around the pole and slipped in through a knot in the wood of one of the Watchmen. He pushed his finger through the knot, and a chunk of wood slipped out. A secret door. He slipped his fingers inside and found a cold piece of carved rock. "Got it." He pulled out a green crescent stone mottled with swirls of white and speckles of black. A leather thong wrapped around both ends allowed it to be worn as a necklace. It smelled sharply of brimstone.

"We did it. Can I see it?" Kayla gave him a grin that lit up her face.

He was suddenly struck dumb, and he handed over the stone.

"How do we know this is it?"

"Smells like the Gate, but I don't know for sure. I know someone who will."

She turned her face to him, hope brimming in those big eyes. Something tightened in his chest. A guy could get used to that look. "So now that we have this thing, you're free, right?" she asked.

The Lady damn him. He'd almost forgotten the point of this little exercise. Kayla didn't know anything. His expression must have scared her, because she took a fortifying breath. "I mean, Rudrick and his Kivati goons will leave you alone," she clarified. "They promised."

"You can't trust—"

"Anyone, yeah, so you've said."

"Well, you don't seem to be listening." He turned his back on her and stormed out of the cemetery.

Behind him, she panted, trying to catch up. "Where are we going?"

"Time to see the Reaper."

"Who is—?"

"Another operative. She knows stuff. Get in the car." Why did she have to do that to him? She made him forget himself. Why couldn't she have been ugly, or slow, or a man? Smart. Capable. Hot as a siren. He never thought he'd go for a smart chick—too dangerous—but Kayla was something else. And he couldn't have her.

Chapter 8

They drove back around Lake Union, through downtown to Pioneer Square. The landscape changed to brick and stone. Nothing that could burn, not since the Great Fire. A predominance of arches and circular towers gave the streetscape a romantic feel. High limestone blocks edged the sidewalks and gas lamps lined the streets. Antique shops sold mechanized appliances from an older era. Humans claimed they were eco-friendly by using hand cranks and washing boards, but they were nothing but practical. Non-electric tools would always work in Seattle's rarified environment.

Near the clock tower of King Street Station, Hart turned onto a seedier side street where the Aether was fecund with magic. It was almost thick enough to touch, and it made him sneeze. Flesh Alley had, at one time, been all brothels, but these days it hosted a wider variety of shops that catered to the supernatural. Wooden dowels protruded from the brick lintels announcing the wares of each store: two apothecaries, a spellbook store, a small armory in a converted stable, an antique shop specializing in dark materials, and an alchemist. The sign for the Drekar brothel advertised "seamstresses." A banner hanging beneath the sign proclaimed HAPPY NISANNU!

SEE OUR SPECIALS! In the upper turret windows, two golden-haired Ishtar's Maidens sat in spindle chairs. They gossiped as they watched the comings and goings in the street below.

Two crows perched on the weathervane above them, squawking to each other. They quieted when Hart's beat-up car turned down the alley and parked in front of Thor's Hammer. Hart got out. Their beady black eyes focused on him. One flapped its wings and rose into the air. Damn spies. He drew a pistol and aimed, but Kayla made a noise on his other side, and he didn't fire. When he glanced at her, her eyebrows were pulled together and she was chewing the inside of her cheek. "Hey, I didn't shoot it."

"Why not?"

He didn't think she would like it, that's why. And what kind of response was that anyway? He didn't care what she thought. Damn woman. He was losing his edge.

"So who is this other operative? Why's he called the Reaper?"

"It's a girl. She hunts aptrgangr and sends the wraiths back where they came from. Someone joked that she harvests souls for hell, just like the Grim Reaper, and the name stuck."

"And she's Kivati, like you?"

"Naw. She's human, but she's got a gift for it. Maybe it's something supernatural, don't ask me. She's a little obsessed." Grace always ran straight into trouble like her ass was on fire, like she had a death wish or something. He knew she didn't, just the same blinding drive for freedom he did. He didn't imagine Norgard would let her ghost go that easily.

"Why?"

"Aptrgangr killed her folks." Though something dark and nasty had killed his mom and you didn't see *him* trying to make revenge his life's work. He shook his head and approached Thor's Hammer, where Grace worked her magic. The special-ized tattoo parlor occupied a narrow storefront. The top of the Dutch door stood open to the cold spring air. The Reaper didn't like to be shut in.

He yanked the tasseled bellpull, and a man's voice yelled, "Go away!"

"Open up, you fucker," Hart called back, "or I'll huff and I'll puff—"

Oscar emerged. "Hart, you bastard!" He rubbed soot off his hand with a handkerchief, then extended it to shake. His sleeves were rolled up, and his forearms marked with grease. People underestimated him, because his face was too pretty and his body lean. He sized up Kayla, with obvious interest.

"Oscar." Hart jerked a thumb over his shoulder. "This is Kayla."

"Aren't you cute?" Oscar gave her a once-over. He blinked at the ragged right leg of her pants, where Cortez had shredded them. "Ripped jeans went out of style decades ago. Or are we trying for neo-grunge?"

"Inside," Hart snapped. The crow on the roof above listened intently.

"A story. Excellent."

"Where's the Reaper?"

"Come in and see for yourself." Oscar held the door open for them. "The boss has her making decorations for Nisannu, as if she didn't have better things to do."

Hart's eyes adjusted quickly to the dark interior. It smelled like an apothecary, overlaid with a thick layer of iron. Shelves of ink and additives lined the walls. Tools of Grace's trade. He didn't know what liquids were housed in the ceramic jars, and he didn't want to. Grace kept close tabs on the Gate with seismographs and steam clocks. Her machines tracked the movements of the earth and measured the currents of Aether. Gears clicked steadily. Needles bounced with seismic readings. Barometers of mercury rose and fell. A metal duct connected each machine to the potbellied stove that powered them. Every so often, the stove belched thyme-scented steam.

Oscar picked up a discarded wrench and waved it menacingly at the stove. "Better part of a morning fixing that blasted thing. I don't know why you need it, Grace. Aren't there enough aptrgangr wandering the streets to make your quota?"

"Stuff it," Grace said without heat. "At least I'll have warning when the whole thing blows. You'll just be a pile of bones under volcanic ash." In her usual dour black, she blended into the shadows. Her blue-tinted hair was tucked behind her ear. Crouching in the center of a circle of salt, she carved runes into red ceramic beads with a silver needle and a small brass hammer. Her work produced a rhythmic *click-click-click*.

"You can't be sure," Oscar said cheerily. "I might fall in a crevasse. Better to be buried alive than survive to be aptrgangr chow."

Grace scowled. "I wouldn't let that happen to you—"

"No, darling, you'd probably slit my throat yourself." Oscar threw himself into a rusty old dentist's chair. It was the only piece of furniture not covered by machines or jars. Restraining straps hung off it like a torture rack. Propping his feet on the foot bars, he picked up his leather flask from the cup holder and lifted it with a theatrical flourish. "To loyalty! May I always have friends like these."

Grace's black-and-white cat sat to her right. He lifted his head at Oscar's pronouncement, snorted disdainfully, and returned to washing one white-tipped paw. The cat ignored Hart.

"Hullo, Reaper," Hart said. He squatted at the edge of the circle, careful not to upset any lines of power she might have drawn. Only the cat could cross threads of magic and not disrupt the balance.

"It's you," Kayla said. She stared from Grace to the cat, questions dancing in her eyes.

"Who?" Grace asked.

"Short girl with a cat. You taught Desi Norse mythology."

Grace paused with her hammer lifted. "Says who?"

"Some kids from the U. Adam and Caroline. Did you know my sister?"

Grace glared at Hart. "What the hell is she doing here?"

"She's cool," Hart said. "She's with me—"

"I can see that." Grace waved her hand to cut him off. She finished chiseling the rune on the bead, threaded it on a leather thong, and tossed it carelessly on a pile of completed Nisannu necklaces behind her. She turned to Kayla. "Your sister's got a big mouth."

Kayla turned white. She gave a tight smile. "Had."

Hart had the sudden urge to grab her hand. The tight pinch of her shoulders made his fingers itch to rub them. Where the hell did that come from? He had to stop this before it got out of hand. The Reaper was prickly on a good day, and they needed her help. "Grace, we've got something for you to check out. Kayla?"

Kayla stepped forward and pulled the necklace out of her pocket. The cat jumped from his lounging position, hissing. The fur along his back bristled.

Grace winced. "That thing reeks."

Kayla lifted it to her nose. "Hart said it smells like the Gate, but I don't smell—"

"You wouldn't. Give it here." Grace stuck out her hand.

"Don't worry," Oscar told Kayla. "I can't smell it either. Grace might be more human than our toothy friend here, but she's not without magic."

Kayla squatted next to the circle and held out the necklace on her upturned palm. The cat retreated behind his mistress's back. Grace gingerly reached out to touch the jade, but snatched her hand back, burned. Fuck. If the Reaper didn't like touching it, what was it doing to Kayla? She didn't have any mental shields, and her emotional state was a mess. Prime picking for any wraith.

Hart wanted to snatch the damned thing from her fingers and hurl it across the room. He reminded himself that this was probably the safest place in the territory. Neither the Reaper nor her cat would let the dead darken their doorway.

Grace braced herself and reached her hand out again. She

muttered under her breath as she picked up the necklace with her thumb and forefinger. "Be quiet." She held the necklace to her ear. Her eyes widened. Her irises flashed silver. Hart had never asked her about her special curse. He didn't understand what she did, let alone how she did it, but he didn't envy her. Bad enough he turned into a half-mad Wolf. With Hart's unnaturally keen nose and tracker instincts, Norgard had his own personal hellhound. He mostly used Hart to find things or people. Hart didn't want to think about the power Norgard might wield through Grace. The Drekar Regent had taken the girl under his wing at the tender age of sixteen, and she wasn't just another operative to him. He taught her special skills. Kept her close. Took liberties he didn't ask from any of his other blood slaves. Thank the Lady.

Hart pushed the thought from his mind, because there was nothing he could do about it. He tried to throw new jobs at Grace when he could, help her earn her freedom a little faster, but he had no power to stop Norgard from taking what he wanted. None of them did.

His eyes fell on the necklace again with the full weight of his future and freedom hanging in the balance. He was so close.

Grace dropped the stone from her ear. She flipped the jade over and studied the carvings that ran in neat columns over its surface. "Where did you get this?"

After a nod from Hart, Kayla told the story. She was much more thorough than he would have been. The sound of her voice was soothing to his beast. Her words flowed over him like a caress. Warm and melodic.

Sitting next to her outside the circle, he was aware of her every movement. The shift of her cotton shirt over her skin. The swish of her ponytail against her nape. The tap of her fingernails against her leg. Rudrick could come in guns blazing, and he wouldn't notice. He'd just sit here quietly cataloging the little noises Kayla made, identifying the complex notes of her unique scent, basking in the melody of her voice.

Fuck him. He was a dead man. He needed to ditch the broad, and quickly.

"The aptrgangr called you 'sister'?" Grace interrupted to ask. "You're sure?"

Kayla nodded. "It must be Desi, right? Since Cortez died, is she gone for good?"

"I wish," Grace said. "Would save me a lot of trouble."

"Will she try to find me again?"

"How the hell should I know? She left you a specific task. Her ghost might be freed when you accomplish it. If she's lucky."

"But she hurt me. How would that accomplish the task she's left me?"

"Probably didn't mean to, but you ran. It takes wraiths a while to gain control of the body they inhabit."

Kayla wiped her sleeve across her eyes, thinking of her dead sister again. As if Hart needed a reminder why emotions were a weakness. He tried to ignore her, but he couldn't stop his hand from reaching out and squeezing her foot. She gave him a trembling smile.

When he turned back to Grace, her eyes were flat. "Get on with it," she said. "How did you fend off the attack?"

"Since I arrived in Seattle," Kayla said, "I've become aware of something else. A light, I guess, inside people."

"You didn't tell me that," Hart said. So much for trust. She was keeping secrets from him. What happened to information sharing and teamwork? And why did he care so much? He expected people to lie to him.

She shrugged. "I didn't understand it. I still don't. Didn't believe in werewolves or wraiths or strange lights."

Oscar offered Kayla his flask, which she refused. "Happens to the best of us, darling. We trust only what we can hear and see and touch."

Kayla's eyes held gratitude to Oscar for his understanding. The beast inside Hart growled, even though he knew Oscar wasn't a threat. Hart couldn't offer understanding. He wasn't human. He'd been born knowing the spirit world existed. Grace tilted her head and studied Kayla. Her gaze was calculating. "Can you see shadows too?"

Kayla nodded shyly.

"You aren't using her," Hart said. Grace ignored him. He wouldn't let her take Kayla into danger. He turned to Kayla and saw her frustration. "You aren't cut out to hunt aptrgangr."

"No, thank you. Violence isn't my style." She rubbed her arms. "I didn't believe you about the aptrgangr, you know."

Grace gave her a pitying look. "Wraiths find people whose spirits are weak, whether from sickness or depression or lack of willpower."

"Or from Dreki feeding," Oscar added. "Some dark spirits follow Drekar around waiting for their leftovers."

Kayla's knuckles whitened as she gripped her arms tighter. "Hart, that's what you meant when you saved me last night. If I had been left drugged in the alley, I would have been a prime target for a wraith?"

He nodded stiffly. She needed to stop looking at him like some goddamned hero. He hadn't explained that his boss tried to suck out her soul. Hadn't mentioned that tonight he would deliver the necklace to that same monster.

"I didn't think she'd get away with it," Grace muttered, when Kayla finished the story.

"Who? Desi?" Kayla asked.

"You knew what she was planning?" Hart asked. Plotting against Norgard? Grace was smarter than that.

"I didn't ask questions. Told her not to tell me anything. Just helped her a bit with her mythology research." Grace walked a fine line. Hart felt his stomach roll in a way that felt suspiciously like anxiety. Worrying for someone else? When had he become an old woman? He was growing soft. "And I can't tell you what happened either. I don't know, and I don't want to."

She set the necklace on the floor next to the cat, who swiped at it with his paws. She picked back up her needle and hammer.

"What was she studying? Norse mythology?" Kayla guessed.

Grace shook her head.

"Babylonian?"

A nod.

"And this necklace is Babylonian, right?"

Another nod. Grace buried her head in her work, carving Nordic runes in dragon's blood onto the Nisannu beads. Her needle carved a thin shaving off the bead, leaving a trace amount of blood to fuel the spell.

"So we can assume it's the right one," Kayla said.

"What's this necklace do?" Oscar asked. "What's so important that the Kivati and Drekar would risk human involvement? You're the tracker, Hart. Is this baby worth a couple billion or—"

"Belongs to Kingu," Hart said.

Oscar whistled.

"It's strongly connected to the spirit world," Grace said. "Focus, and you can feel it almost vibrate with life."

"It's sentient?" Kayla asked.

"Sort of. The Aether is alive with the spirits of our ancestors."

"Aether—you mean the river of light you can see in the Deadglass?"

Oscar whistled again, this time a catcall. "He let you touch his toys?"

All eyes turned to Hart.

He shrugged. "What?"

"Yeah." Grace drew out the word. "Aether is like the soul of the universe. You would be able to see it in the Deadglass, not that *I've* ever looked." She finished the rune she was drawing and blew lightly on the bead. "Anyway. The markings on Kingu's stone tell part of the story of the founding of Babylon."

"It's a piece of the Tablet of Destiny, isn't it?" Hart asked.

"Looks like it," Grace said.

He had begun to suspect as much. Hearing it confirmed raised the hair on the back of his neck. Norgard had a piece of the Tablet of Destiny and had done nothing with it. He must have been setting events in motion for the perfect moment. With centuries at his disposal, he could afford to be patient. The Pacific Northwest was the perfect place to stage a Gate break, after Chief Seattle had laid his curse. Maybe Norgard's war with the Kivati had been deliberately planned to reduce the number of gatekeepers. Maybe . . .

It didn't matter. This job was in Hart's pocket. As soon as he finished one more, he'd be gone. He would lose himself in the deep dark wild of the frozen north. A Wolf—even a packless loner like him—needed territory. A place to call his own.

Kayla shivered. "Hart said Kingu used the Tablet to conquer the world. Doesn't that mean it's evil?"

"The Tablet is a tool," Grace explained, "not good or evil by itself. What's important is the spirit of the person who wields it."

"And it's the second day of Nisannu," Oscar said, raising his flask in a mock toast. "Perfect timing."

Kayla frowned. "What—"

"The Babylonian New Year festival," Grace explained. "Coincides with the spring equinox. The god who defeated Kingu and slew Tiamat was Marduk. He sliced Tiamat down the middle, and her two halves became the heavens and the earth—"

"Her liver became the North Star," Oscar added helpfully. "Her spittle the clouds and rain. Her tail the Milky Way. Her breasts—"

"I get the picture," Kayla said.

Grace continued, "Marduk returned the Tablet of Destiny after he stole it back from Kingu, and was rewarded by the gods. He built his palace between the realms of heaven and earth and named it Babylon, or 'Gate of the Gods.' Every year the King of Babylon performed a ceremony that reinforced the Gate between the worlds."

"So the Gate is at its weakest until the ceremony is performed," Hart guessed.

Grace nodded.

"Desi was researching the ceremony," Kayla said. "I found an article about it in her things."

Everyone looked at Grace. She buried her head over her hammer and bead.

"How is the ceremony performed?" Kayla asked. "Can anyone do it?"

"I don't know the details," Grace said. "I just know what the runes say. Your sister wanted to learn them."

"Can we destroy the necklace so no one can use it?" Kayla asked.

Enough was enough. Hart could feel the gold bands burning his biceps, as if his master heard the traitorous direction of this conversation. "You're going back to Philadelphia," he told Kayla. "You found the necklace—your work is done. I'll take you to the airport."

She blinked at him. "Who died and made you king?"

He raked his fingers through his hair. "Stubborn woman. Wouldn't you rather be alive?"

"I still haven't found out who killed my sister."

She had a point. "What does it matter? She wanted you to find the necklace, not stick around and be buried alongside her."

"My work isn't done. She wanted me to give it to Corbette."

Silence settled heavily across the room, like cobwebs after years of abandonment. No one wanted to be the first to break it. He didn't look at Grace or Oscar. He knew what they were thinking. The necklace belonged to Norgard. There was no way in this world or the next that he would give it to the Raven Lord.

Oscar came to his rescue, laying his charm on thick and fast. "What makes you think Corbette should get it? The Kivati aren't the shining guardians they'd like you to think. Once upon a time, maybe. But now? The Kivati haven't done jack about the cracked Gate. Corbette's too wrapped up in protecting his precious people from dying out. Humans be damned."

Grace only shook her head. She retrieved the necklace from the cat and handed it back to Kayla, pointedly ignoring Hart. He could practically feel the frost in the air. Screw her. She knew his orders. The golden bands tied her hands as much as the rest of them. The blood debt must be repaid.

"Anyway, you can't destroy it," Grace said. She knelt once more in the center of her salt circle. Her shoulders were tense. "Everything is connected. The necklace to the Gate. The Gate to the Aether. The Aether to the volcanic core of the planet. Destroy the key, and it might blow us all sky high."

Corbette stabbed the Norwegian flag that stood for his enemy's camp into the 3-D map of the Pacific Northwest spread out before him. The four Thunderbirds who stood around the table planning strategy looked up with various expressions of surprise. Usually he kept a better leash on himself. "The Ballard Bluff," he said. "So close and yet untouchable if the humans are to remain ignorant."

"Dynamite." Kai leaned back in the leather armchair and stretched his booted heels toward the fire. He had taken off his suit jacket hours ago. His shirtsleeves were rolled up, his cravat undone. His black hair curled around his shoulders like he'd just crawled out of some tawdry bed. Corbette knew he should reprimand the Thunderbird for his lack of decorum, but a migraine was building behind his temples, and for once, he couldn't cough up enough energy to care. "Smoke Norgard out and duke it out once and for all."

Kai had a point. Corbette could order his army to decimate the entire cliff face, and Norgard would have nowhere to hide. Enough of this secretive cloak-and-dagger bullshit.

Jace nodded in agreement. Unlike his brother, Jace hadn't let a grueling strategy session take the starch out of his sails. Proper and sharp as a razor. Corbette wished he had ten more just like him. "The old warriors didn't worry about the repercussions when they annihilated the Unktehila. They answered to no man."

"But the world isn't ready for us," Corbette said.

"Will they ever be?" Theodore, head of the Eastern House, leaned his blond head against the mahogany bookcase in back of him. The same fatigue Corbette felt was mirrored in the tired lines of his eyes. "I'm not suggesting we come out now; the government would lock us up and throw away the key—"

"I'd like to see them try," Will growled. The head of the Southern House moved the flag representing his aerial warriors to the choppy blue waves on the map. He and Theo were the only surviving Thunderbirds to have served under Corbette's father. They knew what Norgard was capable of. They knew the price of open doors and laissez-faire politics. The Kivati had almost been destroyed once. Corbette hadn't worked this hard to let it happen now.

"Maybe if one of the other races came out first," Kai suggested.

Will scoffed. "Fledgling, you don't have a clue what the human government does to 'others.'"

"It's different now, old man," Kai said. "No one's going to hand us pox-infested blankets and stick us on a reservation. Minorities have rights."

"Like hell. No one in his right mind would come out of the supernatural closet. Humans are just as fear mongering as they ever were. They're banning *Harry Potter* in the south, and that shit's not even real."

"Gentlemen." Corbette held his hands up. "Let's return to task: crippling Norgard's industrial capabilities—" An urgent rapping on the study door interrupted him. "Enter."

Lucia's governess stuck her head in, her lined face pinched

with worry. "It's Lady Lucia; she's run away. I found her window open. She can't have been gone more than twenty minutes, but I thought you should know—"

"Thank you, Ms. Harlow." She nodded and ducked back out. Corbette turned to his generals, who were all suddenly alert. "Send out the sentinels. Jace, search the grounds. You three: Spread out. Find her." Corbette stood. He let the anger wash over him and embraced its heat and vitality. Fire burned down his arms as black feathers burst through his skin. They sprouted and lengthened to touch the floor. His nose and mouth jutted out into a wicked sharp beak. Pain skittered over his nerves; he relished it.

A mental push of the Aether opened the French doors onto his balcony, and he shot into the air. Beating his massive wings once, twice, he sailed into the night. His Thunderbirds followed and split off to search. Heavy clouds hung low to the east like sodden cotton balls, pregnant with waiting water. The moon rose fat and bloated over Puget Sound, yellowed and pock-marked like old bone. The humid air slowed him down, and he added that frustration to his burgeoning anger.

What was the girl thinking? He couldn't wrap his mind around it. She didn't take her position seriously. Didn't she realize she was the savior of his people? Didn't she realize how close to extinction they were? Their survival depended on her, yet she chose to dishonor them time and again.

He sent a command into the Aether and ordered the crows throughout the city to rise up and search. He sailed over the gritty metropolis with its towering steel and dingy alleys. He tried to tamp down his anger so that he could focus on finding one small woman in the scurrying streets below.

It wasn't long before the crows located her. He swung west toward the aging seawall. The thick concrete barrier kept out not only the powerful waves, but also the darker spirits of the deep water. He landed near the new tunnel left by the deep bore machine and Changed. Tremors from the cracked Gate were strong here. He could practically see the tattered edges waving in front of him, dark spirits and demons pouring out into the dirty city street. He would have to do something to stabilize it. Would he ever find a permanent solution? These stopgap measures wouldn't hold it much longer.

The princess stood outside the chain-link fence that kept trespassers out of the tunnel. Her long blond hair was unbound, and the harsh sea wind whipped it angrily around her head. Her demure white gown glowed ghostlike in the light of the swollen moon. She clutched a knitted lace stole against the cold and pretended not to notice him, but a slight stiffening of her shoulders gave her away.

Corbette took a moment to calm his anger. He studied her. How often did he take the time to really look at her—the woman behind the title? He knew she resented her lack of privacy. Any self-respecting teenager hated to be told what to do, and Lucia was allowed to do little on her own. He sympathized, though he himself had not known the freedom of childhood. He had been raised to be the Raven Lord. Occasionally, he'd chafed at the heavy yoke of responsibility, but he took solace in the honor of seeing his people safe. Why couldn't she see it the same way?

"I dream," she said in a small voice that broke him out of his musings, "of people screaming. They cry out for help, but I can never reach them." She raised her thin, ungloved hand and placed it lightly on the fence, as if reaching out to those poor souls.

Corbette was startled. Lucia hadn't shown any of the talents the Crane Wife was supposed to possess. But maybe there was still hope for her. Dream visions were the domain of the Harbinger. "Is that why you can't sleep?" he asked.

She nodded. She looked younger without her usual shield of haughtiness. The Aether swirled around her like an old friend. It sparkled over her alabaster skin and danced in the blue depths of her eyes. She seemed ignorant of it.

"You shouldn't have left the Hall." He knew that was the wrong thing to say, but he didn't know how to comfort her in the vision's aftermath.

"What happened here?" she asked. She rubbed her arms against the cold.

"Mayor White is tunneling beneath downtown for a new light rail line. You know that. We've been trying to stop it, but Norgard has thrown up hurdles against all our efforts."

"And before that? In this spot?"

"There was a Drekar brothel that burned down."

"You mean we blew it up." She shivered. "I can feel the sorrow. It's so thick in the air I can almost touch it."

"Yes." And wasn't that one word loaded with uselessness? He wasn't adept at expressing emotion. He knew his subjects whispered that he had no heart, that he was cold inside and out. He felt as much as any of them. He simply lacked the freedom to express anything other than total control.

The crows alerted him to the arrival of his steam car.

"Let us return, my lady," he commanded. He held out his arm to her.

Reluctantly, she took it.

"I will take care of you," he promised. If she would only stay put.

Chapter 9

Deep in the Underground beneath Pioneer Square, Hart felt the first rush of hope. The necklace was in his pocket. Freedom was in his grasp. It was almost too good to be true.

Kayla had given him the necklace for safekeeping. It was too easy. When she learned he'd given it away, she would be pissed. She wouldn't understand. Couldn't. His life was so far removed from anything she knew. A couple dead bodies, a few shape-shifter encounters, a little blood magic—and she thought she'd seen it all. That was the tip of the iceberg. He'd helped her out of a tough spot once or twice, and she thought him some kind of hero. Let her keep her illusions. Let her wonder why he'd done it, but never know the truth.

He passed a trip wire, gave the password to the watch, and made his way into the heart of Norgard's den of thieves. The dimly lit main cave acted as command center for opium running and prostitution. Stacks of stolen and illegal merchandise rose to the ceiling. A mess of cables and monitors in the center displayed video feeds from all over the city, from the mayor and city council offices to the bank vaults and the traffic cams. A passel of ratty kids sat watching the monitors. More were stationed through the city, taking notes with their own eyes in case the power to the monitors failed, as it often did. They were mostly outcasts and runaways. Norgard culled the sharpest from the litter and brought them here under his wing. Trained them to steal, spy, and murder.

A regular Fagan, Norgard was.

The mortality rate was high. Hart couldn't keep track of the current runners, the youngest of the bunch, but he recognized the others.

In the corner, a few operatives watched TV while they cleaned their weapons. Nearby, two men in camouflage pants and white muscle shirts shot pool beneath an antique Tiffany-style lamp. They wore glowing gold bands around their biceps, just as he did, displaying their blood-slave status.

No one looked up to acknowledge him. In the reflection of the monitors, Hart watched the kids' eyes follow him.

Something was up.

He played it cool. Shrugged out of his jacket and tossed it across a stack of boxes. He got loose, rolling his neck, cracking his knuckles, stretching his arms like he was getting good and comfortable. The buzz of machinery and thwack of the pool balls masked the sound of footsteps behind him, but his nose caught the unmistakable stench of sweat and fear.

A second later something sharp whistled through the air toward his head. Hart was ready for it. He caught the assailant by surprise, flipping him over and sending him flying into a stack of boxes against the far wall with a crash.

The kid—a burly teenager with long greasy hair and a face like a Doberman—was back on his feet in seconds, his eyes flashing with shaken confidence. He charged. Hart swept his feet out from under him in one swift kick. The kid popped back up, ready for more. His style was quick and dirty; he was a street fighter, like most of them. He fought like his life depended on it.

It did.

Hart danced around him, light on his toes despite his large

frame, avoiding the desperate kicks and punches the boy threw at him.

"Coward!" The kid breathed fast and hard. "Fight me, you fucker!"

Hart didn't want to hit a kid, but he knew this wouldn't end unless he did. He sidestepped another lunge and tripped the kid again with a heavy boot to the ankle.

The kid grunted as he fell. He rolled. A knife flashed in his hand. His eyes glistened with hate and fear.

"Enough play. Finish it," Norgard said from behind him.

Hart didn't turn around, but he knew the Dreki watched the fight with no emotion. Gone were the charm and winning smile. Unmasked, Norgard was merciless. Lethal. To the world he was a compassionate businessman, leading the community to a better tomorrow. In the shadows he pulled strings, engaged in human trafficking, and sent his trained mercenaries to silence the opposition.

"I can do it, master." The kid wiped his nose, leaving a smear of blood across his cheek.

Hart almost felt sorry for him, but it was no mercy to go easy. The initiation process was brutal, designed to train warriors for a brutal life. Better to show the kid the misery he was in for while there was still a small chance of escape.

Norgard breathed his name, and Hart felt the bands on his biceps tighten. He had no choice but to obey.

He let the emptiness flow through him, erased from his mind everything but the quick elimination of the target. His fists flew. An uppercut rocked into the kid's jaw and an elbow jab to the kidneys knocked the air from his lungs. It was over in less than a second.

The kid lay gasping on the ground, blood trickling down his nose. Angry, fresh bruises decorated his ugly face.

Hart turned from the kid and stood at attention, his feet apart, his hands clasped behind his back. He should have felt nothing, but all he could think was how disappointed Kayla would be.

"You have failed," Norgard said, looking at the boy from his cold, dead eyes. He wore a thick silk robe that swirled around his feet. The sleeves hid his hands. His white-blond hair was pulled back in a ponytail that kissed his shoulder blades.

Around them the circle of operatives and runners tightened.

"No, I . . ." The kid searched each face frantically, looking for a glimmer of mercy. He found none.

"Did you not promise me your fidelity?" Norgard asked softly.

"Y-yes." The kid pulled himself to his knees. His whole body shook.

"And did I not ask that you win this fight for me?"

"Yes." The kid looked younger now that the swagger was kicked out of him. "I-I tried but—"

"Tried? What use is trying?" Norgard raised his eyes and asked the faces around him. A murmur of distain rumbled through the group. "Failure is death in this world, boy." It was cold, hard truth. "What use is a weapon that fails?"

The boy's face paled.

"No use," Norgard said. "No use at all."

"P-please, sir." The kid crawled forward on his knees. "Master, please give me another chance."

"There are no second chances."

"Please! Please . . ." The kid grabbed at the hem of his robe. "I'll do anything . . . anything at all."

Hart stared at the wall straight ahead. He knew what was coming. He had been that boy once. Pleading no longer moved him, if it ever had. He had no pity, no mercy, no goodness left in him. At least, he shouldn't. Last week, maybe, he hadn't. Today? Today his emotions were jumbled together, fighting to rewake the man he'd been half a lifetime ago.

"Please!" the kid begged again.

Rank fear filled the air. Hart's canines lengthened in anticipation, cutting into his lower lip. A drop of blood welled sweet on his tongue, and it reminded him of Kayla. Her blood stark against the cold marble crypt. Her blood racing in her veins as her arousal beckoned. Kayla, her smile brilliant with the success of the hunt. Her nipples pebbled against the cold. Her plump lips parted for invasion.

By the Lady, he should not have let her go. He was a bad guy. A killer. He took what he wanted, when he wanted it. When had he changed?

"I swear to you, I will not fail you again." The kid said the words that would begin his servitude.

"You see this warrior?" Norgard asked, gesturing to Hart. "He made his first kill at fifteen."

Hart remembered. He'd been an angry, hurting kid, more animal than man. Fighting over scraps of food in the street. It had been a cruel winter. Chilblains covered his knuckles. His lips cracked and bleeding from the harsh scrape of wind outside. The moon fever was heavy upon him. In those early days, after his mother's death, he'd steered clear from the cities with their crowded streets. Far safer to let the moon take him in the forest, where he could hunt deer and elk and let the hot fresh blood sate his madness. But that winter the game was scarce. Snow drove him from the safety of the wild. Half dead with hunger, he let his stomach lead him to a truck stop. He'd fallen asleep in the back of a pickup, and woke in the middle of downtown Seattle.

The moon hovered on the cusp of turning, that bitch of a goddess who sunk her claws deep in his soul. Stumbling down an alley, he'd come upon a small group of street kids warming themselves at a garbage can fire. They were cooking hot dogs, and the smell of the meat had made his eyes flash black and his teeth descend.

Sharing was not on their agenda. He still remembered the taunts and threats of the kids defending their territory, then silence once the firelight revealed his inhuman eyes. The knives were out in a wink. The wind moaned through that alley as they surrounded him. The air was thick with desperation.

He might have been able to stop himself, to fight the call of the early moon and drag himself out of that godforsaken alley to die somewhere else. But he couldn't fight both the moon and the boys.

The Change took him. Screams rent the dirty, broken lane. Blood splattered the brick walls of the buildings on either side. He didn't remember the actual fight; he never did in the throes of the madness. The world narrowed to smell, touch, and taste: piss and acrid fear, snap of bone, shred of muscle, the metallic tang of sweet life.

"I found him hunched in an alley next to an overturned garbage can and a dying fire, munching on human bones," Norgard said. "His face and clothes were soaked red and he was half crazed with bloodlust." He laughed. Laugh was too light and happy a word. It wasn't a pretty sound. It was full of malice, tinged with violence. "He growled and snapped at my hand like a rabid pup. But I took him under my wing," Norgard continued. "Gave him shelter and guidance. Training. He has never failed me."

"P-please just one more chance—" the kid pleaded.

"Never. And now he is the most highly accomplished hunter, at the top of his game, my best warrior, a role model for all my children." Norgard smiled at the circle around him, but his eyes never warmed.

The young runners gazed back at their master with idolatry in their eyes, the older operatives with loyalty tinged with wariness.

"Every one of them would give their life for me. Are you not willing to do the same?"

"No, I . . . I mean yes . . ." The kid scrambled to find the correct answer.

Norgard said nothing. The silence stretched.

The kid swallowed. "Yes, I would give my life for you. M-master."

"Good. I am asking for it now."

"B-but I—"

Hart wanted to leave. His stomach churned. He didn't know whether to hope the kid passed the test or hope he didn't. Slavery or death? The choice was not an easy one to make.

"Did you or did you not pledge it to me?"

As realization slowly dawned on the kid, that this was, in fact, the end, a calm acceptance settled over him. Manning up. He stopped groveling and sat up straight. Brushed the tears out of his brown eyes and looked up into Norgard's face. "I did," he said. His voice shook, but whose wouldn't? Most grown men went kicking and screaming to their own death. It took a special kind to accept it as this kid had finally done.

"Good." Norgard nodded once in satisfaction.

The muscled men who had been playing pool when Hart first came in stepped forward. One of them stripped the shirt from the kid's back and the other held out two golden cuffs.

Hart was hyperaware of the bands on his own arms. They seemed to burn his skin.

Norgard shook his long sleeves to uncover his hideous half-Turned hands. His fingers were clawed, his nails black and long. The skin was faintly scaled. He produced a silver knife from the folds of his robe and held it up.

The kid flinched, but didn't back away.

"I accept your offering," Norgard said. The knife flashed, and a ribbon of blood welled on each of the kid's biceps. "I accept your sacrifice." Replacing the knife in his robe, he took the golden cuffs. He clasped one around each arm over the ribbon of blood. "I accept you into my service with the blessing of Tiamat until this mark is repaid."

Few lived long enough to see that day. Those who didn't were forced to serve even after death, trapping them on this side of the Gate. No peace in the grave.

The gold bands were carved with ancient runes. Slowly, the carvings turned red as they sucked the kid's blood out of his body. He cried out in pain and fell onto his hands. Beads of blood sprang from his pores.

The bands began to glow. Norgard raised his hands again and said something in Old Norse. A blinding flash shook the room, and the kid screamed. When Hart could see again, the kid lay on the ground, unconscious. The bands no longer glowed.

"Take him," Norgard ordered the two men who had aided in the ceremony. The taller one threw the boy over his shoulder, and they disappeared into the tunnels at the far end of the cave.

"Back to your work." Norgard clapped his hands, and the troops scattered. He caught and held Hart's eyes, commanding him silently to stay.

Hart knew he wasn't going to like whatever came next. Inside him, the beast tore at its prison. Its thoughts shot like bullets to ricochet through his skull. An alpha was safety. An alpha was loyalty. Norgard was no alpha, with his poisonous protection. Sweat broke on his skin. *Soon*, he crooned to the madness inside him. Soon he'd have enough to pay off Norgard. Soon they would be free.

Norgard wouldn't make it easy on him. Oh, no. Hart fully expected the fucker would use every devious trick in the book to get Hart to repledge himself. Thank the Lady he'd learned a thing or two in the last fifteen years. He wasn't a starving kid anymore, desperate for the smallest scrap of affection. The binding magic required a willing sacrifice, and he had no intention of giving his consent this time.

Death would be better.

"Walk with me, soldier," Norgard said, and Hart fell into step beside him. They strolled down the long row of monitors. Norgard closed his eyes and breathed deeply. "I sense it on you. I would have it now." He held out his palm.

Hart gave him the necklace.

Norgard sighed in pleasure. "Ah, much better. I have another treasure I wish you to reclaim for me."

His final job. Hart held his breath.

"I want my child," Norgard said.

That was impossible.

"You mistake me," Norgard said. "I don't require you to pass beyond the Gate and return my stolen heir. Even if the child had been born, it would take one greater than you to return him to me."

"Then what—"

"The living sister. I wish her to be the mother of my child. Deliver her, and you will earn your freedom."

Hart froze. He wished his hearing were poor, wished Norgard had asked for something else. Anything else. He should be disappointed in himself. After all these years, he thought there was nothing that he wouldn't stoop to do for his freedom. But Kayla . . .

"What am I to do with you?" Norgard asked. His voice was deceptively calm, but a thin wisp of smoke escaped out of one nostril. "You've been loyal, and yet here, so close to your freedom, you fail me."

Hart found himself thinking of ways to get out of it. He could tell her to run tonight. If she got far enough away . . . but no, he'd be sent to hunt her down.

Norgard examined his sharp nails. "We both know you have no choice in the matter. I want her returned to me. Whole and unsullied."

Ah, fuck. Deep inside Hart, the beast growled. Possessive rage boiled up, and he ruthlessly tamped it down. He couldn't afford to say no.

"Perhaps you're not eager to leave my service," Norgard suggested. "You can always repledge."

"No, I got it," Hart promised. He had no choice. His soul—dark and tainted as it was—craved the solitude of the wilderness. Freedom was all that mattered. It had to be.

Norgard glanced at his pocket watch. "It's almost midnight. You have twelve hours."

Hart nodded. Maybe, if he sent Grace to whisk Kayla away, he could give her a twelve-hour head start before the slave magic forced him to comply. He was saved from further questioning by a piercing whistle from a runner monitoring the lair's entrance.

"Reaper at the front gate!" the runner shouted. "She's down! I repeat: The Reaper is down!"

Inside Hart's head, the beast sent up a long, low howl that reverberated across the bones of his skull. If Grace was injured, there was no hope left. Oscar was needed here to patch Grace up. There was no one else Hart trusted to send after Kayla.

The room burst into a flurry of activity.

"Report," Norgard demanded. "How injured? Can she walk?"

"Blood, sir, lots of it," the kid yelled back. "She's crawling down the tunnel."

Norgard's eyes, usually devoid of emotion, sparked in excitement. Hart had to swallow the bile that rose in his throat. Two operatives ran past carrying a stretcher. Runners cleared boxes out of the way, creating a path from the entrance to the private tunnels that branched off on the other side of the cave. Someone pulled out the medic kit, just in case. From the video feed, it looked too late to use it.

Hart turned away. Poor, driven Grace. For such a skinny little girl, she took big risks. She knew the price of failure. Norgard might demand a high price from his male operatives for his healing blood, but from Grace he took it all. Her innocence. Her dignity. Her soul.

Why did Hart let himself care? He didn't. He couldn't. There was nothing he could do to help her.

But damn it, he didn't have to watch.

Chapter 10

Morning dawned red and hazy. There was a bite to the spring air, almost like a crowd full of disapproving ghosts. Hart didn't pull out his Deadglass to see if it was true. Some things were better off not knowing. That was Kayla's problem. She wouldn't let things go. She didn't understand that sometimes self-preservation had to win out over morbid curiosity. And now look at what she'd gotten herself into.

Hart kicked the wheel of his Mercedes. The car didn't want to start this morning, even after a gentle push. It was almost like the car knew with her female intuition what he was about to do—and disapproved. Fuck it, he was a cold-blooded bastard and didn't give a damn about anyone's feelings.

He yanked open the hood and breathed the heavy perfume of oil and diesel. He sprayed starter fluid into the intake manifold, hoping it would be enough to start her under ghostly conditions. One last job. This was it. He could feel the hated golden bands burning through his upper arms. Soon, so soon he could taste it, the blood price would be satisfied. All he had to do was deliver the package to Norgard, and he'd be a new man. A free man.

How could something so ridiculously easy be so hard?

He slammed the hood down and climbed half in the

driver's side door to give the car another try. This time she rolled down the steep hill, and her engine coughed to life. He gave her a loving pat, pulled himself the rest of the way into the car, and slammed the door.

The city rolled awake around him, blurry-eyed against the unusual cloud-free sky. A day like today should be stormy to match his mood, but the Lady was ornery. She liked rainy weddings and sunny funerals.

It should take him no more than an hour to complete this last job. By ten o'clock he would be cruising the open road with not a care in the world. Freedom wouldn't cure the moon madness, but he'd be his own man.

He pulled up in front of Desiree's apartment. His knock on the door was greeted by a vision wrapped in a white fluffy towel. Kayla's gorgeous chocolate hair was piled high on her head, leaving her long neck and shoulders blessedly naked all the way down to the damnably small towel. The rise of her beautiful breasts spilled over the top, taunting, seducing. The towel hit high on her creamy thighs. The muscles in her smooth legs were strong, powerful and graceful like a gazelle. The beast saw those curves and lunged forward, yanking at the Aether to force the Change, one thought ringing in his ears: Mine.

This job might be the end of him.

"Did you forget something?" she asked.

He licked his lips.

She opened the door, just like that. Let the big bad Wolf into her house without a thought to her own safety.

He should throw her over his shoulder and make tail for Norgard before he did something incredibly stupid. But the beast had control of his brain.

He strolled past her into the living room. The door shut firmly behind him. The walls of the little apartment seemed closer than last time. The air thinner. The couch larger. Her scent teased his nostrils. He could hear her blood rapidly pulsing in her veins, like she'd been running. Or was terrified. Or aroused.

All three called to the Wolf inside him. His canines descended.

She came up behind him and boldly wrapped her arms around his waist, obviously having decided to finish what they started the day before.

He swallowed. "Lady be."

Her firm breasts pressed against his back. He wasn't strong enough to resist this.

"Now that you're feeling better . . ." Her soft voice wavered, and he knew she was nervous.

So why couldn't she back off?

Her small hands explored beneath the edge of his shirt. Her touch on his abs was the sweetest torture.

Don't touch me, he wanted to say.

"Lower," slipped out instead.

Her fingers slid beneath the waistband of his jeans, and he let out a groan. With his eyes closed, the world shrank to nothing but her touch, the press of her hand shyly exploring him, her scent, lilac shampoo and soap. He wanted to taste her, to roll his tongue over her folds and spread her fragrance on his lips. Inside him, the beast howled in anticipation.

Before he knew what he was doing, she was in his arms. The towel dropped to the floor, and there was nothing to prevent him from looking his fill, devouring her lush body with his eyes. He needed more.

He wanted to dive into her smooth skin and drown every sense with her essence. They stumbled to the couch, touching and tasting, licking and biting. He blocked out everything but the pleasure of tactile sensation.

"You're wearing too many clothes," she gasped.

He didn't have time to take them off. If he stopped, the real world would come crashing back in. He couldn't let that happen. All they had was this one precious moment, and he didn't want to waste a heartbeat of it.

He pressed his mouth to hers to silence her. Her lips parted beneath his assault. Her tongue slipped against his hesitantly, then grew bolder as she learned what made him moan. Just like the woman—empowered by knowledge, selfless in her mission to help others.

He didn't deserve her kindness.

She protested when he tore his mouth away. He traced his tongue down her throat, paused at her rapid pulse, and explored farther to her deliciously puckered nipple. Lady, but she tasted good. He blew on the wet tip, and she moaned, so responsive to his every touch.

He slid a hand down her smooth stomach and over her furred mound to the center of her pleasure. Her legs parted for him, and her scent shot straight to his head like a bullet. It was overpowering, pleasure and pain. His balls grew tight in response.

She was hot and wet. His beast wanted to dive in teeth first. How had he thought he could resist this?

"Tell me what you like, babe," he whispered.

"You," she said. "I like you."

He growled, more Wolf than man, and moved from her breast down her body, stopping to pay homage to the delicate curve of her stomach and dip into her navel. The closer he came to her core, the closer the Wolf came to the surface. His skin tightened until he thought he would burst out of it. Sweat broke down his spine with the effort to rein in the beast.

The first taste of her on his tongue almost made him explode in his boxers. She wasn't even touching him. His dick throbbed with the need to bury itself where his tongue lodged. Instead, he licked harder, faster. He played with her nerve endings like a fine instrument and drank up every moan, every heated sob.

His vision began to blur with the effort of holding himself back.

Her hands fisted in his hair, driving him on. He loved it. Loved the sounds she made and her uninhibited response to him. Loved the way she trusted him with her body.

His zipper was in his hand before that last thought hit his brain.

She *trusted* him.

Horror coursed through Hart. Shame hit him squarely in the chest, propelling him off the couch and across the room. He pressed his back against the far wall, breathing deeply, trying desperately to keep the beast from bursting out of his skin and claiming what it wanted. The Lady help him. He didn't even realize his arms were burning beneath the gold slave bands until he had a clean breath free from her drugging scent.

Kayla sat up tentatively. She pulled the towel over her, suddenly shy. "What's wrong?"

What wasn't wrong? How could he tell her what he had done or what he intended to do? He couldn't explain the choice he had to make: her freedom for his. He'd made his choice when he'd first pledged himself to Norgard. Now, half a lifetime later, the blood on his hands made him unfit for anything else.

She couldn't understand. She was a healer. He was a killer, and he would always be a killer. Poisoned from birth, unable to control his beast, his very presence pulled death from the woodwork like a leech siphoned blood. The black spot was his calling card. Everyone who got close to him died.

He shouldn't feel guilty. He'd warned her to stay away from him, warned her not to trust him. She hadn't listened, had she? Got roughed up and kept coming back for more. Stupid. Innocent.

"Hart?" Her beautiful chocolate eyes were huge and hurting.

"Get dressed," he said. "We've got an appointment with

an informant. He's got answers for you about your sister. Everything you want to know."

"Shouldn't we talk about this? About us?"

"This was a mistake. It won't happen again." He zipped his jeans and fixed the buttons on his shirt, anything to keep from looking at her. He didn't deserve to breathe the same air.

Still, she trusted him. She rose and went to the bedroom. When she emerged, mercifully clothed in jeans and a concealing red sweater, she had her game face on. That was the woman he knew: strong, tough—nothing could knock her down for long.

He hated to be the one to shatter her illusions.

She walked gingerly, as if her jeans abraded sensitive skin, and he realized he had worked her up and left her high and dry. She had to be hurting something fierce.

He really was a bastard.

"Who is this informant?" she asked as they took the stairs down to the parking lot.

"Someone who knew your sister really well." Intimately, but he didn't want to dwell on that point. He couldn't think of where he was bringing her. He'd perfected the art of living in the moment, and he drew on that skill now. One foot in front of the other, step by step.

Stiffly, she climbed into the passenger seat. The scent of her arousal was suffocating in the small space. He quickly rolled down the windows, but it didn't help. If he'd been free, nothing on earth could have prevented him from pulling her into his arms and ravishing her on the side of the road. Lady be damned. Damned, tarred, quartered, feathered, gutted, and lit on fire.

Hart drove west toward Puget Sound. Crows clung to the trees overhead, watching but not interfering. Sticking his head out the window, he welcomed the harsh salt wind scraping against his face. He gunned the engine. Inside him, the beast whined.

He'd thought he had no conscience left, but each block closer to his freedom dropped another lead weight in his gut. It hurt. Regret, apprehension, guilt, grief—what the hell? He hardly knew the woman, but somehow she'd managed to get under his skin in a short period of time.

And now he was fucked.

If he hadn't intervened with Norgard in the alley behind Butterworth's, he wouldn't be here now delivering her back into the hands of the soul-sucker. His moment of madness had been a colossal waste of time.

It was small consolation, but maybe Kayla would be spoiled and seduced before she entered the ranks of Drekar concubine. Rumor had it the women were head over heels in love when they joined up. Not that Kayla would have a choice. Maybe she'd like it. Norgard would shower her with diamonds and gold. He'd sweep her away to exotic destinations and buy her whatever trinkets her heart desired. Hart didn't think Kayla was the type to want useless glamour, but with her influence she could make Norgard put some of that wealth to good use. He could see her building orphanages and hospitals in third world countries. That would make her happy.

Hart couldn't offer her shit. No house. No money. Stuck with a crazed werewolf every full moon was no kind of life. He wouldn't wish it on his worst enemy.

She shook out her ponytail and refastened it, thinking. She was always doing that, tidying things, ordering things. He could easily imagine her trying to tuck him under her wing to fix him up, like a broken toy.

Right. All the king's horses and all the king's men couldn't put him back together again.

The factory was perched high on a cliff overlooking the Sound. Next door, the turbines of the Ballard Locks whirred and dinged. Two aquifers, one salt and one fresh, brought water from the Ship Canal to power the giant boilers. The brick and stone mansion had been built in the Second Empire style, with a mansard roof and a widow's walk. It extended multiple stories into the hillside below. Five massive chimneys belched steam, filling the air with the tantalizing aroma of chocolate. It masked the telltale iron scent of the Drekar, giving them the advantage if one wanted to sneak up on him. Hart didn't like it. He needed to get in and get out as quickly as possible.

There it lay: freedom.

But he couldn't do it. Jerking the steering wheel, he spun the car in a tight one-eighty. The wheels squealed angrily on the wet road.

Kayla braced herself against the door as she was thrown sideways. "What's going on?"

"Can't do this." He was throwing away his life for a woman he barely knew. Norgard would kill him this time for insubordination. There were no second chances. No forgiveness. No riding off into the sunset, not in real life.

He pushed the pedal to the floor, gunning the engine back down the hill and onto Market Street. He had to get her to the airport, as far away from the chocolate factory as he could before Norgard found them. The Ballard Bridge loomed ahead, sun glinting off the water below with sharp clarity.

Before he could cross it, the drawbridge rose. He didn't have time to brake. Unlike the movies, his car didn't shoot up one side and clear the jump. His engine stalled halfway up as the bridge continued to rise. The car shuddered. Gravity called, pulling them backward like a pendulum, the inevitable end to a broken dream.

Norgard didn't trust anyone. Hart should have known better, should have realized his every move was being monitored this close to completing his final task. He couldn't save Kayla. He couldn't save himself. Now it was too late for both of them.

"What's happening?" Kayla asked. Her eyes were huge, her face pale as she glanced anxiously back toward the ground below. The car slid down the steep slope.

"Brace yourself," Hart warned, seconds before the tail

end crashed into the ground. The bridge ground to a halt. Shaken, he got out.

A black Panther De Ville had pulled across the road behind them, cutting off any escape. Sven Norgard stepped out.

Hart could offer some lame excuse. He could beg for mercy or plead for another chance. He chose to stand his ground. Norgard wouldn't respect anything less.

Kayla got out of the car, and Norgard's eyes snapped to her. Her breathing was rapid, fear raising her pulse. Hart wanted to step in front of her, to shield her from the Dreki's gaze, but what good would that do? Like a starving man, he watched her breasts rise and fall. He closed his eyes and tried to restrain the madness inside him. Inside his skin, the beast lunged and snarled. The musical quality of her voice lured it. Her scent drove it wild. Her touch made it want to claw out of his skin and claim her in the most brutally intimate way.

She'd probably be safer with the Dreki than she would be spending one more minute in his company.

"You've brought me a guest," Norgard said. "Good dog."

"Hart?" Kayla's voice quavered.

The hurt—the implied betrayal—cut deeply. He'd tried, hadn't he? It wasn't good enough.

He opened his eyes, but wouldn't look at her. "Go. Get out of here." Eloquent and polite, he was not, but it was better to break it off harshly than let her entertain these stupid fantasies about him. He was nobody's hero.

Still she hesitated.

"Mademoiselle," Norgard purred, holding out his hand. "I believe you have a few questions about your sister. Let's find more agreeable accommodations, and I'll see what answers I can give you."

She glanced back and forth between them, sensing the tension and knowing something was off. "Hart?" she whispered.

"Go with him," Hart forced himself to say. If she didn't go

willingly, Norgard would force her. He didn't want her hurt. "I've got nothing for you."

In the end she went.

"Loki's Chocolate," Kayla said, reading the sign that hung from a curled iron bar above the factory door. She had gotten into Norgard's car only because she knew there was no other choice. Something was wrong with Hart. She read desolation in his violet eyes. If she could save him by following Norgard, she would. This might be her only opportunity to find out what happened to her sister, but she would keep her eyes wide open. Norgard wouldn't get the better of her this time.

"A Norse shape-shifter god," Norgard said behind her. "Please, inside."

"The trickster god." She might not be as familiar with mythology as Desi, but she knew the basics. Naming his drugged chocolate after the trickster god didn't seem subtle enough for Sven Norgard.

He only smiled. Inside the tower, plates of chocolate were set out on sturdy glass tables. Exotic truffles filled with fig, cardamom, jalapeño, and scotch. Bars made with beans from Ghana, Venezuela, Madagascar, and Ecuador. Chocolate-infused shampoo and hand cream.

"Let me offer you some chocolate, and we'll start on your questions, shall we?" Norgard asked.

"No chocolate for me." *I'm not an easy mark*, she wanted to tell him. Not like last time. At Butterworth's she had been reeling with grief. She was still heartbroken over Desi's death, but she was smarter now. She knew the monsters that stalked the city. The biggest one was right in front of her.

"In that case, let me give you the tour."

Step into my lair, said the spider to the fly. Kayla wondered what her sister had seen in this man. He was beautiful, true, but his beauty was glacial. Ice seemed to flow through his veins, and his eyes held a malevolence that made her want to back away very slowly.

Norgard led her out of the showroom through matching gold foil-covered doors. The long hallway angled sharply down into a windowless tunnel into the earth. The torches lent a medieval air to the place. The walls bore large woven tapestries of the Viking Age: Dragon boats struggled against maelstrom seas; ax-wielding Norsemen attacked terrified monks; hideous serpents guarded a treasure of gold and jewels; above it all flew the giant lizards, raping the battlefield with their hellfire.

Was it myth or truth? Norgard's life story, maybe. She'd seen his dragon form, but the memory was hazy. Her rational brain still found it hard to reconcile the two, man and beast. Yet she'd seen Hart Change. It was much easier to see the man before her as a monster.

After a while the tunnel flattened out, and the ceiling shot higher. They arrived at giant stone doors that were thirty feet high and carved with mythical beasts and Nordic knots. A pattern of slashes that she recognized as runes ran along the outer edge and down the center where the two sides met. Norgard waved his right hand, and bones shot out of either side of the stone doors. They were bleached ivory, curved, and longer than any mammal's bones she'd ever seen. Dragon, probably. Handles, she realized, as Norgard grabbed them firmly and pulled. The stone must weigh a ton, but he opened them easily and pushed her through.

She was blinded momentarily by sunlight; molten gold poured through floor-to-ceiling plate-glass windows on the far wall. When her vision cleared, she stood in a great hall. Awesome and barbaric. Chandeliers of bone and candle hung from the soaring ceilings. Thick fur rugs covered the stone floor. To her left, a crackling fire roared in a hearth large enough to roast a couple oxen. To her right, a raised dais held aloft a throne of gold. The sunlight sparkled from the hundreds of precious gems set into the chair, sending rainbows cascading over the walls. Out the windows lay Puget Sound, turbulent waters stained midnight blue. Across the Sound, the purple-veined mountains sliced upward into the waiting clouds.

But the most impressive things in the room were three huge dragons. Each was three times the height of a man. Each had a narrow snout and vicious rows of teeth. Each had a ridge of sharpened bone from the top of its head to the tip of its very long tail. They lounged near the fire like giant scaly cats, shimmering in the glow and heat.

Around the room, warriors stood at attention, broadswords at their sides. Their faces were fair and untouchable as the angels above. Their muscled bodies might have been chiseled from stone. A handful of pretty young women in red silk robes knelt on either side of the throne. None of them would meet her eyes. She could expect no help from that corner.

"Welcome to the seat of my kingdom," Norgard said behind her.

She had the feeling few humans had ever seen this much of his lair and lived to tell about it.

"Desi would have loved this." Desi's involvement with the Drekar suddenly made sense. But she would have known Kayla wouldn't believe her; no rational person would. Kayla felt some of her anger ease. Desi had kept her secrets to herself simply because the truth was too fantastic, too terrifying to grasp.

"Who wouldn't?" Norgard asked. "A fairy tale brought to life. Every little girl wants to be a princess." He ushered her to the dais, where he settled onto the throne. A silk-clad girl brought a smaller chair for Kayla, and another brought tea. Kayla politely refused the food and drink. She didn't trust anything Norgard had to offer.

"She was beautiful," Norgard said. "Full of light and laughter." There was a slight wistfulness in his voice that caught Kayla off guard. He reached out and stroked his long fingers down her cheek. "You look a bit like her. The cheekbones. The eyes."

Kayla moved her head away, and he dropped his hand with a smile. "Were you the father of her child?"

Norgard's eyes changed. An ancient being peered out, one too old to understand the petty cares of mortals.

Kayla shivered. "Did you ever love her?"

"Love." He smirked. "You sound like my brother. What is love but a tool we use to bend another to our will? I offered Desiree something infinitely more useful: wealth, knowledge, and a place at my side in the new reign. I offered her power, Miss Friday. Power is the ultimate high. It's the closest you'll ever get to the gods."

"You can't be serious."

"Oh, I am. Very. And I'm willing to offer you the same prize. Give me an heir, and I will give you a seat at the table of the gods. A new dawn rises: the rule of the dragons. We will raise an army of the dead to take back the night. There will be no land untouched by our fire. There will be no place free from my rule." He raised his voice so that it filled the room. "Ladies and gentlemen, let me present Kayla, my newest treasure. Please see that she is made welcome. There is much to do before the Nisannu festivities tonight."

"And if I refuse your oh-so-generous offer?" She stood. Norgard was insane.

"You have two options. I recommend choosing the one that will be pleasant for you, but it matters little to me. Either way, I get what I want."

The heavy stone doors were the only exit to the room, unless she wanted to climb out the windows. The drop into Puget Sound would probably kill her. She looked back at the gauntlet through dragons and armed men to get to the doors. Then again, the window might be the less impossible path.

"Looking for someone?" he asked. He pulled something gold out of his pocket and began to spin it around his fingers.

She recognized the gold armbands with their strange rune markings.

"Are those Hart's?"

"These little things?" He spun one into the air and caught it. "Why, yes. Our furry friend finished his last mission, didn't you know? Hart delivered you in exchange for his freedom. He betrayed you."

"Liar," she whispered.

Norgard's mouth broke into a full, satisfied smile, showing a row of perfect, white teeth. He leaned forward and rested his chin on his fist. "You are delightfully naive, just like your sister."

Inside she was screaming, but she didn't let any of her panic show on her face. She embraced the icy calm at the center of her own personal maelstrom. Wordlessly, she held out her hand, palm up. He gave her a gold band. It was heavier than it looked, but not as heavy as the knife of betrayal lodged between her ribs. She didn't want to believe it. She had trusted Hart, and he had betrayed her. If—no, *when*—she got out of here, she would skin that wolf and wear him as a muffler.

Curling her fingers around the gold band, she cocked back her arm and punched Norgard straight in his perfect teeth.

His head snapped back. The impact wiped his smug expression clean off. The soldiers in the room lurched forward, hands on their weapons, but Norgard recovered and waived them away. He pulled a white handkerchief from his breast pocket and wiped the trickle of blood from his lip. "Hold on to that anger, darling. You'll need that fighting spirit to stay alive with my fledgling in your belly."

Chapter 11

The full moon was tonight. Hart could feel it in every pore. The flashing lights of Butterworth's didn't help his already pounding head. He shook like an addict. He should be long gone, but he couldn't bring himself to leave. The familiar smells of opium and tea calmed him. Another of Norgard's dead musicians performed on stage, his spirit invisible to the naked eye. The keys of the piano plunked like a mechanical player, but the music was too passionate and sorrowful to be mistaken for a machine.

"A drink to celebrate," Oscar said. He slid into the booth and poured vodka from a flask into Hart's cup of tea. This evening Oscar wore black pants and a sleeveless shirt that shimmered under the lights. His blond hair was gelled into spikes. "You lucky bastard. You give the rest of us hope."

What a joke. Hart took away hope. The alcohol helped steady his shaking hands, even though he'd already been drinking since noon.

Grace slipped into the booth next to Oscar, a whisper of shadow in her usual black hoodie and black jeans. Unlike Oscar, who graced the dance floor with flamboyant passion, Grace tried never to draw attention to herself. Last night's injuries seemed healed, but her skin was tinged with an unhealthy gray pallor from Norgard's price. She would regenerate the bit of life force he had eaten. It would take time.

"Let's see 'em," Grace ordered. No one wanted freedom more than she did.

Hart didn't blame her. He took off his jacket and pushed up the sleeves of his white T-shirt to show his now bare biceps. After Kayla had climbed into Norgard's Panther De Ville, the Dreki had twisted his malachite ring and the hated gold shackles had slid off Hart's upper arms. He remembered the smirk on Norgard's pretty face. Guilt ate at him.

"Wow," Grace said, little more than a sigh.

"Congrats, man." Oscar clapped him on the back. "I'm green with envy. What are you still doing around here? I thought you planned to jet as soon as the manacles were off."

"I . . . did." How could he tell Oscar that he couldn't let go of his last job? He had done so much bad shit and walked away afterwards, but this one wouldn't leave him alone. Kayla's golden-brown eyes were seared into his memory. Her face lit up in a smile with those bedroom lips parted, welcoming. Her lush body pressed against his. Her scent clinging to his tongue.

And Norgard had her. Norgard was probably now driving himself between Kayla's shapely thighs and ravishing her oh-so-kissable mouth. Norgard was planting his seed inside her womb. Kayla would grow round with Norgard's child and, most likely, die in childbirth.

It was all Hart's fault. He was free from Norgard's command, but he had crafted for himself a prison worse than Norgard's golden bars. Norgard knew it too, which was why he had let Hart go even after his disastrous break for freedom. What a fucking bad time to develop a conscience. No amount of alcohol could cleanse Kayla's image from his brain. Hart wanted to howl. The beast inside wanted to rip and tear Norgard to pieces until his limbs were soaked in blood.

Hart couldn't agree more.

"Watch out. Sentinels, one o'clock," Grace said.

Hart took a swig of his tea as he glanced over. Sure enough, four Kivati sentinels led by Rudrick the Fox were searching the crowds. They weren't technically allowed weapons here in Butterworth's, but that didn't stop them.

"What do you think they're looking for?" asked Oscar.

"What . . . or who?" Hart noticed the sentinels were scanning faces, working the crowd systematically. This wasn't going to be good.

"Grace, get out of here." Oscar nudged her.

But damn, four more sentinels approached from the opposite direction. There was no escaping this particular clusterfuck.

"Wait," Hart told Grace before she could slip away through the crowd. "The back way is blocked. We're going to have to tough it out. Can you do that?" He glanced at her and knew immediately that it had been the wrong thing to say.

Grace bristled. "Fuck you, dog breath."

"She's cool." Oscar pushed Grace's tea toward her and forced her to take a mouthful. "You're cool, right?"

Rudrick spotted Hart and motioned to his men. Lady be damned.

"You know the drill. Don't give 'em a reason to fight," Oscar said to both Hart and Grace.

Did the guy think Hart was going to pick a fight? Hart was good, but he wasn't Superman. Even he couldn't take nine Kivati sentinels. Now that Hart was a free man, there was no threat of retaliation by Norgard to halt violence against him. It was, in fact, one of the reasons he'd intended to get the hell out of Dodge. Everyone in the state who held a grudge against him had been waiting for this moment for payback.

And now he had brought Oscar and Grace into it. Hell's bells.

Rudrick sauntered up and eyed the table. He focused on Grace. "A new bone so soon, mad dog? Even after Friday saved your rotten hide?"

Hart didn't let the fucker see him flinch. He drained his teacup and shrugged.

Rudrick rested both hands on the table and leaned forward. "Doesn't matter. You still owe me the terms of our little bargain. The necklace, if you please."

"Don't have it," Hart said.

Rudrick's nostril's flared. "Where is it?"

"Ask the chick. Your bargain was with her."

Rudrick grabbed the front of Hart's shirt and pulled him halfway across the table.

"Ladies," Oscar broke in. "Ladies. Remember where we are."

Bouncers had noted the disturbance and taken out their cudgels. Thorsson—Norgard's right-hand man—pushed through the crowd toward their table. He'd been looking for an excuse to execute Hart for years, and his eyes glowed in excitement.

Hart needed a distraction for Grace and Oscar to slip away. Maybe he could start a fight between the Drekar and Kivati.

"Talk," Thorsson demanded, his accent thick.

"Hart has something of mine," Rudrick said. "A girl."

Thorsson snorted. "Fighting over a piece of ass? Here." He grabbed Grace's arm and yanked her out of the booth. "Take this one."

"Let go of her," Oscar ordered as he and Hart both rose from the table.

Hart fought hard to keep himself from clutching the table for support. His legs were weak with the moon fever. Fortunately, he was a pro at pretending nothing was wrong.

"Now we're getting somewhere," Rudrick said. He and Thorsson each grabbed one of Grace's arms so that she was strung between the two warriors. She looked so delicate and breakable. If a tug-of-war ensued, she would come out the definite loser.

She turned to Oscar, begging for help.

Had anyone ever looked at Hart that way? As if she trusted him with her life? Yes, actually. Kayla. And he had betrayed her.

"Ladies." Oscar's voice and manner were laid-back and friendly, as if they were discussing nothing more serious than the weather. "Let's all settle down and discuss this like civilized folks. Hart would be happy to tell you anything you want to know, won't you, Hart?"

"Yeah." It was barely more than a growl. He shifted around the table. Rudrick backed up, but didn't let go of Grace. She wasn't a match for two men twice her size.

Hart couldn't watch one more person get hurt because of him. "Let her go, and I'll tell you whatever you want to know."

"We want to speak to Miss Friday," Rudrick said. "Where can we find her?"

"Norgard has her," Hart admitted.

Rudrick growled.

Grace swung, twisted, and kicked. Before Hart knew what was happening, she had escaped and tackled him in the knees. He went down hard, hitting his head against the booth cushion.

"How could you?" Grace swung at his face.

Hart blocked her fist seconds before it smashed his nose. "What are you talking about?" Grace had never had beef with him, nor had she ever touched him willingly. Yet here she was practically straddling him while she lit into him.

"How could you give her to Norgard?" Her voice was hoarse as if she was trying not to cry. Grace never cried. "You . . . you sodding son of a wraith!" She slugged him in the stomach.

"Oof! Calm down, Reaper. It was a job. Just a job. You know that." He managed to grab her slender wrists and restrain her. He didn't want to hurt her. "What would you have me do? Huh?"

The look in her eyes was pure hate. "I thought you were different."

"Yeah? Well, you thought wrong." He didn't need this

crap. Different? Sure he was different. He was a hell-spawned werewolf, for the Lady's sake. He had no scruples, no morals.

He had no choice either. With those slave bracelets he was forced to serve Norgard, and Norgard ordered him to deliver Kayla. If the woman had done what he'd told her—packed up immediately and driven hell-for-leather out of Seattle—she would have been safe.

"I tried," he muttered.

"Trying isn't good enough."

An argument broke out between the Kivati and Drekar, but Hart ignored it. He pulled Grace up and muscled her through the crowd and out the back door. Oscar followed. They broke out into Post Alley. The salt wind was a relief after the stuffy air of the opium parlor.

"What would you have me do, Reaper?" he asked, purposefully using the name Grace hated.

She glared up at him. "Go get her, blockhead."

"I can't—"

"You're free now. You did what Norgard wanted and handed her over, so your *job*," she emphasized the word disparagingly, "is done. Now you can do whatever you want. She freed you, so you can now free her."

Hart paused. Rain misted over his skin, a cool freshness that washed away his anguish. And suddenly his way was clear. Grace was right. For the first time in his life he had the wisdom to recognize the right thing and the freedom to do it.

Kayla already hated him. He couldn't run off into the sunset and abandon her here, because despite what he tried so hard to tell himself, he did have a conscience. He would remember her face in his dreams for the rest of his miserable life.

Grace wheeled around and backed away from him when he released her arm.

"I'm not going to hurt you," he said, hating that she was afraid of him, but knowing that she had a right to be. He was a bastard.

"Please?" Grace—angry, defiant, prickly Grace—had her heart in her eyes. "You're better than this."

"No, I'm not," he said. "I don't know if I'll succeed, but I'll try."

"That's all I ask for."

"I'm not doing it for you," he told her.

"I know." She gave him a short salute, which was all the good-bye he needed.

Hart broke into a run. He needed more weapons if he was going to attempt an assault on the chocolate factory. The Drekar laboratories were housed belowground, which meant entry and exit points would be severely limited.

It was a suicide mission, but his life was worth shit. Kayla, on the other hand, was a ray of light. She had dedicated her life to healing. He'd only known her for a short time, but he knew the world would be a worse place without her in it.

Kayla watched the sun bleed from the sky in harsh streaks of red and purple from her prison beneath the chocolate factory. The elegant room held a brass-knobbed bed, a Victorian, rose-painted vanity, and floor-to-ceiling windows overlooking Puget Sound, but it was still a prison. The floor was covered in another of those barbaric fur rugs. She waited on the vanity's matching stool and watched stars bloom across the heavens. The moon hadn't risen yet, but a dim glow on the western horizon heralded its coming dawn.

Two of Norgard's slave girls attended her, as if she were some gothic romance heroine preparing to be sacrificed. The redhead brushed Kayla's hair, while the blonde rubbed perfumed oil into her skin. Passive as a china doll, she allowed them to dress her in a red silk robe and sat again facing the window. It didn't break—she had already tried. Inside, she steamed. Damn Hart. Damn Norgard. Damn Desi for getting into this mess.

The devil himself entered. She didn't need to turn around; his smell was enough to identify him—iron, with a hint of cinnamon. The women left and shut the door.

"Your sister loved this room." Norgard circled in front of Kayla and leaned against the windowpane, studying her. The light of the candles carved deep shadows on his face. "She named it the Queen's Room. Such a fanciful imagination she had. She used to sit here, just as you are, and point out shapes in the clouds. Never saw anything mundane. No, Desiree only saw dragons and mythic beasts—"

"Don't talk about my sister."

"She wasn't yours to keep. She was mine—"

Kayla stared at him. "Because of you she's dead."

Norgard's smile slid from his face. If she had been fanciful, she might have seen sorrow flicker in his eyes.

"Mine," he said. His hand clenched against his side.

"Did you rape her?"

He recovered his composure and straightened. His lips drew back in a sneer. "Desiree was quite willing. Only the good die young, so they say. And your sister," he said, coming close and brushing his lips along her cheekbone, "was very, very good."

"You bastard." She tried to kick him, but he clamped his hands down on her knees.

"Now, now," Norgard clucked. "Name calling doesn't become you. My parents were married. Though I don't suppose my mother had much choice in the matter. Like father, like son." He laughed. "My father was a berserker. He had quite a few wives. Pale Irish lasses. Dark Russian women. A lusty French wench or two. A dragon's treasure is his most prized possession. We have centuries at our disposal to discern the best of the best."

She spit at him, but missed.

"If you insist." He pulled a handkerchief out of his pocket and stuffed it in her mouth. His hands clasped her biceps hard enough to bruise, and lifted her up. "We might have been civilized, but oh, no. You Americans and your foul mouths. Such a waste when there are so many preferable uses for them."

Her arms ached as he carried her to the bed. Pulling manacles from behind the headboard, he locked her wrists and ankles in cold, hard iron, spread-eagle on the dainty flowered bedspread. He removed the handkerchief from her mouth, stepped back and surveyed his handiwork.

"Mr. Nils," he called out as he twisted the ring on his finger three times. "Please come welcome our guest and alert Dr. Roy that his assistance is required."

No one answered.

"You're crazy," she said.

"Don't be tedious."

A little man in a white lab coat and round glasses walked in. An old-fashioned stethoscope hung from his thick neck. He carried a carpetbag with a half-circle bone handle, out of which he pulled bottles and a syringe. His eyes were glassy.

"Doctor Roy, I believe our patient may need to relax a bit more."

"Don't do this," Kayla pleaded with the doctor, but the man didn't even glance in her direction. "What about the Hippocratic Oath? Do no harm?"

"So naive." Norgard brushed her hair away from her face, and she tried to bite him. "So innocent. What a refreshing change of pace."

The doctor pushed up her sleeve and wrapped a rubber band around her upper arm. He tapped her inner elbow, looking for a vein from which to take her blood.

"Immortality is, as you would say, a bitch." Norgard shrugged elegantly. "You should know about my kind, since you are to bear my child."

"Fuck that—"

"First of all," he said, speaking over her, "I will not tolerate that kind of language. You will reform your behavior. And if you survive the birth, I may let you see the child from time to time. The Drekar will rule the world one day soon, make no mistake. You should consider yourself lucky to be on the winning side." He reached down his shirtfront and pulled out a familiar jade necklace.

Kayla caught her breath.

"Yes, your furry little friend returned to me what is mine."

Hart had said he would keep it safe. Hah. She *was* naive. Stupid. He knew she had promised it to the Kivati. He knew Rudrick would come after her if she didn't deliver. Did he care? Another betrayal. Why should it hurt any more than the first?

The doctor finished taking her blood and measuring her blood pressure. He released the rubber band and secured a cotton ball on the puncture wound with a cloth tie. His movements were efficient, impersonal, robotic—almost like no one was home. He didn't meet her eyes, but from the few glances Kayla got from him, they were dead.

He stuck her in the neck with a syringe.

The world started to spin. All her muscles relaxed as a warm heat infused them. It was the same giddy feeling she'd had before, but twice as strong. Her body sunk into the thick feather mattress. Her thighs fell open. "What . . . what did you give me?"

"Only more of what you took willingly," Norgard said. The pupil of his left eye lengthened, so that only a thin line of blue remained of the oval iris. "A drug based on oxytocin, the chemical responsible for human bonding, trust, and love. I have simply given you a larger dose directly into your vein. The chocolate recipe should have the same effect, but it isn't quite right yet. As you might remember."

She remembered all right. The chocolate at Butterworth's. The alley afterward wasn't quite so clear. "You drugged a minor," she said.

"The Kivati princess knew what she was getting into when she stepped foot inside my parlor. She delighted in the risk, the taste of danger. Naughtily rebelling against her lord and master. If she had stayed, I would've fulfilled all her fantasies."

"She's only a little girl."

Norgard scoffed. "Spare me your cultural prejudices. In my time girls became wives and mothers at puberty. Besides, her own people intend to see her wed in a few short weeks."

He bent over Kayla, bracing himself with one hand on either side of her head, and kissed her. She didn't kiss him back. She tried to keep her lips firmly closed and unyielding. He didn't care. He just barged right in with his tongue and ravished her mouth.

Her body betrayed her. The drugs made her hot and sluggish, made her nipples hard against his chest, made her wet and wanting. That was almost worse than being restrained in the first place. That this psycho could call forth such a response— it was a rape. She hated him.

Norgard covered her lips completely, suctioning them together like he was doing mouth-to-mouth breathing. He began to suck.

There was no other word for it. He sucked in, and she felt herself moving. Not her body, but something that was tangibly *her*—Kayla Friday, her sense of self, her emotions, her life force. Tingles shot up every nerve ending. Electricity jolted through her system. Her body felt both too hot and too cold at the same time. Everything inside her was moving toward his mouth.

He was sucking the soul out of her body.

God help her.

Panic made her seize up, but she knew what she had to do. With sheer force of will, she managed to pull back. A tug-of-war over her soul ensued. She would win. She had to.

She couldn't talk, but she screamed at him inside her head, *Get your fucking hands off me!*

Norgard broke off. He fell back, breathing rapidly.

"Tiamat incarnate," he wheezed, "That was . . . You are . . . quite impressive."

"Fuck you."

"Yes, well," He straightened his jacket and dabbed his mouth with a lace-edged handkerchief. "Perhaps the drug doesn't work quite as well as a good, old-fashioned fucking. Next time we'll try it instead."

"Never—"

"Oh, you will. I'm very impressed with your strength. Very." He had an eager grin on his face like a little boy at Christmas. "You'll do quite nicely for breeding." He tucked the handkerchief into his vest pocket and patted it.

The doctor stepped forward and began poking and prodding her again.

"Get away from me." The room revolved lazily around her. Sometimes she saw two doctors interposed on top of one another: the little man in a lab coat, and a taller, rail thin man in a bowler hat and striped three-piece suit. When she blinked, there was only one again.

"Mr. Nils is currently possessing Dr. Roy, an excellent obstetrician. We lured him away from the most prominent medical research facility." Norgard accepted some sort of report from the doctor and skimmed over it. "It was so kind of you to have the preliminary test results done at Norse Hospital."

Anger rolled through her. Did he own everyone in this city? The "doctor" stuck her with a needle and gave her another shot.

"What are you giving me now?" she asked.

"Something to strengthen your eggs and make you more fertile. I thought you were a nurse. What were you expecting?"

"You're rich. You're handsome. You could have women falling at your feet. Why are you doing this?"

"Ah, here's the crux of the matter. Drekar bodies can live forever, untouched by disease or old age, though we can be killed by an old-fashioned beheading." Norgard drew one thin finger across his neck to demonstrate, and Kayla wished fervently she had a knife to complete the action. "But children are terribly hard to come by. Conception rates are very low, while miscarriage rates and birth fatalities are very high. Desiree stole something very precious. Two things, really. She was eight months pregnant. My child might have survived if she hadn't run off in the middle of a storm and been attacked by wraiths. You will repay me what was lost. I dearly hope strong eggs and a robust constitution run in your family. You'll need it to survive."

Had Desi wanted the baby? Sadness curled in Kayla's belly for what might have been. Desi would have been a wonderful mother, but she had died trying to protect the world from Norgard. She was a hero, though no one would ever know. Kayla had to carry on her memory, and to do that she had to escape.

"In all my years upon this earth," Norgard said, "I have yet to have a single child survive to maturity. My father, damn him, had two." His pleasant smile hid a deeper pain. The muscle in his jaw clenched.

The doctor finished his inspection and stepped back, still and strangely lifeless. His hands hung limply at his sides as if the marionette strings had been cut.

"Mr. Nils," Norgard said. "Please check Miss Friday to see if she's ovulating. I wouldn't put it past that dog to play with the merchandise. Hart did well, didn't he? He's always so prompt at fetching things. Never lets any messy emotions get in the way of his work. Almost Dreki-like in his efficiency."

"Burn in hell," Kayla told him.

Norgard smiled. "That fate was sealed a long time ago. Welcome, dearest Persephone, to Hades."

Kayla watched in horror as a spasm shook the doctor, and something glowing and translucent flowed out of his nose and mouth. Shimmering in the air, it was more an absence of light than light itself. It flowed toward her, and it was all she could do not to open her mouth to scream.

Lights flashed in the back of her eyelids as the thing swooped through her nostrils and possessed her body.

Chapter 12

Hart loaded weapons into his car with shaking hands. The moon climbed toward the horizon, pulling him like a lodestone. He didn't see the Crow in time to raise his sword.

The Crow swooped, extending his claws like blood-seeking blades. Hart raised his arm to protect his head, and the Crow's claws plowed through his leather jacket and hit skin. His arm throbbed. Wet dripped down his sleeve. The Crow wheeled in the air for another dive, but Hart already had his gun out and ready.

"I'll shoot," Hart called up. "Don't try me."

The Crow swooped low and Changed in midair, landing gracefully on his feet. "Found you," Johnny said. "Rudrick wasn't done talking to you."

"I don't have time for this bullshit." Hart swung a black bag back into the trunk and slammed the lid. He kept one eye on Johnny as he shuffled around the side of the car to the driver's side.

"I never pegged you for a coward," Johnny called. He was spoiling for a fight.

Hart wiped his brow with the arm holding his gun. His skin stretched taut across his bones. It felt as if one touch would pop him like a balloon. The beast threw itself against his rib cage with wild desperation. Adrenaline raged through his bloodstream. Rabid thoughts flashed through his head as if someone were sitting on the channel changer of his personal remote: *run, tear, hunt, rip, blood, kill, KILL, KILL.*

Johnny must have recognized the haggard expression and the bloodlust flickering in his eyes. He took a step back. "The full moon. You're close to the Change."

"Ya think?" Hart's voice was little more than a raspy growl. He had to hold on to his humanity just a little longer.

"Hell, man. Don't you think you should get locked up or knocked out or whatever it is you do?"

"I wish." Hart opened the car door and got in.

"Where are you going? Hey, I'm talking to you." Johnny ran around the side of the car and jammed his foot in the door.

"Knock it off, bird boy."

Johnny's face darkened. "Oh, I don't think so. You've got something Rudrick wants—"

"Settle your feathers." Hart took a vile of dragon's blood out of his pocket, uncapped it, and shot it down like cheap tequila. Perhaps it would keep the madness at bay. He had an hour, maybe two if the Lady was merciful. "I'm off to get it now."

"What's that supposed to mean?"

Hart leaned back heavily while the Drekar blood burned down his throat and speared through his body. "Norgard has Kayla."

"Shit. She saved your life, and you fucked her over?"

"Yeah. Not going to fight you. Need"—he took a ragged breath—"all my strength to get her back."

Johnny laughed. "How? That's a suicide mission, even if you weren't half dead. You look like shit warmed over."

Hart shrugged.

"No." Johnny shook his head. "I'm coming with you. Rudrick sent me to protect his asset, and I'm sticking with you till the job is done."

Hart managed to turn his head to give the kid a flat look.

"You have extra ammo in that bag, or what? Where is she?" Johnny asked.

"The chocolate factory."

"Shit."

Hart nodded. There wasn't much else to say.

"So what's your plan? You do have one, don't you?"

Hart grunted. The Drekar blood was working already. The images of blood and death faded from his mind until he could see the gritty street clearly again. His beast stopped tearing at his insides.

Oscar stepped from a nearby alley, followed by Grace. "He needs a diversion," Oscar said.

Hart felt his gut twist. He needed help, but he didn't want anyone else to get killed because of him. "It's not your fight."

"You planning to bust in guns blazing, cowboy?" Oscar asked, irritation pitching his tenor voice higher. "'Cause that'll do the woman a whole lot of good."

"Stand down." Hart took two high-powered rifles out of the backseat and loaded them. "Neither of you are free."

"Whoa. Does that mean *you* are?" Johnny asked Hart. "No one lives long enough to pay off a blood debt."

Hart shoved up the sleeves of his shirt to show his bare biceps. Stark tan lines were all that was left after half a lifetime of service.

"Blessed Lady," Johnny swore. "So what's the plan? We burst in the factory's back door and—"

"No one's going in there but me." Hart cut him off. "You three can set up a diversion to get the troops out. Something big."

"I'll blow up the Locks," Oscar said. "It's a one-man job, and it'll get the guard away from the factory."

"Norgard has ordered me to ink at the bridal ceremony," Grace said quietly.

"No," Hart croaked. He didn't want to think of Kayla married to anyone else.

Where had that thought come from?

"I can pass her a message," Grace said. "She'll be ready for you. Bird boy here can provide you cover."

"Can we trust him?" Oscar asked, staring hard at Johnny.

"My enemy's enemy is my friend," Grace answered, but she didn't look convinced.

Johnny puffed up. He slapped his right hand over his heart. "I swear to the Lady that you can trust me to fight the Drekar. The only good lizard is a dead one."

Hart nodded. Johnny would be there to protect Rudrick's investment, nothing more. Hart didn't mind giving the Drekar another target besides himself. "Oscar, twenty minutes to get into position. Johnny, provide cover," he ordered. "When the soldiers arrive, lead them on a wild-goose chase. Don't get caught."

Oscar grinned. "All right. Let's do this thing. They won't know what hit them."

In Norgard's private chamber, slave girls lit tall, white ta-pered candles. Ten brass sconces stretched over the iron head-board. The king-sized bed was outfitted with red silk sheets and covered with a lion pelt, head intact. A blazing fire in the huge fieldstone fireplace chased the chill from the room.

The wraith infestation had been mercifully, painfully brief. Kayla's limbs still shook with the memory of it. She had fought it and won. She'd thrown it out of her body three times, before Norgard had called off his spirit minion. Thank whatever capricious deities ruled this place; no ghost would get the better of her. She was stronger than she ever knew.

Now the drug hummed through her system, soothing muscles, relaxing inhibitions, easing worries, and clouding her mind. Fear and anger dissipated under a blanket of warm fuzzy feelings. She had to stay alert. She had to try to escape, but it was easier to drift along and watch the candlelight play across the ornately painted walls. Visions of hell from every culture, some gruesome, some peaceful, wove and twisted over the uneven stone surfaces. Ravens presided over bloody battlefields, ushering the dead to a great feast in the clouds above or fiery torment in the caves below. The four horsemen of the apocalypse rode above the headboard, leaving carnage in their wake. Even the ceiling was covered in grotesque images of the afterlife.

The images didn't scare her, though she knew they should. She felt detached, more interested in the colors than the grizzly subject of the painting. The slave girls finished lighting the room and exited, leaving her alone. After a few moments, the door opened again, and a slight figure in a red hooded robe entered.

"Please take off your clothes." The voice was feminine.

Kayla considered the statement. She tilted her head and wrinkled her nose. "I prefer to keep them on."

The figure drew back her hood, revealing blue-black hair and a familiar scowl.

"Grace!"

Grace shook her head, quick but firm. "Your assistance is not voluntary."

Hope shattered. Kayla wanted to recoil from the pain and hide beneath the smothering blanket of the drug. She pinched herself, trying to keep her brain in the here and now. "Not you too," she whispered. "What did I do to deserve this?"

"Must we deserve our pain and suffering? We are all playthings of the gods. If there is a sense of cosmic justice at all, it doesn't balance out until we reach the other side."

Play along, Kayla told herself. *Keep alert for an escape route.* Her fingers fumbled with the robe tie.

Grace pushed her backward until the backs of her knees hit the bed and she sat. Her eyes bore into Kayla's, pleading and commanding at the same time. "Don't say anything," she whispered, moving her mouth as little as possible. "I'm here to help, but you need to follow my orders. Relax your shoulders. Try to look loose and a little drunk." She pulled Kayla's robe apart, baring her to the waist.

Kayla crossed her arms over her naked chest. Part of her was embarrassed to be exposed like this. Part of her wanted to float back to that fuzzy, happy place.

Grace removed a small vial and a long black feather. She uncorked the vial and dipped the feather quill into it. The gold-flecked ink bled up the quill and spread into the feathered shaft until the whole thing glittered in the candlelight. "Sit still," she ordered. She pulled Kayla's arms away from her breasts and knelt on the floor in front of her. Carefully, she raised the quill to mark Kayla's skin.

Kayla tried not to jerk away when the ink burned into her breast. The sting helped keep her focused. "What are you writing?"

"Runic inscriptions calling for Freya's blessing." Grace scratched sticklike marks around each nipple. "She's the Norse incarnation of Ishtar, the goddess of sex and fertility."

"Great." Kayla wiped her sweaty palms on her silk skirts. *Stay alert. Stay strong.* It was a struggle. "Do they work? You don't have to do this. You could write something else—"

"He'd know." Grace marked the skin over Kayla's heart and drew a circle around her naval. The runes spiraled out over her womb.

Kayla's eyes followed the swirls of the feather. She felt herself detaching again, the haze thickening in her brain. She tried to stand up. "You don't have to do this."

Grace took her hands and pulled her back down. "I don't have a choice."

"There's always a choice—"

"No. Not for me. Not for Hart."

Kayla's stomach turned over at his name. Emotions churned beneath the drug's dampening mist. Anger. Hurt. How could the choice not have been Hart's? She wanted to believe Grace.

Grace glanced up from her runes. "We're slave-bonded. I

don't have time to explain." Her voice was low and urgent. "Norgard will come in soon. There are manacles at the head and footboards. Don't make him tie you up."

"Won't he be suspicious if I suddenly agree to his demands?"

"You've been drugged, haven't you?" Grace examined Kayla's pupils and nodded. "You're still dilated. How do you feel?"

"Confused. I want to trust you, but—"

"Swallow this." Grace took a small red pill from the pocket of her robe and slipped it between Kayla's unresisting lips. "Quickly!"

Kayla swallowed. "What was that?"

"Caffeine pill. Might help wake your brain up." Grace stood and began painting runes on Kayla's forehead and cheekbones. "You need to slip out of this room before"—she swallowed— "anything happens. Turn left and go down the corridor. Exit the personal chambers through the wide gilt doors; it will lead you to the main tunnel. Climb up to the second floor and exit. Do you remember the Great Hall?"

Kayla nodded.

"Try to get back there."

"What then?"

"There will be help." Grace stood back and corked the vial again. "I hope."

Kayla pretended she hadn't heard that last bit. The caffeine seemed to be kicking in. Fear roused once more. "Why can't I go now?"

"Because he—"

"Eager to leave already?" Norgard's cultured voice from the open doorway deflated any hope of escape. "The best part is yet to come."

Kayla prevented herself from hurriedly pulling the robe over her naked chest. Norgard couldn't know the drug was wearing off. She stood slowly and let a lazy smile turn up the corners of her mouth.

Norgard looked pleased. "Leave us," he told Grace. He resembled an opium warlord, dressed in a red silk robe intricately embroidered with a Chinese dragon in yellow and green. The open neck left his glistening chest exposed. He had no chest hair, like a snake, and his skin glittered in the candlelight as if made up of a thousand tiny scales.

"What do you think?" Norgard asked when the door closed. He turned in a circle, showing off his toned body beneath the smooth fall of the silk. "Eat some chocolate, darling. It's good for you. Plenty of antioxidants to keep you looking young." He slithered closer, and Kayla braced herself for his touch.

She had to hide her revulsion. If she could pretend it was someone else, someone whose body she was actually attracted to, maybe he wouldn't notice the stiffness in her back and shoulders. Maybe he wouldn't notice her gag when he touched her. *Oh, please don't notice.*

But the only person she could think of was Hart. Hart's broad, muscled shoulders leaning over her. Hart's strong chest against her back, and his warm breath tickling her neck. Hart's arousal pressed against her backside.

Heaven help her. Was it better to remember the man who'd betrayed her than to think of this psycho? And what did that say about her, that even though Hart had abandoned her to this fate, she still wanted him?

She was a fool.

"I can make this pleasurable for you," Norgard whispered in her ear. "Very." He stepped away from her, and she breathed again.

She needed a weapon. There wasn't any furniture small enough to lift, or any spare knives lying around. Not that she knew how to use a knife. A scalpel, maybe. A syringe. If she had an ACE bandage, she could make a mean wrap. Her healing skills were useless. Could she perpetrate violence, even in self-defense?

Yes. Yes, she could. The iron candelabra caught her eye, but it wouldn't detach from the wall without a full set of tools. The candles themselves weren't heavy enough. Would a Dreki burn if he were set on fire? Or did that whole fire-breathing-dragon thing mean that he was flame-resistant? *Think, damn it.* If she got out of here, she was going to sign up for boxing lessons.

A bottle of wine sat in an ice bucket on the bedside table. That might work.

Norgard picked up a box of the vile chocolates sitting next to the wine and held them out. "Eat more chocolate."

Kayla shook her head. "Oh, I couldn't—"

"I said eat."

She took one and popped it in her mouth, because he was watching. "These are so good," she said around a mouthful.

"The future of my people depends on you." Norgard pulled the heavy bottle of sparkling wine from the bucket and poured two glasses. He handed one to her.

She accepted the glass, but didn't drink. Her cheeks hurt from smiling.

"This was Desiree's favorite vintage." Norgard took a sip. He had taken off the monocle. His pupils were elongated, which Kayla was beginning to understand was a sign of his excitement.

She eyed the wine bottle. It was heavy, but portable. If she screwed this up she wouldn't get another chance. Norgard stood between her and it. She had to get behind him.

"Let me help you out of that robe," she said. How would she act if she thought herself a little bit in love? Trusting? Playful? Desi had been the actress, not her. Desi had played the flirt well. She wondered how long Desi had known Norgard was psychotic. How long Desi had pretended to love him, while she plotted behind his back. She must have been terrified.

Kayla could do this. She only had to pretend for a few more minutes. She forced herself to walk up to Norgard—swinging her hips a little—and reached up to touch his chest. The coldness of his skin made her snatch her hand back.

He chuckled and took her hand in his long thin fingers. "Perhaps I should have fed more recently—"

"Oh, no. I'll warm you up." She traced her fingers over his cool skin. Wow. Those were indeed tiny scales. She had pet a boa at the zoo once, and this felt just like it. Smooth and textured. The scales ran flawlessly over his sculpted muscles, and if she weren't looking so close, she wouldn't have known it wasn't human skin.

She shot him what she hoped was a sultry glance from underneath her lashes, and slid around to his back, trailing her hand over his shoulder. He was thinner than Hart, but he was still far bigger than Kayla. There would be no contest in a battle of strength, even if he were human. She'd only have one shot to knock him out. He was almost too tall for her to get a good swing.

The bottle felt cold as she closed her right hand around it. She reached her left arm around his waist, slipped inside his robe, and closed her fingers over his erection.

Norgard groaned.

The bottle slipped in her sweaty grasp, and she had to readjust her hold. Her other hand, well, she didn't care a fig if it felt clammy. If she let go for one second, no power on earth could get her to put her hand back there again.

She pretended to rest her head on Norgard's back, while in reality wiping her brow on his robe. His scent of cinnamon and iron was thick and cloying, making it even harder to take a deep breath.

This was it.

"Darling," Norgard said, twisting his head around to look at her. "Your enthusiasm is more than welcome, but your technique could use a little work."

Of all the . . .

The bottle slipped from her hand and crashed to the ground, spilling wine all over her robe and the rug.

Chapter 13

The bottle hadn't broken, but Kayla had lost her element of surprise. Damn, damn, damn! She used the distraction to let go of Norgard, surreptitiously wiping her left hand on her robe.

"I'm so sorry," she said, trying not to burst into tears. Her one chance at freedom was ruined. "You're right. I was too enthusiastic and knocked over the bottle with my big ass." She laughed. Even to her ears it sounded crazed.

Norgard *tsk-tsked*, but he seemed to buy the dumb-blonde act. He even grabbed her ass, as if measuring it. "I can see how you might be clumsy with that waving around."

She desperately pasted on a flirty smile. "Here, let me get this." She bent to pick up the bottle, knowing she'd missed her chance to knock him out from behind.

Suddenly, the room shook. An alarm went off and a red light on the ceiling she hadn't noticed before began to blink rapidly. A second blast rocked the room. Explosives?

Norgard scowled. He marched over to a panel on the wall, pushed a button and spoke through some sort of hidden microphone. "What are you waiting for? Send out the guards." He listened to someone on the other end. "No, all of them. Now, blast you!"

It took five seconds for her brain to realize this was her big chance. Norgard had forgotten all about her. His back was to her, and he was concentrating on whatever was being said through the intercom.

Kayla grabbed the bottle from the floor and strode toward him. Pure adrenaline fired her body. There was no room for doubt or fear. The floor seemed to stretch for miles before she reached her target. With a shaking hand, she raised the bottle and swung.

The bottle connected with a smash.

Norgard crumpled to the floor with his skull partially caved in. She stared at the blond hair now matted with blood. She had done this. Her hands, pledged into the service of healing, had taken a life. She wanted to throw up, but she forced herself to keep moving. She couldn't think about the sound his head had made when the bottle connected with it. Couldn't think about the warm wetness that had splashed her face when it hit.

The alarm still blared, and the flashing red light cast a bloody glow over the entire room. On the wall, the radio receiver crackled. Someone spoke from it, asking if everything was all right. No, it most definitely wasn't. But she couldn't say that. Soon someone would check to see what had happened to Norgard.

Time to get the hell out.

Hart disengaged the outside monitors—an easy task and one, with electrical outages common, that wouldn't attract attention—and crouched beneath a rhododendron bush against the brick foundation of the chocolate factory. The thickly leaved bush hid him from view above, and he counted on the Drekar being too preoccupied to smell him. Crows watched the other entrances and the street. Johnny kept them quiet. It was one small piece of luck, as long as Johnny wasn't waiting to stab him in the back.

Hart didn't think so. He had no reason to trust a Kivati, but his gut said the kid was telling the truth.

A half mile up the canal, Oscar had lit the C-4 along the Ballard Locks, blowing the concrete barrier between the ocean water and the freshwater canal. Flames from the explosions painted the clouds overhead red and orange. A thick pillar of smoke billowed into the sky. The aquifer that brought water from the Locks to the factory creaked and buckled as a wall of water roared through the narrow waterway.

Hart wondered if it would flood the factory. He hadn't counted on that. He wiped his forehead with a shaky arm. He could do this. Please, Lady, let him last a few more hours. Just until he set things right.

Alarms blared from the factory. A dozen Drekar soldiers, battle ready, burst out of the front doors. Focused on the flames and smoke in the distance, they overlooked Hart's hiding spot. When they hit the wide grassy lawn, their bodies morphed. Thighs quadrupled in size. Spines elongated and turned into thick, muscled tails with razor-sharp spines. Six-foot, leathery batlike wings sprouted out of their shoulder blades. Hard green-black scales sprouted over their skin. The dragons soared into the air and faded against the night sky.

Hart was ready. He slipped onto the porch and through the door before it shut. Johnny flew in behind him and Changed on the tasting room floor.

"You're supposed to lead them on," Hart growled.

"I'm protecting Rudrick's assets," Johnny said. He pulled the Aether to swirl around his naked body, and when it cleared he wore black pants and a long-sleeved black shirt. A sheath of arrows hung at his back and a yew crossbow settled securely in his grip. The arrow shafts were crafted from Thunderbird feathers and—guided through the Aether—always found their mark. The iron heads were dipped in venom of the Giant Spider.

"Just don't get in my way," Hart snapped. He slid through

the dark tasting room and through the production room doors. Inside, the cocoa bean roasters and boilers whirred and clicked, stirring their chocolate all through the night. Not all the chocolate was drugged, just the stuff Norgard gave women. The red alarm lights blinked on and off, bathing the room alternately in red and pitch black. His eyes had trouble adjusting to the assault. He hoped his nose would alert him to danger. The whole place smelled like iron and chocolate, with a faint tinge of brimstone. Typical Drekar scents, but in this enclosed area they were overpowering. He resisted a sneeze.

They wove around machines to the far end of the production floor, where two giant gold doors led to the tunnels below. He'd never been down there.

Grace was waiting. She unlocked the doors from the inside and cracked them enough for Hart and Johnny to slip through. She glared at Johnny, but motioned both to follow her down the slanting tunnel. Her red silk robe billowed out behind her as she hurried along the passage.

It was odd to see her in a color not black. Worse to realize there was nowhere she could hide her blades beneath the thin silk. She must be unarmed. How did she stand it?

The tunnels seemed empty of life. Grace led them down four levels, past thick tapestries depicting Drekar history and many locked doors with dragon bone handles. With each step Hart wrestled his growing fear.

What if he was too late? The image swept over him. He had to stop and brace himself against the wall.

No, Kayla was still alive. He knew it. She was too damn stubborn to quit now.

"Look lively, werewolf," Johnny whispered as he notched an arrow in his bow. "We've got company."

Heavy footsteps echoed from the other side of the hall.

"I can't be seen with you," Grace said quickly. "Norgard's private residence is at the end of this hallway, third door on your right. It'll open into another hallway. Go to the end and turn left. May the gods go with you." She disappeared into the shadows.

Hart knew he had to cover her retreat. He drew his pistol as he slipped into a doorway for cover. Johnny mirrored him on the other side of the hallway.

"Identify yourself," a guard called. There were three of them, each heavily armed.

Time slowed. A bullet whizzed past Hart's head and struck the lintel above him. He aimed and fired, and a piece of wall next to the guard's head exploded.

"Go. I'll cover for you," Johnny said.

Hart eyed him dubiously, but he wasn't about to turn down the offer. Johnny fired a succession of arrows at the guards. Hart used the cover to dash down the hallway. A bullet nicked his leg as he raced around the corner of the hall and reached safety. It wasn't too bad, but it hurt like a bitch. He compartmentalized the pain, letting the adrenaline fire his system.

A faint trace of lilac caught his nose. Kayla had been down this way. He followed her scent down two more corridors, along the path Grace had instructed him to take. As he rounded the corner to Norgard's private chambers, a body slammed into his chest.

"Kayla!" He buried his nose in her hair and breathed in Kayla's unmistakable scent. She was in his arms again. Her full breasts pushed against his chest. The soft curve of her stomach pressed unbearably against his groin.

His woman.

It was a good thing he was retiring from the mercenary business, because his sudden lack of objectivity was a real liability.

The madness boiled up inside him, overwhelming his brain with carnal instinct. If he lowered his head just a bit more, he could sink his teeth into her long, swanlike neck. Her scent called to him, made him wild with lust. It was all he could do to keep himself from bending her over and claiming her right there.

But the moon didn't have control of him yet. He still had a few more hours. It was going to take every shred of his self-control to get her out of here and secure before he lost himself to the madness.

He forced himself to detach from the feel of her in his arms. He swept the dark hallway, gun at the ready. Once he'd confirmed they were alone, he released her.

She scrambled back. Her eyes were wide with fright, her hair a mess, but she looked otherwise unharmed. She wore a long silk robe with embroidered cuffs at the wrists and neck. Viking runes decorated her cheeks, neck, and the back of her hands. The symbol for Freya was written in blood across her forehead.

"Hart?" Kayla whispered. "You bastard!" She rushed him. Her hand connected with his cheek, knocking his head back with a snap.

For a woman who hated violence, she sure had a mean right hook. He wrapped an arm restrictively around her and covered her mouth with his large hand. "Shh," he whispered. "You can light into me all you want, but wait till we get out of here."

Lady, he could drown in her eyes, even full of mistrust and anger as they were now. He wished, not for the first time, that he could be someone else. Almost anyone else. Some normal human without blood on his hands. Someone who could ask this beautiful woman on a date and have a normal, human conversation with her.

But it wasn't going to happen. He didn't deserve to breathe the same air. The best thing he could do for her was get far, far away.

"Do you know how to shoot?" he asked, handing her his second pistol.

She stared at the weapon like he'd handed her a cobra. "No. I'm not going to kill anyone . . . anyone else. I think I killed Norgard."

"Did you cut off his head?"

She shook her head.

"Too bad. He'll recover. Those guards are going to try to kill you, so take it." He folded her fingers over the handle. "It's doubtful you'll hit anything without training, but just shooting in their direction will help. They aren't human."

"Maybe not human, but they're still people."

"They're murderous soul-suckers. Once you're free, you can choose never to touch another weapon in your life, if it makes you happy. But first let's get out of here alive. I left a Crow holding down a position back there. Stay behind me. Stay close. If something happens to me, head up the tunnel to the top. Keep to the walls." He motioned her back the way he'd come, leading the first steps out of this prison.

His biceps might be bare of the gold manacles, but the small fierce woman behind him trapped him more tightly than before. She didn't even know it. He would never be free again. He wasn't sure he wanted to be.

Kayla had slipped beyond fear and into an adrenaline-fueled haze that she'd only read about in medical books. People were actually shooting at her. It was surreal. She'd heard enough gunfire in Philly to recognize the sound, but it had never been directed at her before. The wall in front of her exploded. Hart yanked her down and out of the line of fire. If he hadn't been there, she wouldn't have made it out of the chocolate factory alive.

Of course, if not for Hart she might never have been in the chocolate factory in the first place, but who could say for sure? Norgard could have sent someone else to pick her up. Once he had made up his mind that Desiree's sister could carry his heir, it seemed doubtful that he would let anything interfere with kidnapping her.

Maybe she was being too easy on Hart, but her anger at his

betrayal was nowhere near as strong as her relief at being alive and free. Besides, he'd come back for her.

She could tell it hadn't been an easy decision or execution for him. Lines of strain stood out around his mouth. His face was an unhealthy shade of gray.

They ran into Johnny the Crow a few paces up the tunnel, just past the bodies of three guards.

"I'm going to snoop around," Johnny said. "Can't waste an opportunity like this one to check out Norgard's lair. Don't wait up for me. If you need help, Rudrick will give you safe passage."

"Suit yourself." Leading her back up the tunnel, Hart kept her carefully shielded with his body as they entered the production room floor and crept around giant chocolate machines. From the tunnel, guards shot at them.

"Go! Go!" Hart ordered, giving her a push.

Kayla ran toward the front door and didn't look back. Her ears were deaf from the echoing gun blasts. Hart ran backward as he shot at the guards, forcing them to stay behind the tunnel door and keeping them from shooting Kayla in the back. At this moment she could kiss Hart. He was better than Superman.

"Stay down," he told her when they exited the front door, and Kayla tasted her first fresh burst of freedom. She wanted to skip through the streets and laugh, celebrate loudly and joyously, but Hart was still wary.

"They could have shooters on the roof," he said. But he looked at the crows roosting in the trees around the building as if for confirmation. "Never can be sure," he muttered.

"Be sure what?"

"Whose side they're on." He turned to Kayla, and she saw vulnerability flickering in his eyes. He shuttered it quickly.

The crows covered their retreat by dive-bombing the guards who tried to follow them out of the factory. Hart ran with Kayla down the hill to his car. She leaned against a lamppost while he gave the vehicle a perfunctory sniff.

"What was that for?" she asked.

"Bombs, but it's clean. We're good to go." In the lamplight his skin was pallid. Beads of sweat formed on his brow, and he wiped them away with his sleeve.

"Are you sick?" His skin burned beneath her cool fingers. "I think you have a fever. Is it the flu?"

He shook his head and almost collapsed in the driver's seat.

"Hart? You need me to drive?"

"I'm fine," he snapped. He gunned the engine, universal male code for, *I feel like shit.*

She quickly got in the passenger seat, and he pulled away, tires squealing. "I've seen the macho act before, and it doesn't work with me. I'm a nurse. Let me help."

"Why would you want to help me?" *After what I did to you* hung unspoken in the air.

"Because I . . ." She didn't know. She was still angry. "Because it's my job," she said finally.

A muscle flexed in his jaw. The passing streetlights carved deep shadows in his sculpted face, making him look like a gargoyle. Perhaps that's what he wanted people to think, that he was carved out of stone. But she knew better. The silence pressed on her. Awkwardness thickened the air.

"Why did you do it?" She wanted to hear an explanation, even more than she wanted to hear an apology.

"Sometimes people don't have a choice."

"There's always a choice."

"Sometimes," he said slowly, "the choices were made long ago, and the wheels set in motion."

"Grace said you were slave-bonded."

He was silent for a moment. The muscles in his neck stood out. "Yeah," he finally said. "I was fifteen. Norgard promised he could stop the moon madness. He said he could help so that I wouldn't"—he swallowed—"kill people when I Changed."

"He lied to you?"

"No, he locked me up every full moon. Like clockwork.

Never missed a month. So, I guess he did what he said he was going to. But the rest of the time . . ." He shrugged, as if it didn't matter. "Blood slaves can't choose to obey or not obey. The magic makes us do whatever the master orders."

"Whatever the master orders? To the letter? You couldn't have warned me? You couldn't have—"

"I'm sorry!" He glanced at her and swiftly away. "I tried, but Norgard had me made. Fuck." He wiped his brow on his sleeve. "I didn't want to do it. Do you believe me? I didn't want to."

She was silent for a long moment. It seemed obvious that Norgard had set a trap at the Ballard Bridge knowing that Hart would have second thoughts. Could she fault him for that? They might have escaped if they had left right from Desi's apartment, but who was to say Norgard didn't have the other bridges similarly blocked.

"I came back, didn't I?" There was a vulnerable edge to Hart's voice that leeched some of the heat out of her anger. He might not have had a choice about handing her over. He could have earned his freedom and never looked back, but he had chosen to risk his life to make things right. To rescue her.

Her anger eased. "And now that you're free? What will you do?"

He wiped his brow again. His hands shook as he gripped the steering wheel. "I'm going to get you somewhere safe, then I'm out of here. I'll go where there are no people."

He was leaving her? She felt inexplicably hurt. An hour ago she hadn't wanted anything to do with him. "So, this moon madness, is there a cure for it?"

"You can't fix this."

"Is that a challenge?"

The edge of his mouth quivered.

"I can't help trying to heal everyone. It's more than my job; it's who I am. My great-grandfather was a healer too. It's in the blood. He was some sort of shaman. He'd go from village to village, healing the sick and selling magic powders for protection from evil spirits. He died in the Great Seattle Fire of 1889."

"The Land War," Hart said.

"Excuse me?"

"We call it the Land War, not the Great Seattle Fire."

"Why?"

"This area had been dragon-free for centuries after the Kivati exterminated the *Unktehila*. Then Norgard showed up with his followers and planted his stake. Shit hit the fan. The Kivati thought they'd wipe this batch of scaly soul-suckers off the face of the earth too, but they were disorganized. Not like today. In the battle, which the Kivati lost, downtown burned to the ground. Norgard founded his city of Ballard the next year. They've been at each other's throats ever since."

She smiled. "Now that's what I call revisionist history."

"You really think a little glue pot could have caused so much damage?"

"I guess not." She watched the thick column of smoke pour over the Locks as they drove past. "We humans are a bunch of idiots, huh? We'll believe anything."

"No," he said, looking at her with frightening intensity. "It takes a lot of work to pull the wool over your eyes." He wasn't talking about the glue pot anymore.

"I don't know about that." She turned to look out the window. "Seems like you pulled a fast one on me easily enough. Do all your targets walk willingly into Norgard's lair for you?"

"You're too trusting. That's your problem."

"Yeah? And how is that not-trusting thing working out for you, wolf-man?" she snapped. "Do you enjoy cutting yourself off from everyone who might care about you? Is your life richer for being a one-man army?" She watched his shoulders stiffen as her words hit home, but she didn't care. "I'd rather trust and risk my friendship and affection than live in a lonely prison of my own making. Sure, you're safe there. But it isn't living. It isn't—"

Swearing, he yanked the steering wheel hard to the left. She braced herself as her body was thrown against the door. That was one way of ending a conversation.

"Bridge is out," he explained. "Not surprising when the Locks blow."

She let him change the subject. He didn't want to talk about his trust issues? Fine. As long as he stopped berating her for trusting in people. Her way might be riskier, but his was certainly lonelier. "Will Norgard be searching for me?"

"Yes." He glanced at her forehead and frowned. "You'll want to wash that rune off before we get there." He reached one hand into the backseat and pulled out a gym bag. "Here are some clothes. They'll be big, but—"

"Thank you. I don't want to wear this robe a minute longer." Kayla quickly looked down to cover her blush. There was a large button-down shirt and a pair of sweatpants in the bag. Changing in the front seat of a moving car without flashing other drivers or, especially, Hart, was going to be a challenge. She turned toward the window and slid the silk off her shoulders. She could feel Hart's gaze on her bare back.

Adrenaline was a high she couldn't shake off. She wanted to put this pent-up energy somewhere. He wanted to leave, did he? She shouldn't care. Part of her wanted to turn around and let him see the swirls of runes Grace had painted over her breasts and womb. Let him try to pretend he didn't want her. Let him try to hide the hungry look he got when he thought she wasn't looking.

"I'm sorry it's too big." Hart's voice broke her reverie, sounding uncertain. "It was all I had."

"Oh, no, it's fine." She realized she had been staring out the window half covered, the flannel shirt laying limply in her fingers. She slipped it on over her head and pulled her arms out of the robe from beneath the privacy of the cotton shirt.

The pants were harder. Hart kept his eyes straight ahead, but she had the feeling he saw everything anyway. He wanted to pretend there was nothing between them? Fine. Let him ride off into the sunset like a lone horseman.

She wasn't fool enough to think she could keep him. She didn't want to. Bad boys didn't come home for dinner every night at six o'clock sharp. Bad boys sometimes didn't come home at all.

She'd had enough of people she loved not coming back.

Chapter 14

Hart knew he should be planning a safe destination, but with Kayla sitting three inches from him, her scent filling the enclosed space, it was all he could do to keep his car on the road. If he reached out one hand he could touch her. She looked ridiculous in his big clothes. The shirt fit her like a tent, and she'd had to roll down the waistband of the pants and fold up the legs half a dozen times so that her little feet stuck out.

He'd tried not to peek when she changed. Really. But with the moon madness riding him hard, he had little willpower left. The Change would take him soon. There was nothing he could do to stop it. Kayla had to be far away from him when it did.

His brain replayed the curve of her smooth shoulder and the beautiful expanse of her bare back. He wanted her. Wanted to peel those yards of concealing cotton off her and touch her naked skin. He'd never wanted anything more in his life than he wanted her right now.

Sucked to be him. He'd blown whatever chance he might have had with her when he betrayed her. He was a degenerate. Blood on his hands. His soul black and twisted. Who was he kidding? He never had a chance.

She was good, pure, and innocent, with her passion for

healing and her overly forgiving nature. She should hate him, but when he looked in her eyes he didn't see any of that familiar emotion. He saw only hope.

Hope.

Lady be, had he ever known that emotion? Kayla made him want to. And, damn, he couldn't afford this distraction. He planned to drive her to the airport and buy her the first ticket out of town.

South of the city line, abandoned warehouses ruled the murky streets. The dam on the Green River had been a casualty in one of the violent outbreaks a few years ago. It burst, swamping the streets and creating a ghost town that would rival the Ninth Ward in New Orleans. Airport Way was clear and high. It was a little-used fairway that Norgard wouldn't expect him to take.

He'd just crossed the border when he felt a surge of Aether, and his front tires exploded. He swore and yanked the steering wheel hard to the right. He tried to keep the car from careening into the sludge on the side of the road. The car spun like a demon top. It didn't have air bags. Panicked, he shot his right arm out to clamp Kayla firmly in her seat. He felt her soft body jerk as the car hit a light post and came to a stop. Luckily, there weren't any other cars on the road that might have hit them. Unluckily, there weren't any cars on the road to stop and assist either.

"Are you all right?" The beast beat against his chest, a rapid drum roll full of claws and snarls. It wanted to burst through his skin and attack the unseen assailant. With great effort, he pulled it back.

Kayla looked dazed, but otherwise unhurt. Her smooth skin had lost color. She nodded. She looked down to where his hand still protected her torso, and a rosy blush stained her cheeks. He realized his hand clung to her breast.

He jerked his hand away. "I . . . sorry."

"What happened?"

"Trouble." He pulled his rifle out of the backseat and slid his broadsword out of its scabbard. Nothing moved on the deserted street, but he felt the Aether roll. "You have that gun I gave you? Keep it close. Stay here."

He opened the door and got out. The front tires were shredded. He had a spare, but only one. Someone had wanted him stalled here. He raised his rifle and rested the barrel on the top of his open car door. The car headlights lit the dark for a hundred feet in the distance.

The wait was a short one. A titanium-plated jeep drew into the glare of his lights and headed toward him. He resisted the urge to shoot out its tires. The jeep stopped. Rudrick and Benard the Bear got out.

"Seems you got in a bit of trouble," Rudrick drawled. "Way out here. Lucky thing we were driving past."

Lucky wasn't the word that came to mind. "What do you want?" Hart asked, not lowering his gun.

Rudrick drew his hand to his breast as if hurt. "Me? You're driving through my territory, Wolf. Good thing for you we found you here. No one comes driving this road late at night. You and the little lady might have been stranded." He gestured to the east, where the translucent glow of moonrise gathered like molten silver against the horizon. "Or were you hoping to be caught out under the goddess' pull? Nowhere to run. Nowhere to hide. Perhaps you wanted to chase the girl through these ruined streets and sate your bloodlust—"

"No." The denial was more growl than word. Hart had to drop the gun and cling to the door to steady himself against the seductive image. "I claim the ancient right of sanctuary."

"See? Asking for help isn't that hard, is it? I grant you sanctuary and safe passage. Benard, help move this pile of bolts to the side of the road." Rudrick strolled to the Mercedes and got a good look at Hart's face. "You don't look so hot, werewolf. Looks like we showed up just in time."

Hart managed to nod.

Kayla climbed out of the car. "You okay, Hart?"

"We gotta go with them." He jerked his head toward Rudrick. "He's promised safe passage."

"I've a warehouse not far from here, with a holding cell," Rudrick explained.

Benard walked too close to Kayla, and Hart growled. The beast tensed to spring at this new threat.

Rudrick raised an eyebrow. "I swear on the Lady that neither I nor my men will hurt her."

It was a powerful oath, binding for the Kivati. That Rudrick would offer it unasked was unprecedented. Hart wasn't in the habit of trusting people, but he had little choice. The Lady was vengeful on those who broke their oath to Her.

He gathered his weapons and supplies, and escorted Kayla to the Kivati jeep. Rudrick and Benard pushed Hart's car to the side of the road. They piled in the jeep, Kayla and Hart in back.

Rudrick's warehouse was half a mile north. The old factory stood out from the street by its unusually well-cared-for brick exterior. The two-story building had leaded glass windows with wide arches and ten or more stately chimneys. A high chain-link fence with quality ghost charms surrounded the property.

Hart heard Kayla's sharp intake of breath as she caught sight of the men with guns waiting for them. "They won't shoot us." He hoped. "But don't make any sudden movements."

Two gunmen came out to meet the jeep. They patted down Hart and removed his weapons. He kept a close eye on Kayla on the other side of the jeep, where a Thunderbird was getting a little too personal searching her.

"If you want to keep those hands," Hart growled, "get them off her."

"Better do as he says, Torin," Rudrick called from the porch. "I wouldn't want to be in the werewolf's line of sight when the moon rises in ten minutes."

The Thunderbird quickly removed his hands.

Hart was at her side in an instant. Her lips pressed firmly together, and she didn't look happy, but she didn't look harmed either. He guided her forward with a hand on her lower back, daring anyone to touch her again. When Rudrick's thin face broke into a calculating grin, Hart realized his mistake. He should have treated Kayla like she was nothing special, not parade her around like a valued prize. Problem was, she was his. So close to the moon—ten minutes, had Rudrick said?— his instincts ruled more than his brain, and his instincts definitely wanted to claim Kayla in front of all these potential rivals. Hell, he was practically baring his teeth at anyone who so much as looked at her sideways. Might as well pee in a circle around her while he was at it, really show them who was boss.

But he'd put her in even more danger by showing his cards early. Now that Rudrick knew Kayla was important to Hart, she could be used as collateral.

Over his dead body.

But he wouldn't put it past Rudrick to do exactly that.

"Welcome to my humble home," Rudrick said. "Miss Friday, I had worried you left us without saying good-bye." He took Kayla's hand and kissed the tips of her fingers, an unholy gleam in his eyes. "Stop growling, Hart. You're embarrassing yourself."

Hart realized the sound was coming from his throat, and he forced himself to stop. "Where is the safe cell?" he asked Rudrick. "There isn't much time."

"Yes, of course." Rudrick led the way into the warehouse. A narrow entrance opened up into an armory. Weapons and ammunition were stacked in crisp rows on either side of a long aisle. On the far side, furnaces blazed. Blacksmiths with thick leather aprons and round brass goggles pounded down steel into short swords and wickedly curved scimitar blades. Another pair molded silver bullets.

The production was big enough to be the Kivati main armory—the location of which was supposed to be a closely kept secret. Hart wondered what it would cost him to leave with this information.

"Nothing to see here," Rudrick snapped. "The cell is in the basement."

Hart turned to Kayla. She had plastered a tense smile on her face, and her back was straight as the steel blades being tempered a few feet away. Her wide eyes skimmed over the weapons like they held no fear. The warehouse might have manufactured pottery for all the attention she gave it. But when she looked at him her cool mask cracked. In those gorgeous golden-brown eyes he saw an unshakable trust, even after all he'd done. Crooks like him didn't get second chances. Her forgiveness shook him to the core. Damn, wasn't that a lot of responsibility for a guy to live up to?

"Kayla," he said. "I'm going to go downstairs. Don't come down no matter what you hear, not until sunup tomorrow morning."

"What's going to happen to you?"

"The full moon Changes me into a mindless killer."

"I've seen you as Wolf before. You didn't hurt me."

"That was different. Promise you won't come downstairs, and promise you won't try to leave until after we've talked in the morning."

"I promise," she whispered. Her pink lips lured him, calling him to seal their bargain with a kiss, but he knew it was only the madness talking. She didn't want him to kiss her.

He released her and let Rudrick lead him downstairs. The basement was made of thick slabs of concrete reinforced with iron bars and silver shavings. It doubled as a bunker and a holding tank for prisoners. Even as a full-strength werewolf, Hart wouldn't be able to break out, no matter how strong the moon pulled him. A wall of metal bars split the room in two. There wasn't any furniture. He probably would have broken anything left in there with him.

Hart stepped through the gate, and Rudrick slammed it shut behind him. The gears whirred as the locks thudded into place.

Rudrick turned to go back up the stairs, but paused. "You know, I don't believe you fulfilled the terms of our bargain. It's the night of the full moon, but your little human didn't deliver the necklace as promised."

"No," Hart said, suddenly alert. "But you promised you wouldn't hurt her."

Two gunmen dragged Kayla down the stairs, holding her tightly by both arms.

"What's going on?" she cried.

Hart couldn't look away. She was so beautiful, head held high, eyes flashing with defiance. He knew what Rudrick intended, and there wasn't a damn thing he could do to stop it. "You promised safe passage."

"And I've brought you here safely to this sanctuary. Miss Friday," Rudrick asked, "didn't you agree to personally deliver the necklace to me?"

"Don't answer him," Hart said.

She looked between them warily.

"No matter," Rudrick said. He stroked Kayla's cheek. "I have eight witnesses who said she did. I can't allow her failure to go unpunished. You, mad dog, of all people, should know the value of a reputation."

"Let her go," Hart begged. He'd never begged before in his life, but he did now. "Please. Please let her go. I'll pay you."

"What do you think she'll taste like? Hmm?" Rudrick replaced his fingers with his tongue, licking her. She flinched. He smacked his lips. "Spicy."

"What do you want, Rudrick?" Hart gripped the steel bars of the jail cell door, straining to open it, calling on the moon's power for strength. The silver filaments burned his skin. The bars didn't budge. "Come on. Talk to me. Let's make a deal."

"Oh, I don't think so." Rudrick raked Kayla with his eyes. "I'm doing you a favor here. You think I can't tell how much you want to take a bite out of this tasty little morsel? You practically reek with unfulfilled lust. It's disgusting."

Hart's hands shook like a junky needing a fix. Sweat dripped from his brow. His eyes, he knew, had already turned completely black.

Kayla watched him warily, the edge of fear in her scent. What did she think when she saw him? Did she see a monster?

She should, because what Rudrick said was true; he wanted to taste Kayla so bad it hurt. He'd give anything for the chance to feel those sweet lips beneath his, to hold her in his arms again with her soft curves pressed intimately against him.

But he was the last person she'd want to touch. He'd lied to her, kidnapped her, and now deposited her in even worse danger.

"Stand back, or I'll shoot her in the leg," Rudrick told him. "She won't die of it, and the stink of blood will ensure your immediate Change. I'd like to watch, but it would be over too quickly."

Hart stepped back. The gears whirred again. The locks clicked open. He could make a dash for it, but Rudrick's goons had guns trained on Kayla. Rudrick opened the cell door and threw her in.

Chapter 15

Hart caught her.

"I'm sorry," he told Kayla, his heart in his eyes. "I'm so very sorry."

He let go of her quickly, because up close her scent drove him mad. He was holding on to his human form by the bare tips of his claws. He turned to a grinning Rudrick. "You swore to the Lady—"

"And I will keep that promise." Rudrick let his hand caress the bars lazily. "Neither I, nor my men, will harm her. I leave that to you."

"Let's make a deal. What do you want?"

"I want you to let go," Rudrick said. "Let go of that vaunted self-control and embrace your inner beast. The Raven Lord is wrong about you. You can never be Kivati. You have irrevocably split your animal totem and your human spirit, making both of you weak. Stop fighting it, and be who you are. You are a killer. You will never be anything else. And why should you be? You excel at killing."

"I'll . . . I'll serve you," Hart spoke the words he had promised himself never to utter again. To put himself back into servitude when he had just earned his freedom—it was too painful to contemplate. But he did, for Kayla's sake. She didn't deserve this.

"Now that groveling thing is really tiring." Rudrick yawned. "We'll chat again in the morning."

"No!" Hart banged on the iron bars, frantically trying to get out. "No."

"Good night, sweet Kayla," Rudrick called over his shoulder as he ushered his men up the stairs in front of him. He left a single gaslight burning. "Say hi to your dear sister for me on the other side."

"No! Rudrick, you bastard! Don't do this! The Kivati are sworn to protect!" Hart yelled until his voice was hoarse, and his fingers were raw from tearing at the bars.

But Rudrick wasn't coming back.

The night was silent. The wind whistled in the empty street outside. The world held its breath as the full moon hung a hairbreadth below the horizon. Electricity charged the air. The Aether hummed. He could feel it flickering and snapping over his skin, calling forth the Change that would make him a beast. Ravenous. Bloodthirsty.

Kayla made a noise behind him. It was just a small noise, barely audible. The *swoosh* of cotton against her bare skin and the shuffle of her bare feet on the concrete floor. Her scent invaded his nostrils, pulling him like an alcoholic to the bottle. He turned, slowly, shakily, and pressed his back against the cold steel bars.

"Are you all right?"

Was he all right? Here she was roughed up, knocked around, locked up, and she was worried about *him*. He swallowed. "I'm a werewolf," he said simply. "I . . . have no control over it."

"I see." Her eyes were huge.

"I would give anything . . ." His voice broke. "You were better off with Norgard. I . . . it's all my fault—"

"I forgive you."

"Rudrick swore—you *what*?"

"I forgive you," she repeated.

"You don't understand," he said, searching her face, willing her to listen. "The beast, he doesn't understand logic or reason. He only follows instinct. And he wants you. Terribly."

"Do you?"

"What?" He couldn't believe what he was hearing. She was so calm, so matter-of-fact, when she should have been bawling her eyes out. She should have been screaming. Anything but that calm acceptance. She forgave him?

He would never forgive himself.

"Do you, Hart, want me?"

He couldn't speak. His heart was lodged firmly in his throat.

"Because I want you." She lifted her elegant hands and pushed the top button of the flannel shirt through the button-hole. "And I'm not going to be another black stain on your conscience." Another button followed the first, exposing a thin sliver of smooth latte skin.

He reached out to stop her fingers. The temptation was too much. "I won't be able to stop myself—"

"So don't." She shook off his hand and unfastened another button. "If I'm about to die, as you say I am, I'm not going to waste my last few minutes withholding from myself something I desperately want."

She wanted him? Desperately?

"I'm not going to waste a moment longer arguing with myself about all the reasons you and I won't work." A slight tremor ran through her hands.

He could see a thin strip of beautifully exposed skin from her chin to her small oval belly button. His eyes fixated on it.

"Or thinking about all the reasons I should stay far away from a bad boy who will only break my heart." She opened the flannel. Her full breasts hung free. Paler than the skin of her hands, the milky orbs glowed in the dim gaslight.

He thought his heart had stopped beating. After a moment

he could feel it again, louder, faster. Lust roared in his veins to rival the moon's pull.

"I'm going to take this moment as the gift it is," she said.

She kissed him, or he kissed her. It didn't matter which. All that mattered was that they were kissing, and it was electric. Her lips were as soft as they looked, but, oh, so much sweeter than he had remembered. She made a little moan in the back of her throat. He thought he would die from wanting her.

He traced his fingers up and down her back beneath the flannel, trying to touch every inch of her. Her skin was smoother than silk, but wonderfully warm. Her small hands slipped beneath his shirt and burned like a brand. He loved that she touched him, willingly, and she seemed to get as much satisfaction touching him as he did touching her.

But then she grabbed his wrists and moved his hands from her back to place them firmly on her breasts.

He almost fainted. Big, strong mercenary that he was, he almost fainted at the soft fullness of this small, fierce woman. He wasn't so lucky. He couldn't be so lucky. Nothing in his life had been good enough to make him worthy to touch her.

He tasted her nipples, pulling first one taut peak and then the other into his mouth. She fisted her hands in his hair and pushed her chest forward against his tongue. He moaned his satisfaction. She was delicious. Up close, her skin smelled strongly of lilac and something intimately her, uniquely Kayla. His woman.

He wanted to go slow. He couldn't. Her scent called to the beast, but soothed it too. It rubbed itself again his skin, trying to get closer to her.

She fumbled with his shirt, and he helped her peel it off and over his head. He spread it out on the ground with her flannel to make a softer place to lie.

He kissed her again, holding himself back so as not to scare her. The slow simmer was building. She opened her lips and explored his mouth with her tongue. He wanted to howl with pleasure. He let himself go, plunging his tongue into her and tasting her fully. She was fire and flame, and he was melting.

He needed to taste every inch of her, from her delicate earlobes to the tender backs of her knees to her ticklish toes and everything in between.

"Hart?" she whispered.

"Yeah?"

She laughed softly. "I like that about you. You never make promises you don't intend to keep. You don't sugarcoat or use throwaway terms of endearment you don't mean. You're raw and real. What you see is what you get."

He was startled. "I'm not good at this," he admitted. "I never . . ." He gestured to the attraction sparking between them, to the shirt spread on the floor. "I haven't much experience. I didn't want to lose control. It's dangerous."

She covered his mouth with her fingers. "You are good at this." She kissed him, as if to prove her point. When she pulled back, her face was blissful. "Mmmm, yes. You are very good at this."

"Well, honey pie, I can try." He stripped his jeans off and placed them on their little makeshift bed. "And practice makes perfect."

The smile she gave him lit up the room. "I guess it does, baby cakes."

He chuckled.

"I'm not, you know," she said shyly, "very good at this either. I haven't had much . . ."

"Practice?"

"Yeah." She laughed. "Practice."

"Darlin', that is a situation I can surely help with."

"I hope so." She pulled him down with her and kissed him soundly. Tentatively, her fingers slid beneath the waistband of his boxers.

It was agony, wanting her . . . needing her to touch him.

They were close, her lush breasts pressed against his chest, but not close enough. He made short work of her sweatpants, and then they were skin to skin, only the thin cotton of her panties and his boxers lay between him and ecstasy.

She made him happy, he realized. Relaxed. At ease with a world that had always frustrated him. Anger was his constant companion, but she made that emotion slide right off his shoulders like shedding a heavy coat. Her laughter was a soothing balm to his soul, her touch a magic charm that whistled away his demons. He would do anything for this woman. He would rather die than hurt her.

He broke away. "Kayla, we don't have to do this. If I run at the wall hard enough maybe I could knock myself out and—"

"Shut up and kiss me."

He did. He kissed her eyelids and down her nose, scattered kisses across her wide cheekbones and licked the edges of her sensitive ears. Her small hands on his ass drove him on.

The beast demanded he flip her over and mount her from behind. It wanted to overpower her and claim her irrevocably. Hart fought to remain human. He was so afraid of hurting her. He was hard as a rock against her thigh, and the painful pleasure of it almost took him over the edge.

Every touch of her skin was a gift. Every caress was a taste of salvation. Every breathy moan damned him further to hell.

His skin tingled, restless with the moon's pull. He kissed her, hungrily, skating that thin edge of madness. The Aether roiled around him. The moon magic floated on its shimmering waves, sparking against him like static electricity. The blood hunger caused his canines to rip through his gums.

He tried to pull back from her. "I can't control it—"

"Then don't." She bit his lip.

The sensitive nerve endings on his inner lip exploded, and he almost did too. The world danced around him in flashing colors. He could feel the moon calling to him, and his Wolf reveled in it. Fur rippled beneath his skin.

"Stay with me, Hart." Kayla's hand grasped him firmly, an anchor in the chaos.

Waves of power emanated from her warm fingers, subtle but unmistakable. Her eyes caught his, and he lost himself in those pools of chocolate. The flecks of gold in her irises seemed to grow. They flickered in time to the power coming from her hand.

His body returned to fully human, but the Wolf still called for blood. Somehow, miraculously, she kept the Change at bay.

"How?" The word barely made it out of his hoarse throat.

"I don't know," she whispered. "It's never been so strong before, but still . . ." She licked her lips. "I feel like I'm on the edge of a great precipice. There is so much power building, waiting to scoop me up and carry me into the darkness. I'm terrified."

He wrapped his arms around her, trying to tell her without words that he would catch her no matter what.

She reached between them and wrapped her small fingers around his shaft. His body shook with the effort to hold the Wolf back. He could feel it tearing at his insides, clawing and scraping at his skin to be let out. Every stroke of her fingers distracted it from trying to escape. It wanted to devour her, but it wanted her to keep touching it more.

He couldn't hold on any longer.

"What do you need?" she asked.

"You."

She let her legs fall open and welcomed his hard length into the cradle of her thighs. He growled and surged forward.

Her small gasp and the immediate scent of blood made his eyes roll back in his head.

"Oh, Lady be." He breathed heavily, trying to hold still. His muscles trembled. "Sorry."

"Move," she told him. She thrust her hips forward, and he felt another inch give way into her liquid heat.

It was only a tiny bit of blood, but her sacrificed innocence held enough magic to sate the bloodlust that accompanied the moon madness. He'd never felt anything like it. Thick and sweet, just a little spicy, like the woman herself. He thrust in and out, coating himself with her magic. He couldn't get enough.

Her moans drove him on. The Wolf fell into step within him, acquiescing to his control and his guidance. Both man and beast were one for the first time in memory. Both striving for one goal: to drown in this woman until they found salvation.

Pleasure rose up, a wave of shimmering light. Hart refused to come without her. He reached between them and rubbed her clit. She came calling his name, and he followed quickly after.

They collapsed. His lungs burned as if he had run a marathon. He could still feel the pull of the moon, but it was controllable, no longer the mad fury that raked him across the coals.

He had barely shut his eyes before the beast reared its head again. His lunar mistress could not be denied.

Kayla rocked her hips forward. The new strength of her healing gift filled her with a soft glow and gave her the confidence to take control. The first push of Hart inside her had broken more than a piece of skin; a mental block had fallen away too, revealing a sparkling new world when she closed her eyes. The shadows and light she had sensed before were now crystal clear. Electric currents of gold and silver flowed beneath her and Hart's translucent skin.

Hart might think his soul was doomed, but she could see it glowed softly. She wanted to reach out and stroke it.

A second, smaller light whipped around Hart's larger one. If she glanced at it out of the corners of her eye, she could almost see paws, sharp teeth, and a tail. It was playful, but hungry. How would it feel to have two souls living inside her? The Wolf's energy rose, pulled by the moon and by Kayla's own pulsing light. It sensed her, as she sensed it. It bashed itself against the cage of Hart's skin. She sent soothing waves over the Wolf with her gift, but it needed more.

She rocked her hips against his.

"Are you sure?" he asked, concerned for her well-being first. "You must be sore."

In response, she sucked his nipple into her mouth.

"Oh, Lady," he moaned. He kissed her brow and rolled them over so that she was on top.

She sat up, straddling his hips.

A shaft of moonlight slipped through a small window high in the wall and landed on her naked torso. In her new Other sight it looked like dust made of diamonds. It was a living force that settled on her skin and Hart's upturned face, making them both glitter with magic light.

She reached down and took Hart's hands, guiding them to cover her breasts. His face softened in wonder. She was aware of his heart beating, and she settled into a rhythm to match. The soreness between her thighs quickly melted to delicious pleasure. The sparkling lights inside their bodies brightened with each thrust. The lights rose through their skin and twisted together, wrapping around each other like thick ropes.

Their bodies grew slick. Hart moved his hands from her breasts down her hips and around to grip her ass. He kneaded her, urging her onward, and she increased the pace.

Inside Hart, the Wolf lunged toward the moonlight. Kayla wanted to reach inside his skin and soothe it. Their souls intertwined, but they did not meld. She needed more of him. More skin. More touch. More taste.

"Give me your mouth," she said. She pressed her breasts against his chest, raising her ass into the firm grip of his capable fingers. His mouth tasted like fire beneath hers. His tongue filled her with the same motion of his cock.

Again and again he filled her, until she didn't know where he ended and she began.

The moonlight heightened their pleasure, adding its fire to their souls until they were consumed with it.

He brought her screaming over the edge, waves of pleasure cascading one after the other. He filled her with passion until she was blind with light. Every muscle exhausted. Every nerve raw.

Kayla collapsed on Hart's chest. His heart pounded in her ear. He ran a hand gently over her hair and back. It was a wonder he could still move. She couldn't.

In that other vision, the lights inside him stopped dancing and settled peacefully. The Wolf was finally sated, no longer victim to the demanding moon.

She closed her eyes and faded into oblivion.

Chapter 16

Hart slept little. The moon madness drove him into Kayla's sweet heat every hour. He needed her like he needed air to breathe. For the first time since puberty, he was able to stay human and sane on the night of the full moon. Kayla was to thank for that. She was his salvation. No matter the hour, she always welcomed him into her body. He couldn't imagine how sore she must be, especially given her inexperience, and yet she roused with a smile and open arms.

If anything her soul seemed to grow stronger with every round. Her moans and her passion peaked. Confidence and power filled her supple limbs as he positioned her, behind and beneath and every which way till Sunday.

Through the night her eyes changed. The golden flecks multiplied until they overcame the brown, a hundred different shades of gold: tawny and amber, saffron and flax.

He didn't know what it meant. He didn't deserve her, not her body, or her trust, or her brightly burning soul, but now that he had her he wasn't going to give her up. Not now. Not ever.

By the morning light he could barely walk. Kayla was refreshed, bright-eyed, and ready to go another round. He sat propped against the wall so that he had a clear view of the basement stairs beyond the iron bars, Kayla cuddled in his lap.

Kira Brady

"I'm sorry if I hurt you last night," he told her.

"Don't worry about it," she said. "After the first little bit, hurt was not what I was feeling."

His fingers followed the flush as it spread up her delicate neck and across her cheekbones. He couldn't stop touching her. *Mine*, the Wolf rumbled, but it was sated and calm knowing the man would protect what was theirs. Kayla had settled something inside him, like adjusting two puzzle pieces to make them fit. It was disconcerting, this peace that allowed both souls to coexist. No longer adversaries. Neither fighting for dominance. How long would it last? "How did you do it?"

"I don't know. I can see lights inside you, two souls intertwined, and I can add my light. It sounds silly, but—"

"It's a gift from our Lady. Thank you." He stroked the shell of her ear, making her shiver. He wanted to nip it, to taste the delicate edge beneath his tongue, but he knew where that would lead, and he simply didn't have enough energy to do it again.

"I couldn't do it before. It's almost like something inside me got unlocked with the trauma of losing Desi."

"You sure you're all human?"

"What else would I be?" She rubbed her cheek against his chest as if trying to rub his scent into her. An unconscious gesture, more animal than human. Her smile turned a little rueful. "I don't even know your last name."

"Don't have one. All kids take Kivati as their last name, until puberty when they Change for the first time. Once they get their totem animal, they take their pack's last name. Like the Raven Lord. Corbette means Raven. Each time he does something impressive he gets a new name. Emory Corbette, the Raven Lord, Defender of Innocents, Upholder of Rigid Outdated Rules, General Dickhead—"

She laughed. "What would you have been called?"

"Hart Lupus of the Kivati."

"Were your parents wolves? Is it genetic?"

"No. Animal totems are a gift from the Lady. Mom was

Eagle. She knew a little about being Wolf, because my father was one. I never met the guy. He disappeared after I was born. Followed the last Wolf packs to Canada."

"But your mom raised you."

"Yeah, she defied Corbette's order and ran away with me."

"You miss her." It wasn't a question. She ran her fingertips lightly down his arms, soothing, comforting, leaving a trail of energy that tingled his skin.

He nodded and tightened his hold on the woman in his arms.

She twisted up to look him in the eye. "When I first met Rudrick, he said you killed your own mother."

He was silent for a moment. "If she had stayed in the protection of the Kivati, she would still be alive. But she didn't. She ran. Worked odd jobs and moved from town to town, always keeping her real identity a secret. There are worse things out there preying on shape-shifters than the Drekar. Demons, water spirits, minor devils, harpies, and wraiths. Even demigods. I got home from school one day to find the apartment bathed in blood. It squished in the carpet and dripped off the countertops. She was still alive when I found her." He cleared a catch in his throat. "She gave me the blessing of the Lady and died. I never trusted the Lady again, not after She let that happen."

"It wasn't your fault," Kayla said.

Hart let the edge of a smile creep out. Of course she would say that. "You forgive yourself for not saving your sister yet?"

Kayla smiled weakly and looked away. "Logically, I know it wasn't my fault, but I can't help wishing I could have done something. Like gone with her to Seattle to watch out for her. Or made her stay in Philly."

"My mom believed the Lady chooses our path. We can rage against fate all we like, but everything happens as She wills it."

"Do you believe that?"

He shrugged. He'd never been good with words. If only

there was a dragon to slay or a magic potion to steal—that he could do. But he could hardly battle the thin ghosts of memory, and it made him feel helpless. "Doesn't seem fair that She would will my mom to die like that. Or your sister. Who knows why the gods play the games they do?"

She seemed to take comfort from him. Burrowing into his arms, her body relaxed. She trusted him.

Lady be damned. How could he possibly live up to that much responsibility? He didn't have any experience.

They were both silent for a moment, listening to the splash of rain in the puddles outside. Every once in a while a car drove past.

"What do you think Rudrick will do when he finds us still here, whole and hearty?" Kayla asked.

"I don't know. The Kivati code of honor would demand that he let us go. We passed the test and survived. But . . ."

"Would throwing me to the wolves—literally—follow the code of honor to begin with?"

"Maybe. Corbette would be the one to rule on that. Depends on his mood. He can be a mean son of a bitch. On one hand, you bargained the necklace for our lives and failed. On the other, you're human. Kivati are pledged to protect humans."

She swallowed and shifted her weight in his lap. "It's kind of late to talk about now, but we didn't use protection."

"I'm clean. I'm immune to human diseases."

"What about animal diseases?"

"I'm not an animal," he growled.

"Sorry, I'm a nurse. I have to ask." She sat back, her shoulders tense. He waited for the other shoe to drop. "I'm not on the pill," she said softly, "and Norgard gave me drugs to make me ovulate."

Surprise shook him first, followed briefly by fear. He didn't have anything to offer a pup, but the thought of her holding a little girl with his violet-tinged eyes and Kayla's wide cheekbones and sparkling smile made his chest tighten with an unfamiliar heat. Hope? Pride? Longing?

His sensitive hearing picked up the sound of a car pulling to a stop outside. Doors slammed. He was torn between standing ready and appearing nonchalant. There wasn't anything he could do if they came barreling in with guns. Iron bars locked him in. It would be like shooting ducks in a pond. The best he could do was block Kayla with his body until nothing was left, or they ran out of bullets. Whichever came first.

Fucking worthless options, if you asked him.

"Company," he said, reaching over to grab their shirts and pants from across the cell. "Cover up."

Tension sprang through Kayla's body like a bow pulled taut. Her fear roused the Wolf. "What do you hear?" she whispered. "Has Rudrick returned? What will he do when he sees—"

"It'll be okay." He took over buttoning her shirt from her shaking hands. "We've made it this far, right? After last night I'm ready to take on the world." *For you.*

They dressed quickly and quietly. Booted footsteps passed overhead and spread out across the floor. He caught the timbre of raised voices. Kayla huddled close to his back, as if he could protect her from whatever was coming. The thick basement door opened. Three sets of black combat boots descended the stairs and came into view.

"We'll get through this," he told her in a low voice.

The Aether buzzed. He felt it roll over him, like a caress. Two Thunderbirds came into view, and Hart wasn't sure whether to be relieved or worried. Lords Kai and Jace Raiden were two of the most powerful Kivati, second only to Corbette. The brothers wore long gray dusters—Kai's trimmed in black, Jace's in red—over fitted charcoal three-piece suits, and high black boots. Both had black hair, long faces, and chiseled expressions. Kai was less formal. His long untamed curls brushed the top of a gun belt strapped desperado-style across his chest. Jace was a poster boy for an elegant Kivati Lord—

not a hair out of place, not a crease in his stiff and proper suit. His hand clenched in a fist, and the air molecules tightened and bumped together. A thunderbolt shimmered at the tips of his fingers, waiting only for a reason to strike.

Still, it was the third man to come down those stairs that caused the hair at the back of Hart's neck to rise: Emory Corbette, the Raven Lord. His striking violet eyes stripped away secrets and demanded obeisance. His handsome features were sharp like his animal counterpart, razor nose, fine-boned jaw, stern mouth drawn down at the corners. His ebony hair hung straight to brush his high collar. His dress was severe, yet elegant. A jet-black jacquard tie matched his jet-black, three-piece suit. A tall, black top hat perched on his head. Silver accented the black: cuff links at his wrists; a watch chain hanging from his vest pocket; shiny, silver-toed boots on his slim feet; a cane with a heavy silver handle shaped like a raven in flight. The studs in his ears were nuggets of polished coal.

His hands were graceful and unmarked by scars, but Hart could easily imagine them wrapped around his throat. Here was a man with absolute authority and absolute self-confidence in his right to rule.

Hart fought the instinct to tuck his tail between his legs and bow his head. *Alpha*, the Wolf whined. But Corbette had kicked him out; he didn't owe Corbette fealty. Braver men had fallen before the Lord's terrible power.

Corbette cocked his head to the side. He took in Hart's imprisoned state and Kayla's obvious survival. Locked in with a werewolf on the full moon. She should be a pile of bloody bones. It didn't take a Kivati's heightened senses to smell what had happened recently. Sex hung heavy in the air.

Hart tried to shut out the scent of arousal and carnality. He'd prefer not to fight with a raging hard-on.

The two Thunderbirds moved into a protective position on either side of Corbette, not that Hart could do anything with those iron bars caging him in. If he could have escaped, he would have long before now.

"How unexpected," Corbette said. His voice was dry as autumn leaves. "I had dreamed that one day you would return to us, but on your own steam."

Hart started to say over his dead body, but bit his tongue. Another first.

The edge of Corbette's mouth twitched.

Jace gripped one of the bars and tested it for strength. "She can't have been in there all night. She's only a human."

"Perhaps." Corbette stepped closer to get a better look at the ground. His eyes paused at the small streak of blood on the concrete. "Perhaps not."

All three glanced behind Hart to where Kayla stood partially concealed.

"What is your name, child?" Corbette asked.

"Kayla Friday."

Hart was proud that her voice didn't waver.

Corbette tilted his head again. "Friday," he murmured. "A descendant of Cheveyo Kivati?"

"My grandfather's name was Cheveyo, but he wasn't Kivati."

"Wasn't he?" Corbette asked lightly.

Hart growled.

Corbette raised an eyebrow and cocked his head in the other direction.

"You're wrong. I'm not Kivati," Kayla said. "I can't change into anything. I'm human."

"Are you?"

"Of course!"

"And yet you survived a night imprisoned with a werewolf," Corbette pointed out. "There is more than one power of Change. Hart, chatterbox that he is, might have shared a few details of Kivati lore with you, but even he is not privy to all our secrets. He missed out on so much of his education."

"I didn't miss nothin'." Hart didn't need this crap.

"Didn't you?" Corbette asked. He didn't elaborate.

"Whose fault is that?" Kayla stepped in front of Hart, much to his surprise. She bristled like a wolf defending her cubs. "You threw him out. How was he supposed to learn all this lore?"

"I have admitted my mistake," Corbette said, "and do not have to explain myself to you."

Kayla took a breath to argue, but Hart stopped her with a hand on her shoulder. "Doesn't matter," he said. "You going to let us go, or what?"

"Why," Corbette asked, "are you here?" His voice crooned, and the Aether answered him like a loyal hound. It swirled around Hart, extracting the words, one by one, from his tight lips. Inside, the Wolf gnashed its teeth.

All together, the story was a grim one. Lies. Violence. Betrayal. His freedom in exchange for another's. Corbette's face was impassive, but the air grew hot with his anger. Kingu's necklace. The weakened Gate on Nisannu eve. Desiree Friday's failed escape and last request. Hart tried to keep the words inside, holding on to each until it was ripped from his tongue. The Aether stole every secret from the depths of his tarnished soul.

When he reached the end of the tale—moonrise the night before when Kayla was thrown into the cell with him—Corbette interrupted. "Thank you. That is enough."

Thank the Lady. The tips of Hart's ears burned. He couldn't look at Kayla.

Corbette tapped the tip of his cane thoughtfully. "Rudrick has been keeping secrets."

Hart could think of a few reasons the sentinel might avoid telling his boss. If Rudrick told Corbette of his plans, but failed to deliver the necklace, it would be his life on the line.

"Maybe he wanted to surprise you," Kayla suggested.

A heavy beat of silence.

"And this necklace is now, once again, in Norgard's possession." Corbette turned to his right-hand man. "Lord Jace, alert the four Houses. Level five, if you please."

"Yes, sir." Jace turned and retreated up the stairs. The Kivati princess passed him on the way down. She had transformed from the last time Hart had seen her into the perfect Kivati Lady. She could have walked off the canvas of some Belle Époque painting: a gown of pale blue, blond hair swept back in curls and covered by a beribboned straw bonnet, white lace gloves. A mouthful of bubble gum ruined the picture. Good for her.

"I instructed you to stay upstairs," Corbette said without turning.

"I got bored." She blew a pink bubble with her gum and popped it obnoxiously. She was painfully young. Her bravado was all for Corbette. Her eyes lit on Kayla. "You again! Hullo, there."

"Hi, Lucia." Kayla held up a hand in greeting. A faint blush tinged her cheeks.

Lucia grinned, strolled over to the cell, and leaned lazily against the bars. "Looks like you had fun last night." She gave Hart an appraising once-over.

"Um, yeah," Kayla answered sheepishly. "You could say that."

Lucia laughed. "What're you still doing in the cage? Corbette, let them out."

Corbette closed his eyes. Hart smirked. The girl had balls of steel. No one spoke to Corbette like that. They'd kill each other before the honeymoon was over. Hopefully not before the wedding. His bet with Oscar was still on.

"How do you know Miss Friday?" Corbette asked.

"Butterworth's," Kayla supplied. She turned to Lucia. "You get home okay?"

"Of course," Lucia said. "Hard not to with the X-Men

trailing my every step. I can't sneeze without three of them handing me a tissue."

"Something's come up, Lady Lucia," Corbette said. "I'm sorry, but I have to break our date."

A flash of disappointment crossed her face. She covered it quickly, indifferent as only a teenager could be. "As you wish." She shrugged and blew another bubble. "I'm going anyway. It's so rarely good weather for sailing."

"Take Johnny and Charlie with you," the Raven Lord ordered.

She rolled her eyes and turned back to Kayla. "Darling, may we meet again as the Lady wills it."

"Have a good sail," Kayla said.

The princess gave a parting wave and flounced up the stairs. Corbette turned to Kai. "Take our guests into custody."

"But we haven't done anything wrong," Kayla protested.

Kai pulled the lever to unlock the cell. The gears ground against each other, whining. The lock slid open with a *thunk*. Hart and Kayla weren't handcuffed—that would be too uncivilized—but Kai stalked behind them up the stairs with a heavy hand on the hilt of his scimitar. Hart's body felt like it'd been chewed up and spit out by Mount St. Helens. Kayla, on the other hand, practically bounced up the steps. Kai noticed Hart's strained gait and smirked. Bastard.

In the main armory, the blacksmiths and weaponsmiths had disappeared. Two female Kivati warriors joined their little band: a Cougar named Elinor and a Bear named Nita. The female warriors wore battle dress: leather knickers, sturdy knee-high boots, and boned leather corsets that served to protect the internal organs rather than squeeze the waist. Their leather arm bracers were both black, because they belonged to Kai's Western House. Leather boleros covered their shoulders and bone chokers protected their delicate necks from clavicle to chin. The Cougar was an archer, with Thunderbird arrows and a heavy yew crossbow. The Bear favored brute strength; the ax was her weapon of choice.

If he hadn't been so on edge, Hart would have enjoyed his first trip in a Kivati steam car. The ride was smooth, yet the landscape blurred past as the engine easily topped a hundred miles per hour. The only noise was a quiet bubbling of water in the glass boilers beneath the hood.

Kivati Hall lorded over the city from the top of Queen Anne. The Georgian monstrosity dated back to the early days of Seattle. Diamond-paned windows set off the yellow façade, and a wraparound porch with ionic columns gave the place a deceptively friendly feel. An imposing iron gate surrounded the grounds, each spike topped with little tinkling bells to keep out wandering spirits.

"Nice view," Kayla said when Kai helped her out of the steam car and she stood for the first time on sacred Kivati ground. Downtown Seattle rose in front of them, looking flimsy and fleeting beneath the looming gaze of Mount Rainier. To the west, storm clouds gathered, hiding the Olympics from view.

Kayla didn't seem afraid of the Kivati anymore. She had a new confidence, like a chick after its first flight. When she glanced at Hart, she blushed.

He almost tumbled her to the grassy lawn, Kivati be damned. *Down, boy.* He turned to Corbette. "Now what, oh benevolent Lord? Shall we take tea and chat about old times?" Perhaps sarcasm wouldn't get him what he wanted, but he couldn't help himself. He wouldn't bow to Corbette if his life depended on it.

Kayla's life, on the other hand . . .

Hart shrugged off the queasy feeling in his stomach. The Raven Lord was sworn to protect humans. He might be a bastard, but he was honorable.

"Patience." Corbette led them around the side of the mansion to a long lawn. The colorful daffodils and crocuses in the flowerbeds contrasted sharply with the weapons and siege supplies piled high on the green grass. A small army of warriors sharpened knives and arrows. Most had steadfast rifles and revolvers too. One never knew when a burst of Aether would render more modern guns useless. It was best to be prepared for any situation.

Hart's fingers itched for his broadsword. He wondered what Rudrick had done with it, and if he'd ever get it back.

The perimeter of the yard and upper balconies of the mansion were guarded by modified crossbows. A hand crank turned six barrels in rapid fire. A small steam-powered engine could propel the heavy arrows all the way to the skyscrapers downtown and through the thick scales of a flying lizard. The war preparations resembled those of an earlier age, but they represented the future. Nothing plastic. Nothing requiring electricity. Nothing vulnerable to a large surge of spirits.

Hart looked thoughtfully at Corbette, whose blank expression said he was furiously plotting something within that thick skull. "You planning to attack the Drekar?"

"Not originally, but now—who knows? It's the fifth day of the Babylonian New Year. I like to be prepared." Corbette waved to a man wearing a red armband. The white feather in his hair signified a recent personal loss. Hart wondered if Norgard had lashed out against the Kivati after last night's debacle.

"So?" Kayla asked. She looked warily at the weapon field as if she could already see the future carnage.

"Norgard has taken a special interest this year in celebrating his ancestral festival," Corbette explained, "in addition to stepping up attacks. He set a new record in the past two months for civilian casualties. Indifference or arrangement?" He stopped to speak with the man he'd summoned. The eagle-shifter's red-rimmed eyes and stony jaw reminded Hart of Kayla the first time he'd seen her.

He shook off the thought. He tried to remind himself that emotions made an operative sloppy. He needed to stay sharp.

If the Southern House warrior had lost someone, Kivati honor demanded that he drew first blood in retaliation. The guy certainly seemed motivated. He glared at Hart as if blaming him for the Drekar's strike.

Kayla frowned. "Why would Norgard want to kill more people? Doesn't he eat them? Or can he get their souls after they're dead?"

"No, Drekar need living victims," Hart told her.

Corbette dismissed his officer and turned back to Kayla. "Why does Norgard do what he does? I only knew the attacks had escalated, so gave the order to mobilize. Recent information"—he gave Hart a stern look—"shines new light on his actions. We all know the Drekar seek to return to power. They tell their children bedtime stories of Kingu's glorious battle before Tiamat, goddess of chaos, fell. The Lady knows, many have tried to spring Kingu from the Gate. A few have come terrifyingly close."

"Norgard is trying to weaken the Gate further by flooding it with the newly Dead," Hart suggested.

Corbette nodded tightly.

"What about the Nisannu ceremony?" Kayla asked. "Desi was researching it. Can it stop Norgard from opening the Gate?"

Hart felt a little ill. He squeezed Kayla's hand. Inside, the Wolf rose to its haunches, ready to defend her.

"It can be used to reinforce the Gate, or to open it," Corbette said. "Nisannu occurs on the Spring Equinox, an auspicious time for any great work of magic to be performed. The festival consisted of the Descent, the Sacred Marriage, and, most importantly, the Determination of Destiny. Through the ceremony, the king was able to summon the gods to fix the destinies of the universe."

"Could these gods return the Drekar to power?" Kayla asked.

"Yes," Corbette said. "But the gods are capricious. Norgard must have some way of controlling Kingu once he frees him."

The sun slipped behind a cloud and Kayla shivered. Hart brushed her arm with his, trying to give her some of his warmth. He wished he could hold her. "How would he do it?" he asked. "What's he need for this ceremony?"

"The Descent involves atonement of sins," Corbette said, "for which the king sacrifices a ram."

"He needs livestock?" Kayla asked.

"A human would be better," Hart said.

Corbette nodded his agreement. "Part one—a human sacrifice. Part two—the Sacred Marriage. The king reenacts a 'wedding' with Ishtar, the goddess of love and fertility."

"Sex," Hart said.

"With anyone?" Kayla asked.

Corbette's fingers flexed around the silver handle of his cane. "A virgin sacrifice is the most powerful—"

Kayla's eyes flickered to Hart, and she blushed. He was immediately glad Kayla no longer fit the bill for Norgard's plans.

"—but not strictly necessary."

Damn.

"Should Norgard carry out the first two ceremonies," Corbette said quietly, staring out toward the distant Mount Rainier, "he may summon the gods to do his bidding. The Gate will fall, releasing Kingu and whatever army he possesses."

Hart scratched the stubble on his jaw. Did the gods still listen to mortal requests? Perhaps the magic of the old covenants was strong enough to wake even the most recalcitrant deity.

"Lord Kai," Corbette called to his general, who had been conversing with various warriors off to the side. "Summon the four Houses. Every able-bodied Kivati needs to soldier up. Get the vulnerable to the safe houses."

"What about the humans?" Kayla asked.

Hart snorted. "The humans will never believe this."

"But we have to try. You could tell them it's a terrorist attack or something. Call the military—"

"Miss Friday." Corbette laid a hand on her shoulder, but removed it when Hart growled. "It would be a massacre if the humans got involved. There's nothing we can do—"

"Bullshit! We have to warn them—"

Kai wrapped an arm around Kayla and yanked her off her feet. "Remember your place, human."

Hart lunged forward, canines extended, teeth snapping, but Corbette caught him before he reached them. Hart was no lightweight, but Corbette had the power of the Raven Lord on his side. It packed quite a punch. His skin burned with the need to shift. Corbette's magic held him back, fire against fire. The hair on his arms started to smoke. His eyes rolled back in his head.

Dimly, he heard Kayla yelling, "Stop it! Don't hurt him."

"Calm down," Corbette said in his ear. "I need you alive and lucid." He ordered Kai to release Kayla. Once Kai stepped away from her, Hart backed down, breathing heavily.

Kayla rushed to his side. "Did he hurt you? Let me see—"

"I'm fine."

She insisted on checking his skin for wounds before she believed him.

"As endearing as you two lovebirds are, time is of the essence." Corbette started up the front steps to the mansion, silver-tipped boots clicking on the wide cedar planks.

"You don't need us." Hart's voice was raspy, still close to the Change. His Wolf paced the edges of his skin, growling.

Corbette turned and thumped his cane on the steps. Aether shot through the yard like a ghostly wind. "Don't you care for anything in your miserable life? All able-bodied warriors. This means you."

"I'm not Kivati, damn it."

"You can't escape the apocalypse any more than you can escape your blood. Hate it, rage against it all you want. You will always be one of us. Nothing can change that." He let out an ex-asperated breath. "Forget us—what about her?" He pointed his cane at Kayla, who stood uncertainly at the bottom of the stairs. "Isn't her life worth fighting for? When that Gate falls, Seattle won't be the only city overrun with the dead. Gates are like dominos: one goes down, they all do. Volcanic explosions, earthquakes, tsunamis, hurricanes. Get it through your thick skull: this is not something you can run from."

Kayla's face was pale. The cold wind blew wisps of her pretty brown hair across her eyes and bit color into her cheeks. She deserved to be cherished and protected, but he'd only brought her violence. Out of the frying pan, into the fire.

How could she still look at him with hope in her eyes? He had to man up and do something to deserve that look. "Fine. What do you want?"

Corbette shook his head. "Come inside and we'll talk. You've been in Norgard's lair. My spies have not. We need the layout. How many guards are there? What security systems? What—"

"Hold up there, cowboy," Hart said. He finally had a bar-gaining chip with this bastard, which he could use to secure Kayla's safety. She didn't need to be involved. She should be in a safe house with the other vulnerable ones. Some of the tightness lifted in his chest. This was a whole new ball game.

Chapter 17

Preparation for storming the Drekar lair took considerably longer this time, according to Hart. It made Kayla nervous to hear his tale of sneaking in to get her with only three operatives and a brick of C-4. It wouldn't be so easy a second time. The Drekar were most likely still on high alert. Blowing up the Ballard Locks to pull their warriors away from the factory had been genius, but couldn't be repeated.

"We're going to have to overwhelm the place with troops," Kai said.

"The Lady will aid us." The Raven Lord sat in a throne-like chair in a plush study. Floor-to-ceiling bookcases covered the walls. Red velvet drapes fell from wide French doors that opened onto a balcony. A large wooden table, covered in maps, stood in the center of the room. Aerial photographs marked with red X's showed the best places to access the Gate. All were volcanic sites.

The two Thunderbirds from Rudrick's basement, Lords Kai and Jace, were in attendance, as well as the Cougar Elinor. Elinor was tall and built to run. Her long black hair was plaited in two complex braids, from which hung a feather, tip down. A symbol of mourning. Kayla had seen quite a few Kivati warriors wearing them around the Hall.

Elinor seemed hostile, but mostly toward Hart. Kayla didn't know if it was because he was Wolf, or because he had worked for the Drekar. Probably a little of both.

"These are the best aerials you got?" Hart asked. He bent over the table on the opposite side from Corbette. The two men were more alike than either would want to admit. Both large. Both imposing. Both more stubborn than a pair of rocks.

The Raven Lord was a control freak facing absolute chaos. A casual observer might mistake his even, low voice for calm. He emulated confidence and absolute authority, but Kayla could see—on that other plane when she closed her eyes—the vibrating nervousness of his inner light. A black weight pushed down on him, like the weight of the world resting on his shoulders. Colors swirled within him. Red and purple, a bit of blue, greenish yellow. Were they emotions? Anger at Norgard, fear for his people, annoyance at Hart's grudgingly given help perhaps? She could only guess.

The tightening of his jaw and occasional bursts of power betrayed his resentment at asking Hart for help. "The werewolf" was unstable, unreliable and a traitor—or so the Thunderbirds repeatedly pointed out. They distrusted anything Hart had to say on principle. Corbette was cautious, but he seemed to value Hart's opinion.

Kayla wondered if his power was similar to hers. Was he able to see beyond Hart's tough-guy exterior and tarnished past to the soul that glowed within?

Hart held the chips, seemingly for the first time in his life, and he milked them for all they were worth. He lounged in the wingback armchair, legs stretched out, as if they were planning a picnic in the park. He even rested his feet on the table at one point, but there Corbette drew the line. She noticed Hart's grammar had deteriorated. He was doing it just to piss off the eloquent Corbette.

Kayla didn't have much to add besides her description of

the main hall, tunnel, and private quarters where Norgard had planned her seduction. She felt a strange sense of purpose in the coming battle. Somehow the loose threads of her life were coming together—her mother's death, her nurse training, her sister's sacrifice. The future was still foggy as all get-out, but it seemed right.

Hart wouldn't let her leave his sight.

"Lord Jace," Corbette ordered, pointing to a spot on the map just west of the Ballard bluff where the lair was located, "lead your men through the cliff face windows. They are usually opened only at night, but Theo will take care of that. How long will it take to get his warship and rockets into position?"

"Thirty minutes," Elinor said, "forty, tops. Theo's already onboard with his wet crew."

"I've got point on the eastern front," Kai said. "We'll need a team of cats in first to sniff out where Norgard is hiding."

"Cats?" Kayla asked. "Wouldn't dogs—or wolves—be better? I thought they had a stronger sense of smell."

Elinor gave her a contemptuous glare. "Do you know anything? Why are you here again?"

Hart growled.

Corbette answered, "Only a few left in the Seattle area. Too little hunting ground in the city."

"What about foxes?" she asked, not that she wanted to see Rudrick after he tried to kill her.

"Where is that fucker?" Hart asked. "I've got something for him." He flexed his hand and claws shot out of his fingertips.

"None of your business," Jace said.

"Gentlemen. Ladies." Corbette stood, and the Kivati stood with him. All except Hart, who sat back and put his hands behind his head, just to be ornery. "You are dismissed." Hart jumped up like his tail was on fire. "Prepare the troops. Be ready to depart at eighteen-hundred hours. Not you, Hart."

Hart stayed standing. "What do you need me for? I told you everything."

"And yet, your woman is correct, having a Wolf—especially one familiar with the target site—on the ground will be priceless."

Hart glanced at Kayla when Corbette said "your woman," but quickly looked away. Did he not want her to be "his"? A week ago she would have scoffed at the notion of belonging to someone else. She was her own woman. Independent. Self-sufficient. But after last night she felt stronger than she'd ever been. The pieces of her soul had clicked into place, and she needed Hart as part of that puzzle. It had all happened so fast. It wasn't rational.

She couldn't tell if he felt the same way. Corbette wanted to send him into battle. She'd seen those dragons. There was no way a Wolf, even a large, magic one, could win against one of those monsters. The thought of losing him so soon made her break out in a cold sweat.

"Calm yourself, child." Corbette motioned her to sit again. He rang the bell for fresh tea service to be brought and waited for the Kivati to leave. "Wolf, sit your ass down." A wave of power barreled through the room, and Hart sat. He didn't look happy about it. "We have a few matters to discuss privately."

"I'm getting a little tired of everyone talking over me," Kayla said. "I may be 'just a dumb human,' but I think I've earned the right to an explanation. Or to be let go."

"No," Corbette said.

"She isn't one of yours," Hart snapped.

"No?"

"No!"

The tea arrived. Kayla accepted a fresh cup with a little milk, wishing it were coffee. Corbette took his black. Hart, after watching the Raven Lord, dumped half the milk and a bowl of sugar in his cup. Corbette didn't comment. Once the serving girls left, he took a photograph out of the drawer of his desk and passed it to Kayla. "Cheveyo's blood has returned."

Kayla set down her cup and accepted the tintype photograph. It was her great-grandfather. He wore a handlebar mustache and a cowboy-type shirt. His thick black hair was in two plaits. A medicine bag sat at his side. "Where did you get this?"

"He was one of ours, in my father's time," Corbette said. "Let me start at the beginning. The Kivati were once a great race. The giant animal people of legend. The Lady granted each two gifts—the ability to Change into a totem animal, and guardianship over one of Her five sacred powers: air, fire, water, earth, and heart."

"Does that make you Captain Planet?" Kayla asked.

He ignored her. "Each must be in balance to sustain life. If they fail, so do the walls that protect the Living World from the Land of the Dead. Cheveyo was the last guardian of heart, and he died protecting the Gate in the Great Fire."

"If there hasn't been a guardian for over a hundred years," Kayla asked, "how has the Gate survived?"

"His sacrifice strengthened it. You know something about blood magic, I think. It runs strongly in his family. We thought his blood lost, but it became known he had a half-blood child, who had a half-blood child."

"My mother?"

Corbette took a sip of tea. "I found her at the same time the Drekar did. We were too late."

The old anger rose in her chest. The old nightmare flashed in her mind. Her parents' voices raised in the night. Strange cars pulling in front of their little house. Pushing a chair to the upstairs window so that she could see out. Mama on the lawn below, illuminated in the moonlight, hands raised. A shadow, then fire catching the maple tree and turning the grass to ash. Mama. Fire. And then Daddy's firm hand pulling her away, sweeping up her sleeping sister, urging her not to make a sound as he led them out the back door and into the night.

Corbette's "too late" had shattered a family. How many others had suffered similarly while the Kivati and Drekar played power games, letting violence corrode a city?

"I see." She didn't see. "What did the Drekar want her for?"

"Norgard knew Cheveyo's blood sacrifice secured the Gate for a hundred years, and only Cheveyo's blood could break it. He needed one of Cheveyo's descendants to open it for him."

"So he went after my mother. But he's got the key. Does he still need my family's blood?"

"When he attacked your mother, yes. But now that the hundred years are up, no. Cheveyo's magic still holds, but it is weakened. Any Kivati's blood would do."

"Norgard is big on symbolism," Hart said. He scratched the stubble on his jaw. "He'd get off on using this guy's descendants to open the Gate, especially after fixating on it so long."

Corbette tipped his head in agreement.

"But Desi, did he plan to sacrifice her too?" Kayla's opinion of Norgard was so low there wasn't much room to drop. But she didn't want to believe her sister had been completely duped. She'd seen a blend of grief and affection in Norgard's eyes, however briefly, when he spoke of Desi. She wanted to imagine there was a kernel of truth there.

Corbette offered a cucumber sandwich, which she refused. She wasn't remotely hungry. "Intent is important in magic," he said, selecting one for himself. "Unwilling, the blood sacrifice requires death, or close to it. But if your sister conducted the ceremony willingly, a bit of her blood would be enough."

"Desi would never—"

"The kid." Hart reached over and squeezed her hand. "He could have raised the kid to do the ceremony willingly."

"Possible," Corbette said, "There is the small matter of

controlling Kingu once he is freed. Who knows what devious plan he concocted?"

Kayla shuddered. Hart wrapped his arm around her shoulders. She turned into his warmth.

She wondered when Desi had discovered his plans for her child.

Corbette set down his teacup and turned his heavy gaze on Kayla. "You see why I can't let you leave. You're vulnerable. You need my protection—"

"I'll protect her," Hart said.

"And when you grow bored of her?"

Hart showed his teeth. His eyes turned black, and his canines elongated. "Right. And you do a bang-up job of protecting your own."

The oxygen in the study seemed to shrink. The air grew pregnant with the edge of violence. Outside, thunderclouds rolled in. She wondered who would blink first.

To everyone's surprise, Corbette broke the silence. His expression said he didn't admit defeat, only acknowledged that Hart's accusation was legitimate. "It was an old custom. No Changeling had been moon-marked in over a century. You were the first. You were . . . unlucky."

"Unlucky? You wanted to leave him to die on a glacier!" Kayla said.

"Hart and his mother left precipitously. There was, for certain, a call to uphold tradition in this instance, but not everyone agreed." Corbette sipped his tea, as if they chatted about embroidery or the weather, not murder. "Our culture is on the verge of extinction, and our rituals sustain us."

"Convenient for you," Hart muttered. "'Don't blame me, the rituals made me do it!'"

Corbette gave him a flat look. "Like I said, you left before I ruled on the matter. We would have spared you, but you were already gone."

"And you didn't go after them?" Kayla asked.

Hart made a small noise and sat back slowly in his chair. The angry set of his shoulders eased. Now he just looked tired. "Maybe he did."

Corbette studied the contents of his teacup.

"He did?" Kayla asked.

"We thought they were trying to kill us." Hart ran a hand through his hair. "We were on the run for almost a year."

"I am sorry for your loss," Corbette said formally.

"Yeah, yeah." Hart waved him off. "So you owe me one. Let us go now, and we'll call it even."

"I can't."

Hart settled his arm protectively around Kayla. "I say you can."

Corbette sighed and put aside his cup. "We need her to close the Gate, should Norgard succeed in opening it."

"But I don't know anything." Kayla protested. She hadn't studied magic. She hadn't read any books, attended any lectures, passed any exams. They couldn't depend on her.

Yet this is what Desi had died for. What her mother and great-grandfather had died for. This was her legacy. She couldn't ignore it, even though it terrified her. She couldn't let them down.

"No time to train you," Corbette said. "Trust your instincts. They don't seem to have failed you yet." His eyes flicked to Hart.

Kayla blushed. She couldn't explain last night.

"She's not going in there," Hart said. "She's staying in the safe house, or she's going back to Philly. That's nonnegotiable."

"Is she?" Corbette asked mildly.

"You said her blood's diluted. You can't use her. She's not Kivati—"

"Isn't she?"

Hart slammed his hands on the table. "She doesn't owe you nothing!"

"Get it through your thick skull, Wolf: this isn't about the Kivati or the humans or you or me. If we don't shut the Gate, there will be nowhere she can run, nowhere she can hide from what's coming. There will be no one and nothing left."

Hart closed his mouth, but he didn't look happy about it.

"Hart." Kayla took his hand. "I want to do this. I have to."

He searched her face.

"Perhaps," Corbette said, "she could use another guard to increase her chances of getting out alive."

Sneaky bastard. He had Hart right where he wanted him. The same thought flashed over Hart's face—surprise, then resignation. Kayla wanted to tell him he didn't have to risk his life for her, but she knew it would be a waste of breath. His eyes said as much.

Corbette stood. "That's settled. You've one hour. I'll loan you a guest room where you can get some . . . rest."

Kayla had so many questions, but for the first time in her life she didn't want to waste precious moments gathering information. One hour was hardly time to fit a lifetime worth of living, but it was all she had. She wanted to spend every one of those thirty-six hundred seconds with Hart.

He seemed to have the same idea. He put a protective arm around her, and led her into the opulent hallway.

The guest room was lavishly decorated with an antique four-poster bed and floor-to-ceiling windows overlooking downtown Seattle and Puget Sound. The mountains in the distance were snow-topped and gorgeous, but she couldn't help imagining them exploding in lava and ash in a few short hours. She closed the curtains against the multimillion-dollar view, leaving the room in shadow. She needed the world to be small again, narrowing to touch and taste. Not the fate of the world, just her and her lover. Hearts beating in passion, not fear.

He came to her in the darkness. His hot hands rubbed up and down her arms, soothing and reassuring. She strained her eyes to see his handsome face. She wanted to burn it into her memory, a gift to take with her into the dangerous unknown. Would he still be alive tomorrow? Would she? Would they stop Norgard before it was too late? Would humans rest peaceful tonight, ignorant of the disaster that hung on a knife's edge? Until the next time some hell-bound lunatic tried to blast open the Gate.

"Shh," Hart whispered in her ear. His breath on her sensitive neck sent shivers down her spine. He was so large and hot and deliciously male. She wished she could burrow into his strength and light, and take shelter from the coming storm.

"Don't think," he said. "Stop that beautiful brain of yours for a minute or two. Give me a chance to get started."

She couldn't help smiling.

"Yeah, I can feel that laugh," he said. His hand caressed her breastbone. He probably felt the vibration along her chest. "Stay with me, babe. Tell me what you feel when I touch you here." His fingers dipped beneath her shirt and found the pebble of her nipple.

"I feel . . ." She had to concentrate on what he was doing to put it into words. As a distraction, it worked. Her brain wasn't big enough to both worry and make sense of the sensations cascading through her.

"What?" His teeth nipped her earlobe.

"Oh . . . I feel *that* down my nerves, down my neck and—"

He moved his teeth lower, biting gently over her carotid artery. She shivered.

"I love that sound you make," he said. "A little breathy moan in the back of your throat." His right hand cupped her breast and massaged. His left got to work on the buttons of her shirt.

"That feels . . . nice," she said.

"Nice? That's it?"

"*Very* nice."

"I can do better." He opened her shirt and replaced his hand with his mouth. His tongue and teeth laved her nipple. The sensations quickly overwhelmed her ability to form words.

She wrapped her hands in his hair and held on tight. Her lack of sight in the almost-dark served to heighten her other senses. His smell—musk and pine—shot north to her brain. His touch—calloused and hotter than hell—shot straight south.

Last night their lovemaking had been rushed. A race to the finish before the madness claimed him. A conflagration, burning all at once. This time they went slow, not because they had more time—they had less—but because they didn't want to miss a second of the time they had. Every caress was like the first time and the last. Every inch of body and soul was savored to make it stretch an eternity.

Time stopped.

Hart carried her to the soft feather mattress and carefully laid her down. "A real bed this time. Should have been like this—"

"No." She covered his mouth with her fingers. "It was perfect."

He took her fingers between his lips and sucked on the sensitive tips. Desire pooled low in her belly. She helped strip him of his clothes until they were skin to skin. His hard length burned against her hip. He kissed his way down her torso, stopping along the way to suckle and lick, and made his way between her thighs. His hot breath tickled.

"Touch yourself," he ordered. He dragged her uncertain hands to cover her breasts and showed her how to rub and pinch the alert tips. His head returned to her core. He lifted and spread her thighs for his perusal.

She tried to think of words to describe it, but she could only moan. Oh! *There*, and *Yes, more!* She closed her eyes and lost herself. In her Other vision, Hart's body flared with light. Electric currents pulsed through his limbs and spine, shooting toward the place where his mouth suckled her. It was almost as if his light were feeding into her. It built higher and brighter, matching her body stroke for stroke. She reached the top like a firecracker.

He held her gently as she came back down.

"Is it always like this?" she asked.

"No."

He filled her with one solid stroke. She didn't think she could take any more, but somehow she did. He restoked the fire. Could Hart see how brightly their soul lights blazed? Like a beacon searing the shadows from the room.

"I love you," Kayla said, when at last they lay still in each other's arms.

Hart's eyebrows shot up and his lips parted. "I—"

The door flew open. The sudden light blinded Kayla, but she sensed two figures quickly turn their backs to the room. They didn't, unfortunately, leave.

Hart gave her a wry grin, but didn't move. His body blocked her nudity from the intruders.

Kai stopped in the doorway. "Get the fuck up," he ordered.

"I was up," Hart said. "You should try it sometime, dickwad."

"We're leaving immediately—"

"Why? Corbette said we had an hour—"

"Something's come up."

"Not my problem."

Kai drew his gun. Hart's back was to the weapon, so he couldn't see it, but he must have noticed Kayla stiffen beneath him.

"That's going to do you a lot of good," Hart said, "considering you need us alive."

"Don't try me, werewolf. Norgard has taken a hostage for his sacrifice."

Kayla felt her stomach drop. "Who?"

"Lady Lucia."

"Shit," Hart muttered, pushing himself up. "Smart move on his part. Don't know why we didn't think of it. Poor kid."

Kayla swallowed. "What's he going to do to her?"

"Nothing," Kai growled, "if we get there in time."

"How'd he snatch her?" Hart asked. "Your people sleeping on the job?"

"Ambush. Killed one bodyguard, the other is missing. We found her sailboat scuttled in the Montlake Cut."

Hart kissed Kayla's ear. "I can see you wanting to feel guilty for this one too, but she isn't like your sister. She had trained warriors guarding her. Not your fault."

He knew her too well. Saw her faults and weaknesses, understood her need to help and heal. She felt a burden lift from her chest. She couldn't change what had happened, but she could put all her energy into moving forward with his help.

Kai left clean clothes—Kivati battle gear—and gave them privacy to dress, with the order to "hurry the fuck up."

Kayla's hands shook as she pulled on the black leather pants.

"Leather is tougher for knives and claws to get through," Hart said, when she asked why she had to wear so much black leather. She felt like a wannabe vampire.

The leather corset was a little too tight. It covered a black, long-sleeved cotton blouse that laced up over her breasts. Iron-studded leather arm sheaths protected her from elbow to wrist. The steel-toed combat boots were made for stomping. She could break someone's kneecap with these suckers. She hoped she never got close enough to the enemy to test that theory.

Hart's outfit had a similar leather-bound theme, though his pants were looser and his boots bigger.

"Hasn't someone invented stronger material than leather for battle?" she asked. "Kevlar or something? Military grade."

"Synthetics don't hold up to the spirit world. Only materials that have once been alive work: linen, cotton, hemp, hide, leather. Natural fibers have residual Aether energy, like a memory of having life. It's a small additional barrier to demons and spirits. 'Sides, plastics and other crap just fall apart close to the Gate."

"But plastic is in everything these days. If the Gate opens, what will happen to skyscrapers, computers, modern technology in general?"

"Babe, if the Gate opens we'll have much bigger problems."

Kai returned to bring them to the armory.

"I don't know how to use anything here," Kayla protested. "I'd be more likely to shoot myself on accident."

"I'll be with you the whole time," Hart promised. "But you have to carry something just in case." He picked out a short knife and matching scabbard that had protective runes carved in the weathered hide. Lacing a belt through the scabbard, he strapped it around her waist.

He picked enough weapons for himself to outfit a small militia. Knives in each boot and strapped to each arm bracer. Silver throwing stars at his wrists. A long sword and an ax—well suited for beheading a dragon—crossed over his back. Guns too. Like Kai, he wore a bandoleer over his chest to hold ammunition.

Kayla didn't want to think of him having to use all that stuff. He was armored and lethal, but she'd seen beneath his hard exterior. He wasn't a killer, no matter what he said. He had a choice.

"I choose to protect you," he said gruffly, "I don't give a rat's ass for those other dumb fucks."

How sweet.

Chapter 18

Hart settled weapons against his body. The familiar weight was comforting. He couldn't waste energy thinking about Kayla being in danger. Her scent—following delicately behind him—was comforting too, but it also sent fear coursing through him whenever he thought of her going into battle. All his training had led up to this moment. He was one bad motherfucker with a weapon in his hand. Nothing would get past him to touch her. Nothing.

They followed Kai to the weapon field at the front of the mansion, where Corbette waited. Corbette looked like someone had run over his dog. His face was dark as the thunderclouds above and his knuckles so tight on his cane they looked like bone. His left foot tapped with restless energy.

Hart tilted his head and studied the man. He'd never thought of the Raven Lord as a real person, with hopes and personal dreams, emotions even, before this. Corbette was legendary for his ruthlessness and self-control. He lived to protect his people, but he'd failed to protect the little princess. Was that the only maggot eating his conscience? Or did he have deeper feelings for the girl?

Corbette was supposed to marry the kid, but only to fulfill the Spider's prophecy. Only to combine two strong bloodlines and create the next generation of iron-willed rulers. Convenience, not love. Right?

Hart wasn't so sure about that anymore.

Corbette noticed them finally. His violet eyes pulsed with the killing edge.

"Why Lucia?" Kayla asked. "Why not any Kivati off the street? What's he going to do to her?"

"There's a prophecy about her," Hart said. "She's supposed to be the Kivati's 'salvation.' Norgard would like that, twisting her role so she's their destruction instead."

"He's all about the grand gestures, isn't he?" Kayla asked.

Hart nodded. "If you're gonna do something, go all out. Balls to the wall."

"What's the prophecy say?" Kayla asked.

Corbette stared at the ground. "In an age of Darkness, the Crane will bring a great light. The people who lived in the land of the shadow of death will rise up, and the Harbinger will lead them. Cast off your shackles, oh Changers! See, oh you blind ones! Follow the Crane to destiny, for behind her lies ruin."

Hart paused with "What the fuck?" sitting on his tongue, but he kept his yap shut. He must be learning. Corbette was not receptive to smart-ass questions.

"Destiny," Kayla asked, "like the Tablets of Destiny? You're saying her prophecy and the Drekar's Tiamat legend are connected?"

Corbette and Kai both stared at her.

"No?" Kayla seemed uncertain.

Hart grinned and said to Corbette, "Now who's a stupid half-blood, huh? Never thought of that, did you?" Nope, he couldn't keep his yap shut apparently.

"No," Corbette said slowly, "never thought of that."

Kai swore.

"What's he going to do to her?" Kayla asked.

Corbette stiffened. Ignoring her, he spun on his booted heel and began snapping out orders left and right. Kai followed. Apparently it was time to move out.

"Norgard will rape her, won't he?" Kayla asked quietly. "He needs a virgin sacrifice."

Hart put his arm around her and drew her close. He couldn't stand the horror in her eyes. Would confirming the truth make her feel better or worse? He rubbed her arms, wishing he could take away some of the pain.

In the center of the field, Corbette raised his hands for a moment of silence. All the warriors bowed their heads.

The Kivati Spirit Seeker stepped onto the porch. She held a white feather in one hand and a fistful of earth in the other. She spread her arms wide to encompass the army and prayed. "May the Lady lift our wings today. Grant us the strength to overcome this great evil, and the courage to pass into the world beyond should we fall. May She hold us in Her heart whatever path lies before us."

Hart had never paid much attention to the Lady, except to curse Her name. She'd marked him as a Changeling, after all, and cast him out. Damned him to the moon madness and forced him to fight for his survival. For the first time he listened to the words of the prayer and it didn't rub him the wrong way. Perhaps She had set him on a different path, but not a damned one. He'd met Kayla, hadn't he? He'd learned to fight better than most of these Kivati solders. Maybe he'd be able to keep her safe, with the Lady's help.

A third of the Kivati force Changed and took to the sky. The rest piled into steam-powered jeeps. Kayla and Hart rode with Kai, Corbette, and another soldier. They drove northwest from Queen Anne to Ballard, over the Aurora Bridge and along the Ship Canal. The sky was eerily quiet. No rain. No wind even. The clouds hung low, pregnant with tension. Trees bent away from the sky as if frightened of the coming storm. Humans could feel it too. Few braved the open streets. Even the lifeless buildings seemed to hold their breath.

The Kivati who had remained human let their consciousness soar across the Aether into their black-feathered spies. Their eyes filmed white. A murder of crows took to the air until the sky was black with them. There was no hope in pulling off another surprise attack. Corbette was simply going to flood the Drekar lair with soldiers, like the beaches of Normandy.

The Locks still smoldered; a thick column of smoke rose into the air, joining the dirty cotton clouds stretching across the sky. The fresh water in Lake Union and the Ship Canal, without the Locks to hold it back, had dropped by a good four feet, bleeding into the sea and exposing yards of slimy green lake bottom. The closest boats to the shore in Fisherman's Terminal were grounded; they floundered like beached whales on the mossy rocks.

Next to Hart, Kai's eyelids fluttered as he connected his mind to a crow. "Jace is in position," he told Corbette. "Theo waits for your signal to launch."

"And Rudrick?"

"Still no word."

Corbette gripped the head of his cane, which Hart realized was his tell. The Raven Lord was considering an attack without one of his top sentinels. Rudrick was probably lying dead in a gutter somewhere, an early casualty of Norgard's grand plans. Nothing else could keep a Kivati sentinel from the coming battle. One more reason to hate Norgard. For what Rudrick had done to Kayla, Hart wanted to kill the bastard himself.

"Give the launch order," Corbette said. "We go in firing. Take no prisoners—"

"But what about the other women?" Kayla protested. "I wasn't the only one Norgard kidnapped—"

"They chose their path."

Kayla looked like she wanted to argue more, but Hart quieted her with a quick kiss. Old Ironsides there wasn't going to change his strategy, and Kayla needed to be in control of her emotions if she had a prayer of using her gift. He still thought this idea was crazy. She wasn't trained in blood magic. She didn't know anything about her power. Though he had to admit, she'd used it pretty good last night.

That thought had him adjusting his leather pants. He hated this getup. Didn't allow his boys to breathe. It had gotten to the point that the mere thought of this woman sitting next to him made his dick sit up and take notice. Forget the alluring smell of her. Forget the feel of her small, soft hand clinging tightly to his.

The coming battle should act like a bucket of cold water, but the adrenaline pumping through his system had always had the opposite effect on him. He wanted to grab her hips, lift her onto his lap, and thrust into her for one last good-bye.

Lady be damned.

Loki's Chocolate Factory came into view at the top of the hill. No time to indulge that carnal daydream; the attack began. Crows filled the sky with premature night.

This was his last chance. "Kayla, I . . ." He cleared his throat. "I . . . hell." He couldn't do it. "I don't want to jinx you. Just . . . just stick close."

"Like glue," she promised.

Rockets exploded from the Sound side into the cliff face, sending up a shower of dirt and sparks. The ground shook. Thunderbirds dove from high above, the undersides of their giant wings reflecting the rocket's orange glow. Jace—his Thunderbird form recognizable by his sheer size and the red tips of his wings—disappeared with six others behind the now smoldering building. The plan was for them to fly in through the windows Theo had blasted open and enter the Drekar Great Hall.

Other Thunderbirds covered the exodus from the jeeps, which screeched to a halt in front of the building. The invading force poured out of the vehicles, Changing mid-leap. Fur and claw ripped from human bodies. The Change started at the

extended arms and rippled down the torso and legs. Tails grew
last. Men left the jeeps on two feet and landed on four paws.

The beast army didn't stop. It stormed the factory doors
before the Drekar knew what hit them. Some dragons escaped
to jump into the sky and grapple with the Thunderbirds hundreds of feet above the ground. Wings of skin met wings of
feather, both beating rapidly against the cold salt air. Scales and
feathers rained down upon the predators below. The Thunderbirds called thunderbolts from the sky and hurled them at their
enemies. The dragons spewed fire in response.

Elinor—in Cougar form—bit a chunk out of a Dreki's thigh,
causing the creature to stumble. She was a runt, but her claws
were sharp. No soulless lizard could match her in ferocity.

The Raven Lord hadn't Changed. He stood facing the
ocean with his arms extended. Kai hovered over him in Thunderbird form, protecting his back. Corbette called on the
power of his people. The earth trembled. The wind blew in
from the north, shaking the trees. Waves crashed against the
base of the cliff, forming hands of water that grasped and
clawed at the lair from below.

Hart didn't Change either, though the Wolf inside him
tore at its tether. His swords unsheathed, he protected Kayla
with his body and waited for Corbette to give the word to
enter the lair.

In the Drekar Great Hall, Sven Norgard lounged in his
throne made of gold and bone. A killing mood throbbed in his
temples. He dreadfully missed the days when he could fly over
Europe and burn everything in his path. This civilized pretense
was a bore. He couldn't wait until Kingu broke free and took
the earth back from these wretched sheep. In his daydreams, he
slaughtered them one by one, until only those with beautiful
burning souls were left.

Like Desiree. She had been a breath of fresh air in his stifled existence. Her smile was infectious and without artifice. Truly, she hadn't seemed to care about his treasure or political power. He remembered the first time he saw her. A day of sun breaks, when the mountain was out and the air tingled with the call to fly. She was buying strawberries at Pike Place Market. Her yellow frock, so innocent and pure, set off her tanned skin beautifully. He was attracted to the brightness of her soul, of course, but as he drew closer it was her eyes that captivated him. Caramel and set too far apart, they took in the world with almost childlike wonder.

Later, after he'd seduced her and she lay naked, twisted among his gold thread sheets and jeweled belongings, it was the sound of her voice that had called him. It was light and lulling, like a lyre played by Freya's hand, and he had been content to let it wash over him. To warm himself in it, lazily, like a dragon basking in the sun.

He should have thrown her out like he had with others, but she had seemed . . . special, somehow. A diamond among pearls.

Desi's sister was a conniving bitch. He could almost admire her cunning, bashing him with that blasted wine bottle. He shouldn't have tried to romance her, but he'd been swept away having a bit of Desi back.

Tiamat smite her.

Norgard kneaded his temple. He needed to be patient. Couldn't lose his wits to this burning anger. His plans had led up to this moment. He was so close, but the threads of his machinations were quickly slipping through his grasp.

Thorsson rushed into the Hall moments before an explosion shook the windows. "Kivati!"

More rockets hit the cliff face and glass shattered. Thunderbirds swooped in through the broken frames, calling gale-force winds at their backs.

Thunderbirds in the middle of the day? What had happened to Corbette's strict hide-from-the-humans policy? The Kivati's actions had always been sadly repetitive. Dependable.

Predictable. Small-scale retaliation on Drekar businesses or individuals. But this was a full frontal assault like a shootout at high noon. There would be no way to hide this atrocity. The humans could explain away a single overly large airborne bird as a plane or a mistake of the eye. The six that flew in his window, with most likely more on the way, were impossible to ignore.

What had changed?

His interest piqued at the new challenge, even as his stomach dropped. His people were unprepared for an annihilation attempt. Perhaps this was his destiny. Death was the only great adventure he had yet to try.

"Move, my liege!" Thorsson yelled. He unsheathed the broadsword at his back. His first swing clipped a Thunderbird neatly beneath the wing, crippling the creature so that it crashed to the ground.

Its talons scraped for purchase along the stone floor. The sound was awful: a bow across a saw magnified a thousand fold. The Thunderbird slid the length of the hall and crashed into the dais at Norgard's feet. Its feathers began to shiver. A milky glow appeared at the creature's neck. It flexed its shoulders, and the light fell down its wings like a blanket being shrugged off. Bone, muscle, and feather disappeared behind the ripple of light, leaving a brawny human body behind. Blood dripped down the left arm from the man's armpit. He tossed his Thunderbird head, and the long hooked beak fell backward like a mask and disappeared, leaving square features and close-cropped dark hair. His violet eyes flashed with hate.

"Bravo," Norgard said. "I haven't had such a close demonstration since I captured that ravishing Kivati female back in 1900."

The Kivati curled his fist as if to conjure a thunderbolt from the Aether. A few sparks shot from between his bloody fingers, but he didn't have enough strength. He drew his lips back in a snarl and rushed the throne. Naked as the day he was born. Weaponless. He would have made a fine berserker.

Rockets continued to bombard the cliff face, destabilizing the ground. The Hall shook.

"Let's make this more interesting, shall we?" Norgard said. The arms of the gilded throne ended in two bone hilts. He seized these and pulled up, lifting the swords from their secret resting place. He tossed one to the Kivati and raised his own. The man grabbed the sword mid-arc and rolled. He slashed out at Norgard's legs. Norgard parried the thrust.

"What prompted this foolish mission?" Norgard asked as he sliced the Kivati's injured arm. A thin ribbon of blood welled from the cut.

"The Gate must . . . unh!" The Kivati lunged, but the ground shuddered beneath them at the same time, and his sword slipped.

Norgard evaded easily with a step left. "Keep your tip up. Must what?"

The man held his injured arm tightly against his side. Blood had dribbled all the way to his knee. He would soon expire all on his own. Norgard glanced around the Great Hall to see his men in battle with the other five Thunderbirds. Three had Turned to dragon and flew about the ceiling. Bone chandeliers crashed to the ground in their wake.

Where were his other soldiers? The battle must be in more places than this.

The Kivati in front of him took advantage of his momentary distraction. The man tossed his sword to his left arm, which appeared to be not as injured as he had let on. Norgard blocked the offensive thrust, but while his sword was engaged, the Kivati Changed his right hand to claw. He raked Norgard down the right side of his face, drawing blood. He dug his talons into Norgard's throat and held tight.

Norgard couldn't move. He swallowed. "Good show. Now tell me, must what?"

"The Gate must stay closed."

"Ah, yes." Norgard saw Thorsson sneaking up behind the Kivati. He didn't let his face betray anything. "I assume you found out about the necklace? I've had it for quite a few years. Why now?"

The Kivati squeezed his talons. "The princess—"

Thorsson plunged his sword between the man's shoulder blades. His body stiffened. His eyes bulged and his mouth fell open. His fingers released the sword in his left hand, and it clattered to the floor. Norgard used the opportunity to raise his sword and slice off the man's clawed hand that still grasped his throat. Blood splattered Norgard's chest and face, but he felt immediate relief in his poor pincushion of a neck.

"Bloody hell, Erik. Let the man finish his thought. The Kivati princess . . . what? She's had some new blasted prophecy? She's sneezed, and they blame me? What? Answer me, damn you!"

Red spittle appeared at the corners of the Kivati's mouth. His lungs wheezed like a ruptured bagpipe. Thorsson braced his foot against the Kivati's back and yanked out the sword. The man crumpled to the ground.

Thorsson bowed his head. "Oops."

Norgard turned to survey the Hall. The storm blasted through the broken window. It hurled glittering hail, leaving a blanket of ice on the stone floor. Knife-sharp winds ripped through the room, tearing the tapestries from their hangings and knocking about the few remaining chandeliers. Three of his men and two of the Kivati lay lifeless on the floor like colorful piles of modern art: splattered with red and blue paint, bone and sinew torn open to the air. The others still fought.

"Check the Hall doors," he ordered. "Something has prevented my men from making a dramatic entrance."

Thorsson wiped his bloody sword on the skin of the slain

Kivati. "Ja, Regent." He returned shortly. "Locked from the outside—"

"Seems our recent guest has been busy spilling all our little secrets. The window it is."

"Ja, but, surely, it is a trap—"

"Of course. Corbette stands atop the cliff directing this storm. It would be rude to ignore him." Norgard staggered as the cliff took another hit. Precious jewels from the ceiling rained down. "Besides, I believe the roof is about to cave in." He felt his skin stretch and his jaw jut out. The familiar burn ran down his spine as his body grew. The air crackled with magic. His shoulder blades ripped through the skin of his back and sprouted wings. He flexed his new dragon body, flapped his wings, and pushed away from the ground with his muscled thighs.

It would take more than a spot of bad weather to take down a dragon as old as he.

Chapter 19

Kayla crouched over an injured Kivati warrior and pressed gauze tightly against his wound. He'd been gouged by a dragon from his sternum to his groin. She tried to ignore the battle, pain, and death surrounding her.

Hart stood over her with his arsenal of weapons slaying anything that got too close. He really was good at his job. The thought sent a sick jolt through her gut. She was a healer. He was a killer. She'd always abhorred violence, but this time she appreciated Hart's skill. He was using it to protect her. Nothing got past him, except the weather. Hail beat on her back as she tried to shield her patient's body.

The Raven Lord had called a storm to ravage the cliff face. He didn't seem to care about the damage to the rest of the city. Boats in the marina far below crashed against the rocks; their timbers bobbed in the angry waves like the bones of drowned sailors. Trees were pulled up by their roots, and the larger branches whipped against neighboring houses like giant battering rams.

The screeching wind masked the battle cries.

Her patient was dying. She could feel the light inside him flicker and slowly fade. "No, damn it!" She drew on her own soul and tried to give him strength as one would stoke a dying fire. It didn't work. He was losing too much blood.

Her eyes flitted over the battlefield and landed on a fallen dragon twenty feet away. "Hart!" she yelled over the wind. "I need blood."

He scowled back at her, not wanting to leave her side. Who else in her life had ever tried to protect her? She had always been the strong one.

"Please." She saw the struggle in his gorgeous eyes, but he couldn't refuse her. He checked the sky and surrounding field. No enemies were near. With a backward glance, he sprinted to the dying dragon. He cut the monster's throat and filled his scabbard with the blue-black blood. When he returned, she accepted the scabbard. The Kivati was too far gone to drink it. Would it work applied topically? She had to try. She poured it over the deep wound in the Kivati's chest.

His eyes shot open. The blood on his chest seemed to bubble. He cried out and flailed on the slick grass. Before her eyes, the skin regenerated and knit together over the deep cut. He clutched his left breast, but it seemed to be in surprise more than pain. A deep moan reverberated in his throat.

"I think you'll live," she told him.

The next moment the sky erupted in a fountain of flame. Kivati and Drekar on the field threw themselves to the ground to escape the sparks. Iridescent purple wings emerged from behind the cliff, followed by a long, rusty snout and row upon row of sharp, jagged teeth. The dragon that rose into the sky was the largest she'd seen yet. Powerful too, for the Raven Lord's weather didn't blow the creature off course. Oval scales glittered over its sleek muscles. It hung suspended over the battlefield, beautiful and terrible at the same time. The ancient being surveyed the field almost lazily, until its eyes caught Kayla.

"Norgard," Hart said in her ear.

She'd seen him as dragon before, but her brain had blocked

the memory. She tried to connect the urbane gentleman she'd met to this nightmare creature. Something in those hollow eyes gave him away. Her presence seemed to enrage Norgard as the attack on his lair hadn't. The dragon's huge chest inflated as if to breathe a mouthful of fire. Kayla could already smell the burnt meat and cinders, along with a peculiar hint of cinnamon.

Hart threw himself over her. His weight crushed her into the scorched grass, knocking the breath from her lungs. From beneath Hart's arm, she watched the dragon lurch toward her. Its tail caught on something, and it jerked in the air. There was a general cry from the field. Kayla pushed Hart's arm out of her view. A second dragon had emerged from behind the cliff and sunk its teeth into Norgard's tail. They had similar builds, though the second dragon was slightly smaller. Its red scales were tipped in green, as if moss had crept over them with the rain and damp. It seemed younger somehow, but it was deadly serious about its attack on Norgard.

Who could this be? Which of Norgard's men would side with the Kivati?

Hart seemed to read her mind. "His brother, Leif Asgard," he shouted in her ear.

"Why would he help us?"

"Don't know."

Norgard's long body twisted in the air until he reached his brother's left wing. His teeth tore into the thin membrane, but Asgard didn't let go of his tail. Asgard's weight pulled Norgard toward the ground. They rolled in the air, shimmering coils moving smoothly over and around each other, gripping, squeezing. Kayla glanced around the field. The other dragons didn't seem to know whether to continue fighting the Thunderbirds and Kivati, or to come to their leader's aid.

Asgard was tilting heavily toward his injured wing. He needed help, but the Kivati didn't seem eager to interrupt the fighting dragons.

"Get up," she hissed in Hart's ear. Norgard had been distracted by her before, maybe he could be again.

"Don't think I can't tell you're plotting something," Hart growled.

"Trust me."

He didn't give his trust easily. His skin grew hot to the touch. She knew how much he hated Changing, but he would do it willingly to protect her. One Wolf couldn't take down an army of Kivati and Drekar. She had to do something before he tried. She couldn't live with herself if anything happened to him. How could one man grow so important to her in such a short time?

His body suffused with a golden glow. She felt fur sprout beneath her fingers. His jaw lengthened, and his teeth grew. She used his distraction to slither out from beneath him. When she turned, a huge timber Wolf with eerie violet eyes growled behind her. He lunged in front of her. His head reached her breasts.

"I have to help. Come with me if you want, but don't stop me from trying." She buried her hands in his fur and tugged.

He allowed her to move, but shadowed her so closely that her knees knocked against him at every step. She clutched his fur for courage. He wouldn't let anything happen to her. Slowly, they made it across the field to the edge of the cliff. It was idiocy to get closer to the battling dragons, but she had to do something.

"Norgard!" she shouted. Her cry was lost in the howling wind.

Corbette noticed her perched on the edge, and the first bit of color flashed over his gaunt face. She wasn't sure if his visible fatigue was a result of the battle or his worry for Lucia. He motioned to his men. Suddenly Kayla found herself caught between the cliff edge and a line of predators. Kivati who hadn't Changed held guns cocked and pointed at her.

Hart's flank pushed against her hip as he tried to bare his teeth in all directions. The fur on his back stood straight up.

Above them, Norgard noticed the movement and twisted around to glare at the ground. He hovered with Asgard's long head between his sharp talons.

"Norgard!" Corbette shouted. "I'll blow her to pieces if you move a muscle." The wind carried his voice so that it boomed over the battlefield.

The dragon raised its head and screeched. It sounded halfway between a bird of prey and a tiger.

"We only want the princess," Corbette yelled over the crash of the waves. "A trade: Lucia for the human."

Anger washed through Kayla's fear. Corbette had planned to sell her out. No, he wouldn't. She was partially Kivati, and he needed her to close the Gate. Didn't he? No wonder Hart had so much trouble trusting anyone. No one in this city seemed to be worthy of it.

Norgard still hesitated.

"She's untouched, dragon," Corbette lied. "Going once . . . going twice . . ."

Hart snapped his teeth in the Raven Lord's direction.

Norgard dropped through the air with Asgard clutching his back. His claws scraped for purchase along the edge of the cliff. He hauled himself over, and his brother followed. Both were the worse for wear, covered in blood and broken scales. Asgard Turned and collapsed to the ground. Norgard was more graceful; one moment his talons gouged the soaked earth, the next his bare feet padded softly forward. No hitch in his gait. Even naked and in human form, he radiated power. The rain slicked his blond mane back from his face and drizzled down his sculpted body.

"Hold your blasted fire," Norgard ordered.

The brothers resembled each other, though Asgard was slightly swarthier. He panted on the ground as his wounds slowly healed in the open air. The hurt in his eyes as he looked at his brother shocked her. She had thought all Drekar were evil, but Asgard seemed more human than most.

She kept her eyes raised as Norgard strode toward her. He had nothing she wanted to see. Hart crouched between them, prepared to attack if Norgard didn't halt. A small, vicious part of her wanted Hart to attack. This was the man responsible for her sister's death. The man who kidnapped and drugged her, as he had countless women. A soul-sucking monster.

Norgard stopped ten feet from Hart's sharp teeth. "You think so little of my intellect, Corbette? A blind man could see that the Wolf has taken a mate."

A mate? The word sounded more permanent than boyfriend, but she and Hart hadn't discussed the status of their relationship. It had happened so fast. Hart was protecting her at the moment, but what happened once they made it past this madness? When the adrenaline faded and real life began again, would he stick around? Or would he grow tired of her calm, boring lifestyle? The thought of him leaving made her heart squeeze unpleasantly in her chest.

Corbette widened his eyes a fraction, as if Norgard's accusation was a surprise. "You know Kivati are forbidden from taking human mates. This girl is yours for the taking."

"In exchange for my surrender, of course."

"Of course."

A hundred paces behind Norgard, Asgard stirred. Achingly, he rose to his feet, his body now smooth and whole as if he'd never been scratched. The glacial cast of his face seemed devoid of emotion. His sea-green eyes fastened on his brother as if the rest of them were shadows. His long, sure strides narrowed the gap. "Sven, what have you done?" His voice held such pain and rage that even the Kivati took a step back.

Norgard drew himself straighter and turned to face his brother. "Only what was required for the survival of our people. You lack the courage, little brother. I have shielded you for your own sake."

Asgard's eyes changed from green to fire. His grip on humanity hung by a knife's edge. "Raping women? Slaughtering innocents? Plotting to unleash the Horde? This is what is required for survival? At what price?"

Norgard snorted. "Humans are plentiful as grains of sand beneath the sea, and twice as expendable."

Corbette crossed his arms over his chest. "Do you have any idea what would happen if the Gates open fully? You would lay waste to the world. There would be nothing left to rule but ruins and refugee camps. Much more profitable to concentrate on your business empire—"

"It will never be enough," Norgard snapped. "I will not accept crumbs when I am owed an empire. Don't you tire of living in the shadows? Don't you chafe at serving humans who would despise you if they knew what you were? Don't you weary of upholding a compact with gods who have forgotten you?"

Corbette's lips thinned, but he didn't disagree.

"I thought you might be interested in joining my little cause." Norgard sauntered closer to Corbette until he stood just out of reach. The air crackled with power between the two. Norgard smiled lazily. "Have you ever taken down a human in animal form? No? It's a wonderful feeling. The bones snapping in your teeth. The hot blood streaming down your throat." Norgard's half-lidded eyes glowed. He licked his lips. His naked body swayed toward the other man, a sensual offense that was either mad or brilliant.

It put the Raven Lord in an uncomfortable position, though his stoic expression hid it well. He obviously wanted to take a step back, but couldn't. He would not retreat from his enemy.

Norgard took a step closer so that their bodies were a hairbreadth apart. His pale skin contrasted sharply with Corbette's black leather. He tilted his head down, nose to nose with the shorter man. Corbette ground his teeth and held his ground.

"It's the hunt that truly gets the blood running," Norgard

crooned. "Hearing those little human heartbeats race and their pitiful mews of panic—ah! Nothing can compare. Especially as you press those soft bodies to the ground and take what the good earth has given you. Our goddesses are not so different, Tiamat and your Lady. Both sacrificed their bodies for their children to live upon. Both gave their wombs to create the bounty of the earth. It would be rude to ignore their sacrifice by refusing that bounty." He bent his head to touch his lips to Corbette's ear. "When you plunge into your human prey, whether with teeth or cock, you worship your goddess. She doesn't want your silly celibacy, your barren self-restraint. She is fertility. She is blood. She didn't build this world with hands and hammer, but birthed it bloody and heaving for her children to rule."

Corbette wrapped his hands around Norgard's neck and threw him to the ground. "Enough!" His fury caused the clouds above to bash into each other. Thunder filled the air. The waves crashed angrily into the cliff face. It was suddenly apparent why the man kept his temper so tightly leashed. His uncontrolled emotions sent the weather roiling. He could cause tsunamis and hurricanes without thinking.

Hart growled. Fur raised, he backed into Kayla's legs, pushing her away from the confrontation.

Norgard might have been thrown to the ground, but he quickly turned it to his advantage. Lying on his side, he propped his head up on one hand as if he was lounging on the wet dirt of his own accord. He was unself-conscious in his nudity. The power humming through the air excited him. He turned his head to Kayla and smirked. "Going so soon, my love?"

Hart snapped his teeth. Kayla dug her hands in his fur to try to keep him from lunging at the Dreki.

Norgard laughed softly. "I never thought I'd see the day. Mad dog, attaching himself to another weak woman. You'll get yourself killed that way, don't you know?" This he addressed to the Wolf. "Women can't be trusted. I've often thought they were gifted their capriciousness from the goddess herself."

"Maybe if you weren't such a monster, you'd find women more interested in sticking around," Kayla told him.

The muscles around his eyes tightened. "Your sister seemed to like me as I am. But perhaps you're right. She turned out to be just as much of a whore as you. Must run in the family." He rolled to his feet with feline grace. "I propose a different trade. Your body is useless to me now, but you have something else that belongs to me. Return it—"

"Return what?" Kayla asked.

"Don't be coy. I want my necklace."

Kayla felt her mouth fall open. Norgard didn't have the necklace anymore? She'd seen it around his neck. He had to be lying. All the facts pointed to his culpability. His history of violence, kidnap, and rape. His admission that he'd planned to use the necklace to open the Gate. Fear shivered over her skin. She wished she could curl up next to Hart's warm pelt and sleep through this nightmare. Nothing she had done since she stepped foot in Seattle had gone as planned. Where was Lucia?

No one spoke for a long moment. Norgard turned from her to Corbette to Hart and back again. His brows rose slowly as the silence lengthened. "Who, pray tell, has it now?"

Overhead, lightning flashed. "Where," Corbette asked, his voice low and menacing as the thunder that shook the ground, "is Lucia?"

"How should I know?" Norgard snapped. "I don't have her. I never did."

His admission clawed through Kayla, sudden and deep. He had to be lying, but Drekar couldn't lie. Lucia was gone. Kayla felt blindsided, just like she had with Desi. Though she hadn't known Lucia well, she had felt a connection to the young woman. Lucia reminded her in some ways of her sister: brash, beautiful, and wild. They both lit the room. They both leaped before they looked. Kayla hadn't made the connection before, but Lucia's disappearance drove it home. Kayla had failed her as sure as she had failed Desi. Was everyone who came in contact with her doomed? She looked at the Wolf in front of her, and her eyes teared up. Hart should run now while he still had a chance.

Yeah, real logical, Nurse Friday. She shook her head. God, she was a mess.

Think, damn it! It was the eve of the equinox. She had been so certain of Norgard's guilt, she had ignored everyone else. Who had the motivation to steal the necklace and open the Gate? Who had the opportunity? She searched her memory for clues she had missed. Sleep-deprivation and terror didn't make for brilliant deductions.

Hart turned his head to look up at her, worry plain in his eyes. If Norgard didn't have the necklace or Lucia, they were already too late.

Chapter 20

Lucia was underground, that much she knew for certain. Where and when escaped her. The walls were rough-hewn and crumbled around the edges. The small alcove was carved into the wall of a larger cave. Steel bars set into the mouth imprisoned her. In the main cavern, a large, rectangular, flat-topped boulder rose from the center of the floor. From each of the four corners dangled iron manacles. She tried not to stare at it, but she couldn't seem to drag her eyes away.

The smells of damp earth and rotten eggs permeated the stale air. There must be a hot springs somewhere nearby. It was warm enough that she didn't need her wool cape, but still she wrapped it tightly around herself and shivered. Her butt was falling asleep on the stony ground. Some Kivati lady she turned out to be—when the going got rough, she fell apart. Skirt wrinkled and torn. Blond hair a tangled bird's nest. Scrapes on her manicured hands. If only the Raven Lord could see her now, he wouldn't want her.

She tried not to rock. The sulfur might mask the scent of her fear, but she couldn't let *him* see it in her body language. "What the hell, Rudrick? Let me go."

"How can I do that, princess?" Rudrick leaned against the bars, anticipation etched keenly on his face. "You are the salvation of our race. It's time to fulfill your destiny. Only a month sooner than you thought."

"What are you talking about?" And where was Johnny? He had blindfolded her on the sailboat, right after shooting poor Charlie through the heart with his crossbow. She hadn't seen him since.

"You will fulfill your duty as gatekeeper," Rudrick said, "allowing our people to recapture our rightful place on the earth. We shouldn't have to bow to humans any longer."

A small gasp escaped her lips. "But the Raven Lord—"

"Is weak."

Lucia laughed. She couldn't help it. She pictured Emory Corbette, his dark shining hair pulled back from those sharp cheekbones and high, royal forehead. Many unflattering words could be used to describe the Raven Lord—inflexible, heartless, cruel—but weak was not one of them. He might not be as tall or broad-shouldered as his Thunderbirds, but his aura took up every molecule of space. His tanned, coppery skin seemed to exude power. His dark, violet eyes were like looking at death itself. Calling him "weak" was like calling the Lady "barren."

Rudrick didn't like being laughed at. He wrapped his hands around the bars to her cell and squeezed. "Uppity little bitch. I've noticed you aren't so snotty in his presence, are you? You hate him as much as the rest of us. You can't hide it."

She didn't hate the Raven Lord; she was terrified of him.

"I'm saving you from him, princess. He would waste you. You, for whom prophesies are made. You, who have been given to us as the savior of our people." Rudrick's knuckles turned white on the bars. "He is weak. Too weak to do what is needed to defeat the Drekar. Too weak to take back our rightful place as rulers of this world. Too weak to use you as you were meant to be used."

Lucia flushed and turned her face away. Being talked about like a tool, not a person, was nothing new, but that didn't mean it hurt any less. She knew why the Raven Lord wanted to marry her. It wasn't because of *who* she was. It was because of *what* she was.

"Little Crane Wife." Rudrick's voice developed a mocking edge. "He would keep you chained to the bed, on your back for his pleasure—"

"Shut up."

"—as he ruts between your thighs and keeps you so full with child your body will die long before your little spark of a soul is ready to go. He thinks you could repopulate the Kivati, just the two of you. How can that be called anything but weak and shortsighted?"

"Shut up!" She glared at Rudrick, who only smiled knowingly. How could she defend her sovereign lord? Rudrick voiced what she had always feared in her heart. She couldn't repopulate the Kivati herself. She didn't want to. "He never said that," she mumbled.

Rudrick only raised an eyebrow. Corbette might never have said that was his plan, but everyone guessed it. Why else did he want to marry her? He might have made a match with one of the other supernatural races and joined their people together, but he didn't. He might have chosen a powerful female warrior from among the Kivati. Elinor, perhaps. Their children would certainly be the strongest and smartest of the new generation. A much better, more powerful match. But he didn't.

Instead he'd chosen a thirteen-year-old child. Untried. Without any magical power besides turning into a Crane. Not even a predator. Prey. A timid, peaceful Totem. In the past five years nothing had changed. Lucia showed no value except what that stupid unintelligible prophecy had said about her.

Rudrick's eyes turned soft and sympathetic as he watched the emotion flickering over her face. He knew. When he spoke, his voice had lost the edge of mockery. "You see. The Raven Lord is jeopardizing the future of the race. You are not the only person who realized it. I've seen the growing burden you carry, knowing you injure all of us by going along with this mad plan of his. Don't keep it to yourself any longer. I'm here to help you, sweetheart."

She bit her bottom lip. It was treason to listen to his silken words.

"You're not alone anymore. Many of us disagree with his choice. Many of us see it's time to emerge from the shadows and take back the power of the land. Corbette has sat back and watched our sacred powers wane. Fewer and fewer of our children find the power to Change at puberty. Fewer and fewer can master the wind, rain, and sun to nurture the earth as our Lady bade us. If we continue to neglect our steward duties, will She remove Her blessing entirely? If we continue to let the humans rape and pillage the land, how can She not? We have failed Her under Corbette's rule—"

"The decline started before Corbette came to power," Lucia objected, but her traitorous heart wasn't in it.

Rudrick shook his head as if disappointed in her. "But he has done nothing to reverse it, and the Lady's blessings have continued to disappear. You do Her disservice by defending him."

Lucia brushed her snarled hair back from her face and took a deep breath. No one spoke ill of the Raven Lord and lived to tell about it. She had grown up thinking all Kivati supported him. She had been raised to think of him as infallible. But what if she was wrong?

As shocking as it was to hear Rudrick speak of their lord with disrespect, deep down his words rang true. She didn't think the Raven Lord was willfully leading their people to destruction, but what could she think when all his plans seemed hinged on marrying her?

"Your people need you, Lucia. Your Lady needs you. Are you willing to help?"

She swallowed, and nodded. Her stomach turned over at the thought of the Raven Lord learning of her rebellion.

"Good choice." Rudrick smiled. He stood and unlocked the gate. "Come out and let me get you something to drink. Hot tea, perhaps?"

She nodded again. Her mouth was too dry to speak. She stood and brushed the dirt off her skirt. She tried to put some of her usual spunk into her spine. The Lady knew she'd had enough practice pretending to be brazen when all she really wanted to do was curl up in a ball and cry. She refused to be the downfall of her people.

A soft rain dampened the battlefield, washing the blood into the earth like some sacrificial offering. Slowly, the Kivati and Drekar Changed. Kayla helped collect the wounded from the battlefield. The dead were put to the flame, with a minimum of words spoken over the corpses. No one wanted wraiths to descend and possess the fallen bodies of their comrades.

The Thunderbird generals were in an uproar over the loss of one of their own. Jace hadn't survived the battle. He'd been gutted on the end of Norgard's own blade. Only the Raven Lord was able to keep Kai from killing the Drekar Regent. They needed Norgard alive, for now. The generals circled around Corbette, shutting Kayla out of their meeting. Angry voices lashed on the wind. Heightened tempers caused the clouds overhead to buckle and smash against each other, sounding like a drum circle of drunken giants.

Kayla watched Hart Change. Light collected at the ends of his fur, starting at his snout and rippling down over his body to the tip of his tail. It looked like a golden blanket that was shrugged off, revealing a very sexy, very naked man underneath.

"Hi," she said, when he lay panting on the ground.

"Hi." He pillowed his head on his hands and grinned wickedly up at her, reveling in his nudity. The slivers of rain didn't seem to bother him. They ran over his sculpted chest, trickled between the rocky muscles of his abs, and pooled in the soft hollows of his hips.

How could she still blush after all they'd done together? This intense attraction had to wear off eventually, didn't it? The sexual energy was only part of what drew her to him. He pretended not to care about anything, but he rushed into danger for her again and again. He was protective, possessive even, making her feel cherished. He didn't try to lock her away from the world, but trusted her to make her own decisions.

"What's buzzing around that beautiful brain of yours, huh?" Hart asked.

She gave a lopsided smile and turned to the urgent matter at hand. "Norgard had the necklace," she said. "I saw it around his neck before I clobbered him with the bottle."

"Johnny was in the lair too. He said he wanted to snoop around, remember?"

"You think he stole the necklace while Norgard was unconscious? What would he want with—" Suddenly the missing pieces fell into place. "Rudrick." Desi had been bringing him the necklace. He'd told Kayla to find it, and not tell anyone but him. He'd kept news of its existence from Corbette. He'd sent Johnny to sneak into the lair with Hart. He'd tried to get rid of the witnesses by locking her and Hart together on the full moon. "But why? Why would Rudrick want to open the Gate?"

"Power." Hart stood up and stretched the kinks out of his neck and back. She tried not to stare. "Rudrick has no love for the Raven Lord."

"Do you think Corbette has figured it out?"

"Who cares?"

"I do."

He rolled his eyes. "If it's important to you, then it's—"

"Werewolf!" Kai snapped from a few yards away. Grief

ravaged his face, turning handsome planes into something pained and shadow-wrought. "You trying to blind us?"

The meeting had apparently ended. Generals ordered their troops and began to evacuate the field. In the distance Corbette argued with Norgard.

"I can only hope," Hart called back. He raised his face to the falling rain and licked at the water falling in his mouth. A second later the air around him trembled and black battle clothes appeared on his body. His eyes widened in surprise. "I've gotta learn that trick," he muttered.

"You're welcome," Kai told him.

Hart gave him the bird. He turned back to Kayla as he adjusted the weapons that had also miraculously appeared on his person.

"Should we tell the Raven Lord that Rudrick is behind this?" she asked. Kivati moved around them as if they were invisible.

Hart shrugged, but turned to Kai. "Rudrick and Johnny have the necklace."

"We know," Kai said. "The deepest level of Hell has a place reserved for him, and I mean to send him there screaming."

"What's happening now?" Kayla asked.

"We've narrowed it down to five potential targets where the ceremony would be most effective: Rainier, St. Helens, Adams, Baker, and Lassen Peak. Our forces are splitting, each taking one target. We'll hunt him down."

"What about us?"

"You don't need us anymore," Hart cut in quickly. "Isn't that right?"

"Rudrick won't use the key. He's posturing. But just in case, be ready to mobilize. You need to stay here in a central location. We'll send the crows." With a shimmer of light, he turned one finger into a sharp talon, which he pointed at Hart. "Don't think of skipping out."

"We'll be ready," Kayla said. Hart grunted, but she knew

he wouldn't leave her side. His body radiated warmth, and she wanted to curl into it, away from the cold and damp.

"Good," Kai said. "May the Lady protect you." He leveled a flat stare at Hart. "And *you*. I don't like you much, werewolf, but may She protect you anyway."

"May She grant you justice," Hart told him quietly.

Kai dipped his head in acknowledgment and marched off without a backward glance. He Changed to Thunderbird mid-stride and launched into the air.

Hart stepped in front of Kayla to block the harsh wind that ricocheted through the field in the Thunderbird's wake. "Let's go," he said.

"Where?" It felt as if the rug had been pulled out from under her. The buildup and the battle had adrenaline rushing through her. They were being left behind, and it felt like giving up. She'd be anxiously waiting for the crows to come knocking this time around. She'd be ready, if the wait didn't kill her first.

He tugged on the lock of white hair, as he did when he was uncertain. "You could, ah, come home with me. There's a stocked bunker in the Underground. We'll be safe from the earthquakes. Safer, at least, than up here in the open." He glanced at her sideways, gauging her reaction.

She slid her hand into his. "Of course."

He let out a breath. "Come on then."

"How will we get there? We don't have a car."

He swore. "We'll have to ask his royal pain in the ass for a favor."

Corbette hardly gave them a second glance when they approached to ask for a lift. His face was stark, like a man facing the firing squad. He motioned for an underling to toss them a set of keys. Then he Changed. A brilliant white light shot out of the tips of his fingers and spread down his arms, engulfing his body like flame. When she could see again, a man-sized Raven hovered above the battleground, beautiful and terrible. His wings shimmered like an oil slick, while his razor-sharp beak snapped at the air. He rose into the gray sky with an army of Crow and Thunderbird at his back, and flew south toward Mount Rainier as if the hounds of hell were on his tail.

Hart and Kayla headed toward a black topless roadster parked down the hill. Grace appeared as they strolled away from the battle scene. Her hair was disheveled and a thin scrape marred one cheek. Her eyes narrowed when she saw Hart. "Thanks for the heads-up," she said with an edge of bitterness. "I thought you two would be long gone."

"Believe me," Hart said, "if I could have warned you, I would have. You made it through okay. You always do."

She seemed soothed by this. "The cat's out of the bag, thanks to Corbette. The humans won't be able to ignore this. They're probably scared shitless, but they won't have the good sense to hide. They don't know what's coming. Things are going to get ugly. I'm going to warn emergency services. Twenty bucks says they'll laugh me out on my butt."

"I'll see that and raise you a vial of dragon blood. After all the hours you've put in charming the firemen, I'd think you earned a few favors." He winked at her.

"Yeah, well, the Reaper has saved those idiots once or twice before. Payback time."

"Good luck," Kayla said, hugging the smaller woman. "May whatever deity you worship protect you."

Grace laughed. "You're getting the hang of things around here, aren't you? Take good care of this mangy mutt. He needs a keeper." She gave Hart a playful grin, though stress lined her eyes.

"I will," Kayla promised. They watched Grace mount an old motorcycle and roar off in the direction of downtown. "Why does it feel like we're always saying good-bye?" she asked Hart.

"I'm not going anywhere."

The ride back to Pioneer Square took them through Interbay and along the water. Kayla watched the skyline rise before them and wondered if it would still be there when the sun rose again. Corbette's storm had wreaked destruction from Ballard to the edges of downtown. Trees and downed power lines blocked the road, forcing Hart to drive creatively on the sidewalk and through alleys.

She let her eyes unfocus as they drove along the water. Whitecaps broke on the Sound. A stiff wind stung her cheeks. As they passed the sculpture park, her skin began to tingle. A concrete barrier rose on either side of the road. The air shimmered, stronger now as they passed beneath a bridge and approached the giant bore hole made by the new light rail tunnel.

"Lady be damned." Hart yanked the car to the side of the road and parked. "They're going to the wrong place."

"How do you know?"

"Can't you smell it? This place reeks of the Gate."

She sniffed the air and caught the faint edge of sulfur.

"Norgard had men guarding this hole. I got out of it, because I was on special assignment. He was a big financial backer for the light rail. Thought he was just looking after his investment. Should have known better."

"What's down there?"

"Downtown's built on infill. There's a lot of crap down there. Old buildings. Old burial grounds. Tunnels upon tunnels. Way down deep, legend has it, the Spider's lair." Hart looked at her and looked back at the tunnel mouth. He sighed.

"We have to tell Corbette."

"Sure." He threw the door open and climbed out.

"Then we have to go after Lucy."

"You aren't coming." Searching the skies for crows, he missed her grimace. Spotting two crows that had been trailing them from the Drekar lair, he called out to them. "Hey, birdbrains! Yeah, you. Tell his royal majesty he's going the wrong way. He's on the way to Mount Rainier. Tell him to get his royal ass over here. I'm going down."

The birds cawed, their grating voices echoing against the concrete barrier on either side.

"Get out of here!" Hart threw a rock at them, and they flew off. "Dumb birds. Now, you take the keys and go—"

She tried to rein in her temper. "And how are you going to help Lucia if she's injured? How are you going to close the Gate without my powers?" It felt funny saying that. Powers. Desi would have gotten a kick out of it.

He ran a hand through his windblown hair. "I don't want you to get hurt."

"You'll protect me."

"What if I can't? No, really Kayla." He put both hands on her shoulders and searched her face. "If anything happened to you . . ." He swallowed.

"You need me."

The ghost of a smile passed over his features. "Yeah, I do."

"You need me to help in the tunnel," she clarified.

"Fine. Can't fault me for trying. I want you safe." He released her shoulders. "But stay behind me. If I tell you to run, don't argue. Run like hell."

Hart wished for the first time that he had a silken gift with words to persuade Kayla not to follow him into the bowels of the earth. Fear ate at him. Hart had never feared death. It was why he was so reckless—and the key to his success as a mercenary. Even now, facing the very real prospect of all hell breaking loose, he didn't fear it for himself.

He feared for Kayla. He had turned his back on the Lady half a lifetime ago, but he prayed to Her now. *Please, Lady of Life, Mother of the World, please protect this small, defenseless woman.*

Fear put a target mark over his heart. He shook with vulnerability. How could anyone stand this? He wished he could go back to being an island. Alone. Independent. Accountable to no one but himself.

Then he looked at her sparkling golden-brown eyes and those generous lips smiling up at him and he was lost. He couldn't go back. Even if he didn't see the Lady Sun rise again, it would be worth it. His spirit would treasure these precious memories as he floated along the Shining Path.

"Thank you," Kayla said. She crouched behind him at the entrance to the light rail tunnel. The dark bore hole opened threateningly like a giant maw. Sulfurous gasses disbursed on the wind.

He tried once again. "It's a trap," he growled. "One way in. One way out. We'll be crushed. What would your little sister say if you threw your life away like this? Where's the logic? Where's your rational thinking? This is crazy."

Kayla ran a slender hand along his arm. His skin tingled where her cool fingers touched. He wanted to take her right here in the open, so many times that she wouldn't be able to walk. Then let her try to follow him into danger.

She covered the back of his hand and squeezed. "Desi would be the first in line. She always told me to follow my heart instead of my head. Some things are worth dying for."

He turned and grasped her upper arms with his large hands. So much bravery from someone so small. He wanted to shake her, but he just held on. "Some things are worth living for," he whispered.

Her lower lip trembled. "I trust you to keep me safe."

A strangled noise emerged from his throat. He turned back to the tunnel and closed his eyes. "Stay behind me."

He let his Wolf free from its restraints. It rubbed against his skin. The excitement of the hunt pumped in his blood. Beneath the sulfur his nose caught the smell of a recent kill. Blood and death lurked somewhere around the next bend in the tunnel. The scent aroused his wolf, and he tugged hard on the beast to keep it confined and on task. He sifted through the macabre

bouquet, searching for his targets, and found them: Fox and
Thunderbird had passed through here. A young female had left
a telltale path of some expensive perfume. It made him sneeze.
He would be able to follow it in his sleep.

"My phone is dead," Kayla whispered behind him. "Are
there ghosts about?"

Probably. He pulled the Deadglass out of his pocket and put
it to his eye. As he adjusted the gears, the thick opaque forms
of the recently departed came into view. Three men in security
guard uniforms. They gesticulated wildly and shouted something no one could hear. It looked like "No trespassing."
Rudrick's victims didn't even realize they were dead yet. Hart
took the Deadglass away from his eye and handed it to Kayla.
"Put it in your pocket for later," he told her.

The tunnel was circular and even, thanks to the boring machine. Tree roots had been ruthlessly sliced off. They poked
through the ceiling like mutilated limbs, oozing sap. Their
blood added to the malevolent feel of the tunnel. Around the
bend, just out of sight of the opening, the bodies of the three
guards lay where they had fallen. Their faces were frozen in
fear, their throats torn open. The blood soaked the ground, an
offering and a sacrifice to the Gate. Hart could feel the vibrations coming from deep beneath his feet. The earth moved as
the Gate cracked farther.

Kayla saw the bodies and gave a little cry. He helped her
over them, and moved on. He drew his sword. The light from
the entrance faded until the darkness swallowed them. The
warm, humid air embraced him. A heartbeat deep in the earth
matched itself to his. He fought to keep his senses sharp against
the urge to sleep. If it wasn't for the odor of death and sulfur,
he could almost pretend he was deep inside the Lady's womb.

After a mile, the floor sloped sharply down. The angle didn't
make sense for a light-rail line; it was too deep. Any doubts
he'd had about this tunnel leading them to the ceremony site
vanished. Norgard must have dug it for a secret purpose. The

walls became slick. Water dripped from the roof—as if the earth itself were crying. Mud climbed up their legs with a will of its own.

Hart gripped his broadsword in his right hand and used his left to feel out the tunnel wall. He was guided by scent through the blackness. The dark was his friend. Kayla stumbled behind him. She tripped over roots and divots in the floor. Sucked in every cry. He wished he could carry her, but he needed his hands free.

The pounding heartbeat grew louder the farther down they traveled. Magic thickened in the air like long forgotten cobwebs. Sparkling threads were visible when he closed his eyes. They danced over his skin, teasing the beast to come out and play. He wiped a thin layer of sweat from his brow. He reached behind him to take Kayla's hand. Her touch centered him. He could feel her strength flowing up his arm and into his chest. It calmed his racing heart until he could breathe easily again.

Soon they came to the giant drill. It lay abandoned on its side like a beached whale of some machine-aged future. The rotating heads were silent now, but their razor edges seemed coiled to strike. Hart hesitated to touch it. It appeared to block the entire tunnel, but he could feel a light current of air from somewhere to the right. He let the Wolf tease the air and follow the faint scents of his prey across the tunnel to a narrow slit between the bore and the tunnel wall.

"Let me go first and scout it," he said. "If I don't come back, I want you to know—"

She covered his mouth with her small fingers. They smelled of earth from where she had reached out to steady herself against the dirt wall. "Don't jinx us. You're coming back."

He thought of how far she'd come. Three days ago, she'd refused to believe in supernatural creatures she'd seen with her own eyes. Now, she didn't dare risk naming her fears aloud in case some malevolent spirit heard and made them come true. She really did learn quickly.

He wondered if he had changed as noticeably to outsiders. From enslaved to free. From solitary to part of something greater than himself. Did she realize how much she had changed him?

He kissed her fingers and turned away, folding in on himself to slip between the metal teeth and the packed dirt of the tunnel wall. He led with the broadsword, not that there was room to maneuver, but he hoped he would have a brief moment to skewer anything that tried to get in his way. His back cramped, but he pushed on. The smell of magic was even stronger here. Finally he slipped free.

His eyes adjusted to his surroundings. Lady be *damned*.

Chapter 21

Rudrick let Lucia out of the small prison and into the larger cavern. It was older than she'd first thought, though the ceiling lacked roots and the usual debris one expected from an old cave. It was a perfect circle with a vast domed ceiling. Far above, a forest of stalagmites hung threateningly, the pointed tips poised to skewer unsuspecting victims on the floor below. They glittered in the torchlight like tiny stars. Not rock then, but diamonds. She wondered why no one had mined this place. The dragons, in particular, should have been drawn to the forest of priceless jewels like bees to honey. Especially given the sulfur and deep-earth vents that must be nearby.

"Where are we?" she asked.

Rudrick's eyes shifted to her and away, and she wondered if he was going to tell her the truth. "Deep underground," he said, finally.

She scowled at his non-answer. "No! Reee-ally?"

"The princess has recovered her irascible charm," he said. "Good. You'll need it."

Great. She stuck her chin out instead of letting him see her shiver. "We're in a cave, underground. Where is the cave? Are we still in Washington?"

"Can't you feel it?"

She opened her mouth, but closed it when she noticed the slight vibration beneath her feet. When she closed her eyes, the darkness sparkled with a million tiny phosphorescent lights. If she had been better at her studies, she might have noticed the connection sooner. Aether clotted the air. They must be standing at a node where the strands of power that wove around and through the earth connected. She opened her eyes again and took another look at the cave walls. Except for the stalagmites above, they were smooth as an eggshell—not a natural occurrence, nor made with rough human tools. Only an Earth mage could have shifted this much dirt and left behind these glossy walls.

Rudrick led her to the other side of the cave where he'd left a backpack and a few boxes. He took out a water bottle full of yellow liquid and handed it to her. "Here, drink."

"What is it?" She still wasn't sure if she could trust him.

"Orange juice. Finish it. You'll need all your strength."

She swallowed some and immediately felt better. Her stomach grumbled. She didn't know what time it was, or when she'd eaten last. Rudrick pulled a small takeout bag from one of the boxes and handed it to her. She opened it and found chicken chow mein and three vegetarian egg rolls. "My favorite."

"I know." When she glanced up at Rudrick, he looked away. It seemed suspicious that he had discovered her favorite food and brought it to her. Was it a sort of apology for kidnapping her? She dismissed the thought as paranoia and dug in, famished.

"What's the plan?" she asked between bites. "The Gate must be strong through here. Are you planning to do something to it?"

"Not too witless after all." Rudrick smiled and reached out to tuck a strand of blond hair behind her ear. She tried not to recoil. "You're beautiful, princess. Who can blame you for leading Corbette astray?"

Lucia swallowed. "You think it's my fault?"

"Many powerful men before him have been distracted from their duty by a woman's wiles. You can't help it, can you?" He removed the to-go bag from her nerveless fingers and set it on the cave floor. He opened another box and took out a sleeveless white robe and a sash striped in the four sacred colors—white, green, red, and black—which he handed to her. "Put this on."

"Why?"

"You said you wished to help your people. Put it on."

"Turn around."

He smiled slightly, but did as asked. Lucia shrugged off her jacket and slipped out of her skirt.

"Nothing but the robe," Rudrick said.

She glared at his back, but took off her panties and bra before tugging the robe over her head and belting it with the sash. It fell to mid-thigh. The low V-neck showed the tops of her breasts. "You can turn around now."

He did, and she shifted uncomfortably under his too-close appraisal. This was Rudrick, she reminded herself, one of Corbette's sentinels. He was Kivati. Even if he opposed the Raven Lord, he still had the Lady's honor. Didn't he?

His smile this time showed all his sharp teeth.

"I changed my mind," she said quickly. She tried to cover herself with her jacket. "I don't want to wear this. I don't—"

"Princess, how can you abandon your people in their hour of need? Look at you. You don't have any powers. You've failed or barely passed the basic tests in all the five powers. Your instructors report you're not particularly bright or clever. You show no talent at weaponry or combat."

"I do all right at healing and herbal lore—"

"But nothing to distinguish you from your fellow students."

His words flew like arrows. The poison tips lodged deep in the secret crevices of her heart, piercing her fears with their malice. With their truth. It was as if he'd reached into her mind and snatched her worries, waving them in the air for all to see.

She was useless. She was worthless. If she was the cornerstone of her people's future, they were doomed.

Why hadn't the Raven Lord seen her for the failure she was? Why had he gone on with this mad plan to make her the queen of his people, when anyone could see she wasn't worthy of the position?

Rudrick pulled the jacket away. "Your body is your only power."

"But you said—"

"Corbette's judgment might be clouded by lust, but his general idea was correct. What else do you have that could be of use to the Kivati? Your body is what will save our people. The Raven Lord was wrong in how to use it."

Lucia wanted to cover her ears. She took a step back toward the center of the room. Rudrick took a step forward. The nervous twisting in her stomach was growing more pronounced. The few bites of food she had eaten wanted to rebel.

She took another step back, and Rudrick advanced.

"Your people need you," he said again. "Corbette refused to read the prophecy as it was meant, because he wanted to keep you selfishly for his own use. The Lady has greater plans for you. She gave you to all the Kivati, not one man. Corbette didn't have the balls to do what is necessary."

Lucia didn't like the fervor she saw in Rudrick's eyes. She didn't like the direction of his thoughts. "And what is necessary?"

Her backward progress was halted when she ran into the stone table. It bit into the back of her legs. Too late, she realized that Rudrick had herded her to this spot. He crowded her with his body. His leg pressed between hers. Lucia reached her hands behind her, searching frantically for something to use as a weapon. A stone. A torch. Anything.

Rudrick's eyes glowed. "You will open the Gate—"

"No!"

"—and I will call upon our ancestors to set things right. The army of souls will sweep over the earth, ridding us of the Drekar and tainted humans. The Lady cleansed the earth once before in the Great Flood. It's long past time to do it again."

"Shouldn't the Lady decide such a thing?" He couldn't open the Gates. It was madness. She might agree that the Raven Lord was wrong to marry her, but she knew Rudrick wasn't right about the Gates. Her hands were clammy. Her skin itched with the need to Change and fly out of here, but she'd never been so great at Changing when she wanted to. The tranquil state required was beyond her.

"The Lady has always selected tools to do Her bidding. I am Her servant. You and I are Her instruments. Why do you think She put us together? Why do you think She distracted Corbette and allowed Johnny to bring you here? She knows what needs to be done and blessed us." Rudrick reached forward on either side of her, pressing her back against the altar with his body. She tried to squirm away, but he was too strong.

Too late she felt the cold bands of metal at her wrists. Too late she heard the sickening catch of the lock shackling her to the stone altar.

Rudrick stood back and smiled. "The Kivati will name you Salvation, Deliverer of the People. Don't cry. It's an honor to walk in our Lady's footsteps. Just as She did long ago, now you too will sacrifice your body so that your people may live."

Kayla felt the dark and the earth pressing in on her until she thought she might suffocate. She hadn't thought she was claustrophobic, but with a ton of dirt above her and only a thin, stuffy airflow to breathe, she was hard-pressed to keep from panicking. If the tunnel collapsed . . .

She tried to remind herself that something much worse was about to happen if she didn't hurry. The seconds stretched out. She wanted to call out through the narrow passage to make sure Hart was still there, except she didn't want to alert anyone else

who might be listening. Her pulse pounded in her ears, growing loud in the muffled silence until it felt like the whole
tunnel throbbed with the beat of her heart. She had thought life
in the ER was as fast-paced and high-stress as it got. She had
been wrong. How did Hart deal with this much adrenaline on
a regular basis?

Finally a shape blacker than the darkness detached itself
from the drill. He came to her and wrapped her in his warm
embrace.

"What's that for?" she whispered.

He squeezed lightly and let her go. He tilted her chin up as
if he could make out her features in the dark. "Do I need a
reason?" He bent and pressed his lips to hers. The kiss tasted
warm and desperate. Something had scared him. "Come on.
Keep your knife ready. Don't make any sudden movements.
Don't call her attention."

Whose attention? she wondered, but she knew better than to
ask. She followed Hart through the narrow gap into a wider,
older tunnel. Unlike the perfectly round bore hole, this tunnel
was flatter and highly irregular. Boulders jutted out from the
walls and floors. At first she was glad at the increase in light,
until she saw where it came from. The tunnel was awash in
sparkling spider silk, beautiful and gruesome. It hung in
curtains across the ceiling and down the walls. Objects the size
of cows were suspended from the roof, cocooned in a glittering
shroud. A few of the mummified bundles held smaller, human
shapes. She shuddered and stepped closer to Hart.

"Don't say her name," he whispered. "Don't even think it.
Try not to touch anything."

He led her through the tangled webs. The air was thick
with the cloying sweet smell she was beginning to associate
with magic. Someone had been through here before, ripping
a path for them to follow. Bends and dips shaped the tunnel
with no rhyme or reason. She couldn't keep the cobwebs out
of her eyes. The spider silk stuck to her hands and body,

coated her hair, drifted in every breath she took. It melted on her tongue like spun sugar, but left a bitter aftertaste. Her eyelids grew heavy.

She felt someone tugging her hand, and realized she had fallen asleep for a moment. Warmth and twilight surrounded her, soft and soothing. "Want to rest," she sighed.

"Not yet," Hart growled. "Just a few more steps. We're almost there." He pulled her away from the sticky boulder where she had rested her head. She stumbled into his arms. He set aside his sword and rubbed the webbing off her face, wiping his hands on his filthy pants. He took a small flask of water out of his pocket and a clean cloth, wet the cloth and wiped her eyes with it.

Her mind cleared. "God. What is that stuff?"

"We're in the lair of the Spider Woman. Her webs hold the world together and keep out the Birds of Torment. She is the dreamer of dreams, the future seeker, the king killer."

Kayla bit the inside of her cheek. She didn't want to meet the monster that had created this place. The tunnel ended around the next bend. Four archways were set in the wall, each framed by a totem pole. Kayla recognized some of the carvings: Thunderbird, Raven, Crow, the Watchmen, Killer Whale, Bear. It looked as if there was one for each of the first Animal People. A stripe of paint adorned the top of each doorway: red, white, green, and black.

Hart dropped to his knees in front of the wall. He lifted his nose in the air and scented through each doorway. His shoulders tensed in frustration. Finally he lay his sword down before him like the needle of a compass. "Lady, I know I am unworthy, but if it be Your will, please show us the way."

It was the first time Kayla had ever heard him pray. His derisive tone was gone, replaced by urgency and something close to pleading.

A scream ripped the air. High and undoubtedly female, it

vibrated with shock and betrayal. Kayla's heart lurched like a fish on a hook.

"West," Hart said, turning to the black arch. He grabbed his sword and jumped to his feet.

"Wait." She drew out the small curved knife Hart had given her and stuck it point down in the packed earth beneath the black arch, marking the way. If Corbette and his men made it this far, the knife would tell them which passage to take.

"Come on." Hart stepped through the arch. The ceiling was only a little taller than his head, and he would be able to touch either wall if he stretched out both hands. He started running. She followed as quickly as she could. The scream still echoed in her ears, sending icy phantom claws skittering over her limbs. The tunnel turned sharply. Light flickered on the wall, reflected from something in the passage ahead. It smelled like rotten eggs.

Another scream filled the tunnel, weaker this time, pain and heartbreak evident in the sobs that echoed in the tight space. The floor lurched up to greet them a moment later, as an earthquake shook the ground. The walls buckled. Dirt rained from the ceiling. Hart grabbed her hand. He pulled her down the tunnel and around the bend.

They flew out of the narrow passage and into an airy domed cave. Torchlight illuminated pillars of stone around the edges. The earthquake rumbled through the underground cavern, loud and low like a steam train, tossing the stone pillars as if they were nothing more than matchsticks in a box. A boulder jostled free from the ceiling and dropped. Kayla ducked right, and it slammed through the space where a moment ago her head had been. Hart grabbed her hand and pulled her down into a protected alcove, shielding her with his strong arms, a bit too tightly.

She peeked out between his muscular forearms.

An altar sat at the center of the room. Lucia was strapped to the top in a spread-eagle fashion. Her long straight hair fell over

the side like a waterfall of gold. The white robe she wore was
parted at the waist to expose her lower half. A thick stream of
blood dripped from her wrists into a stone trough around the
edge of the altar.

They were too late.

Kayla covered her mouth. Hart's arms tightened around her.

A man stood at Lucia's feet. Rudrick, the Fox, dressed in a
flowing white tunic and pants, the white now speckled red,
marked like Cain with a symbol of his betrayal. He faced them,
but was too caught up in the ritual to have noticed their entrance. The roar of the earth and falling rocks hid their
presence. The altar stone slanted downward, directing the
blood in the trough to pool in a long thin basin in front of
Rudrick. He raised the jade necklace in his right hand. Its
sharp edge glittered like a knife in the torchlight. He flicked
it and droplets of blood flew from the tip. He was chanting, but
the words were indecipherable over the roar of the earth.

"We have to stop him!" Kayla shouted, but already she
could see a thickening of the air above the stone basin.

Rudrick reached over the girl's prone form and sliced the
inside of her right thigh. She cried out. Lucia was alive! Kayla
swallowed her choked sob. The rise and fall of Lucia's chest
was shallow and uneven. She was weak with blood loss. They
had interrupted the human sacrifice part of the ritual.

Rudrick still hadn't noticed them. He raised the necklace-
knife again and flicked blood at the condensing air. The blood
hit it and was absorbed. A shimmering curtain of Aether drew
up from the blood-slicked stone, like a sheet of bubble liquid
drawn from a vat of soapy water. Swirls of light danced over
it. Who knew the Gate would be so beautiful? Kayla had
imagined something gruesome, a rotting shroud holding back
the Dead. The Gate spread up and out, stretching to the shaking ceiling and crumbling walls. Falling rocks encountered its
glittering edge and were sliced in two.

She didn't need her gifted sight to see the terror that lurked

behind that filmy screen. The translucent curtain bulged as
claws and tentacles pressed on it. Dead faces leered at her.
Dead hands scratched, trying to dig their way to freedom.

Was Desi one of them? Was her sister there, just out of
reach, or was her soul free to pass into the land beyond?

The altar stood between them and the Gate. She pointed to
Lucia and yelled—over the roar of the earthquake—in Hart's
ear. "We have to rescue her."

He shook his head and yelled back, something that sounded
like "Too late."

Kayla refused to take no for an answer. She struggled
against his embrace, trying to break free like those damned
souls. He set his jaw—hesitant to leave Kayla unprotected—
but she gave him a push.

Relenting, he dodged out and sprinted across the open floor.
The Gate was so thick that Rudrick—trapped on the other
side—was obscured. Hart snapped the chains that held Lucia
to the altar, lifted her carefully, and shielded her with his body.
He dodged falling debris to return to their alcove, and laid
Lucia gently on the ground with her head cushioned in Kayla's
lap. Sweat beaded on his brow with the effort to hold back his
Wolf around so much blood. He crouched, blocking them from
the Gate with his body.

Kayla quickly checked Lucia's vitals. Her skin was white
and clammy. Her lips were almost blue. Deep black gashes
marred each wrist. The blood flowed down her limp hands and
stained the virgin white of her gown. She whimpered. Shadows
flickered behind her closed eyelids. Her hands and feet were
icy as her body pulled blood away from the extremities to
power her weakly beating heart.

"I need something to staunch it," Kayla yelled over the
rumble.

Hart pulled something from her hair and shoulders. "Use
this." It was the spider silk. The thick webs clung to her fin-

gers as she took the handful from him. Strong, stretchy and absorbent, it was nature's perfect gauze.

"But what about the magic? The sleepiness? Is it safe?"

"It'll ease her pain."

Kayla didn't have anything to clean the wound. She twisted the spider silk together in a long rope and wrapped it around the girl's wrists. It took five wraps before the blood stopped soaking through. She used every piece she had, pulling it off Hart's back and shoulders as well as her own.

"I'll get more." Hart stood and, keeping to the walls, crept back to the mouth of the tunnel where they had entered the underground cavern.

Kayla thought he left partly to give Lucia some privacy. She swallowed and reached down to part the robe again.

"No!" Lucia muttered. Her head thrashed back and forth. Her hands clenched weakly at her sides.

"You're safe. You're safe. No one is going to hurt you anymore. It's me, Kayla. I'm a nurse. Please let me help you." Kayla repeated calming words, reiterating that Lucia was safe even as the Gate bulged outward twenty feet away. There were worse things than death, she thought. Worse monsters than the ghosts that haunted the living.

Carefully, she pulled back the blood-soaked robe, hoping desperately that Rudrick hadn't completed the Sacred Marriage part of the ritual. The flecks of blood and semen between the poor girl's legs crushed that hope. Rudrick had cut the femoral arteries in each thigh. Kayla pressed the robe against the freely bleeding gashes and held them tightly while she waited for Hart to return. She murmured soothing words. Lucia was losing far too much blood. Even if the spider silk succeeded in staunching the bleeding, the injuries to Lucia's fragile spirit might still kill her. Sometimes, even if the body was whole, a soul gave up interest in living. She'd seen it in the ER.

Kayla closed her eyes and shut out the noise from the earthquake. She banished her fear of the opening Gate. Behind her eyelids the world sparkled with a million threads of gold. Either they were stronger in this place of old magic, or she had shed the last of her self-made blinders and embraced the power that surrounded her.

The sparkling light of Lucia's soul pulsed dimly. It was no longer whole. Cracks rent the ethereal substance, as if claws had torn it apart. The pieces beat with great effort, slowly, erratically, as the body fought to pump too little blood.

The gashes on her wrists and thighs were black in Kayla's gifted sight, as if some malevolent substance had taken residence in her wounds and now sought to penetrate the body. Viscous, like molasses, it crept up Lucia's arms. The soul-light fragments cringed away from it. Kayla tried not to shake in horror. She didn't want Lucia to sense that anything was amiss. The poor girl needed every scrap of hope she had left.

Chapter 22

Nose full of the scent of blood, Hart stumbled at the entrance to the narrow tunnel. He hung on to his human self by a single claw, knowing if the beast took over they were all lost. How could one small body hold so much blood? He had known what to expect. He knew the ceremony of the old Babylonian kings to restore the Gate involved sacrificing a ram and a ritual mating of the goddess Ishtar and the king, but seeing it was something else. He'd thought he was immune to violence. He'd been wrong. Seeing that poor girl strapped down with her virgin blood staining her pale white thighs made the bile erupt from his gut and tore at his not-so-sensitive self-control. How could Rudrick justify it? How could the Lady allow it to happen?

The Wolf usually rose at blood, wanting to dive into the fresh kill himself, but not this time. This time the Wolf wanted to hunt the bastard who had ravaged the poor pup and strip his skin from his muscle slice by slice.

Hart felt blind without his sense of smell to guide him. The ground rolled beneath his feet. Steadying himself against the tunnel wall, he ran through the dark passage toward the Spider. The Wolf whined. It knew they'd been lucky to make it through

her webs the first time. Would the earthquake be enough to
distract the Spider a second time?

He passed through the doorway into the Totem Hall and
arrived at the beginning of the webbed walls. The spider silk
was strong enough to keep the walls from crumbling. It
dampened the roar of the earthquake. The air whistled and
moaned through the dark webs like the cries of the dead.

No, it was only his imagination. He couldn't get the sight of
the bulging Gate out of his head. He bent to tear spider silk off
a rock. Years of webbing had accumulated into great tufts that
whispered seductively to him.

Sleep, it said. *Rest a moment.*

He fought it off and gathered until he couldn't carry any
more. He prayed to the Lady that the Spider wouldn't feel his
vibrations wherever she hid in her secret lair. She had predicted
the Crane would usher in a terrifying new future, but holy shit.
She should have been clearer, because Corbette and his cronies
had been way off. Where had they gotten the bright idea that
the girl would be a spiritual leader of her people? That was true
only if you counted leading a shit-ton of spirits through the
Gate into the living world.

The wailing grew in volume. Hart stood up and peered
through the dimness. He thought he saw shadows flailing
past the veils of web. A moment later, the tip of a sword
sliced through the sticky strands. A magic blade, he realized.
The bearer came next, his black greatcoat covered in a white
film, purple eyes blazing in the dim light of the cave. The
Raven Lord cut a swath through the tangled webs with the
sword he had removed from his silver-knobbed cane.

Hart closed his eyes and could see the Aether swirling
around the cane and its master, severing the matter that crossed
its path. He had to moisten his parched lips before he could get
the words out. "Lucia. Help."

Corbette didn't seem to notice the ground rolling beneath

his feet. The air sizzled with his anger. The Wolf inside Hart cringed.

"Lead the way," Corbette demanded. He didn't raise his voice, but it rolled on the Aether directly into Hart's ear.

A handful of Corbette's men climbed through the webs behind him. A moment later a burst of fire incinerated a large hole through the spider veils, and Norgard stepped through. Unlike the others, no silk stuck to his skin or clothes. His blond hair was perfectly coiffed. He smiled toothily. "Where is that bastard Fox? I'm going to tear out his entrails and feed them to him."

Hart turned and led the way back through the crumbling tunnels. *Lady, please let them not be too late.*

He knew in his gut that they already were.

The Spider attacked before the small troop was safely through her lair. Her swollen abdomen blocked half the tunnel, and her spindly, razor-sharp legs were each taller than a man. Serrated and dripping with venom, her pincers were the stuff of nightmares.

Hart ran, Corbette at his heels, as screams filled the silken tomb. He had a brief glimpse of rock falling in front of Corbette's men, blocking them off from following, and of Norgard partially Turning to fend off the Spider's poisoned jaws.

Hart realized he had expected the Raven Lord to fix it. All that power had to be good for something. *Alpha*, his Wolf whined. *Protection. Safety.* But even a half-mad Wolf could tell Corbette was off his game in a big way. It was a shock; he didn't much like Corbette, but he'd counted on the Kivati leader to be a rock.

Hart hoped Kayla pulled another surprise out of her sleeve, because he was all out of tricks. He wasn't going down without a fight.

* * *

Helpless was not a word familiar to Emory Corbette, but it summed up the sour feeling churning his gut. He could do nothing for his men, trapped on the other side of the Spider's lair. Norgard could take care of himself.

Aether poured through the tunnel, a Sparkling Path guiding Corbette's footsteps to the other world. His anger shot out in short bursts, frying the spider silk that brushed against him. Deep inside, ice encased his heart. A frozen cube of sorrow and pain, trapped forever in a cage of guilt.

His deepest fears had been realized. All his plans, his ambition to bring his people into a new Gilded Age, were for naught. Even his slug of a father hadn't screwed up this royally. The Gate crashing down around his ears. The souls of the damned free to walk the earth on his watch. His fiancée slaughtered under his very nose.

If only he had paid closer attention to dissent and whispers of broken protocol. If only he had taken decisive action to halt the digging of this tunnel into the forgotten lair of the Spider Woman. If only he had come here first instead of tearing off after a white rabbit down a false rabbit hole. If only . . .

He burst through the narrow arch into the Sacred Cave. A wave of sulfur and twisted rage engulfed him. The Gate had solidified and thinned, so that only a faint smear of Aether separated the two worlds. A storm of unholy spirits brewed on the far side, pushing and clawing and battering against the Aether to break free. Their wrath had already passed through. It thickened the air of the cave with malevolence and hate. Demons—their solid black shadows distinguishable from the iridescent wraiths—waited with weapons ready. Scorpion men, storm demons, manticore, harpy, and the rest of Kingu's banished horde.

Behind them, Kingu himself rose up. Twice as big as any dragon and thrice as twisted. Steam curdled from between his steely jaws. Hellfire burned in his eye sockets.

Corbette turned away. He let the heavy mantle of the

Raven Lord slip from his weary shoulders and fall, tattered and soiled, to the quaking ground. All that was left was a heartbroken man to follow the trail of blood.

He found her in an alcove in the cave wall.

Oh, Lucia! The world faded. The light narrowed. His eyes only saw the poor mangled form of the girl who might have been his future. Her blond hair flowed like a river of gold over the crumbled earth. Her skin was pale as alabaster, her white gown smeared with blood. She lay unmoving on her back, her bandaged hands crossed over her bosom.

A cry broke from his constricted throat. A terrible sound saturated with a lifetime worth of grief and regret. He fell to his knees by her side. Lights flashed in the corners of his vision. He saw only her still form and knew that he had failed.

"Get him off her!" Kayla shouted to Hart. The Raven Lord was like a man possessed, his mind encased in dense spider silk, unreachable. She needed him to release her patient.

Hart pulled him back. Corbette's eyes were points of violet fire. She was afraid to touch him in case he turned that dangerous gaze in her direction. She gathered the webbing Hart had collected and dressed Lucia's remaining wounds. The blood was staunching nicely. The girl wouldn't bleed out. Unfortunately, her spiritual wounds weren't so easily patched up.

"Use him," Hart yelled, jerking his thumb at Corbette. "He can manipulate the Aether."

"What?" She wrinkled her nose.

"The Aether is connected to the sparkling light of her soul."

Kayla took a deep breath. She tried to sift through the snippets she had heard over the last few days about Aether and souls, but it was so convoluted. She didn't have time to study the problem or find answers to her questions. She had to rely on instinct to show her the way. But what if something went wrong? What if she made the problem worse? She wasn't

trained in paranormal healing. She hadn't even believed in the
supernatural until a few days ago. Doubt made her hands shake
until she stuck them under her armpits and clamped down.

Hart gave her a crooked smile. He believed in her. She'd
managed to earn his trust and his admiration. She'd helped him
during the moon madness. Could she do the same with Lucia?
She didn't have a strong emotional tie to Lucia, except perhaps
guilt that she hadn't been able to stop what had happened in
time. But Corbette did.

"Rouse him," she yelled.

Hart picked up the thin silver-knobbed sword and smacked
the flat end across Corbette's shoulder blades. Corbette released
the air in his lungs with a *whoosh*.

"Wanted to do that for a long time," Hart said. He lifted the
sword to do it again, but Corbette raised his hand and clenched
it into a fist. A wave of sparkling air rushed out of nothing to
surround the sword and snatch it from Hart. The sword floated
down to Corbette's now upturned fist.

"Enough," the Raven Lord snarled.

"Lucia needs your help," Kayla said. "Physically, she'll
live. But inside she's a mess. I need you to concentrate on your
feelings for her. Affection, respect, love. Anything positive.
Picture her in your mind at her healthiest and happiest. Focus
on who she is, on her best qualities, on her essence of self. Can
you do that?"

Corbette nodded roughly. A vein throbbed at his temple.

Kayla pulled down the top of Lucia's gown, careful not to
expose her breasts. Corbette growled, but she ignored him. She
picked up his hands and placed them on Lucia's pale chest
above her heart. Corbette broke out in a fine sweat.

"You too, Hart," Kayla ordered. "Put your arms around me.
Envision yourself sharing your strength with me."

With Hart's strength at her back, she put her hands over
Corbette's and closed her eyes. Immediately, light blinded her.
Her first impression was prisms floating in the air, casting

rainbows on everything they touched. The light was fluid. It spread across the universe in an infinitely more brilliant Milky Way. She understood, in a flash of clarity, that this was the Aether. It was the fabric of the universe, weaving through everything: the molecules of air and earth, light and sound, gravity and force. It was matter. It was energy. It pulsed to the beat of a phantom heart, ticking through the very fabric of time.

Was this the way Corbette saw the Aether? A sense of wonder stole her breath away. She wanted to let her consciousness drift into the sparkling light, to lose herself in its warm embrace. She wanted to let the rainbows cocoon her, to be rocked to sleep to the sound of the heaven's heartbeat.

The rainbows thinned near the Gate, revealing a darkness that lurked behind. The clustering stars shied away from it. She had to heal Lucia before that darkness broke through. If she could pour enough Aether into her, it would overwhelm the shadows. Beneath her hands she felt the Aether gather. It felt like a fizzing liquid, bathing her arms to the elbows. She imagined herself pulling at that liquid and pouring it down through her fingers, through Corbette's hands and into the chest of her patient. A waterfall of shimmering light to buoy Lucia's own broken soul.

A tingling sensation began where Hart's hands wrapped around her forearms and flowed down her bones. Corbette chanted under his breath. She breathed deeply, letting the Aether fill her lungs. As she exhaled, she pushed. The sparkling water emptied into Lucia's body in a flash of heat like a supernatural defibrillator. Lucia's chest jerked up off the ground. Her eyelids flew open, so wide the whites showed. She opened her mouth in a silent scream. A wave of light poured from her lips. She gasped. Coughed. Breathed.

"We did it," Kayla said. The shadows inside the poor girl's body had fled.

Corbette scooped Lucia up in his trembling arms. He buried

his head in her soft golden hair. "Oh, Lady," he mumbled. "I thought I'd lost you."

Exhausted, Kayla sat back into the circle of Hart's arms. She felt safe there, even if the ground still shook beneath her and the Gate stretched to breaking a few feet away.

"You did good," Hart whispered in her ear. "Real good."

Norgard appeared. He strode around a pillar and into the alcove, looking decidedly worse for wear. Dirt and spider silk covered his head and shoulders, and his clothes hung in tatters. "What the bloody hell is going on here? Corbette, get off your ass and help me. The Gate is breaking, and that idiot hasn't laid any spells to leash the demon!"

Corbette blinked up at him. It was an odd sight: the powerful Raven Lord sitting on the dirty ground with cobwebs in his hair and a smear of blood on his cheek. His steely command had abandoned him. He was helpless to do anything but clutch Lucia to his chest.

"Ye gods, man!" Norgard looked helplessly between Kayla and Hart. "What did you do to him?"

"A sacrifice opened the Gate," Kayla said. "Maybe a sacrifice is what it takes to close it?"

"Good thought." Norgard pointed at Lucia. "Let's throw them the blonde."

"No." Corbette bounded to his feet with the girl held protectively in his arms. Electricity crackled from his skin. Everyone took a step back. Eddies of Aether swirled around him. The sparkling lights caught on the spider silk wrapped around Lucia's wounds. Her wrists, thighs, and chest were bathed in a soft glow.

Kayla dragged her eyes away and turned to Norgard. He stood tall and haughty, a king who hadn't yet realized his kingdom was lost. She shouldn't be surprised by his coldness, not after all he'd done. But she couldn't help wondering, yet again, what her sister had seen in such a monster. He had to have some redeeming qualities, didn't he?

"Hasn't Lucia been through enough?" she asked.

"Exactly. Sacrifice the weak so that the strong may live." Norgard looked at each of their shocked faces and landed on Hart's. "What's wrong with you, mad dog? You've always been detached, able to get the job done no matter the cost. This shouldn't be a difficult decision. This makes the most logical sense!"

Hart shook his head. His hand tightened on Kayla's arm. "I'm free now. Free to make my own choices. Free to do what's right—"

The next moment the air shattered. The earth split open down the center of the cavern, breaking the stone altar in two. A crevasse opened. A river of light and shadow poured out. Inside the river floated an army of screaming souls. The river rushed along the cavern wall, spinning around the room in a circle, trapping Kayla and the others in the center of a giant turbine.

A wild drumbeat pulsed in the rocks and air. The pounding took over her breath and seemed to anchor in the rhythm of her blood. A terrible wave of power rolled through the cave, knocking everything to the ground. Hart fell on top of her, protecting her with his body. She clung to him as the floor undulated violently beneath her.

Fear broke along her skin. The wall of the alcove crumbled and fell as the river of souls carved into the sides of the cavern. Around and round the river flowed, gnawing into the rock walls like a demonic merry-go-round. Kayla watched the stalagmite spears overhead break off and fall toward them as if in slow motion. She clutched Hart and cried out.

If only she could protect him. But there was nowhere to go. If it hadn't been for her, he would be far away from here. He would be in Canada by now, safe. It was her fault he had stayed.

The stalagmite dropped straight over Hart's back. Midway it froze, suspended in the air. She watched, horrified, as the rock shattered and disintegrated into dust. The molecules of earth and air were sucked into the vortex of spinning souls. The raging river picked up speed, pulling rocks and pillars out of the ground into a giant tornado of spinning matter. So many souls were packed together that they were only a blur. Horrific shapes solidified and were gone. Men with the tails of scorpions. Half-lion, half-bird creatures with human faces. Dragons and clawed beasts too hideous to imagine.

The drumbeat rose. The twister spun around them and shot higher. Its hungry maw consumed the roof of the cavern and began to eat through the layers of dirt and rubble below the city streets. Its terrible force radiated outward and upward, destroying the cave around it.

In the center, where they lay, the air was still. Quiet even.

Kayla moved beyond fear. All the worries of the past melted away. All the loneliness and guilt separated like atoms in a centrifuge and dissipated into the swirling light. She wrapped her arms around Hart and held on. If the tornado picked him up, she wanted to go too. Maybe if she held on tightly enough, the shattered world would fling them together into the great unknown.

Chapter 23

The eye of the storm was a circle about ten feet across. The deep crevasse cut across one edge. Soul-soaked light poured out of it to join the whirling vortex. Hart pushed himself off the trembling ground and helped Kayla stand up. She burrowed into his chest. He wrapped his arms around her.

Fear had always been a foreign emotion, but now it dug its claws in deep. He had come to protect Kayla. He had failed. How could he save her from this swirling prison?

Our Lady, he prayed in his head. *I've never asked you for much. I know I haven't lived according to your laws or kept the sacred vows. But, please . . . please save Kayla. Please let her live through this. I don't want anything for myself. Just . . . save this woman.* He closed his eyes and kissed the top of her head. She smelled of lilac, even covered in dirt and spider silk. If it came down to the wire, and there was no other option, he would sacrifice himself to the crevasse for the chance to save her.

He opened his eyes and examined the wall of swirling Aether. Could he cross it?

"Don't touch it. You'll get sucked in." Corbette's voice rasped. The Aether bathed his face in an unholy glow. Shadows flickered over his angular features. He didn't look like the feared Kivati leader anymore. Something had broken in him.

Hart tried not to feel disappointed. He'd never depended on the Raven Lord before; why should he now?

"This is magnificent," Norgard said, inspecting the giant funnel. "But where is Rudrick? Who is controlling this glorious machine?"

Rudrick had disappeared when the Gate opened. Either he was trapped on the other side of the swirling vortex, or he had been sucked into the great river itself, just another string of molecules powering the twister of souls.

Hart looked up and watched the twister bore through the ceiling of the cave. It ate through centuries of debris like a giant drill. The Aether sucked in the grave dirt and bones of his ancestors that lay beneath the city streets, and grew stronger from their magic. Soon, the concrete foundations of buildings could be seen overhead. Broken pipes and rebar were exposed one moment and disappeared the next into the rapacious funnel.

The tornado broke out into the open sky and shot upward to join the churning storm clouds above. It had eaten sideways into the cave walls, removing enough earth around and above them that they no longer stood underground. Lightning crashed around the funnel. Hart could see through the thick Aether walls onto a scene of destruction. The earthquakes had left a city in ruins. Once-tall skyscrapers had crumbled into the sea. Jagged asphalt lay over crushed cars. Gas leaked from broken streetlights, and water gushed from burst mains. Bridges had collapsed in pieces like discarded Tinkertoys. Fire lit the skyline, destroying what was left of a once-great city. The air was hazy with smoke and particulate matter.

Hart hurriedly searched the southern horizon. A cloud of thick black ash obscured Mount Rainier.

"What happened?" Kayla asked in a whisper. She trembled in his arms.

He wanted to lie. "We fell into a burning ring of fire," he whispered. "Down, down, down . . ." His voice broke.

"The mountains . . . you said they would erupt."

He could only nod. Every active volcano on the planet would have lost its top.

In the cavern, Norgard hadn't seemed worried, but now in the burning light of the open air he lost his cool. The blood drained from his face. His eyes dulled to hollow pits. Horrified, he took in the annihilation of the world he'd hoped to rule. His hand tore through his hair, again and again.

"Dust to dust," Corbette said. He still hugged the princess to his chest. "The Gate kept the balance. Allowed the world to survive. You see this?" He thrust one hand out to the sky, where overhead the twister grew ever taller. "It will start moving and destroy the earth. Until nothing is left, and we are all once again part of the Sparkling Water as we once were—"

"Shut up!" Norgard marched to Corbette and tossed Lucia from his arms. The girl fell to the ground like a broken doll, and her eyes blinked open. He grabbed Corbette by the shoulders and dug in his claws. "Fix it. Fix it!" He shook Corbette until his teeth rattled in his jaw, but the Raven Lord's face was impassive. "Damn you! What about the compact? What about your famed power to manipulate the Aether? Use it! Use it, goddamn it!"

Corbette began to laugh. If the Raven Lord couldn't save them, no one could.

"Don't lose hope." Kayla turned in Hart's arms and raised a cold hand to his cheek. She smoothed her fingertips across his wet lashes. "As long as we're together, there is always hope."

Hart had to clear his throat twice before he could speak. "I'm not going anywhere." *Not yet.*

"Good." Kayla had a choice. She could sit here and wait for help—which was looking less and less likely to appear—or she could do it herself. Slipping out of Hart's arms, she took a step toward the Raven Lord and slapped him. He stopped laughing.

"Thank Tiamat, someone else has sense here," Norgard said.

"You, shut up." She knelt by Lucia, who had woken and was staring wide-eyed at the swirling tornado around them. "Can you focus?" She moved her finger in front of Lucia's face from side to side. The girl tracked it just fine.

"Yes."

"Good. Corbette said we needed five powers to close the Gate." Plus a blood sacrifice, but she spared the girl that information. "What's your power?"

"Water."

Thank the Lady, Tiamat, and whoever else was listening. Kayla stood. "Corbette, pull it together. You're a Raven, so I'm assuming you can do air." He nodded. "Norgard, dragons breathe fire. I don't care if you aren't Kivati. Make it up." She turned to Hart.

"Earth," he said. "Wolves run on four paws."

She breathed a sigh of relief. "All right. Let's do this thing." She had always done everything by the book. There wasn't a book for this. No directions. No instruction. No logic or reason. She had to be like Desi for once in her life—take a running jump and hope she landed somewhere soft.

The tornado of souls twisted around them. Shadow shapes lunged and beckoned from the Aether. Hart squeezed her hand. He believed in her. She could do this.

"Close your eyes and visualize the Gate closing, whatever that looks like to you," she ordered. "Picture your own energy joining with mine. Imagine the souls returning to the crevasse, and the crevasse shutting." She shut her own eyes and focused on the swirling Aether. Around her, the life energy of the others sparkled. She tried to direct it toward the tornado. *Slow down,* she ordered.

Nothing seemed to change.

Hart moved closer to her. The heat from his body enveloped her. She felt warmth and smelled pine. The soothing calm of the forest as light filtered through the leaves. Wet earth beneath her paws and the wind on her face as she raced through the underbrush. The call of an owl, and the howl of her own voice as she answered, wild and free.

Kayla opened her eyes from the daydream to see the center of the twister filled with light. It poured, sparkling, from each of them and rent the twister's walls. The shadows in the Aether cringed away. The momentum of the twister slowed. The whole funnel began to wobble.

A ghostly figure slipped free from the crevasse. It eluded the rushing river that fed the twister, and stepped inside the eye of the storm. It solidified somewhat, still transparent, but now recognizable as a young woman. Her familiar heart-shaped face sent a spear of pain through Kayla's chest.

"Desi." Her concentration broke. She took a step forward and stumbled. Hart caught her arm and steadied her on her feet.

The apparition stretched out her hand. Her sister's eyes were sorrowful. "Come," she breathed. "Come with us." She motioned for Kayla to follow her back into the crevasse.

"No!" Hart shouted. His fingers cut painfully into her arm.

Kayla turned to him and saw the anguish in his face. "Don't you see? It's the only way to free you. The Gate needs a willing sacrifice—"

"No!" He shook his head violently. "If anyone's to do it, it will be me."

"You? But my sister—"

"Let go, sweetheart." Hart cradled her face in his large hands. The lines around his eyes and mouth stood out against his pale face. Longing and frustration warred in his eyes. "Your grief anchors her ghost. Let go of your guilt and let the dead rest."

She glanced back toward her sister's outstretched hand. She could be with her family again.

"You will be with her again in the world beyond," he said. His voice was ragged. His hands shook. "But not yet. You're going to live. There are patients who need your help and puzzles that need your brain. A lifetime of adventures wait for you. This is not your time. When you die, you'll be a contented old woman surrounded by grandchildren and great-grandchildren who will inherit your beautiful stubbornness."

She turned her eyes back to Hart, letting her gaze caress the familiar angles and faded scars on his handsome face. How could one person become so integral a part of her in so short a time? She couldn't live without him. "Does your vision have a handsome husband by my side?"

He lowered his lips to hers. His mouth tasted of bitter desperation and the sweet tang of hope. "There is nothing for me without you."

Kayla took a deep breath. "Lend me your claw." She cut her left palm on his sharp claws and pictured the rune that Hart had taught her—Ehwaz. Dipping her finger into the blood, she drew the rune in the air. It burned white-red in her other vision, illuminating silver strands that wrapped around her heart and through the Aether to tie her sister to her. She hadn't known they were there. She wondered if she had hurt Desi this whole time by tethering her to the living world. Sweat broke on her brow as she worked to untangle the knots that bound them. Hart lent his strength, much as he had done to heal Lucia. With each strand, she felt a constriction around her chest ease.

When a single strand remained, she turned in Hart's arms and faced her sister. Desi's ghost lingered near the crevasse, her hands at her sides. Her lips parted, approval stamped plainly in her familiar, mischievous grin. Her gaze flickered to Hart, and she winked.

Kayla picked up the last silver strand and let go.

Ice moved sluggishly through Sven Norgard's veins. How could his plan have been so misguided? He'd been so sure he could control the demon horde. Sure his magic would be powerful enough to leash the dead. Sure the breaking of the Gate would cause just enough destruction to shake up governments and ensure him a smooth takeover.

Not this. Never in his wildest dreams had he imagined this. Leif had been right: it was Ragnorök. The doom of the gods. The end of the world. There was nothing left to rule. No treasure left to collect. Only a broken kingdom of barbarians and dirt. He joked about the glory of the Dark Ages, but he liked civilization. This was so much worse than the Dark Ages he had lived through. Had his brother survived the cataclysm? Had his people? He hadn't wielded the key that opened the Gates, but he had set it all up. Rudrick had followed his plan to the letter.

Except, of course, leashing Kingu. Bloody hell. The demigod was loose in the world.

Norgard turned as though drawn by invisible hands toward the dark crevasse. His cold heart shuddered in his chest at the vision before him: Desi, pale and withdrawn as she had never been in life. Her lush curves were insubstantial, forever out of his reach.

"Damn you." The harsh whisper escaped his lips. "Why did you leave me?" He took a shaking step toward the ghostly form, and another. She turned and saw him. Her lips slowly curved up. A smile, after all he'd done. Didn't she see the damage he'd wrought? "I offered you everything, and you threw it away. This is your fault," he said, needing to cast blame. The pain of her loss cut fresh. "If you hadn't left me . . ."

She stretched her thin hand out to him.

"If you had stayed we might have ruled the world together," he said. "We might have soared above the clouds with our child. If only—"

He was caught off guard when she took his hands in hers. She had material form. Her skin was cold and silky. Her lips tilted in that charming half smile that had first pierced his cold, dead heart.

"Come with me," she said. Her voice was as melodic as he remembered.

"I can't," he whispered, humiliated. "I have no soul." Drekar only existed in the Living World, an empty body but no spirit.

She shook her head and smiled to herself, as if he had said something funny, not bared his deepest shameful secret.

"Come with me," she said again. She squeezed his hands.

Looking into her eyes unlocked something in his chest. *Why not?* he thought. Why not take her hand and leave this wretched, lonely existence once and for all? He didn't know what waited on the other side, but there was nothing left for him here. Why not follow the only woman he'd ever loved into the dark unknown?

"Together?" he asked.

She smiled, turned and wrapped her hand in the crook of his arm. "Together."

Norgard took a deep breath and kept his eyes glued on his lady's face. He didn't look back. He didn't look down. He held onto her hand and let her pull him over the edge of the crevasse. He felt himself falling and clung to her hand more tightly. A shadow passed above him—a nightmare shape with eight spindle legs—and was gone.

The darkness rose up, terrifying and vast. Its drumbeat pulsed in his bones and took over the beating of his heart. Soon his vision cleared. Not darkness, but a million sparkling lights, more brilliant than the finest treasure. They wrapped him in their embrace. He squeezed Desi's hand, and together they faded into the Aether below.

"Desi!" Kayla screamed as her sister disappeared with Norgard into the crevasse.

Hart clutched her to him. He wouldn't let her go. She was his life, his breath. He didn't care if her family waited on the other side. He was her family now. He would create a new family here with her. Would do whatever it took to make her happy, as long as she stayed with him.

As Norgard disappeared, a flash of lightning shot up from the deep. Inside the great twister of souls and Aether, the shadows jumped back as if burned. The ground shook again. The sides of the crevasse groaned and strained. With a great screech, they slammed together, cutting off the river of souls and Aether from the other side.

"Hold on to me," Hart yelled at Kayla. He didn't have time to worry about Corbette and Lucia.

The earth shook once more, tossing Hart and Kayla to the ground. He rolled so that she landed on top of him. The twister drew up, growing thinner at the base. In a few moments it would pull off from the earth, and there would be no more safety in the eye of the storm. They wouldn't be able to keep from being sucked up into the great whirlwind.

In that last moment he imagined all he would miss. Lazy mornings in bed with Kayla. Watching her belly grow round with his child. Watching the sunset over the Olympics, hand in hand, two graying heads bent together.

The twister left the ground. Kayla's body strained in his arms toward the whirlwind, and he tightened his grip. He felt his molecules pull up.

A shadow crossed his vision: a swollen abdomen with a deadly point, eight thin legs for weaving the magic silk that bound and dreamed. Before he could fly apart and join the river of souls, a web fell over them, trapping them to the earth. Its soft silk severed the pull of the monster twister. He felt the land singing below him. It sung of freshly washed earth after a rain and the dry hot bake of summer. It sung of spring grasses and the mulch of fall leaves nourishing the soil for the long sleep of winter. He was vaguely aware that Corbette and Lucia had been snared in the webbing too. He didn't care. Kayla was in his arms. She was safe. It was enough. He let the web's spell pull him under, and he dreamed.

Chapter 24

Kayla stepped out the imposing brass doors of Norse Hospital and rested her head against one of the cold, stately columns. It had been forty days since the Gate had broken. Forty days of death and mangled bodies. Forty days of fearing the dark. Survivors were still being located in the rubble of the city and brought to the Drekar-run facility. A small unit of doctors, nurses, EMTs, and volunteers did what they could to save the injured. There was no electricity. Not here. Not anywhere. An army of wraiths had escaped before the Gate closed, forever changing the balance of Aether between the worlds. If the Raven Lord could be believed, the living world would never fully recover.

She had spent most of her time working beside the Kivati healers, watching miracles happen before her eyes. It no longer surprised her. She had worked a few miracles herself.

Staring out over the devastated city, she tried to calm her shaking hands. The air was thick with volcanic ash. Half the Cascade Mountains had exploded, but she couldn't see them through the gloom. Ash landed on her hair and skin like a smoker's pall. The Raven Lord thought his people could use the wind to get rid of enough ash to plant food in the spring, but at the moment all their energy was engaged tending to the wounded and beating back the wave of dark spirits that had taken over the city.

She wondered again how much of the world was like this. There was no television, no radio, no phone. No means of communication with the outside world to see how other cities had fared. Corbette had explained, tiredly, that a disruption of this magnitude would have rocked the world over. Supernatural races would have felt the earth shift and known to find shelter. How many humans had made it? There was no way to know. Unimaginable destruction. It would have been unbelievable, if she hadn't seen the twister with her own eyes.

Strangely, she felt more at peace with herself than she ever had. It was as if something deep inside had shifted and clicked into place. She was using her gifts—both her supernatural ability and medical knowledge—to save lives. Whole and complete, she was stronger and more effective than she had been before. She knew whom to thank.

He strolled up the hill, hunched against the wind in his worn bomber jacket. The breeze tugged at the tuft of white hair, now only a memento of his years of moon madness. He and his Wolf had joined completely, two halves of a coin, each adding his strength to the whole.

Every morning Hart escorted her to the hospital from the home they now shared with other Kivati healers. He spent the day hunting through the rubble for bodies and salvageable goods. It was grisly work, but his keen nose made him an invaluable asset. Every evening before curfew he trudged up the hill to pick her up.

She felt the sun break out over the bedraggled hillside when his eyes met hers, even though the sky was gray and streaked with soot. Her inner light warmed at the sight of him. The heavy burden of the day slipped off her shoulders and she smiled.

He caught sight of her and his lips curved in answer. He lifted a hand in greeting, but she was already bounding toward him. She threw herself into his arms and kissed his eyelids, cheeks, and nose. He tasted of soot and ash.

"Tough day?" he asked.

She nodded. "You?"

"I've got a beautiful woman in my arms. My day's looking up." He gave that crooked grin she had grown to love so much.

"I saw Lucia again today," Kayla said. "She stares out the window, refusing to speak. Like a little china doll: a lovely body, but no soul. If I didn't know better, I'd wonder if a wraith got her."

Hart squeezed her hand. "Will she recover?"

"Given time, maybe. She's hidden herself deep. I don't know what it will take to reach her." Her parents and friends had failed to do so. They had alternately wept over her and yelled at her to snap out of it, until Corbette had roared in and ordered everyone from the room. The Raven Lord had taken her injuries personally. Guilt cut deep furrows across his brow. He could hardly bear to be in the same room as her.

"How are things in the streets?" Kayla asked.

Hart helped her navigate through a maze of broken concrete and steel, the bones of a once-great skyscraper. "Grace says the aptrgangr are rising faster than we can burn the dead. We need to train civilians to fight them, but the human population is still reeling after the Kivati and Drekar came out to them. At least half have withdrawn to various human-only conclaves. A couple hundred are holed up at St. James Cathedral. Some fire-and-brimstone minister is preaching that the Gate breaking was the Rapture. He says the mass disappearances are all people who have ascended into heaven and that Corbette is the antichrist."

Kayla couldn't help but laugh. "If only he could have met Norgard."

Hart's mouth kicked up. "He claims he was chosen to remain on earth to pray for the salvation of those left behind."

"Interesting."

"Some Drekar are claiming Norgard is a martyr. They're talking of building a gold statue in his honor."

She tried to repress a flash of anger. Anger attracted wraiths. "I suppose his sacrifice did close the Gate."

Hart pulled her to a stop and brushed a lock of hair back behind her ear. "You still thinking of your sister?"

"No." She was surprised to realize it was true. She missed Desi, but her grief faded in the knowledge that she would see her again when it was time. Hart was her family now.

They made their way up Capitol Hill and along the ridge. The air was warm from the smoke of the still partially burning city.

"Has the council made any progress on locating Kingu and his horde?" Kayla asked. Government had fallen in the wake of the cataclysm and a consortium of supernatural beings and human militia had stepped in to fill the power vacuum and try to restore order. The Kivati and Drekar were best able to handle the new world, with their intimate knowledge of the paranormal and head start on steam-powered technologies. The humans were wary of cooperating with them.

"No sign of him," Hart said. He helped her climb over a half-buried Volkswagen Bug and onto a higher path. Empty, partially standing buildings hunched on either side like ancient mausoleums. Shadows flickered in the ruins, waiting for darkness to come out and hunt.

"Hopefully he's plotting to ransack some other poor city. Is it wrong of me to say that?"

Hart's eyes crinkled at the corners. "You evil thing, you. Wishing harm on others. Where's the Goody Two-shoes I rescued from giant birds oh so many weeks ago?"

"I guess I've been hanging around with a bad crowd, huh?" She threaded her arm through his and grinned. "Besides, you're remembering it wrong. I rescued *you* from being pummeled into the ground—"

"Is that right?"

She shrieked as he swept her feet out from under her and threw her over his shoulder. "Let me down!" she ordered, but he was already running toward the brick mansion on Millionaire's Row that was now home.

The street of Victorian-era houses had survived better than most. Patched roofs and replaced windows had been all that was needed to make them habitable. The Kivati had put them at the top of the list for renovation, as they had been outfitted for both gas and electric power. The new Drekar Regent—Sven Norgard's brother Leif Asgard—had promised to renovate the Seattle Gas Works to provide gas power to light the city in the new post-electricity world.

Home had a whole new meaning. It wasn't a place anymore. Home was a person. As Hart set her down on the wide front porch, she realized that despite the destruction, the uncertainty of the future, and the threat of demons plotting revenge, there was nowhere else she'd rather be. She held out her hand to the handsome, stubborn, endearing man who had rocked her world and said, "Let's go home."

Night blanketed the city, but Kivati charms and shields protected the grassy lawn where Hart stood from the dark spirits that stalked the night. He gave a mental salute to Kai for this bit of weather magic. The conjured wind blew the volcanic ash from the air, enough that the waning moon could be seen in the sky once again. He rubbed his hands nervously on his jeans. This was it. *Trust*, Kayla had urged him. But putting it all on the line was like facing the hell-born twister all over again. He was trying. *Trust.* She might have saved his twisted soul, but could he trust her with his fragile heart?

He didn't have a choice; it was already hers.

Checking his preparations one last time, he raised his head and let the Wolf surge through his blood. His head fell back, his eyes closed, and a pure howl poured from his throat. The song vibrated through the Aether, a harmony of Wolf and man, soaring up to the stars above. As the notes flew through the night sky, he felt the answering hum of the earth beneath his bare feet and the sweet melody of the distant ocean crashing against the shore. The fire by his side crackled in rhythm. The Aether sparkled and swirled around him, dancing with his spirit in joy and love.

He heard the front door open and Kayla's soft approach onto the mansion's wide front porch. *Mine*, the Wolf growled.

"Hart?" she asked. Her scent teased him.

He let the notes go, drifting on the wind, and turned to her. Kneeling by the stairs, he held out a slipper for her foot.

"What is this?" she asked, slipping her foot into the soft deerskin.

"I will carry you when you grow weary." He held out the matching shoe and helped her into it. Taking her hand, he led her down the stairs to the fire he had laid and set her on an up-turned log. "I will warm you when you are cold."

Her eyes sparkled in the flickering firelight, the many flecks of gold marking her awakened gift.

She was his gift. His to treasure and protect. His to hold. His to cherish. His to love until the end of time.

He picked up a thick woven blanket and placed it gently around her shoulders. "I will shelter you when you seek refuge." Kneeling by her feet, he placed his hands over his heart and took a deep breath. His pulse raced. His mouth was dry. "I pledge my body to your protection, my soul to your happiness, and my heart to your keeping. May the Lady witness my troth. Kayla Friday, my love, my mate, will you marry me?"

The moment seemed to stretch forever. Teardrops glistened from her thick lashes, sending a jolt of fear through him. Had he made her cry?

But in the next heartbeat she fell into his arms, nearly

toppling him into the fire. He rolled, keeping them safe from the dancing flames.

"Yes! Oh, yes." She rained kisses over his cheeks and jaw. His heart started beating again. The sudden ice in his limbs thawed under her warmth and joy. "I love you."

He grinned. "I know."

She made a face and tickled him between his ribs.

Laughing, he said, "All right. Mercy! I love you too." He cradled her beautiful face in his hands and studied every curve and dimple. "By the Lady, Kayla, I love you more than life itself."

The mate bond snapped into place as if it had always been there, as if their souls had always been one. It lit up like a firecracker, blazing between them, brighter than the brightest stars. The Aether hummed.

"Shiny," Kayla said. Her skin glowed with magic. "It's brighter than before."

"Before? Before what?"

She tilted her head shyly. "Than it was in Rudrick's dungeon."

He blinked at her. "You saw the mate bond then?"

"Is that what it is?" She kissed the questions from his lips. "I think I need a reminder. What happened that night?"

He felt his blood rush south. Her teasing caresses broke the thin leash he had on his patience. Sweeping her into his arms, he took the stairs two at a time. There was one way to finish the Kivati mating ceremony, and for once he intended to follow the official protocol to the letter. The bond coursed through his spirit like a living thing. He wanted it secure, safe, and unbreakable, to chain him forever to this sparkling, vibrant woman.

Freedom had never felt so good.

Keep reading for a special preview of the next

Deadglass Novel,

HEARTS OF SHADOW,

available soon in paperback and as an e-book.

Leif Asgard looked up when the blood slave slipped into the crowded council chamber. No one else noticed. Leif noticed, because he felt the ring on his finger softly thrum. It was his brother's ring, and Leif couldn't figure out how to get the damned thing off.

One more thing to curse Sven for. Worse, his brother had the balls to die and leave Leif to this madness. Six months since the Crash. Six months since the world turned upside down. Six months since all hell had broken loose, literally, and brought down the civilization he had come to depend on.

Six months since Sven had died and left Leif shackled at the reins of this gods-be-damned runaway circus train.

From his seat at the defendant's gate, Leif watched Admiral Jameson ranting across the room. In his mind he turned the sound off like an old black-and-white movie. He was tired of listening, tired of having to defend himself and his kind, tired of having to prove his right to exist when some moments he didn't even know if he believed it himself.

Admiral Jameson wore his navy uniform like a shield. Frayed about the collar and threadbare in some places, it was a nostalgic symbol of authority in the once-great United States of America. The fallen government had few spokesmen left.

Those that chose to fill the void were frightened, bullheaded, and incredibly paranoid. Jameson pointed his gavel at Leif, and Leif tuned back in. "—Let me remind you, sir, that you are under oath. Do you mean to say you have never killed?"

Leif didn't think anyone could survive two hundred years without shedding blood, but the human admiral was having difficulty wrapping his head around the idea of immortality. There were any number of honorable reasons for killing in the course of his two centuries. There had been revolutions, riots, duels. Insults that couldn't be borne. Revenge. Justice. But Leif refused to be tried for past deeds in this laughable shoestring mockery of a court, judged by a mob of terrified mortals.

He wouldn't die for his brother's sins either.

"Dragons are not killers," Leif said, "any more than the lion on the Serengeti is a killer. A predator, yes, but man is also at the top of the food chain."

"Humans don't harvest souls!" Jameson shouted, and the mob in the council audience murmured its agreement. Leif could almost imagine them with pitchforks, right out of Shelley's tale. Time might progress, but humans stayed as ignorant and xenophobic as ever.

"But you kill to eat," Leif said. "The imbibing of souls doesn't require the death of the donor. Think of it as a blood transfusion."

"You steal—"

"Our donors are willing." At least his were. "And this really isn't the point of contention, is it? Humans could choose to be vegetarians, but most of you don't. For a Dreki to choose not to eat souls would be suicide."

Tiamat blight him. He'd told Astrid this was a mistake. She sat on one side of the long council bench separated from the Kivati by Jameson and his fellow human representatives. It made a pretty tableau: two shape-shifting races forced to play nice beneath the terrified watch of the humans. Everyone had pulled together to help put the world back to rights after the Crash. Leif had left the political wrangling to Astrid, because she was experienced in this bullshit. She had served Sven's interests on the Seattle City Council for four decades, right here in this room beneath the blithely ignorant noses of the humans. Since the Crash, she'd stopped dyeing her hair gray. She wasn't pretending to be human anymore. None of them were.

Leif didn't have Sven's silver tongue or Astrid's slippery morals. He shouldn't be here debating his people's right to live when he could be doing real work in his laboratory. He was a scientist, not a politician, and he was a damned good one. There were people dying in the streets. People cold and hungry without jobs, without the skills needed to live in a world without electricity, without shelter from the wraiths. Leif could help those people, but not *here*. He needed to get back to work inventing tools that could make a difference.

"Your kind put us into this situation," Jameson accused.

"Not *my* kind. Not the Drekar." Sven might have set up the fall of the Gate, but a Kivati man pulled the trigger. "Please stop lumping all supernatural races into the same group—"

"You are all killers!" Jameson shouted.

"Please." Emory Corbette, the leader of the Kivati, was elegant in a coal-black three-piece suit, silver rings in his ears. His ebony hair brushed his straight shoulders. A thin circle of violet—the tell of all Kivati shape-shifters—ringed his jet-black eyes. A vein ticked in his temple. His people were an ancient race who could shift into a totem animal: Thunderbird, Crow, Wolf, Bear, Fox, and the like. Corbette's totem was the Raven, and his sharp beak of a nose gave him away. He raised his hand, and a silent wave of Aether licked through the room, quieting tempers, easing the rabid murmurs of the crowd. "This is unproductive. We are all here to help rebuild civilization. We have the same goal. The new Regent is not his brother."

Thank Tiamat for that, Leif thought. But what if he were? He'd felt the darkness swirling in his breast in the empty space where his soul should have been. He could easily follow it down and get lost somewhere between despair and madness. It happened to all Drekar eventually. But Sven had always seemed so sane.

Corbette rapped his silver-tipped cane on the banister. Since the Crash, everything about the Kivati leader was sharper, crueler. "As a scientist, Leif Asgard was building steam- and coal-powered technology in its heyday. He is an invaluable resource for reviving our technological capabilities and building a new world. Even if the Drekar deserve to be exterminated"—and his tone said they did—"we can't afford to lose his skills."

Leif granted Corbette a tight smile. After more than a century of bloodshed between their two races, he was hesitant to trust Corbette. Leif didn't want to be the Regent, and he had good reason. His people still needed a wartime leader, and it would never be him. Dragons might have survived the apocalypse better than most, given their thick hides and imperviousness to fire, but how many would want to live on in this barren new world? Their treasure hoards lay beneath miles of collapsed rubble and dirt. Their once-clear skies were constantly gray with thick volcanic ash. They needed someone to rally behind. A Machiavellian leader who could wield fear to keep them in line.

Not Leif.

Astrid finally decided to intervene. About damned time. She rose. With her black hair undyed, she didn't look a day over twenty-five, though she'd seen the fall of Genghis Khan. *Act charming and a little clueless*, the elder Dreki had coached him. *Humans don't trust anyone smarter than them.* She should be the one standing behind the defendant's gate answering questions, not Leif. "Admiral, Lord Raven, gracious members of the council." Her smile caught their attention. Gorgeous like all dragon-kind, she had the cat eyes of her Mongol father and the fair skin of her Norse mother. Few could resist her charm, even before she opened her mouth. "The Drekar bring many invaluable resources to the council. The Regent, in particular, is almost finished restoring the Seattle Gas Works so that we may have functioning gas to light our city."

Out of the spotlight for a moment, Leif spared a glance for the blood slave. Hidden in the back of the mob, the slight figure blended with the shadows in a black sweatshirt with the hood pulled forward over his or her face. A few blue bangs stuck out from beneath the hood. Leif could pinpoint the kid with his eyes closed. The invisible tether burned across the room like a live wire.

"Regent?" Astrid called his attention back to the damned meeting. "Why don't you share your progress on this project with the council. I'm sure they will understand how generously we put our resources toward the good of the whole."

"Right." He shuffled his notes. This is why Astrid insisted he come. She wanted him to be the face of the Drekar. She needed him to explain the technical details of his project, not that Jameson would care. He could smell a ruse as good as the next fellow. But she wore him down until he agreed. She could be as bad as Sven. "The Gas Works is an old coal gasification plant built in 1906 to create luminous gas for houses and streetlights. Though decommissioned in the 1950s, I've spent the last six months restoring it. Corbette has reopened his coal mine at Ravensdale." He nodded to Corbette, who acknowledged the fragile partnership with an answering nod. This was where the project got sticky. The city needed light. The Kivati had the coal; Leif had the factory. Both sides expected a knife in the back at any moment.

Another human on the council, the charismatic, but slightly fanatical prophet-minister Raphael Marks, raised his hand. "And where do you expect to put this gas? Who gets it first?"

"The old Victorian mansions on Capitol Hill and Queen Anne make the most sense. Many of them were wired for both gas and electric, as the victor in the gas/electric battle had yet to emerge at the time they were built. I've placed those houses at the top of the list for renovation."

"And how many humans live in those mansions?" Marks asked.

"Ah," Leif hesitated. He'd walked right into that trap. "Retrofitting regular houses for gas will take time."

The mob, who was mostly made up of Marks's rabid followers, hissed.

"Resources for mankind first!" someone yelled.

"Send Satin's minions back to hell!" another shouted.

Leif did his best not to roll his eyes. He sent Astrid a pleading glare. She raised her eyebrows a fraction. She wasn't going to take over and save this thing. Damn the woman. "First we need to get the Gas Works back into commission, then we can identify the most suitable buildings." He raised his voice to be heard over the crowd. "I need resources and manpower to finish the job."

"What about wraiths?" a woman called.

"I don't think a few ghosts should be an insurmountable obstacle to retrofitting the—"

"Bullshit!" the woman shouted. The mob started throwing things. More anger. More anti-supernatural hate mongering. The tide had definitely turned. After six months of working together, the survivors needed someone to blame. Leif made a convenient scapegoat.

"Please," Leif said. "Please hear me out. Light will help. Secure shelter out of the darkness—"

"Resources should be used for training human civilians," the woman called.

"We don't need more armed civilians," Jameson growled. He banged his gavel, but no one minded.

Leif slowly turned in his seat to locate the woman. It was the blood slave. She was still half hidden in the crowd, still hiding behind her black hood and hunched posture. He wouldn't let a coward derail his project. "Show yourself," he ordered. The bond between them cracked like a whip.

She jerked forward and threw back her hood. He was startled to find such a delicate face. Long, blue-black hair framed a heart-shaped chin. Coral lips were a slash of anger across her smooth skin. Thick, sooty lashes framed almond eyes. Those eyes sparked with defiance.

Interesting. "What do you want?" he demanded.

"Safety," she said, and seemed startled.

Admiral Jameson rose. "That's what we're working on. Thank you. Please save your comments for the citizen petition session."

But she kept talking. "We must train citizen soldiers to recognize the aptrgangr and take them out. Establish a tougher curfew—"

"The what?" Marks asked.

"Quiet, please!" Jameson commanded.

"—Gas lighting is a waste of time until we address the direct threat. Wraith attacks have tripled. Hungry, weakened humans are easy prey for possession," she continued, seemingly unable to stop. Her hunched shoulders were defensive. In those black jeans and baggy sweatshirt, she looked like a skinny punk kid. Leif would never have given her a second glance on the street. Perhaps that was her intent.

On his finger, Sven's ring hummed. Leif wondered what his brother had used her for. She looked too small to be trained as a fighter. Perhaps an assassin or thief? He tried to keep his mind from exploring other possibilities. The words "pleasure slave" rose unbidden to his brain.

Her face had grown red. Each word seemed pried from her lips. "And also to prevent weakened humans, the soul-suckers should be ki—"

"Stop," Leif ordered before she could rally the mob in a direction he most firmly did not want to return to. "Stop. Thank you. You're correct. Safety is more important than power, but wraiths fear the light. The two tasks go hand in hand."

She glared at him with both parts hate and fear. Ye gods, it cut him. This hatred born of prejudice he had little control over, but he never wanted to inspire fear. He would never be a leader like his father or brother. Fear was not something he would seek out. She made him want to jump out of his chair and apologize, but he didn't know what for. For not being able to solve all the world's problems? For "sucking souls" as she so unflatteringly put it? For existing?

Her dark eyes flashed silver.

Leif caught his breath. It might have been a trick of the light.

But the mob swallowed her up in the next instant, and Admiral Jameson reclaimed his attention. "The girl has a point. What we really need is protection against your kind."

Leif ran a hand through his disheveled hair. "And if I designed something like that, then could we stop this damned waste of time?" He heard Astrid suck in a breath, but he was too tired to care. He'd botched this meeting, and he might as well continue.

Corbette, who'd been quiet all this time, gave a slippery smile. "It would be a show of goodwill."

"Fine." Forget wraiths, aptrgangr, and demon men, *Leif* was the monster here. The world might have turned upside down, but some things never changed. "Are we done?"

"Go." Admiral Jameson dismissed him. "But the council will be watching you."

Leif stood. "Good day, gentlemen, ladies." He strode to the council doors, and the crowd parted to get out of his way. The hall was empty. He concentrated on the malachite ring and reached out along the invisible tether that connected him to the blood slave. It pointed toward the stairwell. "Mademoiselle?" he called out. His unnatural hearing caught the slight sound of a door closing, and he ran to the stairwell, following the faint scent of rose petals. The need to find her drove him.

He told himself it was because her eyes had flashed silver, and he had questions. A purely scientific inquiry. But his pursuit of science burned with a cold flame.

This need burned hotter.

Leif opened the door onto a wide circular staircase that was open in the middle. He peered over the banister and caught a glimpse of a dark-hooded figure five floors below. Nothing else moved in the stairwell, so he threw his legs over and jumped.

Air *swooshed* past him. One flight passed. Two. Three more in close succession.

Bone and sinew shot out of his back, sending the sound of ripping fabric echoing in the tower. His wings unfurled and caught the air, halting his free fall. He beat them once, twice, before dropping to his feet on the stairs below the woman.

Who scrambled backward like her feet were on fire. She pressed her back against the wall as if she could tumble through it to escape. The whites of her eyes showed, reminding him of a little black mouse in the paws of a cat.

She was terrified.

"Excuse me." He pulled his wings back into himself. He couldn't do much to repair the ripped suit. "I was under the impression you were familiar with my kind."

She said nothing, but he caught the glint of light off the knife in her hand.

"I need to ask you some questions. Tell me—" He stopped himself. "Please. Please tell me what you know about aptr-gangr. About wraiths. Did you know your eyes flash silver?"

"*Pah-lease*," she mocked. Spinning, she would have run back up the stairs if he hadn't caught her by the hood of her jacket. She tried to knife him. He was faster. Defending himself, he grabbed her and pinned her arms so she couldn't move. So small compared to him, but surprisingly strong. Her loose black clothes hid muscle. The top of her head barely hit his sternum. He remembered the spark he had seen in her eyes in the council chamber. Her spirit called to him, heady and filling. He barely felt her struggle in his arms.

Leif hardly knew where he was, or what his body was doing, before he felt her lips beneath his. Ye gods, they were soft and so very sweet. She tasted of cardamom, like *glögg* at Yuletide, reminding him of warm fires and happier times.

He couldn't help himself. He dipped his tongue between those lips, seeking more, seeking deeper penetration and a fuller taste of her spirit.

Pain lanced through his tongue.

"Bloody hell!" He pulled back. The metallic taste of blood spread through his mouth. The minx had bit him.

She scuttled back out of his reach. "Stay the fuck away from me." The knife shook as she wiped her mouth with the back of her hand, hard. She spit on the stairs. The bit of blood and saliva sizzled when it hit the worn wood.

With effort, he reined in the baser part of his being. What was wrong with him? He'd practically raped her soul in a stairwell. If he wanted to prove her fears correct, there was no better way to go about it. "Forgive me. I don't know what came over me—"

She laughed. It was a grim sound. "I know your kind. You're all the same."

"That is patently untrue." Though his actions a moment ago hardly supported that statement. He knew perfectly well that his brethren weren't in accord on the need for consent, but he had always held himself to a higher standard. This caveman routine was beneath him. "But I suddenly understand the need for chaperones. Instinct, in the face of a beautiful woman, turns a man into a flaming idiot."

"Fuck off."

"I only wanted to talk to you."

She snorted. "I know what you wanted."

"No, really. I—"

"Save your lies for the council."

Wasn't that a damning indictment of his honor and professional conduct? "Please. Let's start over. I'll introduce myself properly, will that do?"

"I don't give a—"

"Leif," he said over her. "Leif Asgard. Younger brother to your former—ah." He scrambled to find something reassuring. Announcing he now held her slave bond wasn't the correct way of going about it. "I'm a scientist. With your silver eyes, you could be a Shadow Walker. Am I right?"

"I don't know what you're talking about." She tried to inch past him in the stairwell without touching him. Stubborn woman. He admired her spirit. She might be scared, but she wouldn't be cowed.

Still, he needed her to cooperate. She'd sabotaged his session in the council, and he was still mad. Whether he liked it or not, they were tied together. He had stayed out of her way for the last six months—he'd avoided all the blood slaves since he'd inherited that blasted ring—and things had been going swimmingly. Now was not the time for her to muck things up.

The dragon in him disagreed. He growled at the thought of letting her go now that he had a taste of her. But that was his baser self talking, and Leif ruthlessly tamped it down. The girl seemed to want to bite any hand that reached for her, even one given in aid or kindness. Tiamat damn him, but he wanted to reach for her anyway. He could still feel the heat of her lips, still taste her sweetness on his tongue.

She caught sight of his face and took a hasty step back.

Bloody hell. He shut his eyes quickly and prayed for self-restraint. Why would this skinny, pugnacious girl have such an effect on him? It must have been too long since he had last fed. He would have to resolve that issue immediately. This poor woman seemed to have enough on her plate without being ravaged by his demonic hunger. "I'm really not a bad sort," he said softly.

"Look, if you're so good, why don't you donate your blood

to ward houses? Runes could keep those"—she swallowed—
"*things* outside. People would be able to tell if their friends and
loved ones had been taken. Possessed bodies wouldn't be able
to pass over the threshold."

"You know runes?" he asked. "What kind of runes? Old
Norse or Druidic? Who taught you? Which would you—"

She scowled. "Forget it.

"Would a human be able to conjure enough magic to use a
rune? Perhaps a Shadow Walker could . . ." The puzzle hovered
in front of him, so striking in his mind that he barely noticed
his informant slipping away.

Until she tried to stab him in the balls on the way past.

He caught her arm a hairbreadth away from turning him into
a eunuch. Her wrist twisted in his grip, and she dropped the
knife. It clattered to the side. He overbalanced, and they fell,
locked together, crashing down the oak stairs. He tried, despite
the fact that this woman had attempted to castrate him, to
protect her delicate skull from cracking on the hard ground.
His large body curled around her so that he took the brunt of
the impact.

Pain blossomed along his back and arms, shooting up his
spine and along his limbs with red florets of blood beneath
the skin. In a human those flowers would metamorphose into
ugly purple bruises, but his Drekar blood sparked into action,
healing the broken blood cells and reinforcing the torn skin.

The woman moaned when they hit the ground. Leif lay still,
praying the world would stop spinning sometime soon. He
didn't let go of her. He couldn't. His muscles refused to work.
His brain was foggy from being hit, repeatedly, on each step on
the way down.

Beneath the fog, his body knew, instinctively, that she
belonged there in his embrace. She felt good in his arms. She
felt right. Her lithe body was soft and warm. He buried his
face in her blue-black hair and breathed in her fragrance

hungrily. She must use a rose petal shampoo. He wanted to run his tongue over her skin.

His heart drummed loudly in his ears, drowning out all logic, all self-control.

Forget all pretense of civilization. Throw out all notions of decency. At this moment he wanted to spirit her away to a mountain cave where he could hoard her as treasure all for himself, like the dragons of old had done.

If he chose to do so, no one and nothing would stand in his way. He was a creature of power. Might made right. Besides, she had fought him and lost. By the ancient laws, she owed him forfeit.

She belonged to him.

Slowly, his head cleared and he realized she was whimpering in his arms.

Devil take him. This attraction was one-sided.

"Who hurt you?" It was obvious someone had. Someone like him, apparently. Leif wanted to cut out the bastard's heart and skewer his head on a pike.

"*You're* hurting me."

He was indeed. "I apologize." Again.

Leif grasped the banister and pulled both of them from the ground. He set her gently away from him. Digging in his pocket, he pulled out a card. "I truly would like to ask you a few questions in the name of scientific research. I also have information about the Shadow Walkers, should you be interested." He watched her face, but it was carefully blank. He couldn't tell if she knew who or what she was, or might be willing to answer some questions for answers of her own.

She didn't take the card.

"Please?"

"You could order me," she whispered. "I have no choice."

"But I won't," Leif said. So she knew he now held her slave bond. How could he assure her that he wouldn't abuse it? She would never believe that he sought a way to free them both.

"So polite now, huh?" she laughed darkly.

"I . . . ah . . ." Last time he checked accosting a woman twice in a public stairwell wasn't considered polite. He reached out, and she flinched. He carefully tucked his card in the pocket of her sweatshirt and brushed a strand of sleek hair back behind her ear.

He wanted to cup her smooth cheek and pull her close for another taste of those luscious sweet lips.

But it was not to be.

"Take care of yourself, Walker." Leif stepped away slowly, not giving her his back in case she had another knife, but not moving as if he worried for his own physical safety.

He didn't. His emotional safety was another matter entirely. This young woman had much too strong a pull on his baser instincts. Like the moon's call to a werewolf, she brought out in him something he didn't recognize. Something monstrous.

Leif couldn't afford to become a raving lunatic. His experiments were too close to breakthrough. His people needed him. It was the only value of his damned soul. To betray his people would be unforgivable, for any reason.

"My name is Grace," she said softly, before he stepped through the door.

"Grace," he repeated.

The irony was not lost on him.